The Woman
ON THE
Bridge

By Sheila O'Flanagan

Suddenly Single
Far From Over
My Favourite Goodbye
He's Got To Go
Isobel's Wedding
Caroline's Sister
Too Good To Be True
Dreaming Of A Stranger
The Moment We Meet
Anyone But Him
How Will I Know?
The Season of Change
Yours, Faithfully
Bad Behaviour
Someone Special
The Perfect Man
Stand By Me
Christmas With You
All For You
Better Together
Things We Never Say
If You Were Me
My Mother's Secret
The Missing Wife
What Happened That Night
The Hideaway
Her Husband's Mistake
The Women Who Ran Away
Three Weddings and a Proposal
What Eden Did Next
The Woman on the Bridge

SHEILA O'FLANAGAN

The Woman

ON THE

Bridge

REVIEW

First published in Great Britain in 2023 by
HEADLINE REVIEW
An imprint of HEADLINE PUBLISHING GROUP

1

Cataloguing in Publication Data is available from the British Library

ISBN 978 1 0354 0277 9 (Hardback)
ISBN 978 1 0354 0278 6 (Trade Paperback)

Typeset in ITC Galliard Std by Palimpsest Book Production Ltd,
Falkirk, Stirlingshire

Printed and bound in Great Britain by Clays Ltd, Elcograf S.p.A.

Headline's policy is to use papers that are natural, renewable and recyclable products
and made from wood grown in well-managed forests and other controlled sources.
The logging and manufacturing processes are expected to conform to the
environmental regulations of the country of origin.

HEADLINE PUBLISHING GROUP
An Hachette UK Company
Carmelite House
50 Victoria Embankment
London EC4Y 0DZ

www.headline.co.uk
www.hachette.co.uk

In memory of my grandmother Winifred O'Leary Burke
and my grandfather Joseph Burke

Chapter 1

Dublin, summer 1920

Winifred was measuring out a length of fabric, pushing the sky-blue silk along the brass ruler at the edge of the wooden countertop with the tips of her fingers and enjoying the feel of the delicate material as it brushed her skin. She didn't need to use the ruler; she instinctively knew exactly how much she was measuring out. But Mrs Kelley, the owner of the city-centre drapery shop where she'd worked for the past five years, insisted on fabrics being measured exactly, no matter that Winifred's estimate was as precise as any ruler. And so Winifred did as she was told, even when, like today, Mrs Kelley wasn't in the shop and there was nobody to check if she followed the rules or not.

Her fingertips moved to the rhythm of the large white enamel clock on the wall behind her, its slender second hand ticking by the black Roman numerals, while she lost herself in visions of how the blue silk dresses would look when they were finally made. She wished she could afford to have a silk dress of her own, but Winifred's clothes were hard-wearing and practical, for a life that was hard-working and practical too.

Nevertheless, she was imagining walking down a long staircase in a blue evening gown, picturing herself smiling graciously at the people around her, when the enormous stone came crashing through the shop window. She shrieked as it rolled along the narrow display area before thudding onto the wooden floor like a miniature cannonball. She abandoned the billowing waves of silk to duck beneath the counter, while razor-sharp shards of glass cascaded around her.

The shouts and yells of the people running along the narrow street outside grew louder and angrier. Then she thought she heard a shot being fired.

'No, no, no,' she gasped as she tried to slow the frantic beating of her heart. 'Please let it not be anything to do with Mrs Kelley. Please let them keep running. Please don't come in here. Please.'

Although the reasons to target Kelley's Fine Fabrics were slim – Alice Kelley wasn't blatantly taking one side or the other in the War of Independence that was raging across Ireland – it didn't mean that someone, somewhere mightn't have regarded the shop as fair game. The atmosphere in the city was becoming more tense with every passing day, and the least thing could lead to unexpected violence. Last month there'd been a skirmish between republicans and the Royal Irish Constabulary right outside the door, which had led to it bursting open and two men rolling across the floor before the republican was arrested and marched outside again. Winifred was beginning to think that working in a drapery shop was almost as dangerous as being a Volunteer.

The shouting grew louder, and beneath the counter, Winifred tried to make herself smaller. All she wanted was a quiet life, she muttered to herself, but how was anyone supposed to have a quiet life when the last few years had been so emotionally charged and explosive?

It had started with the Easter Rising in 1916, when groups of republicans seized control of buildings across the city, and Padraig Pearse, one of the leaders, had read the Proclamation of the Irish Republic on the steps of the General Post Office. The resultant military action by the British, who vastly outnumbered the Volunteers and kept them under siege as they pounded them with artillery, did more than anything to turn the tide of public opinion against their rule. Until then, many families had been, if not supportive of the British presence, at least ambivalent about it, and a large number had regarded the Rising as unnecessarily provocative, but the high civilian casualties and the subsequent execution of the ringleaders by firing squad changed many minds and hearts.

Winifred, who'd been fifteen at the time and hadn't much cared who was running the country, had been shocked at the executions. But listening to her parents, she'd also thought that an armed uprising was a dangerous way to go about things. Her father, Thomas, insisted that there had to be a peaceful political solution, and would often bore Winifred and her sisters with his thoughts on what type of solution that could be. Not, he would admit, that the British seemed unduly interested in such a thing.

In any event, the Rising had let the republican genie out of the bottle. Almost three years later, a new provisional Irish government was formed at the Mansion House in Dublin, where a declaration of independence was read out and a new constitution established.

And that had led to war.

There were still people shouting and chanting outside the shop. Winifred realised she was holding her breath. As though they could hear me breathe over their own yelling, she said to herself. I should go outside and tell them to move on.

But she stayed where she was.

The War of Independence was a guerrilla war. And much as Winifred's views had evolved to agree with its ideals, she was tired of the escalating raids and reprisals. She was tired of never knowing what she might get accidentally get caught up in. She was tired of the fighting on the streets, of the restrictions and the curfews, of the undercurrent of anxiety that was with her from the moment she woke up in the morning until she finally went to bed each night, relieved at surviving another day without a major incident. She desperately wanted the fighting to be over, but as she hugged her arms around her knees and continued to shelter beneath the counter, it seemed that peace was as far away as ever. The British had no intention of leaving, and as long as they were in the country, not a day would go by without trouble of some sort. It was a permanent feature of living in Dublin, no matter how hard she tried to avoid it. Not just of living in Dublin, of course. Of living in Ireland. Of living. And it was exhausting.

She recognised the names that were being chanted. They were all prisoners in Mountjoy gaol who'd died on hunger strike earlier in the year. The hunger strikers were considered to be martyrs by most people, and even her father (who remained a pacifist despite – or maybe because of – what had happened to him in 1916) had read the reports of the deaths with fury at an administration that had allowed them to happen. Winifred couldn't imagine what it would be like to voluntarily stop eating. In the course of her nineteen years, her family had gone through times of extreme hardship, when her parents had struggled to put food on the table. And even though they were now, if not well off, certainly in less straitened circumstances, the idea of refusing food was almost impossible for her to imagine.

Perhaps, she conceded as she pulled at a loose thread in her calico skirt, if it was for the sake someone she loved, she'd consider not eating. And then she would have to chain herself to the gates of Dublin Castle like some of the more militant women had done to highlight the sacrifice she was making. Perhaps she'd even have her photograph on the cover of the nationalist newspaper, *The Freeman's Journal*.

Who am I kidding? she asked herself as she banished the image from her mind. She was as much of a pacifist as her father. Her mother, too. 'Keep out of harm's way,' Annie O'Leary would beg her every day, and every day Winifred promised she would. There'd been enough pain and suffering in their lives already. No sense in adding more.

She took another deep breath and tried to control her racing heart. But it was hammering in her chest and pounding behind her eyes, making her dizzy. 'Everything will be fine,' she repeated over and over again. 'Nobody will hurt you. Nothing will happen to you.' But even when she realised she was right, and nothing would, because the shouts and the running footsteps had receded, she stayed where she was, unable to move.

Feckers, she thought, when she finally found the courage to lift her head and blink away the tears of relief that filled her wide brown eyes. Scaring me like that.

The bell over the shop door rang as someone pushed it open. Winifred gasped and remained motionless, her arms hugging her knees, the metallic taste of fear in her mouth.

'Hello? Anyone here?'

It was a male voice, deep and rich, and the accent was a Dublin one.

Winifred stayed where she was.

'Anyone? Are you all right?' A pause before he continued. 'If you're unhurt, I'll leave. I'm not here for trouble.'

Winifred emerged slowly from her hiding place. Splinters of glass fell from her dark hair and rattled onto the wooden floor. She shook out her skirt and more glass landed at her feet. Then she looked at the young man in front of her. In his twenties, she estimated, he was tall and thin, his arms and legs seeming too big for his body, his face gaunt yet composed. Black hair peeked out from beneath his flat cap, and he wore a green serge jacket over a faded shirt and matching trousers. The buttons on the jacket were brass, and she could see the harp etched on them.

Relief that he seemed concerned rather than aggressive flooded through her, and she allowed herself to feel angry. She exhaled slowly and drew herself up to her full height.

'And what's all this about?' She put her hands on her hips. 'Do you think that throwing stones through the windows of decent working people is an acceptable thing to do, no matter what you're protesting about? Is this your idea of—'

'Stop!' He put up his hand. 'The stone was a mistake. I'm here to tell you that. And to make sure you're not injured. Although,' he said with a note of concern, 'you are. Your face.'

'My face?' Winifred whirled around to look in the mirror behind her. She saw a thin line of blood from a cut just above her eyebrow tracing its way along her cheek. 'Disfiguring us is the plan now, is it?' She turned around again. 'When people aren't safe from their own kind in their place of work . . .'

'You think you were safe before?' He raised an eyebrow.

'The Brits never sent a rock through my window,' retorted Winifred.

'I really do apologise, Miss . . . Mrs . . .'

'O'Leary,' she said. 'Winifred O'Leary.'

'Are you the owner of this shop?' He was unable to keep an element of surprise from his voice. Winifred knew that this was because she looked even younger than her age, and certainly didn't have the presence of someone like Mrs Kelley, even if she already knew enough to be a shop owner herself. She'd worked there ever since she'd turned fourteen, and there wasn't a question about fabrics she couldn't answer.

She looked at the man again, struck by the fact that although his eyebrow had moved earlier, his eye hadn't. In fact, she realised, only one of his hazel eyes moved at all. The other remained staring at a fixed point behind her head. It was disconcerting.

'I'm not the owner, but I *am* the person in charge,' she replied. 'And I can tell you now that someone is going to have to pay for the damage, and it's not going to be me.'

'A minor inconvenience for Ireland's cause,' he said.

'Oh for the love of all that's holy!' She glared at him. 'A minor inconvenience? The window has to be replaced. The name repainted. The displays redone. The shop cleaned. And as for my fabric . . .' she gestured towards the blue silk that now lay flat and limp on the counter, 'I have to get rid of this. Nobody wants a dress with glass fragments as decoration.'

He smiled.

'And you can take that smirk off your face too,' she added.

'It's not a smirk,' he assured her. 'I was just smiling because of course you're right, you shouldn't have to pay. Even if many people and businesses are willing to accept that these things happen in a time of war.'

'Spare me!' cried Winifred. 'When Mrs Kelley returns, she'll want her shop looking as perfect as it always does, and how am I supposed to do that with no money to pay for repairs?'

'If you're the person in charge, surely you can find some?'

She gave him a withering look. 'You think business is easy right now? More than a year into this damn war and you imagine droves of women are rushing in here to buy nice fabric for clothes or for their homes? When they're afraid they could be pulled off the street at any time? Or that their house could be raided? You men are all the same! It doesn't matter where you're from. Every single thing has to be resolved by fighting.'

'Not our choice,' he said. 'And not only men either. There are plenty of women ready to fight for the cause.'

'I'll give you that,' she conceded, knowing that women's organisations like Cumann na mBan were active in the struggle and protested daily outside the prisons. 'But it would be better to negotiate.'

'They don't want to negotiate. When we win, and we will, you'll appreciate us. However,' he added, glancing towards the blue silk again, 'straitened times or not, you clearly have customers willing to spend a lot of money on fine cloth. Who would they be?'

'None of your business,' she retorted. Then her brow creased with worry. 'It's an Irishwoman,' she said. 'A good woman. Yes, she has some money, but the fabric is for dresses for her and her daughters, and I don't —'

'Forget it.' His tone was impatient. 'I don't need the details of your customers. I don't care who's buying your silk.'

'I bet you do,' she said in return. 'But it really is nobody you need worry about. Nobody of interest to you.'

'Nice material.' He rubbed it between his fingers, then murmured, '"Had I the heavens' embroidered cloths . . ."'

'Poetry now, is it?' Winifred snorted. 'The rest of us are having to put up with bullets in the streets and rocks through our windows. But Yeats can write poetry to a married woman and people think he's a genius.'

'You're not an admirer? But you know his poetry?'

'You sound surprised.' She shook her head, and more fragments of glass fell from her hair. 'I'm an educated woman, my mother sent me to school. It means I can't be swayed by honeyed words. Only by actions. And the action I'll be swayed by is if you fix the window of this shop.'

He lifted his eyebrow again.

'What's bothering you now? My words or my demands?'

'Neither.' He nodded. 'You're right in every respect.'

'So?' She glared at him. 'Will you give me the money?'

'I'll do more than that,' he said. 'I'll arrange for the window to be replaced for you.'

'You will, will you?' Her tone was sceptical.

'What time do you open in the morning?' he asked.

'Half past nine,' she said. 'Nobody buys fabric before half past nine.'

'Someone will be here,' he promised.

'And in the meantime?' She put her head to one side. 'I'm missing a window. The shop isn't secure. You think I can go home and leave it open to any aul' bowsie who walks by so that he can help himself to bales of my fabric?'

9

'No,' he said slowly. 'But I don't see how . . .'

'That's the trouble with revolutionaries and rebels,' she said. 'You think of the moment and not the aftermath. Once you've got what you rebelled about, there's no plan.'

'I assure you, Mrs O'Leary, we always have a plan,' he said.

'A plan to fix my window before the morning?'

'I can't fix the window until then, but I can secure the shop. Do you have wood? Or old crates? I can use them to board it up for you. But before that,' he added, 'you really should attend to your face.'

'There are crates in the storeroom,' said Winifred, opening the door that led to it. 'And there are nails and a hammer too.'

'I'll get on with it then, while you do something with that cut.'

Winifred shrugged and turned away from him. She looked at her face in the mirror again. The gash above her eye had already begun to crust over, but she knew it should be disinfected. She followed the man to the storeroom, where she found the antiseptic lotion and cotton wool that Mrs Kelley kept in a small tin box that had once contained Oxo cubes. She dabbed her face, wincing at the sting of the antiseptic, and then fixed a small bandage over it. She wondered if she'd have a scar. Not that it mattered; a scar wouldn't mar her beauty, because Winifred wasn't beautiful. Even her own mother described her as plain, although Annie O'Leary would occasionally concede that she had nice eyes. Which was true. Winifred's brown eyes added a spark of mischief in a face that might have lacked conventional beauty but was full of character.

Those dark eyes narrowed as she watched the republican bring slats of wood onto the shop floor and begin to survey the broken window. He was so sure of himself and his cause, so sure he was going the right way about it. And so insistent that he had a plan too. Everyone has a plan, she thought, until they run into the opposition's better one.

He whistled as he hammered the wood into place. He was a quick, efficient worker, and it didn't take long until the gap was covered by the wooden slats. The interior of the shop was now dim, and she turned on the single electric light so that she could see to clean up.

'Do you have another brush?' he asked when she began sweeping the glass.

'In the storeroom,' she said.

He fetched it and began sweeping too. They worked in silence until the counter and the floor were free of glass.

'Tomorrow,' he said. 'Half past nine.'

'I'll say thank you when it's done,' she told him.

'Of course.'

'But in the meantime, I'm obliged for you helping me tidy up.'

'You're welcome, Mrs O'Leary.'

He tipped his cap to her, opened the door and left the shop.

Winifred leaned against the countertop and released a breath she didn't even realise she'd been holding. She was trembling now from the shock of it all. The stone through the window had frightened her, but the shop door opening had terrified her. She hadn't known who might come in and what might happen to her as a result.

She'd been lucky.

She smoothed down her skirt again, then looked at the clock. There was still an hour to go before she was supposed to close the doors, but nobody was going to come into a shop with a boarded-up window. And nobody was going to come in while there was still trouble in the streets. So she turned out the light, walked out of the door and locked it carefully behind her.

She turned onto an almost deserted Sackville Street and crossed the bridge, stepping carefully between the tram tracks before walking along the quays. The city was quiet; whatever flash-point had caused the riot was now over. The sun shone from a milky blue sky and a light breeze carried the strong malty smell from the Guinness brewery further up the river, causing her to wrinkle her nose in disgust. The few people still around were walking with a sense of purpose, clearly eager to be somewhere else. Winifred walked with a sense of purpose too.

It took her just ten minutes to reach her family home in East Essex Street; two adjoining rooms in a tall building facing north towards the Liffey. It was a well-maintained property in a city that had many seriously overcrowded tenements, and the rooms were surprisingly spacious. Just half a dozen families lived in the building, and each tenant had an individual door. Years ago, eight O'Learys had lived together, but now it was only Thomas, Annie and Winifred. Her oldest sister, Katy, was married and living in the country along with her younger brother, Tom, who Annie had sent to stay with her at the start of the war. She had hoped he would be safer there than in the city, but there were daily reports of fighting in the country too, and Winifred knew that her mother was torn between wanting her son near her and hoping that he really was better off with his older sister.

Katy had only been to Dublin once since her marriage, and Winifred thought that living outside the city didn't really suit her, because although she was unquestionably the prettiest of all the O'Leary girls, with her long curly hair and soft, creamy skin, she'd looked thin and worried when she visited. And it wasn't that anyone wouldn't be worried with the country in the state it was in, but Winifred couldn't help wondering if it was married life, living in the country or the war that had put the frown lines on her sister's forehead and left dark circles under her eyes. But they hadn't had time to share confidences, not that they ever had very much. Katy had always kept her own counsel.

Two other sisters, Mary-Jane and Rosie, had moved to England shortly after the Rising. Their reasons for leaving weren't political. The two girls had worked at the Jacob's biscuit factory on Bride Street, but had been fired for inappropriate behaviour and had struggled to find anything else. When their mother learned that their inappropriate behaviour had been laughing as they packed biscuits, she'd asked the Irish Women's Workers Union to help. But after Rosie admitted that their laughter had been because their supervisor, Mr Potts, wore his few strands of hair in a way that tried to hide the fact that he was almost completely bald, the union representative had suggested that protecting workers who laughed at the boss was hardly what it was set up for. She told Annie that their aim was to improve working conditions for women and girls, not intercede for those who'd mocked their employers. Annie had been furious, retorting that young girls were entitled to have a bit of fun at work. 'But not at the boss's expense, Mrs O'Leary,' the rather austere woman from the Union had said. 'Not for being disrespectful.'

Annie hadn't wanted her girls to leave the country, but in the end, the move to England had been a good one for both of them, because they'd found well-paid jobs. At first, Annie had worried how two Irish girls would fare in London, especially given the attitude of the British press, which frequently portrayed the Irish as ungovernable drunken louts. But after a year, Mary-Jane had married an Englishman and was now settled in Kent, and Rosie, who was working in a London hospital, had recently written to say that she was seeing a young man herself. A pilot, she'd said, underlining the word four times. From Belgium and very handsome. This last had been underlined four times too.

In any event, as both Annie and Winifred sometimes said to each other, it was all very well fighting to get the British out of Ireland, but the girls were doing well in England and it seemed churlish to shout slogans when they were benefiting from being there.

As for Winifred's youngest sister, Marianne, she was no longer living at home either, being in service to a doctor's family in Pembroke Road. Annie hadn't particularly wanted Marianne to go into service, but the Desmonds were good employers and Marianne talked about learning what she could from the doctor so that perhaps one day she could work for him rather than the household. As a secretary, she'd said, or an assistant. Annie had her doubts, particularly as Marianne's writing was poor and she'd been known to faint at the sight of blood, but she kept them to herself. Her daughter was happy and that was the most important thing. It was, in fact, Mrs Desmond who'd ordered the blue silk from Kelley's. Marianne was due to pick it up before the end of the week.

And now there's just me, thought Winifred as she climbed the stairs and put her key in the lock. The last girl at home. She pushed the door open. Her mother, who was scrubbing the wooden table with carbolic soap, looked up at her in surprise.

'What are you doing here so early?' she asked, a note of concern in her voice. And then, as she saw the bandage on her daughter's face, 'What happened?'

Winifred told her about the stone through the window and her encounter with the Volunteer.

'Dear Mother of God.' Annie shook her head. 'Will it ever end? What was today about?'

'I'm not really sure. They were shouting the names of the hunger strikers, but I don't know why. They were released weeks ago.'

'Though more have been imprisoned since,' remarked Annie.

Winifred nodded.

'Yer woman was supposed to be giving a speech today,' Annie recalled. 'The Countess.'

'Markievicz?' Winifred looked surprised. 'I thought she was on the run.'

'Still giving speeches.' Annie dropped her scrubbing brush into a metal pail and put it in the corner before drying her hands on a well-worn towel.

'She's brave,' acknowledged Winifred. 'Stupid, maybe. But brave.'

'She has the luxury of being stupid,' said Annie. 'We don't.'

Stupid wasn't really the right word for the woman who was a leading light in the republican movement, Winifred mused as she slipped off her shoes and rubbed her tired feet. Perhaps rash was a better description. Nevertheless, Winifred couldn't help admiring the fact that the Countess had the courage of her convictions. She very much doubted that if she herself had been born to an English baronet and brought up on the family's country estate in County Sligo she'd have thrown her lot in with the Irish freedom fighters and taken up arms against the considerably better-financed and organised British.

Even more to admire was that the Countess had been appointed as Ireland's Minister for Labour. It was heartening, Winifred thought, to see women in positions of power. Not that the Countess could do much, given that at the time of her appointment she'd been imprisoned in Holloway, but Winifred liked her ideas. Now, despite her release, she was staying at safe houses, only emerging to make rousing speeches about women's rights and Irish freedom.

'Your head's in the clouds again,' said Annie as she reached past Winifred to get her coat, which was hanging from a peg on the door.

'Just thinking about the Countess,' Winifred said. 'She's amazing really. She could be living in luxury, but she's true to her beliefs. You don't need that coat, Ma,' she added. 'It's a warm day.'

'It won't be warm by the time I'm coming back,' said her mother.

'I suppose not.'

'There's coddle for your daddy's tea,' added Annie. She nodded at the pot of potato and sausage stew suspended over a fire of barely glowing embers. 'Yours too, of course.'

'Thank you,' said Winifred.

'You're a good girl.' Annie smiled at her and suddenly looked younger than her forty-eight years. 'I hope that so-called freedom fighter does what he says.'

'If he knows what's good for him he will.' Winifred's voice was firm, but she smiled in return.

'Would you mind lining the drawers in the dresser for me while I'm out?' asked Annie, indicating the old scratched kitchen dresser propped against the wall. 'I left a newspaper for it.'

'Of course.'

'I know you. You'll read it first.' Annie laughed as she opened the door. 'That's all very well, but don't forget to do the drawers too.'

When her mother was gone, Winifred walked into the other room and pulled back the heavy curtain (fabric supplied by Kelley's at a discounted rate) that separated her bed from that of her parents, then lay down. She'd once shared this bed with two of her sisters. Now it was hers alone. Lining the drawers could wait. It was nice to have time to herself. It was nice to have the bed to herself too. Winifred enjoyed solitude, and she was glad that she had a couple of hours alone while her mother cleaned the steps of the Empire Palace Theatre. Annie O'Leary was a strong woman and she'd brought her daughters up to be strong too. But right now, with the cut above her eye throbbing, and feeling suddenly overwhelmed by the events of earlier, Winifred didn't feel strong at all. She felt tired.

But at least she could rest until her father came home looking for his tea.

She surprised herself by falling asleep. In her dream she was wearing a blue silk dress, hiding behind an upturned table beside the young rebel who'd come into the shop that day. He was telling her to take aim, and she shrieked in horror at realising she had a rifle in her hand. The shriek, whether aloud or merely in her dream, woke her, and she sat upright in the bed, her heart thumping in her chest once again.

I'm spending altogether too much time in a state of panic, she told herself as she swung her legs over the side of the bed and got up. Things aren't as bad as all that. It's just been a hard day.

She pushed the sash window open a little further, allowing the malt-scented air into the room. Then she took the neatly folded paper her mother had left on the shelf for her to line the drawers with.

The newspaper was an old copy of *The Freeman's Journal* and the lead story, coincidentally, was about the hunger strikers. Despite already knowing how things had turned out – there had been a general strike in support of the prisoners, who were looking for political status and better conditions, and as she'd said to Annie, they'd already been released – she still read it. The country had come to a standstill in the two days of the strike; even Mrs Kelley had decided it was better to close the shop than stay open. And the result had been worth it, although the British had in fact made a mistake and released all the Irish prisoners, even the non-political ones, much to the horror of the authorities and the amusement of the hunger strikers.

As she read, Winifred wondered how it was that the British managed to control so much, given that they were forever making strategic errors. And she wondered too how the young Volunteer she'd met earlier and his comrades could possibly prevail. Because the War of Independence was only one more step in the continued battle between the Irish and the British over the control of the island. From even before the beginning of the Plantations, when English lords were given Irish lands, there had been nothing but rebellions, uprisings and battles. It was impossible to keep track of them all, but each one had left its scars and resentments. Winifred couldn't help wondering why the British thought it was worth it. Was it because they felt they'd lose face if they left? Or did they really believe they had a right to control a smaller country close by?

She closed the paper with a sigh. One day, perhaps, people would look at the old newspapers and wonder about the events that had taken place years earlier. In the meantime, though, she'd do as her mother asked and use them to line the drawers of the kitchen dresser.

Chapter 2

When Winifred arrived at the shop shortly after a quarter past nine the following morning, two men were leaning against the boarded-up window. One was tall and sinewy, the other shorter and squat, but both looked strong and capable, their rolled-up shirtsleeves emphasising the muscles in their arms. Beside them was a sheet of plain glass.

'We're here to do your window, missus,' said the shorter of the two. 'Padraig Shanahan and Anthony Walsh at your service.'

'I'm glad you're punctual,' said Winifred as she unlocked the door. 'And I hope you're as good at replacing it as you were at breaking it.'

'It wasn't us that broke it,' said Padraig. 'But the lieutenant felt responsible.'

'The lieutenant?'

'You met him yesterday.' This time it was Anthony who spoke. 'He's in our battalion.'

'And what battalion is that?' she asked as she watched them take down the boards that the young lieutenant had so carefully nailed in place the previous day.

'The third battalion Dublin Brigade.' There was a note of pride in Padraig's voice.

'Well, you need to be more careful in future,' she said. 'It's one thing fighting the RIC, it's another destroying local businesses.'

'It wasn't anyone from the battalion who broke your window,' said Anthony. 'There are always elements—'

'I really don't care,' said Winifred. 'All I want is for it to be fixed.'

She went into the storeroom and poured herself a glass of water. After a moment's hesitation, she poured two more glasses and handed them to Padraig and Anthony.

'Thanks, missus,' said Padraig.

'Much obliged.' Anthony smiled at her.

He was the best-looking of them all, she decided, with his taut frame, angular face and bright blue eyes. The image of yesterday's lieutenant and his fixed hazel eye came into her head. She suddenly realised that it was a glass eye and that was why it hadn't moved. She supposed he'd lost his own in a guerrilla attack somewhere.

She understood it, she admitted to herself as she cut away the blue silk that had been damaged in yesterday's incident. She understood what drove people to fight. But it was so relentless, and the victories so short-lived, that it was hard to know if it was worth it. Besides, she wasn't entirely sure she believed the speeches by people like Cathal Brugha, the Minister for Defence, or even the Countess herself, insisting that having an Irish government would turn the country into a place where men and women were treated equally and poverty would be wiped out. From what Winifred could see, people changed the moment they got power. It was they and those around them that prospered. As for everyone else, they still had to get by as best they could. And Winifred reckoned that despite having a female Minister for Labour, it'd be a long time waiting before women were truly equal. How could they possibly be equal when men could vote at twenty-one whereas she had to wait until she was thirty. Thirty! She wondered if that age had been decided because most women should be married by then and would vote how their husbands told them to? Not her, she thought. When she got the vote, she'd use it whatever way she wanted.

All the same, she conceded, if you were going to mistrust powerful people, it would be better to mistrust your own and not those who took what was good from the land and left the rest. She wondered if the British believed everything they read in their newspapers about Ireland. And how many of them thought they had a right to run another country as they saw fit because they were told the people who lived there were somehow lesser than them. She couldn't believe the majority did.

Rosie and Mary-Jane's letters from London contained nothing but cheerful comments about the English, and their love of order and tea and their royal family. Rosie occasionally mentioned that the Irish girls working with her at the big hospital in the city often did the jobs that the English girls didn't want to do, and that the English could be rude and dismissive towards them from time to time. But most were pleasant, and she didn't complain. She was happy. From their letters it certainly seemed that London, in the wake of the war to end all wars, was a vibrant and glamorous place to be, and that the people were kind and generous. It was so hard to reconcile that with what was going on in Ireland.

Dublin was probably as exciting as London right now, but it was the wrong sort of excitement. Tense was probably a better word to describe the atmosphere of the city. But how could you not be tense when the streets were full of policemen and soldiers and you could be stopped and arrested for nothing at all? And when the papers were full of war talk? Winifred wanted to read about people having fun, not battles. She wanted gossip. She wanted pictures of the latest fashions. She wanted excitement of her own. But she wouldn't go to England for it. Even though she liked a nice cup of tea as much as the next person.

'There you are,' said Anthony, bringing her out of her reverie. 'One window, good as new.'

'It'll be good as new when you clean your grubby finger-prints off it,' said Winifred. 'And when you paint the name of the shop on the front. Kelley's Fine Fabrics. Prop. Mrs A. Kelley.'

Anthony looked startled. 'The lieutenant didn't say anything about painting names,' he said. 'We don't do painting.'

'Neither do I,' said Winifred.

'I'm sure you'll get someone, missus,' said Padraig.

'It's miss,' snapped Winifred. 'Miss Winifred O'Leary. Your lieutenant promised to put everything to rights, and it's not to rights until the name is painted on the window.'

'He only asked us to replace it,' said Anthony. 'But I'll speak to him for you if it keeps you happy.'

'You do that,' said Winifred. 'If I don't hear from him, I'll go looking for him. And he'll wish I hadn't.'

Anthony's mouth twitched.

'Don't you laugh at me either.' Winifred gave him a stern look. 'You'll find more sympathy from the Crown forces than me if you do.'

* * *

23

It was later in the afternoon, and Winifred was folding yards of yellow chiffon for delivery to one of Mrs Kelley's best customers, when the brass bell jingled and the door opened. She looked up and saw the lieutenant, this time wearing a dark brown suit buttoned over a heavy cotton shirt.

'Miss O'Leary,' he said. 'I heard you weren't happy with the work.'

'I'm perfectly happy with the work,' replied Winifred. 'But it's not finished. The name has to be painted.'

'I never said anything about painting.' The lieutenant echoed Anthony's words of earlier.

'Replacing the window without replacing the lettering isn't much good to me.'

'I think I've been more than generous,' he protested.

'Your band of merry warriors put a hole in my window, cut my face, ruined yards of my fabric and caused me to have to close the shop early and lose sales,' Winifred said. 'So the least you can do is paint the name of the premises.'

The lieutenant laughed. It was a surprisingly infectious laugh that completely changed his austere appearance and made him seem less autocratic and more approachable. Winifred felt a desire to laugh bubble up inside her too, but she clamped down on it firmly.

'You're the toughest negotiator I've ever had to deal with,' he said as he composed himself. 'We could do with you over in England talking to Lloyd George on our behalf. You'd reduce his government to agreement in no time.'

'Possibly,' agreed Winifred. 'Most women have been negotiating forever. Negotiating good behaviour with our husbands and our children. Negotiating with our neighbours. Trying

24

to fix the mess men have left behind even though they think they're in charge of us.'

'Are you an activist?' He looked at her with interest. 'You certainly seem to have a low enough opinion of men to be one.'

'I don't have a low opinion of men; I just don't have the time to keep running after them to make sure they've done things properly. And I don't have time to be any sort of activist either,' Winifred added. 'Right now, I haven't time for anything other than my job and my family.'

'But you don't actually have a family, do you?' he asked. 'I called you Mrs O'Leary yesterday and you didn't correct me.'

'It's of little relevance to you whether I'm Miss or Mrs,' said Winifred. 'Besides, I don't know your name at all.'

'Joseph,' he said. 'Joseph Burke. 'You'd get on well with my older sister,' he added. 'She's just as outspoken as you. She's in Cumann na mBan. I'm sure that's right up your street.'

'Didn't I tell you I don't have time for protest groups?'

'They do a lot more than protest,' Joseph said. 'They were an integral part of the Rising, which shows how equal we want women to be in the new Ireland! They also raise money for prisoners' families and—'

'And my main concern is going about my daily life without being shot at,' she interrupted him. 'Do I think things could be better here? Yes. Do I think it will change? Not quickly enough. Do I think violence is the best way to do it? No. Can I change anything? Unlikely. Because you know what, Mr Fancy-Pants Lieutenant? All the people who are writing about change and talking about change and getting other people to put their lives on the line for change – no matter what happens, they'll be all right. Like your poet Yeats and his outrageous swooning over Maud Gonne MacBride, and her a married woman, and like the Countess too, no matter that I might agree with her. It's a game to them. Will their change really do anything for me or my mother or father? Or for you and your family? I sincerely doubt it. Because the people doing the real, proper fighting instead of just talking about it are the working class and will always be the working class, and you can set up all the soup kitchens you like, but unless you change things for people who have to work for a living, then you're not really changing things at all.'

He stared at her, his natural eye as fixed as the other. 'The Countess has been in and out of prison for the past five years,' he said. 'So she's certainly made some personal sacrifices. You should definitely meet my sisters. A woman like you is wasted behind a counter. You should be out there encouraging people to fight for their rights.'

Winifred was conscious that this might be a dangerous conversation, and she usually steered away from dangerous conversations. Her whole upbringing had been about avoiding conflict. But there was something about Joseph Burke that made her want to keep talking, to argue her points with him.

'I think the Countess is a brave woman, but I don't think I'd actually have anything in common with your sisters,' she said.

'You absolutely would,' insisted Joseph. 'They want a better life for all of us. Yes, there's protest. Yes, it can be difficult. But nothing happens without sacrifice. Don't you agree?'

'I . . . of course I do,' she said in a sudden rush. 'Of course I do, and of course I want Ireland to be a free country, but people are being killed every day and that'll keep happening if we stay on this course. Each death is a tragedy for some family, and I read somewhere that more than a thousand have been killed so far. I don't know if it's worth it.'

'You always have to pay the price for freedom,' said Joseph. 'No matter how high.'

'It's easy for you to say,' said Winifred, and then, remembering that he'd been injured in battle, felt herself flush slightly. 'I'm sorry. That makes it sound as though I don't think you put your money where your mouth is when clearly you already have.'

'I like being challenged,' said Joseph. 'People don't challenge assumptions enough. We get ourselves stuck in our opinions and we all start to think the same way. Perhaps it's not always the right way.'

'Are you telling me I've steered you from the path of violence, Mr Burke?' She looked at him in sudden amusement. 'To one of peace and enlightenment?'

'Not quite yet.' He smiled. 'I should also have asked about your injury, Miss O'Leary. How is it today?'

'I've had a lot worse,' she said. 'And I feel as though I've done my bit for independence now that I'm scarred for the cause.'

He laughed again.

This time she did too.

'So,' she said, when they were serious again. 'What about my window painting?'

'I'm very sorry, but I don't have anyone to do it,' said Joseph. 'I do know some arty people . . . I met them when

27

I was in Frongoch. They did lots of brilliant drawings. But I don't think they'd be any good at painting shop windows.'

She nodded at his mention of the detention centre in Wales where many men who'd participated in the Rising, even peripherally, had been imprisoned.

'Were you there long?'

'Six months.'

'I'm sure that was difficult.'

'It was a mistake putting us all together so that we could plot and plan.' He laughed. 'To be honest, bad though the conditions were – the place was overrun by rats, and I hate rats – it wasn't the worst experience of my life. I made some good friends. Decent men with shared ideals.'

'My father was shot in 1916,' remarked Winifred.

'He was a combatant?'

Thomas's involvement was a story that was frequently recounted with amusement within the O'Leary family. But Winifred wasn't sure if she should share it with Joseph Burke.

'It wasn't like that.' She decided to tell him the truth. 'He was walking past Boland's Mill during a lull in the fighting, and a stray bullet hit him in the leg. He's walked with a limp ever since.'

'I'm sorry,' said Joseph.

'Unless you were the shooter, it wasn't your fault. He was lucky. He lost his job at the docks but knew someone who got him something at the Custom House. But that's the problem with violence,' she added. 'It doesn't discriminate. You aim for the enemy, you can still hit a friend.'

'What do you want, Miss O'Leary?' he asked.

'Right now, all I want is that you get someone to paint my window.'

'I thought we agreed that it wasn't your window?'

'It's the window of the shop I work in. And I told you that Mrs Kelley won't be happy if she comes back and finds things not as she left them. As it is, I'm having to get rid of this silk.' She gestured at the bundle of blue fabric behind her. 'So that's another sacrifice. It's nothing but sacrifice from us.'

He smiled, then put his hand in his pocket and took out some coins.

'Will this cover you getting the job done?' he asked.

She looked at the money he'd placed in front of her.

'It'll do,' she said.

'I hope so.'

She picked up the coins and put them carefully in her purse.

'I'll come back in a day or two,' said Joseph. 'To check on the work.'

'You think I'll squander your money on feminine fripperies?'

'You might.'

'You don't know me.'

'No,' said Joseph. 'And you don't really know me either. Good day to you, Miss O'Leary.'

Then he turned on his heel and walked out of the shop.

Thomas O'Leary arrived home at six o'clock every evening. By then his wife had already left to clean the steps of the Empire Palace Theatre, but he knew Winifred would be waiting for him, ready to serve the dinner that Annie had left ready. He was lucky with his wife, he thought, and his daughter too. Annie was the love of his life. His soulmate. They were there for each other no matter what. And Winifred was a gem. You could always depend on her. She wasn't beautiful like Katy. Or flighty like Rosie. Not cheery like Mary-Jane or headstrong like Marianne. Winifred was the serious one who cared for others, who solved their problems, who put her family first. She was the one he leaned on.

But when he opened the door and walked inside, the small wooden table in the corner of the room still hadn't been set with a knife, fork and enamel mug for his tea.

He called out for her as he took off his boots. After nearly thirty years as a labourer at the docks, he was now a porter, and the work was less demanding on his footwear; the boots were serviceable enough for years to come and there was no need to waste money on anything else. As he put them neatly beside the chair, he massaged the top of his leg where the bullet had entered four years earlier. The injury might have been deadly but for the doctor who'd been running towards him and had been beside him when he fell. It had all been so sudden, Thomas hadn't even realised what had happened, although, he often told himself afterwards, being shot was hardly unexpected given the number of casualties that had resulted from what had turned into a bloody battle. The doctor, William Desmond, had dragged him from the pavement to the shelter of the shrubbery near the canal. He'd staunched the bleeding and brought Thomas to the nearest hospital, where they'd removed the bullet and cleaned the wound.

It was a twist of fate that Thomas's youngest daughter, Marianne, had recently found employment with Dr Desmond. Thomas knew of Marianne's dreams to be more than just a housemaid. He had faith in them too, because even though she had a tendency to look before she leaped, Marianne had inherited her mother's iron will and strength of character.

Every one of his daughters had. Nobody ever stood in the way of his girls.

I'm surrounded by women, he thought as he stretched his leg out in front of him, while my only living son is on a farm in County Meath. Hopefully Katy and her husband can keep him out of trouble there. Boys got caught up in battles and this damn war could go on for years yet. The world would be better off run by women. He laughed at himself. Men would never take orders from women, no matter how intelligent they were. Men always wanted to be the ones in charge.

He took out his watch and frowned. Winifred was now very late, and he worried that something had happened to her. He'd been shocked to learn about the stone coming through the window of the shop the previous day, and relieved it hadn't been anything worse. Alice Kelley had been married to an Englishman, and the Volunteers, the rebels, the republicans – he was never sure what he wanted to call them – knew things like that. So they could easily decide to sack Kelley's Fine Fabrics and make an example of a young girl working there if they chose. His stomach tensed at the thought of what they could do to Winifred. At what he knew had been done to other women, especially if it had been decided that they were in some way collaborators or spies. Rape, and he shuddered to think of it. Murder too – even though they called it execution and often left the bodies to be found by relatives.

He got up and walked to the window, his big toes poking out of his socks. There were plenty of people in the cobbled street below, but he didn't see his daughter. And then, just as the knot of worry was working its way into something bigger, he heard the door open and she walked into the room.

31

Winifred wasn't his favourite. That honour had been reserved for Mary-Jane, who, Thomas thought, was the sunniest of them all. But Winifred was clever and independent, which was probably why she was leaving it a bit late for find a husband for herself. Not that she needed to rush into marrying anyone – Annie had preached that to the girls often enough – but Winifred didn't seem to care about men or marriage, even though at nineteen she should surely be looking for someone. Although as he remembered again the things men did, he couldn't entirely blame her.

'You're home,' she said to him as she closed the door behind her.

'Where were you?' he asked.

'Working.'

'Until now?' He frowned.

She reminded him about the window in the shop and told him of her discussion with the young lieutenant about painting the name on it. 'And so,' she said as she counted out coins onto the table in front of him, 'I thought you could get your paint and your brush and do the job tomorrow, as it's Saturday.'

He looked up at her and smiled. Not the prettiest daughter. Not the sunniest. But definitely the smartest.

'I didn't tell Mr Burke that you'd once done a bit of painting at the docks,' she added. 'It wasn't something he needed to know.'

'You're a good girl, Winnie.' He scooped the coins into his pocket. 'Thanks for thinking of your aul' Da.'

As he took his seat at the table and she ladled the tripe and onions that had been simmering in the pot onto his plate, Winifred was glad that although there were many men in Thomas's position who'd spend any spare money on drink,

32

her father wasn't one of them. He rarely touched alcohol, and for that she was grateful. She'd seen how some men became after it, their inhibitions loosened, the baser parts of themselves released. Like Katy's husband. Winifred wondered with a sense of shock why she'd never thought of it before. Reid was a drinker, and his words turned coarse when he'd had a few pints. Perhaps that was why her sister now wore a permanently worried expression and had dark circles under her eyes. And maybe that was why Winifred herself had never liked her brother-in-law.

She would write to Katy, she thought. Suggest she pay her a visit. Just to check things out for herself. See if she wasn't putting two and two together and getting five.

'Have you forgotten about the bread, Winnie?' asked her father, his words bringing her back to what she was doing.

'Sorry.' She cut a slice from the loaf. 'Will you paint the window tomorrow?'

'First thing,' said Thomas. 'Don't you worry, Winnie my girl, it'll be as good as new when Mrs Kelley comes back.'

'I know it will.' She kissed him on the head.

'And now, if I'm going to be doing all that extra work, how about a second slice of bread?'

'Coming up,' said Winifred. 'And after that, I'll darn your socks for you. I can't have my father walking around like Bigfoot.'

'You're a wonder,' said Thomas.

'I know,' she told him, and handed him his extra bread to go with the tripe.

Chapter 3

The moment she arrived at her drapery shop on Monday morning, following her annual visit to her in-laws, Alice Kelley knew something was different. It took her a minute to see that the window was exceptionally clean; despite her best efforts, the dust of the city meant it was usually grimier than she'd like. But more than clean, she thought as she went inside. It was positively sparkling. And the interior of the shop was positively sparkling too. The floor was swept and the wooden counter polished. The bales of fabrics – linens, cottons, velvets and silks – were neatly stacked on the shelves, and the boxes of sewing patterns and trays of buttons had been tidied. Winifred had been busy. Although, Alice said to herself as she took out the ledger, if Winifred had had time to clean and tidy so well, she couldn't have been selling much fabric. And indeed, she saw as she traced her finger along the assistant's neat looped handwriting, after a busy start to the week, things had tapered off towards the end. She sighed. The shop was profitable, but only if their sales stayed above a certain level. And thanks to that fall-off, Winifred's first (and probably only) week in charge had barely kept it on the right side of the red line.

Alice looked up as the bell rang and Winifred herself stepped inside.

'What on earth happened to your face?' she asked after they'd exchanged greetings.

Her eyes opened wider and wider as Winifred told her of the riot outside, the stone coming through the window and her efforts to have it replaced.

'That's dreadful,' she said. 'You poor girl. You must have been terrified.'

Winifred admitted that she had been.

'And there was no talk of . . . well . . . me? As proprietor of the shop.'

'No.' Winifred shook her head. 'It seems it was a protest that started somewhere else, and when they tried to break it up, people ran in all directions before regrouping. But they weren't trying to intimidate business people or anything like that.'

Alice looked relieved.

'And all's well that ends well,' said Winifred. 'Because we have a new window and the old one already had a crack in it.'

'You've done very well.' Alice smiled. 'Very well indeed.'

'We lost sales, of course.' Winifred knew exactly what was most important to her boss.

'Yes. But at least I didn't lose you. I really don't know why there has to be all this violence,' Alice added peevishly. 'Why we can't all just get along. My mother-in-law thinks those republicans are just louts trying to force change that nobody wants. What exactly is wrong with what we have now?'

Winifred said nothing. She wasn't going to argue with her employer and say that she was mistaken, or naïve, or both. Like many of her friends and customers, Alice seemed to think that the desire for independence was temporary, driven

35

by a minority of the population. She didn't want to believe what was happening around her.

'These thugs do what they do, and we honest people trying to make a mere living have to get on with it,' Alice continued.

Winifred remained silent as she rolled out a bale of cotton and began to measure four lengths. She knew her employer saw herself as an impoverished widow, but she had her own home in the relatively affluent suburb of Rathmines and, as far as Winifred could tell, was financially comfortable. Admittedly the shop was a business venture and needed to be properly run, but Winifred was aware that Mrs Kelley had an annual income from her late husband's estate, provided for her by his parents (which was why she made a yearly visit to see them). Edward Kelley had been killed in the Great War, unlucky to have survived most of it only to be caught in an ambush in late 1917. Alice always said that at twenty-seven, he'd lived through most of the war precisely because he was old enough to know better than to end up in the line of fire. It aggrieved her that he'd been unlucky when victory was just around the corner.

'Well now,' she said to Winifred, 'best get on. We need to make up for lost time. I'm going to write letters to our customers. If any of them have heard about our misfortune, I want them to know that Kelley's is open for business as usual. And you must have orders to get on with.'

Winifred nodded, but before she could start on the orders, Mrs Beatty, one of their regulars, walked in, and she and Alice started talking about the stone through the window as though it was Alice herself who'd been there and not Winifred.

*   *   *

It turned out to be a day that kept both of them busy. Alice wrote her letters while Winifred finished with the cotton order and parcelled another three of muslin. Then she calculated and cut the correct amount of green and blue brocade needed for an entire house in Sandymount, a sizeable order for Kelley's as the house had nearly two dozen windows. She enjoyed making the calculations, being able to tell to the inch exactly what a customer would need and always getting it right.

She was tired by the end of the day, and by the end of each following day that week, because customers had reacted to Alice's letters by calling in and supporting her, buying something small or asking for greater amounts of fabric for different needs. By the time Friday lunchtime came around, Winifred was counting down the hours until closing. Alice, noticing that the younger woman looked pale, told her to go for a walk to get some colour back into her cheeks. After being on her feet all morning, the last thing Winifred felt like doing was walking, but she wasn't going to pass up the opportunity to have some unexpected time outside, so she left the shop and walked briskly across O'Connell Bridge, past Trinity College and on to Grafton Street. She stopped briefly outside Weir's jewellers, wondering if she'd ever have enough money of her own to buy items like the decorative peacock brooch or the emerald ring, as green as a shamrock, that were displayed in the window.

Winifred's dream, though it seemed very far off, was to have a drapery shop of her own, where she could stock the latest fabrics and designs and where she didn't have to answer to anyone other than herself. She never told anyone about this dream because, despite the rousing speeches of women like the Countess, it was an impossible one for somebody like her. The only way it might happen would be for her to marry a man with money, and the last thing Winifred wanted to do was marry for money. Not that she was likely to meet any men with money. Not that she met many men even without money. After all, despite the animosity of the republicans towards British rule in Ireland, nearly 200,000 Irish men had gone to fight in the world war on their behalf, and it was estimated that around 30,000 had lost their lives. Now many of those who had returned were fighting against the Crown forces at home. The pool of available men wasn't particularly deep, she would say when Marianne teased her about her lack of a beau, and she wasn't going to pick an unsuitable man out of desperation.

'If the right fella comes along, I'll know,' she would retort whenever the subject came up. And then she would sometimes add that too many young girls settled for second best, simply to be able to put a ring on their finger and Mrs in front of their name.

'I'll get married if I fall in love,' she said one day after another debate with her younger sister. 'But he'd need to be exceptional.'

'As if you're all that exceptional yourself, Winnie O'Leary, and you who doesn't even wear a little bit of rouge on your cheeks,' Marianne said, and flounced off.

Winifred continued her stroll along the city's most important commercial street, smiling at other pedestrians, whose good cheer was enhanced by yet another pleasant day. She paused again outside the Hodges Figgis bookshop and looked at the books lined up in the window. She didn't even have money for a book, let alone a peacock brooch, she reminded herself. So she wasn't doing much to help trade. And then she recalled her mother once saying to her father that the bookstore, which had been founded well over a hundred years earlier, survived on rich Protestants. In which case they certainly weren't depending on her to keep going.

She carried on walking until she reached St Stephen's Green, which was already busy with people promenading around the neat lawns, and past the carefully tended flower beds, the duck ponds and the fountains. She found a seat near the empty bandstand and allowed her eyes to flicker closed beneath the warmth of the summer sun.

'Miss O'Leary.'

Her name spoken aloud jolted her into wakefulness, especially when she recognised the voice of the person saying it.

'Lieutenant Burke,' she said. 'What are you doing here?'

'I had some free time, so I decided to take a walk,' he said. 'I saw you entering the park.'

'And you followed me?' She sat up straight, her voice indignant.

'Yes,' he said. 'I wanted to talk to you, and I hoped you would talk to me too.'

She looked at him. 'Go on then. Talk.'

'Would you like to walk around the park with me?'

'I've been standing all day,' she said. 'And I walked here from Sackville Place. I'd prefer to sit. But you talk away, I'll listen.'

'It wasn't just talking,' he said. 'I wanted . . . well . . . perhaps you'd like to have tea with me some day?'

'Tea?' Laughter bubbled up inside her. 'D'you think you're a society lady, inviting me to afternoon tea?'

'People have tea,' he said. 'In a tea shop. I thought you might like it.'

'I might,' she conceded.

'After your work this evening?'

'And what about you, Lieutenant?' she asked. 'Will you not be too busy planning ambushes and raids to have time for tea?'

'I have a job as well as being a Volunteer,' said Joseph. 'I work in a printer's. I also help my father. He's a boiler man.'

Winifred considered this. His father being a boiler man somewhat contradicted her earlier assumption that Joseph and his sisters lived a comfortable middle-class existence that allowed him the time to play at being a soldier. Yet he seemed, if not prosperous, certainly not destitute. And he'd had sufficient money to pay for the fixing of Mrs Kelley's window as well as the repainting of the name. Of course he probably hadn't paid for that himself. The money had likely come from some republican fund. Though that would've been unlikely if they'd done a bit of research on Alice Kelley and realised that she was a Protestant and that her husband had fought for the British.

Joseph sat in silence beside her as she weighed up the merits of having tea with him. The truth was, she was tempted. Despite his membership of the republican army, Joseph Burke was an interesting man. She suddenly thought of Katy, whose marriage to Reid might not be as good a thing as she'd first believed, and Mary-Jane, who seemed happy with the Englishman none of them had met, and Rosie, who was besotted by her Belgian pilot and whose most recent letter had been peppered with French phrases and their translations.

Winifred was the only one who hadn't a man in her life. But here, now, was an opportunity to go out with a man, just like every other woman her age did. She'd been asked. The least she could do was say yes.

'Thank you for the invitation,' she said finally. 'I'd be delighted to have tea with you. But not this evening,' she added. 'They're expecting me home.'

'Tomorrow?' suggested Joseph. 'Do you work on Saturday?'

'Of course. And tomorrow would be fine, thank you.'

'Excellent.' He smiled at her. 'I'll wait outside the shop for you.'

She nodded.

'In the meantime, would you like me to escort you back there?'

'That would be very kind,' she conceded as she stood up beside him.

Mrs Kelley noticed the following day that Winifred was wearing a different blouse, white with a scalloped collar, and that at the close of business she spent a lot of time fixing her wavy brown hair before dabbing a few drops of her precious 4711 eau de cologne behind her ears and on her wrists.

'Are you going somewhere, Miss O'Leary?' she asked.

When Winifred said she was meeting a man, Alice's face lit up.

'How lovely for you!' she exclaimed. 'Do I know him?'

'It's the man who fixed your window,' replied Winifred. 'Maybe he was feeling bad about me getting cut and wanted to make it up in some way.'

'Or perhaps he just likes you.' Alice beamed at her. 'Although he's a republican, so you want to be careful what you say to him.'

'He seems like a nice man,' said Winifred.

'In that case you must . . . Wait here.' Alice disappeared into the storeroom and emerged with a bright apricot scarf in light organza. 'Here,' she said. 'For luck.'

'Oh, Mrs Kelley, you don't have to . . .'

'No, I don't,' agreed Alice. 'But I want to. I want you to look good and have a nice time with your young man, and I want you to tell me everything about it on Monday.'

'I don't know that there'll be anything to tell,' said Winifred.

'There's always something to tell.' Alice winked at her. 'Go on. Enjoy yourself.' And she hustled her out of the store a little earlier than Winifred had intended.

Even though she was early, Joseph was waiting for her, leaning against the facade of the building next door. When he saw her, he straightened up and smiled.

He had, thought Winifred, a very nice smile.

'You look well,' he said.

'So do you.'

He was wearing the same brown suit as before, this time with a grey tie and highly polished brogues. He looked distinguished, she thought in surprise, a very different man to the one who'd come into the shop the day of the riot. Not an army man. And definitely not a boiler man.

'I thought Bewley's in George's Street,' he said.

'Good choice.'

Their conversation as they walked along the quays and then up Crown Alley to Dame Street stuck to topics like the weather (beautiful for the time of year, although the smell from the Liffey was over-ripe), the number of people on the streets (surprising given the continuing violence), the business of the city (erratic, also because of the violence) and, as they arrived outside the café, their personal preference for coffee over tea whenever the opportunity presented itself.

'It's so enriching.' Winifred stopped at the window and looked at the big vats of roasting beans as the aroma, hot and slightly bitter, filled the air.

Joseph held the door open and she stepped inside, hesitating for a moment as her eyes adjusted to the darker interior after the brightness of the late-summer day. A waitress in a button-down black dress with a white collar and starched white apron led them to a table.

After consulting with both the waitress and Winifred, Joseph ordered a pot of coffee and two sticky buns.

'I used to meet my friend Esther here once a month,' said Winifred in answer to a question from him. 'But she got married last year and doesn't have much time for outings since she had a baby. And you? Is this your preferred spot for coffee with lady friends?'

'I don't have many lady friends.' He grinned at her. 'In fact, Miss O'Leary, you're only the third woman I've had coffee with here. The other two were my sisters.'

Conversation with him was easy, she reflected as she ate her bun. He was clever and witty and clearly well educated. When the discussion almost inevitably veered towards the War of Independence, he didn't reduce it – as she thought he might – to a simple question of Them and Us, but had a nuanced viewpoint about how it was the British acted as they did and why it was that some Irish people were happy to allow it.

'But not you,' she said.

'Look, I'd prefer to be living a peaceful life,' he said. 'I don't want to be involved in planning raids on military barracks or hiding Irishmen on the run or debating questions of freedom.

I'd like to read my books, play my music, be in my garden and grow vegetables without a care in the world. But that's not how it is right now.'

'Music? You're a musician?'

'I play the mandolin,' he said. 'And the harmonica.'

'While you plan raids and hide men on the run.'

'I'm a good planner,' he said. 'I have to be because my fighting capacity is limited.'

'Because of your eye?' She put the question cautiously.

'My peripheral vision isn't good,' he said. 'That's a disadvantage when you're trying to . . .' He stopped and laughed. 'I was going to say "keep an eye out", but that's a grim kind of humour.'

'How did you lose it?' she asked. 'An ambush?'

He exhaled slowly but didn't speak. Had it been something so awful he didn't want to recall it? she wondered, feeling embarrassed at having asked him.

'I'm sorry to say that the loss of my eye had nothing to do with Ireland's struggles,' he replied eventually.

She looked at him inquisitively.

'It was a childhood accident,' he said. 'It happened at school. Another boy hit me with a stone from a catapult. It's why I was so anxious when the stone came through your window,' he added quickly. 'I was afraid for you. For whoever was inside.'

'Oh.' This time her look was sympathetic. 'Well, we know that I was fortunate. I'm sorry you weren't.'

'So am I.' He gave a rueful shrug. 'I feel that I can't give my all.'

'And yet you were in Frongoch,' she said. 'So you gave enough to be arrested.'

'Oh, everyone with even the slightest connection to the signatories on the 1916 Proclamation of the Irish republic was rounded up,' he said. 'I knew Pearse. It wasn't surprising.'

'And hiding people on the run?' She returned to his earlier comment.

'Only occasionally,' he said. It was clear he wasn't going to elaborate any further.

'You're a rebel family,' she remarked.

'We don't call it rebellion,' said Joseph. 'We call it the fight for freedom.'

She acknowledged his comment with a nod.

'And we'll win eventually,' he added. 'I'm quite sure the British would get out of Ireland now if they could, only it would be such a loss of face for them and their empire. Imagine the feeling – they couldn't hold on to one of the smallest parts of it, right next door. And if they can't keep us, how can they expect to retain India? It's not about what's best for them or for Ireland. It's about having power, wanting to show it and wanting to keep it. That's why we fight, Winifred. We want to control our own destiny.' He picked up his spoon and stirred his coffee. 'You know, I didn't ask you for tea to talk politics. I get enough of that at home. Tell me about your family.'

She didn't want to talk about politics either. And she rarely spoke about her family. She sat back in her chair.

'There's Ma and Da,' she said. 'Ma has cleaning jobs and Da works in the Custom House. He used to be a docker, but when he got shot . . .' She shrugged. 'He's a decent man, my da. Ma is exceptional. She made sure all of us went to school even when it was very difficult. She taught us herself too. She says it's the most important thing in the world for a girl to have education.'

'She's right,' said Joseph.

'Oh, Ma is always right.' Winifred smiled. 'At least, that's what she tells us. Anyhow, I have four sisters and a brother. None of them live at home now. Katy and Mary-Jane are both married, and I think Rosie will be soon. She's seeing a Belgian air force pilot. She always goes for the adventurous types. Marianne is too young to be married yet, but because she's in service she doesn't live with us either. To be honest, although it's a lot more peaceful and I enjoy having time alone, I miss my sisters. Tom, my brother, is twelve, and living with Katy at the moment. I miss him too, of course, but what can you say about young boys? Sometimes you miss them the same way you'd miss a fly buzzing around you.'

'That's a little harsh.' Joseph laughed.

'But true.' She smiled again. 'It's an odd feeling when you've spent a lot of your time so close to people and then suddenly they're gone.'

'Do you feel a responsibility towards your parents?' asked Joseph. 'To stay with them? Look after them?'

'Love many, trust few, always paddle your own canoe,' said Winifred. 'It's my mother's favourite saying. I think she's telling me that I've got to live my own life. So I don't feel responsible for them, no. But they've been wonderful parents to all of us and I'll always want to be close to them.'

'You're a caring woman, Winifred O'Leary,' he said.

'Call me Winnie,' she said. 'Everyone who knows me does.'

She thought of him that night as she lay in her bed listening to the gentle snores of her father on the other side of the curtain. Annie and Thomas had asked her about the young man she was seeing, and she'd shrugged and told them that he seemed nice and was very polite.

'He should have asked my permission to take you out,' said Thomas.

Winifred had laughed at that. So had Annie. They weren't the sort of family where anyone asked permission to do anything.

But when they were alone, Annie had asked her more about him and Winifred told her about his family's involvement in the war. Annie had looked concerned.

'Everyone's involved in some way or another,' Winifred pointed out.

'Be careful with him,' said Annie.

'I will.'

And she would. But she didn't want to be. Because there was something about Joseph Burke that made her feel like throwing caution to the winds. Something that made her feel like nobody else had ever made her feel.

I can't love him, she decided as she turned over once again. I hardly know him.

But what I do know, I really, really like.

Chapter 4

Agnes Burke had almost finished cleaning the small room on the ground floor of the house. Having stripped the narrow bed and put the sheets and pillowcase in the big laundry bag, she was now mopping the floor, pushing the galvanised metal bucket with her foot as she went. She was glad he was finally gone. Unlike some of the more grateful men she'd sheltered in the windowless room, Phelim Flynn had been arrogant and demanding, and – despite strict instructions to the contrary – had smoked his pungent cigarettes whenever he felt like it. Agnes hoped that the distinctive smell of Jeyes Fluid would eventually overcome the lingering aroma of cheap tobacco.

She heard footsteps in the hallway and froze for a moment, her eyes scanning the room for signs of recent occupation. The fact that it was empty didn't detract from the presence of a bed, even one with a thin, uncomfortable mattress.

'Ma! Are you home?'

Agnes released her breath. She picked up the bucket and mop and walked out of the room, locking it behind her.

'I'm here,' she said to the young woman standing in the hallway. 'Just cleaning up.'

'Is everything all right?' Her daughter, May, looked at her from grey-green eyes that held a hint of anxiety.

'And why wouldn't it be? Take this.' Agnes thrust the mop at her while she headed towards the scullery with the bucket. May followed her.

'We shouldn't have said yes to him,' she said as her mother emptied the dirty water into the Belfast sink.

'We didn't have a choice.'

'We always have a choice. Mostly we've made good ones.' She hesitated. 'We need to make another. It'll only be for a few days.'

Agnes rinsed the bucket and left it under the sink.

'Where's Baba?' she asked her daughter as she dried her hands.

'In his perambulator. Rosanna is looking after him.'

Agnes opened the scullery door and both women stepped into the garden. The sweet scent of clematis reached them on the lightest of late-summer breezes. Agnes looked appreciatively at the flowering plant that covered the wall dividing their half of the garden from the adjoining convent building, and took a deep breath to banish the aroma of smoke and bleach from her nostrils.

'When?' She breathed out again and began to walk along the gravel path that led towards the rose bushes.

'Tomorrow night.'

Agnes dead-headed the tired flowers without speaking.

'It's someone very deserving,' added May.

'They're all deserving. Even that cocky so-and-so of the last few days.'

'So . . . will I say yes?'

'The transfer will be at night?'

49

'Of course.'

'And you're sure it won't be for long? Because we're in their sights and it's getting more dangerous.'

'I know. We'll be very careful.'

'All right.' Agnes nodded.

'How's Da?' May asked as they passed the door of the boiler house.

'You know your da.' Agnes smiled. 'Never happier than when taking something apart and putting it together again.'

The two women laughed.

'He loves that boiler more than he loves you,' remarked May, though her eyes twinkled.

'And I love your da because the only thing he loves more than me is his boiler.'

May chuckled and put her arm around her mother's waist.

'Will you have some tea?' asked Agnes.

'Yes. I even brought fruit cake to have with it,' said May.

The two women went back into the house, where Agnes boiled a kettle on the enormous cast-iron range.

'Maud Gonne wrote another piece for the *Bulletin*,' said May when they were sitting with tea and cake in front of them. 'It was very powerful.'

'She's a good writer,' acknowledged Agnes. 'And a good republican too.'

'She said in the piece that our children are being neglected by the British.'

'Some of them are being neglected by the Irish. Not that you can blame them; the level of poverty in the city is shocking.'

'Our family is lucky,' said May.

'And that's why we help,' Agnes said. 'Because we can. And because we should.'

She poured them both another cup of tea just as fifteen-year-old Rosanna walked into the room carrying May's baby daughter. And the conversation shifted to children and their needs, which suited Agnes just fine.

Chapter 5

Dublin, September 1920

Dear Ma and Pa and Winnie,

I'm getting married. Sorry, was that too abrupt? But what else can I say? I'm getting married to Léonard next week and we're going to live in Belgium. He's been offered a job at an air school near Brussels and he's taking it. He's always wanted to go back. It's very exciting. My French is improving all the time! Je m'appelle Rosie. That means my name is Rosie. After I'm married, I will be Madame Rosie Voorspoels. Doesn't that sound good? I'm sorry I can't come home first but I hope to see you all very soon. I love Léo very much and I hope you'll be happy for me.

You're the only girl left, Winnie!!!!

Don't leave it too late.

Lots of love and bonne chance (that means good luck!).

Your loving daughter and sister,

Rosie xxx

Winifred thought she might be in love too.

Her weekly walks around St Stephen's Green and Saturday visits to Bewley's for coffee with Joseph Burke were events she looked forward to more and more each time. She enjoyed tidying her hair and wearing her blouse with the scalloped collar and her best shoes whenever she met him. And she liked that he always wore his best suit to meet her. Annie, noticing the new lightness of mood in her daughter, had asked about Joseph, and Winifred told her that he made her smile.

'I can see that,' Annie said. 'Are you two serious about each other?'

'I've only known him a couple of months,' said Winifred.

'More than enough time, Winnie,' said her mother. 'Bring him home.'

'Oh Ma! I don't know if that's a good idea.'

'Are you ashamed of our home?' asked Annie.

'Of course not.' Winifred shook her head. 'But having him meet you . . . doesn't it make it all seem . . . well . . . very formal?'

'We're not a formal family, but I'd like to meet him all the same,' said Annie. 'Bring him here next Sunday.'

'All right,' agreed Winifred, although her tone was doubtful.

But when she issued the invitation to Joseph on their mid-week walk, he said he'd be delighted to come to East Essex Street.

'It's not for much,' warned Winifred. 'Just a cup of tea.'

'I can't wait to meet your family,' he said.

'You won't meet them all. Only Ma and Da.'

'I still can't wait to meet them.'

On the day he was due to arrive, Winifred was in a state of complete agitation, which made Annie think that her young man really meant something to her. She was glad. For all Winnie's independence, a girl needed a man in her life. Married women were treated with much more respect.

'Is that the shirt you're wearing?' Winifred looked at her father in dismay.

'It's my Sunday shirt,' said Thomas.

'It's missing a button,' Winnie told him.

'Nobody'll notice.'

'Winnie just did. Take it off and let me replace it,' said Annie.

'All this for a young fella,' Thomas said as his wife took a matching button from a wooden box on the mantelpiece. 'Are you sure you wouldn't like me to run out to Fitzpatrick's and get fitted for a suit?'

'Da!'

'It would be money well spent,' he teased, 'if it means I get you off my hands.'

'Da!'

'Are my boots shiny enough for you?' he asked. 'Is my face smooth enough? Would you like me to shave again?'

'Leave the girl alone, Thomas.' Annie threaded a needle and began to sew on the new button. 'Polish your boots, comb your hair and this will be ready when you are.'

'I suppose as you're wearing your good blouse it's the least I can do,' said Thomas. 'And you, Winnie – have you been off to the dressmaker's for something fancy?'

'She's got a lovely new skirt,' said Annie. 'She had it made from some remnants Mrs Kelley gave her.'

'Now there's a decent woman,' said Thomas. 'Shows that

those Protestant types aren't all bad. But that doesn't look like a new skirt, Winnie. You wear it every day.'

'I'm going to change into the new one now,' said Winifred.

As soon as she went into the other room, Annie made a face at her husband.

'Be nice,' she whispered. 'Don't tease.'

'Oh, all right,' he said. 'But it's a bit of an event, Winnie and a young man.'

'So let's make sure it goes well.'

'Anything for my girl.' And Thomas stood up and combed his hair in front of the mirror.

Winifred was pleased with the new cardinal-red skirt, which looked well with her white blouse. She'd bought herself an inexpensive cameo brooch that she pinned at the neck, and even though her hair wasn't long enough to put up in the elegant style that Katy wore, she thought she was almost pretty.

She was nervous, though. It seemed silly to be nervous when all that was happening was that a friend was coming for tea, but she knew that Joseph was more than a friend, and she also knew that she wanted her parents to like him. She wasn't really nervous about that – Joseph was very like-able. But whether they'd approve of him or not was another question entirely.

He arrived exactly on time, wearing his dark suit and his flat cap and carrying a small posy of flowers, which he gave to Annie, much to her delight. She put them in a jar on the table, and then they sat down to a tea of cheese sandwiches.

'Tell me about your work,' said Thomas. 'A printer. And a boiler man.'

'My father's the boiler man,' replied Joseph as he took one of the sandwiches that Annie offered him. 'For the convent in St Anthony's Place. It fires their radiators and makes sure they have hot water.'

'Well for them.' Thomas glanced at the grate with its barely glowing embers. 'Those nuns know how to look after themselves.'

'They do,' agreed Joseph. 'But they also do a lot of good work.'

Thomas snorted, but Annie agreed that the charitable work the nuns did was important.

'And the printing?' asked Thomas.

'*The Freeman's Journal*,' said Joseph.

Winifred's eyes flickered between her parents. Her father already knew that Joseph's family were republican; that he worked for a newspaper sympathetic to the cause made it even clearer. He made no comment, but simply asked Annie for more tea.

'And what about your family?' asked Annie when all their cups had been refilled.

'I have three sisters,' said Joseph. 'And a brother who died when he was a baby.'

'Like me, you're surrounded by women,' said Thomas.

'Yes,' agreed Joseph.

'Strong women?'

'Opinionated, that's for sure.'

The two men laughed.

'Are they married, your sisters?' asked Annie.

'May is, and she has two children, a young boy and a baby girl,' replied Joseph. 'Rosanna and Ita are still living at home. They're just children themselves.'

'Not exactly children.' Winifred, who'd stayed mostly silent during the meal, suddenly spoke. 'Ita is seventeen. Rosanna is fifteen.'

'They're young yet,' said Joseph.

'And neither working?' Annie sounded surprised.

'Ita is delicate,' said Joseph. 'She caught the flu last year and hasn't fully recovered. Rosanna helps my mother with . . . with things around the house.'

'God knows your sister was lucky to survive the flu,' said Annie. 'Was she the only person in the house to get it?'

'Thankfully yes,' said Joseph. 'I know my mother was afraid for me, because I had bronchitis when I was in Frongoch and I seem to catch colds and coughs more easily since. But maybe I built up a resistance to the flu, because it passed me by. Anyhow, we're fortunate that it seems to be abating now, even if the war isn't.'

'What's the story about your position as a Volunteer?' Thomas asked. 'Because that's how you met our Winnie, isn't it? Attacking the shop where she works.'

'Da!' Winifred couldn't stop the exclamation. 'I told you, it was an accident. We weren't attacked.'

'So he says.'

'It was a bit of overexuberance by the participants,' said Joseph. 'The stone hit the window by mistake. And we did replace it.'

Winifred shot her father a glance. She hadn't told Joseph that it was Thomas who'd painted the name, and she didn't want him to blurt it out now and make her look conniving. But Thomas merely asked him how likely it was that he'd be killed in the near future.

'Da!' cried Winifred again.

'It's a fair question,' said Joseph. 'The truth is, Mr O'Leary,

I'm more of a planner than an active member. But I'm a good planner. My speciality is logistics and commandeering equipment.'

'Won't stop them coming for you,' said Thomas.

'I'll try to stay one step ahead.'

Thomas nodded, then Annie turned the conversation again, asking about Joseph's mother. He replied that she was a woman very like Annie herself, who cared deeply for her family as well as for the future of the country. Then he thanked her for the excellent tea and for looking after him so well.

'I should be going.' He took an old pocket watch from his jacket and checked it. 'I've taken up a lot of your time.'

'I'll walk you out,' said Winifred.

Joseph shook hands with her parents and then the two young people walked down the stairs and out onto East Essex Street, where Winifred exhaled loudly.

'Are you all right?' he asked.

'Are you?'

'Of course.'

'It was an ordeal,' she said.

'Not for me.'

'Really? They peppered you with questions.'

'Your parents are good people, Winnie. I liked them. I hope they liked me.'

'How could they not?' She smiled suddenly. 'You see the good in everyone.'

'I'm a Volunteer in the fight for independence,' he reminded her. 'I hardly see the good in everyone. But,' he added, 'I certainly see the good in you, Miss Winifred O'Leary.'

Then he kissed her on the cheek and walked away.

* * *

'I don't like that he's so involved in the struggle,' said Thomas when Winifred returned. 'He'll get himself killed and he'll put anyone who knows him in danger. Which means you, Winnie.'

'Like he said, he's a planner, not an active participant,' said Winifred.

'It's all the same to the Brits,' her father pointed out. 'If they suspect him of something, it won't matter if he has a rifle in his hand or not.'

'They seem to be a well-to-do family,' observed Annie. 'Two girls at home not working, delicate or not. And a mother who doesn't work either.'

'That's because Mr Burke has a cushy job with the nuns,' said Thomas. 'I've always said it's the religious that have the money in this country. They ask people to give them what they have, and we do so that they can keep their seminaries and their convents a good deal warmer than we can keep our houses.'

'That's true,' said Annie.

Winifred stayed silent. Her parents were ambivalent about religion, although her mother went to Mass every Sunday at the church of St Michael and John on Essex Quay, and made offerings to help the priests and nuns. But she didn't, as the majority of the congregation appeared to, believe that they were almost as infallible as the Pope.

'I believe in the message,' she sometimes said. 'The messengers are a different kettle of fish altogether.'

'But he seems a nice young man,' said Thomas. 'You could do worse, Winnie.'

'She could do better too,' remarked Annie.

'Who says I'm doing anything at all?' Winifred turned on her heel and walked into the other room.

She sat on her bed and opened the little notebook Joseph had given her, and read the inscription inside: *To Winifred: When you smile and it's just for me, I know my heart will never be free.*

Alice was delighted by Winifred's romance. She thought Joseph was very handsome and manly, although she never spoke about his involvement in the War of Independence. Winifred knew that this was because her employer liked to pretend that it was nothing but a skirmish, and that riots, ambushes and shootings were isolated incidents even though they occurred daily. She couldn't blame her. It was easier to think that events were less serious than they were, to tell yourself that it would all be over shortly, than to think that the country could be engulfed in war for years.

It was easier, too, for Winnie, to accept Joseph's word that his involvement was minimal, even though she was well aware that the Burkes knew many of the more prominent military figures and were probably on some kind of watch list. She tried to pretend it didn't concern her, but it did. The recently enacted Restoration of Order in Ireland Act, passed after the British government had discussed but rejected the idea of imposing martial law, had heightened tensions in the city, and the arrival of supplementary forces to support the RIC had enraged the population even more. The Auxiliaries and the Black and Tans (almost immediately given the name because they wore surplus uniforms left over from the Great War in those mismatched colours) brought a new level of brutality to interaction with the public. The Black and Tans were ex-soldiers who were attached to the RIC, but the Auxiliaries had a paramilitary status. As far as most people were concerned, they were as bad as each other.

'And when they attack women, that's not keeping the peace,' Winnie said to Joseph one afternoon as they sat on a bench in St Stephen's Green. The leaves on the trees were just beginning to turn from green to gold, and occasionally floated to the ground beside them. 'They're just being bastards.'

He looked at her in surprise. While he was used to the occasional swear word from her, he'd never heard her sound so angry before.

'Not all of them,' he said.

'Too many of them,' Winifred retorted. 'We're not men's possessions, you know.'

'I never thought you were,' said Joseph. 'Besides, lots of women are working alongside men in the cause of freedom. None of them are treated like possessions.'

'Some are, I think,' said Winnie. 'But what I'm more upset about is the men who use women as part of the battle.'

'How?' Joseph looked puzzled.

'Women are used to get their menfolk in line,' said Winifred. 'They're assaulted in front of their husbands. I read a report . . . It was more what wasn't said than what was. But the soldiers . . .' she hesitated, unsure whether she could say the word, 'they tied a man to a chair and raped his wife while he watched and said she was now soiled goods. As though she was a thing and not a person. It's . . . shocking.'

'You're right,' agreed Joseph. 'It's shocking and unacceptable. In the new republic, violation of women will be a crime. And the men who do it will be dealt with accordingly.'

'Sorry.' Winifred sighed. 'I get carried away sometimes.'

'I love that you do. I love your passion.'

'Misplaced maybe.'

'Not at all,' said Joseph. 'I told you before, my mother, my sisters – they're equally passionate about women's rights.'

'I'm worried about my own sister,' admitted Winifred.

'Which one?'

'Katy. Her husband drinks a lot and I think he treats her badly. She was always the prettiest of us, but the last time she visited, she looked pale and worn. I don't know if that's because of him or for some other reason. I do know she's been pregnant a couple of times and lost the babies, so it might be that that's getting her down. But I worry all the same.'

'Perhaps you should visit her. If you need transport, let me know.'

'Thank you. That's really kind. I'll think about it.'

They got up from the bench and walked around the lake, silently feeding the ducks with stale breadcrumbs.

'Are you too angry with all men to come to tea on Sunday?' he asked after they'd emptied the brown paper bag of crumbs and begun to walk towards the park gates.

His mother had issued the invitation shortly after he'd been to East Essex Street and Winifred had accepted. Subsequently, there was some talk of changing the day, which had worried her because perhaps Mrs Burke didn't want to meet her after all, but Joseph had assured her that she did, and confirmed the date was unchanged.

'I'm not angry with you.' She tightened her arm around his. 'You're a decent man. I'm just frustrated at . . . well . . . how things are, I suppose.'

'Me too,' said Joseph. 'That's why I'm fighting to change it. And those changes will be good for women too, Winifred. I promise.'

She looked up at him, and when he smiled at her, she wanted to believe that he was right.

Chapter 6

The following Sunday afternoon, Winifred dressed in her red skirt and white blouse again, and spent an age in front of the mirror brushing her hair until it gleamed. Annie had loaned her a pair of earrings – the only jewellery she possessed apart from her narrow wedding band. Winifred loved how the tiny pearls swung from her ears, and made sure that her hair was pinned back enough so Mrs Burke would see them and know that the O'Learys weren't impoverished workers. Once again she fixed her cameo brooch to her blouse, and she also wore the scarf that Alice Kelley had given her, along with a brown hat with a cream fabric band that Rosie had left behind when she and Mary-Jane had headed off to England. She had no qualms about pinching it, because it finished off her outfit to perfection. Meanwhile her father had polished and shined her ankle boots until they gleamed.

'You're a picture,' Annie told her while they waited for Joseph to arrive. 'Any man would be lucky to have you.'

Joseph wasn't any man, thought Winifred, but he was wise enough and polite enough when he turned up in his best suit to tell her that she did indeed look beautiful and that he was lucky to be escorting her across the city.

His home was almost a mile and a half away and she was ready to walk, but when they went outside, she saw that he had come by bicycle. It was a delivery boy's bicycle, with a basket on the front and a panel attached to the crossbar that said *Brown's Butchers*. The basket was filled with flowers.

'For you.' He presented her with one of them. She smiled as she tucked it into the buttonhole of her coat, but then looked at him in disbelief.

'You're not expecting me to get up on that, are you?'

'It's a lot quicker than walking,' said Joseph as he fixed bicycle clips around his trousers. 'I'm good on a bike. I'll look after you.'

'This is against my better judgement,' said Winifred, who squeaked in terror as she sat on the crossbar. The bicycle wobbled slightly before Joseph picked up the pace, and she held firmly onto her hat. She'd used multiple pins to hold it in place, but she didn't trust it not to blow away, and she was determined it was going to stay on her head no matter what.

Joseph cycled along the quays, crossed O'Connell Bridge and continued past the General Post Office, where the pockmarks of the bullets fired at it during the 1916 Rising were still plainly visible. A group of police officers stood outside, and Winifred heard Joseph's sharp intake of breath as he spotted them. Please don't do anything foolish, she thought, pushing her hand down hard on her hat. Please keep going.

And he did, whistling cheerfully as he rode up Sackville Street, past the Rotunda maternity hospital, which catered for impoverished women, and along Rutland Square into St Anthony's Place.

'Here we are,' he said as he helped her down from the bicycle.

She looked up at the house. It was much bigger than she'd expected from the description he'd given, a brown-brick two-storey building with multiple windows. She'd imagined something akin to the rooms she and her parents shared in East Essex Street, but this was a proper house in the grounds of a large convent that took up a sizeable part of Temple Street. Joseph hadn't given the impression it was anything other than small living quarters supplied by the nuns for the family's use as part of his father's contract, but perhaps that was deliberate. She'd often spoken of him and his family as being better off than the O'Learys, and he'd always tried to disabuse her of the notion.

'Are you going to keep staring or are you coming in?' He unlocked the iron gate set into the wall. She followed him wordlessly as he opened the door into the house itself and stepped into the wide hallway.

The floor was covered in black and white tiles, while the walls were painted a pale salmon pink and hung with rather dull landscape paintings. A small chandelier on the ceiling threw multicoloured shards of light across the hallway. Sideboards along the walls were topped with vases of flowers and small ceramic ornaments. Winifred was speechless. This was riches, she thought. It was unlike anything she'd ever seen, except perhaps at Dr Desmond's Pembroke Road home when she'd visited Marianne and her sister had allowed her to peek upstairs.

If, as Joseph said, his family weren't wealthy, then all this largesse was courtesy of the nuns. And if this was a house owned by the religious order and rented out to a worker, what on earth did the convent itself look like?

She heard footsteps, and a tall, statuesque woman appeared at the end of the hallway. Her auburn hair, liberally sprinkled with grey, was swept up and held by a tortoiseshell clip, and her eyes, hazel like Joseph's, looked at her appraisingly from a somewhat severe face. She was wearing a dark green skirt, pale blouse and shiny black shoes.

'Miss O'Leary, I presume,' she said as she walked towards them. 'So good to meet you at last.'

'And you, Mrs Burke.' The woman was so regal that Winifred felt as though she should drop a curtsey; but even though her family wasn't half as republican as the Burkes seemed to be, her mother always said that the O'Learys would never bow or curtsey to anyone. Not even a bishop, she had declared, and they think they're more than royalty!

The older woman's face broke into a smile and Winifred felt relief wash over her. Because when Agnes Burke smiled, the severity left her and her gaze softened.

'We're having tea in the Yellow Room,' she said. 'Would you like me to take your hat?'

'Thank you.' Winifred unpinned Rosie's hat and Mrs Burke hung it on an ornamental hook on the wall along with her coat and chiffon scarf.

'This way,' she said.

Winifred shot a quick glance at Joseph, who smiled at her and gave her hand a surreptitious squeeze. They followed his mother along the corridor and down two steps before turning into an alcove. Mrs Burke opened the door and ushered Winifred inside.

It was indeed a yellow room, papered in a pale primrose

flock with heavy drapes in harvest gold. Winifred recognised the material in the drapes; she'd cut yards of it herself the previous summer for a client. It wasn't the most expensive material that Kelley's sold, nor was it the cheapest, but its floral pattern was very popular. A couple of large Axminster rugs covered the floor, and either side of a wide fireplace were a pair of high-backed armchairs occupied by two young girls whom she assumed were Joseph's opinionated sisters.

The slimmer of them, her red-gold hair clipped into a loose bun at the back of her head, stood up and introduced herself as Ita. Winnie could see a certain pallor in her face, the legacy perhaps of her brush with the dreadful flu. The other girl, her darker hair worn in an untidy plait, was far sturdier and said her name was Rosanna.

Ita extended her hand to Winifred and told her it was good to meet her at last. 'My brother has told us a lot about you,' she added with a smile.

'I have not!' Joseph gave his sister an irritated look.

'Oh but you have,' Ita told him. 'It's all Miss O'Leary this and Miss O'Leary that and "I've never met a woman quite like Miss O'Leary" – as though you hadn't grown up with us and May.'

'That part is true.' Joseph turned to Winifred. 'I haven't met a woman like you before.'

'So what sort of women do you normally meet?' Winifred's eyes danced with merriment.

'Oh, Joe's very much into his literary women,' said Mrs Burke. 'He's a big fan of Maud Gonne.'

'I am not!' Joseph's expression was hunted. 'I invited Miss O'Leary for tea. Not to hear scurrilous – and false – stories about me.'

'We're teasing you,' said his mother. 'Do sit down, Miss O'Leary.'

She indicated a straight-backed chair pushed against the wall, which Joseph brought forward. He fetched another for himself while Mrs Burke said that she would organise the sandwiches.

'We do give him a hard time,' admitted Ita. 'Because he's our only brother and he needs the lightness of mood that a woman can bring. He can be very serious sometimes.'

'We're living in serious times,' said Joseph.

'It doesn't mean we can't have fun,' said Rosanna. 'It gets so boring listening to you and May and Ma going on and on about the struggle and God knows what else. I bet you have poor Miss O'Leary's ear bent off her with your talk.'

'Oh, he's not the worst,' said Winifred.

'Damned with faint praise.' Ita laughed, and then coughed.

'I suppose it's better than no praise,' said Rosanna, ignoring her sister, who got up and walked to the corner of the room, where she managed to get her breathing under control just as Agnes returned with a large teapot and a tray of fish-paste sandwiches on china plates. The sandwiches were cut diagonally and not straight across as Annie always did, which made Winifred wonder if Joseph thought the O'Learys' cheese sandwiches and tea in mugs had been uncouth.

Ita sat down again, and as her mother poured the tea, another woman walked in, a baby in her arms and a toddler pulling at her skirt.

'May,' said Joseph. 'This is Miss O'Leary.'

Winifred knew that May was the oldest of the Burke girls, eight years her senior, married and living to the north of the city. Like her mother she was tall and statuesque, with a sense of purpose about her that was contagious. Her hair was drawn into a tight bun, her hazel eyes were sharp and penetrating. Her only jewellery, apart from a locket around her neck, was her wedding ring.

'Good to finally meet you, Miss O'Leary,' she said as she settled into a comfortable chair and loosened the bonnet on the baby's head while her mother took the little boy onto her lap and fed him some bread.

Winifred got the impression that Joseph's older sister was merely being polite and that she wasn't pleased to meet her at all. But then May asked her about her job at Kelley's and Mrs Burke questioned her about fabrics, because, she said, she was thinking about changing the curtains in the Yellow Room, and the conversation flowed more easily again.

'You'd need about twenty yards,' said Winifred, eyeing up the windows. 'I'm sure Mrs Kelley would be able to offer a discount.'

'We'd have to get the windows properly measured,' said May.

'Of course,' agreed Winifred. 'It's still twenty yards, though.'

'And your Mrs Kelley. Tell us about her,' said Mrs Burke.

Winifred felt a nagging sense of anxiety. She was having tea with a republican family, and no matter how sympathetic Alice Kelley might or might not be to the cause, she was still a Protestant who'd married an Englishman.

'She's good to work for,' she said eventually. 'She's an honest woman and her fabrics are excellent quality.'

'Another sandwich, Miss O'Leary?' asked Ita, who'd noticed her plate was empty.

'No thank you. In fact . . .' Winifred looked around nervously, 'I wonder is there a . . . somewhere I can wash my hands?'

'Of course.' May stood up and opened the door. She lowered her voice as she spoke to Winifred. 'If you walk to the end of the hallway, you'll find a WC there. It's the blue door,' she said.

'Inside?'

'Yes,' said May.

Winifred was astounded. The toilet facilities in East Essex Street were outside and shared. The luxury of a private room indoors was almost too much to believe. She followed the corridor and came to the blue door, which was up a short flight of steps. The WC was tiled in white and green, the cistern of the lavatory high up on the wall. She spent a lot more time than she needed enjoying the privacy of it.

When she emerged, she was immediately distracted by a sudden crash, followed by an exclamation of 'Damn it all to hell!' that came from another short corridor to her left. She turned towards the sound and saw an open door.

'Hello.' She spoke tentatively. 'Are you all right?'

'Is that you, Ita? I've made the most awful mess. Your mother will never forgive me.' A woman appeared at the door and looked out. 'Oh. Hello. Who are you?'

Winifred stared at her.

She recognised her.

The woman was Countess Constance Markievicz, Minister for Labour in the Irish government. Only the second female government minister in Europe. On the run from the British forces since her release from Cork gaol earlier in the summer. And she was here, in the Burkes' house.

Winifred felt sick.

*   *   *

The Countess was in her early fifties, and although her various stays in prisons had dulled her complexion and left her with deep lines on her face, she was still a commanding presence, wearing a dark green skirt and a cream blouse, her pseudo-military jacket with its brass buttons and epaulettes hung over the back of a chair. Winifred was totally tongue-tied in front of her.

'Are you another daughter?' asked the Countess. 'There seems to be a never-ending stream of Burke girls. I haven't met you all.'

'I'm not a Burke,' said Winifred. 'I'm a friend.'

'A good friend, I hope,' said the Countess with narrowed eyes. 'One who'll help me clear this up.' She stepped to one side and Winifred saw a pool of blue ink staining the tiled floor. Sheets of paper covered in small handwriting liberally blobbed with ink spots were strewn across the narrow bed. 'I shouldn't have been writing with nothing but a book to lean on,' observed the Countess. 'But what else can I do here?'

'Is there a cloth?' asked Winifred. 'I don't think the ink will stain the tiles.'

'Probably not,' said the Countess cheerfully. 'But the blanket is ruined. Not that it was much to start off with.' She nodded at the charcoal-grey cover on the bed. 'Mrs Burke will have my guts for garters.'

Winifred smiled. The Countess was probably right. Imposingly aristocratic as she was, Mrs Burke was even more majestic.

'There's ink on your blouse too,' she murmured.

'Bother.'

72

'Oh, don't dab at it, you'll make it worse,' she cried as the Countess took out a linen handkerchief. 'It needs to be soaked. Milk is best.'

'Seriously?'

Winifred nodded. 'Let it soak in the milk then scrub it and wash it in warm water.'

'I'm not sure Mrs B is running a laundry service,' said the Countess.

'Nor am I.'

'Thank you for the information.' The older woman smiled. 'You'd better let my landlady know the trouble I've caused.' She tilted her head to one side. 'You won't be mentioning my presence here to anyone else, will you?'

'I don't know who I'd mention it to,' said Winifred.

'Good girl.' The Countess gathered up her sheets of paper and put the lid on the now almost empty bottle of ink.

'What on earth is going on? And what are you doing here, Miss O'Leary?'

Mrs Burke stood in the doorway. Behind her was Joseph and his sister May.

'I do apologise, it's all my fault.' The Countess smiled at her and then explained about knocking over the ink. 'Miss O'Leary was attempting to help me. Did you know soaking in milk can remove ink stains? Isn't that fascinating?'

'Go back to the Yellow Room, Miss O'Leary,' said Agnes Burke. 'And don't move from there.'

Winifred did as she was told.

She felt sick again.

*　　*　　*

'I wasn't poking my nose in,' Winifred insisted when everyone, including the Countess, wearing a blouse loaned to her by Agnes, joined her.

'It really is entirely my fault,' the Countess confirmed. 'I shouldn't be allowed paper and ink because I'm such a messy person, but I wanted to write to de Valera.'

'In America?' asked Joseph.

'He's doing such great work raising funds for the cause,' said the Countess. 'I wanted to encourage him. He's going to be a great, great leader of this country one day. He's an icon already. And I wanted to let him know what good people there are here, like yourselves—'

'You didn't mention our name!' May looked horrified.

'Of course not. I just called you a devoted republican family.'

'But Miss O'Leary isn't part of our family,' said Agnes. 'And we don't know if she can be trusted.'

Winifred's eyes widened. Was Joseph's mother implying that she would inform on them? She'd already assured the Countess she wouldn't, and she repeated her promise quickly.

'But you might say something unintentionally,' said Agnes. 'To your own family.'

'Miss O'Leary's father was shot at Boland's Mill,' said Joseph. 'I don't think you need to worry about her credentials.'

Winifred glanced at him. Joseph knew the true story of her father's injury, but when his mother asked for more details, all he said was that Thomas had been wounded in the leg and had nearly died on the spot.

'Defending the Mill?' asked Ita. 'How brave.'

Winifred kept her mouth firmly closed.

'It seems we have no choice but to trust you,' said May.

'Of course we trust her,' said the Countess. 'I have complete faith in Miss O'Leary. She's surely one of the Inghinidhe na hÉireann, the daughters of Ireland. Plus she knows sensible things like how to get ink out of fabrics. So definitely trustworthy.'

'I am,' Winifred assured them. 'You can have faith in me, you really can.'

She said the same to Joseph as he cycled back across the city with her after she finally said goodbye. It hadn't been the Sunday afternoon tea she'd expected, but it had been a good deal more interesting.

'I liked the Countess,' she added. 'She's a bit . . . eccentric, but you can't help being drawn to her.'

'When we knew we'd have her in the house, my mother wanted to cancel your invitation,' said Joseph. 'Not because she thought you'd discover her in the way you did, simply that we wouldn't normally have anyone else here when we're sheltering someone. But I thought you might think it was because I was reluctant for you to meet my family, and I didn't want you to think that, Winnie. It was important to me that you met everyone.'

She'd met his father too, after Constance Markievicz had returned to her room with a book and a promise that she'd finished writing letters. John Burke was an amiable-looking man with grey hair and a grey moustache who, when told of the situation with the Countess, asked if the entire afternoon's conversation had been taken up with politics. When Winifred had said not the *entire* afternoon, he'd laughed and said that it was an exhausting topic and if she ever wanted to talk about books or music or gardening, he was the one to come to.

His arrival had lightened the atmosphere immensely, and Winifred had taken to him straight away.

'Well?' said Joseph when they arrived at East Essex Street.

'Well what?'

'Did you like them? My mother, my father, my sisters?'

A variety of answers crowded Winifred's head. But as she noticed the anxious expression in Joseph's eyes, the only reply she gave was 'Yes.'

'And they liked you,' he said. 'So, Winifred O'Leary, will you marry me?'

Chapter 7

Dublin, Autumn 1920

Dear Rosie,

You're not the only one getting married. I've met a man, his name is Joseph Burke and he's the handsomest man you've ever seen. Well, maybe your Léo is as handsome, we will have to put them side by side and judge. Just think, all of us will be married soon and Ma won't have to worry about us. We haven't yet set a date but I hope it will be soon. I'm very excited and I'm sure you'll be happy to know that I won't be left on the shelf after all.

Much love,

Winnie

Following Joseph's proposal to Winifred, and her acceptance, Agnes Burke invited the O'Learys to St Anthony's Place for tea.

'What does Mrs Burke mean by tea?' asked Annie when Winifred handed her the written invitation that Joseph had given her. 'Sandwiches in her parlour or something more than that?'

'She gave me sandwiches.' Winifred knew that her mother was worried that Agnes's offering would be far superior to the casual afternoon at East Essex Street. 'I told you, they were fish paste, nothing grand. Although they do have fancy china and they're getting better bread than us. I don't know from where.'

'Nobody's ever invited me for tea before,' said Annie. 'A cup of tea, maybe. But not tea.'

'They're nice people.' Winifred wasn't sure if she was saying this because she believed it or because she didn't want her parents to let her down by not meeting the Burkes.

'Tea it is, so,' said Annie. 'I'll wash and press my good blouse.'

They walked together from the tenement to the house in St Anthony's Place. There were fewer people on the streets than usual, because autumn seemed to be hurrying into winter without any of the golden days that September and October usually brought. The air was cold and damp, and a hazy fog had settled over the city. Winifred shivered despite the warmth of her fawn coat, a second-hand gift from Mrs Kelley, who'd replaced it with a new one two winters previously. Annie shivered too, and tried to keep her hands warm in the crook of Thomas's arm.

A patrol van of British soldiers, looking cold and miserable, drove slowly along Sackville Street. Winifred felt her stomach clench. Although they were a regular feature of the landscape, she was much more conscious of them than she had been before she'd met Joseph, and she wasn't at all sure that was a good thing.

'Here we are,' she said as they drew up outside the gate in the brick wall beside the convent. 'There's a bell.'

'A bell, is it?' Annie snorted. 'When did we ever have bells?'

Winifred pressed the enamel button in its brass surround, and they waited for a few minutes until Joseph arrived and opened the gate.

'Mr and Mrs O'Leary,' he said. 'Thank you for coming.'

'Thank you to your mother for asking us,' said Annie, in a warmer tone than she'd used all day.

Winifred took Joseph's arm and they went ahead of her parents to the house. She could sense her mother thinking the same as she herself had when she'd first seen it – that it was big and imposing and far grander than anything she'd ever imagined. And when they went inside and Annie was looking around at the well-furnished interior, Winifred could almost hear her father thinking that she'd landed on her feet.

But they didn't know about the strength of the Burkes' republican sympathies, or that they hid political refugees on the run. She hadn't told them that. She'd made a promise and she'd kept it.

'Mrs O'Leary.' Agnes appeared from one of the hallway's side passages. 'I'm sorry I wasn't here to let you in myself. It's good to see you.'

'And you,' said Annie.

As she had when Winifred had visited, Agnes took the women's coats and hung them up. Thomas didn't have a coat – he'd worn his only suit with a tweed cap, which he'd removed and was holding in both hands.

'This way.'

Once again they were brought to the Yellow Room, but this time the only other person there was Agnes's husband, John.

'It does you well,' said Thomas when John had introduced himself as the boiler man to the nuns. 'Coming with this house.'

'Mr Burke is on call for the nuns twenty-four hours a day,' said Agnes. 'That's why they housed us, and they take a deduction from his wages for rent.'

'I'm sure it's hard work,' acknowledged Thomas. 'When I worked in the docks—'

'You were a docker?' Mr Burke looked at him with interest.

'For a time,' said Thomas.

'I had a friend who was the harbourmaster there for a couple of years,' Mr Burke told him. 'Sidney Riordan.'

'I knew Mr Riordan,' said Thomas. 'A good man. A fair man.'

Mr Burke nodded.

While the men talked about the docks, the women talked about the wedding.

'The spring, I think,' said Agnes. 'It's late in the year now to get married.'

'It doesn't matter, does it?' asked Annie. 'They'll be in the church, they'll have a breakfast . . .'

'But it would be nice if we could celebrate,' said Agnes. 'Joseph is my only living son.'

'What do you want, Winnie?' Annie turned to her.

'Whatever is best,' Winifred said.

'Early summer,' suggested Agnes, putting the date even further into the future. 'May. The garden is always beautiful in May.'

'That's a long time away.' Joseph frowned.

'You'll need time to find a place to rent,' said Agnes. 'And Winnie will want to save for a wedding outfit.'

'It's hardly a society wedding.' Joseph laughed. 'She won't need a trousseau.'

'I want it to be a nice day for you,' said Agnes. 'I'm sure Mrs O'Leary wants the same for Winifred.'

'I want whatever Winnie wants,' Annie said.

They all looked at Winifred.

'I want to marry Joseph as soon as possible,' she said. 'But if you really think—'

'May it is, so.' Agnes beamed. 'I knew you had a sensible head on your shoulders, Winifred.'

'It seems we're in agreement,' said Annie. She looked at Winifred, who shrugged.

'Good. That's settled.' Agnes looked at her guests in satisfaction. 'And now let's have some sandwiches.'

This time the sandwiches were thin slices of corned beef, on the same good-quality bread as before.

'We get it from the convent,' Agnes said when Annie commented on it. 'The nuns bake every day. Well, except Sunday, of course, so this is yesterday's, but I have a good pantry to keep things fresh.'

'There are lots of unexpected rooms in this house,' Winifred told her mother.

Agnes shot a sharp glance at her, and Winifred, flustered and thinking of the Countess, took too big a mouthful of her tea and began to cough violently.

'Are you all right?' Joseph looked at her in concern.

'Yes.'

'Perhaps you'd like to take a turn around the garden while our parents talk?'

'That would be nice.'

Although it wasn't, not really. The misty haze had turned into a fine drizzle, and despite the big umbrella Joseph held over her head, she could feel the insidious dampness seeping into her bones. It was ruining her hair too, she knew, because every time it rained it seemed to puff up like a wire ball.

81

'You always look lovely to me,' said Joseph when she complained of this. 'I'm very proud that you're going to be my wife, even though it won't happen as soon as I thought. My mother interferes too much and she's used to getting her own way. I can talk to her if you like . . .'

'I'm proud you asked me to marry you. And if it keeps your mother happy to wait a while, I don't mind.'

'*I* mind,' confessed Joseph. 'But if you're all right with it, so am I.'

'It's best to keep the peace,' said Winifred. 'There's enough fighting going on without bringing your mother into it.'

'You're a good woman and I'm very lucky to have you.'

The two of them were laughing when the gate opened and May came hurrying along the gravel path.

'Was it you?' she demanded as she stopped in front of Winifred, who looked at her in puzzlement. 'Was it?' she repeated.

'What's the matter?' asked Joseph.

'They've arrested the Countess,' said May, 'and we don't know who betrayed her.'

Winifred and Joseph followed May into the house, where they went immediately to the Yellow Room. May broke the news of the Countess's arrest to her mother, whose expression changed from horror to anger and then to fear.

'Did you say anything?' She looked at Winifred. 'Did you tell anyone?'

'Of course I didn't,' said Winifred.

'Tell anyone what?' asked Annie.

'The Countess was a guest in our home,' said Agnes. 'Your daughter knew that. She may have informed on us.'

'Winnie!' Annie looked at her in horror. 'You were here when that woman was being hidden? And you said nothing.'

'I promised to say nothing.' Winifred looked angrily at Agnes. 'If I didn't tell my own mother, I certainly didn't tell anyone else. Why would I?'

'You tell me,' said Agnes. 'All I know is that we've never had any trouble before, not even when Cathal Brugha was here.'

'Cathal Brugha?' Thomas said. 'I met him once. He came into the Custom House. A gentleman. He—'

'Oh for heaven's sake!' Agnes exclaimed. 'Knowing a man like Brugha isn't the point. Informing is.'

'Stop using that word about my daughter.' Annie was furious. 'She didn't even tell *us* that you were harbouring an insurgent.'

'Countess Markievicz is the Minister for Labour, not an insurgent,' said Agnes. 'You'd do well to remember that.'

'Don't you tell me what I should and shouldn't remember,' retorted Annie. 'Winnie, you told us that Joseph was involved in planning raids, and that's dangerous enough. But this . . . What are you getting yourself into? Would you be expected to keep fugitives yourself when you're married?'

'Of course not!' cried Winifred, although she couldn't help wondering if her mother had a point. But she and Joseph would be renting rooms. They wouldn't have the space or the privacy to hide anyone. 'You well know that everyone's involved in some way or another,' she continued, her tone a lot calmer than she felt. 'Except perhaps us.'

'Indeed,' said Agnes. 'Why is that? Because Mr O'Leary works at the Custom House? Keeping records for the British? Where exactly do your sympathies lie as a family?'

'I'm a porter,' said Thomas. 'And regardless of who's keeping them, records are important.'

'Nevertheless, we don't know what sort of information you might be passing on,' said Agnes.

'Winifred, get your things. We're leaving.' Annie almost spat the words out.

'You're not going anywhere until I know—'

'Agnes.' This time it was her husband who spoke. 'Miss O'Leary has told you that she didn't say anything to anyone about the Countess. Her parents were unaware. It seems to me that you're being unfair on the young lady and her family.'

'My fiancée,' said his son. 'The woman I'm going to marry. Not just any young lady.'

'You won't be marrying her if she's betrayed us.' Agnes's words were tight, her mouth a firm line. 'Because I don't care who she is and how much you think you care about her, if she's put our family in danger . . .'

'Don't you think you're putting yourselves in danger?' asked Thomas. 'It's your right, of course, and you should be commended for your support for a republic, but harbouring fugitives is a fraught business and I'm sure Winifred isn't the only person who knew about your illegal lodger.'

'The Countess isn't illegal!' cried Agnes.

'No. But she is, or at least was, on the run,' pointed out Thomas. 'There are a lot of people with a vested interest in making sure she's behind bars. It happens that we're not those people.'

'Indeed we're not,' said Annie. 'Winifred, are you ready to go?'

Winifred glanced at Joseph, who was standing beside his mother with an anguished expression on his face.

'Winnie,' he said, and then stopped.

'I'm ready.' She swept out of the room, followed by her parents, bumping into a small table as she went, which caused it to tip over and send the porcelain ornament on it rolling across the floor. She didn't wait to see the damage that might have been caused, but continued into the hallway, where she took her coat from the peg and put it on. Her mother retrieved her own coat, and Thomas his hat.

'That's the last we'll see of them,' said Annie as they let themselves out. 'And a good thing too.'

'How could you?' Joseph glared at his mother and sister. 'How could you accuse her like that without any proof?'

'Who else knew the Countess was here?' demanded May. 'Only her.'

'Only her and half the Dublin Brigade,' retorted Joseph.

'Only her and the people who brought the Countess here,' said Agnes. 'And we know they're utterly trustworthy. They were involved in helping de Valera escape from Lincoln gaol two years ago.'

'But there are spies everywhere,' said Joseph. 'And even those who share our ultimate aims might not think as we do. As for Dev, he's not the most important person in the world, you know. We're here fighting, but he's living it high in the States, putting up at the Waldorf Astoria—'

'While he drums up money and support,' interrupted his mother. 'He's the kind of leader we're going to need in the future, with his American connections, and he's raised far more than we ever could have hoped for the cause.'

'Regardless,' continued Joseph, 'Dev isn't the issue here and Winifred isn't the one who betrayed the Countess. Besides, the woman left the house two days ago. If Winnie said something to someone, don't you think they would have been around here before now?'

'They might have had us under observation.'

'And let us come and go as we pleased?'

'They would've wanted to see what we were doing.'

'They would've wanted to arrest the Countess here so that they could arrest us too,' said Joseph. 'You're not thinking straight. You've taken against Winnie for some reason I don't know and you're determined to see the worst in her. That's why you didn't want us to get married until next summer. You're hoping she'll change her mind.'

'She's not one of us,' said May. 'We don't know her or her family.'

'They're good, hard-working people,' said Joseph.

'The boy is right.' His father spoke up. 'I like Winifred and I liked her parents. You know that I've never stood in your way about giving shelter to fugitives or those who need it, but I won't have you slandering other people who don't think the same as you do.'

'I didn't—'

'That's enough.' He got up from his seat. 'I'm quite sure that young woman didn't have anything to do with the arrest of the Countess. Joseph is right, the Crown has spies everywhere. You should be looking elsewhere for your traitor.' He turned to his son. 'You should apologise to her on our behalf,' he said. 'Not today. Let them cool down. But apologise all the same.'

'It's Ma who should apologise,' said Joseph. 'Her and May both.'

'Let's see if she accepts your apology first,' said his father. 'Because if not, there isn't going to be a wedding and it's not going to matter one way or the other.'

'There damn well will be a wedding,' said Joseph. 'I love Winifred O'Leary and she's going to be my wife and none of you are going to stop us.'

He strode out of the Yellow Room and slammed the door behind him.

Neither Winifred nor her parents spoke on the walk home. Winifred was too busy trying not to cry, more upset by the fact that Joseph hadn't stopped his mother from saying the things she had than the fact that she'd said them at all. What an absolute harridan she was, she thought. It had been clear to her when she'd first called to the house that Mrs Burke hadn't warmed to her – not that Winnie had warmed to the woman either, but Agnes Burke was too convinced of her own rightness to take account of anyone else. And she had both her husband and her son under her thumb. There was no doubt that she ruled the roost. After all, Mr Burke had been adamant that he liked a quiet life. Agnes and that equally horrible May were the ones who put everyone's lives at risk by hiding rebels in the house. And not that Winifred didn't agree that the Countess deserved to be protected, but what other less savoury characters had they given refuge to? What danger had she put herself and her parents in by going to St Anthony's Place?

She swallowed hard. And what about Joseph? If he'd tried to stop her leaving, would she have listened to him? Yet he hadn't. He didn't care enough, didn't love her enough to stand up for her. Well, better to know now rather than later. Better not to be married at all than married to a mammy's boy.

Annie glanced occasionally at Winifred, but kept her counsel, afraid of saying something about the Burkes she might regret. Meanwhile, Thomas, who'd got on well with John, was of the belief that the problem was entirely due to firebrand women and was rapidly revising his view that they should run the world. Instead he was thinking that John Burke should have more control over his wife. Not that he himself was much better, he mused. Annie certainly knew her own mind and didn't hold back from expressing herself, and his girls had all done their own thing. Though he was grateful that didn't include helping rebels on the run. And not, he thought also, that he should consider them as rebels. That sounded like they were in the wrong. They were freedom fighters, they had a just cause and they deserved to be cared for. Winifred would never have betrayed one of them.

It wasn't until later in the evening, when they were sitting around their rather smoky fire, that she explained about her prior meeting with Countess Markievicz at St Anthony's Place.

Her parents listened in amazement.

'She does a lot of writing for the newspapers,' conceded Annie, when Winifred had finished. 'She gives good speeches too. And she makes valid points.'

'She'd be a good minister if she wasn't spending her time hiding out,' said Thomas.

'I wonder who else besides her and Brugha the Burkes have hidden,' mused Annie. 'What other connections they have. And what else Joseph could get himself into.'

'It doesn't matter now, does it?' Winifred's voice was flat. 'I'll probably never see him again.'

'I'm sorry,' said Thomas. 'He seemed like a nice young man.'

'He didn't speak up for her,' said Annie.

'Nobody could get a word in edgeways with that mother of his,' remarked Thomas. 'Even Mr Burke himself stayed silent.'

'It's not a good sign,' Annie said. 'He's weak and his son is weak too.'

'Joseph isn't weak,' protested Winifred. 'He's a fighter.'

'He'll hardly succeed in getting us independence from Britain if he isn't independent in his own home,' said Annie.

'Ah, but it's not his own home,' commented Thomas. 'It's his parents' home.'

'Jaysus, you're an awful nit-picker.'

'Come here.' Thomas held his arms out towards his daughter, and as she moved close to him, he pulled her into a hug. 'If things are meant to work out, they will. If not, you've had a lucky escape.'

'I favour a lucky escape myself,' said Annie.

But as Winifred lay on her thin mattress and stared up at the cracked ceiling that night, she didn't feel like she'd escaped at all. And she didn't know what her next step was going to be.

Chapter 8

Dublin, autumn/winter 1920

'So how did it go?' asked Alice Kelley the following morning when she arrived at the shop half an hour after Winifred. 'Did your families enjoy meeting each other?'

'There were a few differences of opinion.' Winifred hefted a bale of calico onto the counter and began to measure it out.

'Oh dear. But perhaps they'll come around.'

'I'm not so sure about that. The Burkes don't approve of me.'

'In that case why did they invite your parents to tea?'

Winifred supposed that Alice had been envisaging a social occasion where Agnes filled elegant china cups while chatting about everything to do with the wedding. She wouldn't have imagined heated debate about rebels and fugitives and betrayals and God knows what else.

'I'm not sure,' she said eventually. 'I don't know if I'll ever see Joseph again.'

'Don't give up if you heart tells you different.' Alice's voice was suddenly firm. 'Do what you think is right, Miss O'Leary.

Life is short. If you love someone and he loves you, well, you've got to fight for it.'

'That's the thing.' Winifred took out the pinking shears and began to cut the fabric. 'I'm not sure that this is the fight he wants to be in.'

Despite the fact that they were busy, Winifred felt the day drag, and she was glad when Alice finally turned the sign on the door around to 'Closed' and told her to have a nice evening.

If only, she thought as she stepped out onto the street. Her evening would be spent mending the bed sheets at East Essex Street, which were getting thinner and more frayed by the day, cutting them in half then sewing the ends to the middle. Although she was good at calculating widths and lengths of fabric, she wasn't an especially good needlewoman, and she found sewing tedious. She suddenly saw the appeal for women like Agnes Burke of helping the rebels and fugitives. It was far more exciting than trying to make sheets last another year.

'Winnie.'

He was at the corner of Sackville Street, his cap shielding his face as he stood beside the damaged wall of Clerys department store, the once imposing building that had been almost totally destroyed in 1916.

'Mr Burke.'

He took her arm and she shook his hand away.

'Winnie, I'm sorry.'

'For what?'

'For yesterday.'

She walked quickly along the street and he hurried after her.

'My mother was very wrong in what she said to you.'

She continued to walk towards O'Connell Bridge and the other side of town.

'Winnie, for the love of God would you stop!'

'Why?' She was on the bridge before she turned around to face him. 'So you can pretend you care that my parents and I were insulted by someone who doesn't even know us? So you can pretend that your mother didn't call me a traitor?' Her voice wobbled. 'I've never been so wronged in my life.'

'She had no right to say what she said. In her defence' – he saw the flash of anger in Winifred's eyes and hurried on – 'she's been under a lot of strain over the past months. It isn't easy hiding people in your home knowing that a wrong word at the wrong time could bring everything crashing down.'

'And that means she can throw accusations around at everyone else?' Winifred's anger was unabated. 'She can imply that I'm some kind of British spy?'

'Listen to me! She—'

'No, you listen to me. My family might not live in a big house with a vast number of rooms, but we're good, honest people. And I won't have your mother or your father or you thinking that somehow you're better than us. You're not.'

'I never thought . . .' Joseph looked at her appealingly. 'Honestly, Winnie. I didn't. I wouldn't. I wanted to . . . I got you these.'

He reached into his pocket and took out a pair of elegant grey gloves with buttons at the wrist. They were expensive, she knew, and would be far warmer than the fingerless mittens she normally wore during the winter. She took them and could immediately feel the seductive softness of them, but she didn't put them on.

'And how are these supposed to make me feel better?' she asked.

'They're part of my apology,' said Joseph.

'Oh for God's sake. I don't want stuff from you!' She balled the gloves in her hand, then flung them over the balustrade into the dark waters of the Liffey. 'That's what I think of your apology. That's what I think of your meaningless words. And that's what I think of you believing that you can buy me off with a pair of feckin' gloves!' She turned away from him and began to walk again.

Joseph stared in disbelief at the gloves now being carried downriver towards the sea like a couple of pale fish. Then he looked up. Winifred was already turning onto Aston Quay.

'Wait!' he called.

She ignored him.

'Listen to me, Winnie. Please stop!'

She turned to face him.

'You do know they were very expensive gloves, don't you?'

'I don't care how expensive they were.'

'I can't afford to replace them.'

'I don't want you to replace them.'

'What *do* you want?' he asked.

'Respect,' she said.

'Winifred O'Leary.' He put his hands on her shoulders. 'There's nobody in this city I respect more than you. And if you'll still have me, I'd be honoured to be your husband. For better for worse. For richer for poorer. In sickness and in health.'

'Fine words.' But her tone had softened.

'I love you, Winnie. I want you to be my wife.'

'And your parents?'

'You're not marrying my parents.'

Suddenly she laughed. He smiled. And there and then, ignoring the catcalls of passing Dubliners, he kissed her.

Agnes Burke tried to persuade them to stick to the plan of marrying the following May, when the garden at St Anthony's Place would be filled with blossom and there was a better chance of a sunny day. She offered to have the wedding breakfast at her house, saying that the Red Room would be a beautiful setting for it.

But Winifred was adamant. She wanted to get married as soon as possible, and she didn't care about wedding breakfasts or cherry blossom or photographs in the garden. Nor, if she was entirely honest, did she trust Agnes not to throw some kind of spanner in the works between now and then. She still harboured doubts about her future mother-in-law's apparent change of heart. In any case, she didn't care that it was winter and that they'd be scurrying from East Essex Street to the church in inclement weather. All she wanted was to marry Joseph and move into the rooms they planned to rent in Dorset Street. So they agreed on 22 November as the date, and she began to make her plans.

Her married friend Esther Boland also had rooms in Dorset Street, and the following Wednesday afternoon Winifred went to visit her. She had every second Wednesday afternoon off, and before Esther had married, they used to go on trips to the coast on those afternoons. It had been a long time since they'd managed that, but she was dying to share the news of her engagement and wedding with her friend.

'It's so exciting!' beamed Esther, a petite blonde with blue eyes and dimples in both cheeks. 'I'm glad you're finally getting married, Winnie.'

'You recommend it, so?' Winifred looked around the rooms. She hadn't been here since Esther and Henry had first moved in, and the space seemed smaller than she remembered, although that might have been because it was mainly taken up by a rug where baby Arthur, now nearly nine months old, was sitting banging wooden bricks together. Esther scooped him into her arms and popped him onto her breast to feed.

'I love being married,' she confessed. 'I love when I go to the shops and people call me Mrs Boland. I love that they're more respectful of me. And I love when Henry and I go out together, not that we do very often because of Arthur, but when we do and I'm on his arm, I feel . . . oh, I don't know, Winnie, I just feel more important.'

'He's good to you?'

'He's the best,' said Esther. 'I'm really lucky, I know.'

'And is he involved in any . . . well, you know . . . politicking?'

'Politicking or rebellion?'

'Rebellion.' There was no point in beating around the bush.

'Oh Winnie. It's too tiresome to even think about, isn't it?' Esther sighed. 'You know, I don't properly remember 1916, but I do remember that most people thought Pearse and his friends were a bunch of losers. My mother couldn't stand him. As for de Valera . . .'

They both grimaced.

'. . . long streak of misery that he is,' continued Esther, 'he needs a good woman to cheer him up.'

'In fairness, the current situation would have anyone miserable,' said Winnie.

'Michael Collins now,' continued Esther dreamily, 'I can imagine him all right. He's a handsome man and no mistake.'

Winifred grinned at the mention of the charismatic revolutionary and politician. Collins was widely accepted to be a highly intelligent strategic planner, but most of the women she knew were more taken with his boyish good looks than his republican credentials.

'Whether you fancy them or not is irrelevant,' Winifred told Esther. 'What I was asking was if Henry is involved in any way. But you don't have to answer if you don't want to.'

'Who isn't involved in some way or another?' Esther shrugged. 'After all, Henry's a maintenance worker at Dublin Castle. It's a tightrope he has to walk.'

'Joseph is involved too,' said Winifred. 'I'm terrified that one day they'll arrest him.'

'Which is why you're marrying him now?'

'His mother wanted us to wait. She's an absolute witch, Esther. But what's the point in waiting when we might all be dead tomorrow? I'd rather be Mrs Burke than Miss O'Leary.'

'Well, yes, but I don't want to think of . . .' Esther held her baby close. 'I want it all to be over tomorrow.'

'So do I,' agreed Winifred. 'But it won't be, will it?'

'Feckin' Brits,' said Esther. 'If they'd feck off home and leave us alone, we'd be a lot better off. Still, at least when you're married and you have children, yours and mine will be able to play together.'

'I don't want to rush into having children,' said Winifred. 'I want to spend time with Joseph first. Doing things with him.'

'What sort of things?' Esther gave her a knowing look.

'Not . . . not improper things,' said Winifred. 'Just, you know, ordinary things. Going to the theatre. For walks. Sitting together.'

'Planning raids,' said Esther. 'Blowing up barracks.'

'More likely,' admitted Winifred. 'But I want us to have time together most of all. Because when I'm with him, I feel happy and alive. Nobody ever made me feel like that before. And it's wonderful.'

Esther smiled. 'I'll tell you something, Winnie O'Leary,' she said. 'It's just as well you *have* found a man. Because between the Great War and the Spanish flu and now this War of Independence, there's sure to be more women looking for husbands than men available to *be* husbands. So you're right to get your oar in.'

Winifred laughed, and then nodded at the truth in her friend's words.

'You'll love being a married woman,' said Esther as she adjusted the baby at her breast. 'And you'll love being a mammy too.'

Alice Kelley gifted Winifred the material for the aubergine skirts and cream blouses that the bride, her mother, Mrs Burke, Ita and Rosanna were to wear for the day. Winifred, being a clever cutter of fabric despite her lack of needlework skills, managed to have enough for an extra skirt and blouse for Anthony's girlfriend, Bridget, who was also invited. Although Winifred had met Anthony on quite a few occasions since he'd replaced the window of Mrs Kelley's shop, she was yet to be introduced to the latest young woman in his long list of conquests. She sometimes teased Anthony about his ever changing girlfriends, and he teased her back about having

97

fallen for Joseph instead of him, though he always conceded that she'd made the right choice.

Nevertheless, despite the close friendship between Anthony and her fiancé, and the fact that he was to be Joseph's best man, she worried that the two of them were increasingly at odds over the course of the War of Independence. Anthony wanted the Irish army to be more aggressive in their tactics against the British soldiers, while Joseph favoured more targeted ambushes.

'We don't need things to get even bloodier,' he would respond whenever Anthony said this.

But on the day before his wedding to Winifred, they did.

Joseph was helping his father in the boiler house when May arrived with the news that the republican army had carried out an operation aimed at eliminating British spies.

'Eliminating?' asked Joseph as he wiped his dirty hands on his trousers.

'They've assassinated at least half a dozen army officers,' May told him. 'Pembroke Street and Mount Street.'

'Jesus, Mary and Joseph,' said her father. 'They won't take that lying down.'

'McKee and Clancy were involved.' May named the leaders of the Dublin Brigade. 'Apparently Michael Collins had a list of about fifty, but Brugha cut that down because there wasn't enough information on the others.'

'Fifty assassinations!' Joseph stared at her. 'Are they mad? Six is bad enough. Not that they might not deserve it, but all the same . . .'

'There'll be more than six by the end of the day,' said May.

'They'll take reprisals.' Joseph wiped his hands again.

'They've been dealt a blow. Collins is one hundred per cent sure they were spies.'

'I hope he's right,' said John.

'I trust him.' Joseph looked at his father. 'He's a good man who thinks things through. But this murder squad of his . . . assassinating spies . . . I don't like where it's going to lead.'

'D'you want to go to Winifred?'

'I think I should,' said Joseph.

'I'm finished here anyhow,' said his father. 'And it's a Sunday. So go now.'

He was five minutes from East Essex Street when he felt an almost palpable murmur within the city. People were stopping other people, sharing hurried confidences, turning to each other, turning away, looking scared.

'What's happened?' He waylaid a man running along the quays. 'What have they done?'

'It's a massacre,' the man said. 'At Croke Park. Those fucking Black and Tans.'

Joseph caught his breath. The Black and Tans had a deserved reputation for cruelty. But what could they have done at the sports ground where the Dublin and Tipperary teams had been scheduled to play a match that afternoon? There'd hardly been protests in the stands, had there? Or celebrations of the assassinations? People weren't stupid. They wouldn't agitate at a GAA match. They were just there for the sport.

He found out when he reached East Essex Street. The O'Learys' neighbour in the adjoining rooms had been at the stadium.

'They opened fire on us,' said Jerome Murphy. 'For no damned reason. The Auxiliaries surrounded the stadium to stop people leaving, and those murdering Black and Tan bastards ran through the turnstiles and started shooting.'

'Who were they shooting at?' asked Joseph.

'Anyone who moved,' replied Jerome. 'I know they were brought over to support the police, but those so-called soldiers have no sense of discipline to speak of. Our Volunteers are more professional than them. We tried to run, but we were hemmed in and they kept on shooting.'

'Jesus Christ.' Joseph was horrified. 'How many were killed?'

'I don't know. It could be dozens. The man beside me was hit. He went down and I couldn't help him.' Jerome began to shake. 'People were trampling over him to get out. It was . . .' He couldn't finish the sentence.

Winifred was listening to him, her eyes wide with horror.

'I have to go,' said Joseph.

'Tomorrow,' she said. 'You'll see me tomorrow. At the church.'

'Yes,' said Joseph. 'I will.'

The events of the day before were playing on her mind as Winnie prepared for her wedding the next morning. The sense of joy she wanted to feel was tempered by the pall of sorrow and fury that hung over the city. Nevertheless, she couldn't help the thrill of excitement that ran through her as she dressed in her new blouse and skirt.

Annie did her hair for her, putting it up and pinning it with a pearl clip that was her wedding gift to her, while her father polished her shoes to a mirror shine.

'I love you and I hope you'll be very happy with Joseph,' Annie whispered as she put the clip in place.

'I love you too. And I know I will,' murmured Winifred.

And then the knock came on the door.

It was John Burke, who told them starkly that Joseph had been arrested. The police had raided St Anthony's Place shortly after he'd returned home the previous night and had discovered the stencil machine that was kept in the boiler room, along with copies of the Proclamation of 1916 and the Declaration of Independence of January 1919.

'Why didn't they arrest you?' asked Winifred. 'You're the boiler man, after all.'

'I was in the convent,' John told her.

'And Mrs Burke? And the girls?'

'Fortunately May had taken all her Cumann na mBan posters home with her,' replied John. 'Which at least kept them out of it. But they knew Joseph was a lieutenant in the 3rd battalion. You heard about Dick McKee and Peadar Clancy, did you? They've been executed. They said they were trying to escape, but that's just an excuse.'

McKee was the commander of the Dublin Brigade with its four battalions. If he'd been arrested, it wasn't surprising that other members of the brigade had been too. Winifred groaned softly.

'I'll let you know when I have more information,' said Mr Burke.

When he'd gone, Winifred looked down at her cream blouse and aubergine skirt and started to cry.

'He'll be grand,' said Annie. 'Nothing bad will happen to him.'

'Are you taking me for an absolute fool?' asked Winifred. 'The Black and Tans slaughtered civilians yesterday. They shot an eleven-year-old boy in the chest, for God's sake. I heard the name O'Leary being mentioned and I was afraid for a moment it was Tom, that Katy had brought him to Croke Park for the match. I was frozen inside. If they can shoot children in cold blood, don't you think they'll want to make an example of anyone at all they suspect was involved? Especially young men? It's a campaign of terror and intimidation and it's reprisals for Collins and his so-called assassination of spies.'

'Do you suspect Joseph was involved in that?' Annie looked at her in shock.

'No!' cried Winifred. 'He was as horrified as me when he found out. Besides, it was the number two battalion that was involved.'

'I don't think it matters much who was involved,' said Annie.

'Nor do I.' Winifred swallowed anxiously. 'Are they going to charge him with anything? Or are they just going to hold him like they did with the hunger strikers?'

'Try not to worry,' said Annie.

'The last time he was arrested, he was sent to Frongoch,' said Winifred. 'That was bad enough. Who knows what'll happen this time.'

'I'm really sorry,' said Annie. 'If only you'd married him sooner . . .'

'I might have been arrested too,' finished Winifred. 'And whatever my feelings about the rights and wrongs of the situation, I don't think I'd make a very good political prisoner.'

She went into the other room and took off her wedding clothes. She was terrified that she'd never see Joseph again.

She was heartbroken at the cancellation of her wedding. And she was devastated by the slaughter of what was already being called Bloody Sunday. As she sat on the end of her bed, she didn't even try to stop the tears that were rolling down her face.

The atmosphere in the city was febrile. Following the massacre, opinion had shifted. Those who'd been ambivalent about the War of Independence had changed their view, horrified at the thought of people being trampled in the stampede to escape, or being shot in the back as they ran, and enraged that children had been part of it. Reports in *The Freeman's Journal* said that the venue had been 'a mass of running and shouting men and shrieking women and children', and those words had brought the scene to life not only for Dubliners, but for the wider world, where shock was expressed at the actions of people who were supposedly there to keep the peace.

'I don't want to say it's been good for us,' Agnes told her daughters a couple of days later. 'But it's definitely swung popular opinion our way.'

'Popular opinion is all very well, but what about Joseph?' Ita looked at her mother. 'What's going to happen to him?'

'I don't know. But I do know that he'll be brave and strong.'

'And Winifred?' asked Rosanna.

'She'll have to be brave and strong too,' said Agnes.

Joseph was being held in Kilmainham, the dark and gloomy prison that dated from the eighteenth century. It was where most of the political prisoners were held, and everyone knew that conditions were grim. Despite her confident words, Agnes was worried for his health, which had been impacted by his previous incarceration at Frongoch. It was almost inevitable that anyone involved in the fight for independence would find themselves in prison sooner or later, but possibly for the first time, she wished that her family hadn't been part of anything to do with it over the last few weeks, that her home hadn't been raided and that her son had been able to marry Winifred O'Leary just as he'd intended.

Forty-eight hours after what should have been her wedding day, Winifred was back working in Mrs Kelley's, carrying out all her usual tasks while feeling as though her body and her mind were two separate things. She knew she was rolling out fabric, measuring it and cutting it, but it seemed to her as if she was watching herself do it. Because her head was in Kilmainham with Joseph. She pictured him in one of the shared dark, damp cells she'd read about in the newspapers, and worried about diseases like tuberculosis that the prisoners could pass to each other. Despite being held, he hadn't actually been charged with anything, and she didn't know when or if he would be. Even more worrying than the potential illnesses he might pick up was the talk of further hunger strikes by the inmates. She remembered the strikes of previous years, in which men had died.

She didn't want Joseph to die. She wanted him to live and to come back to her. She wanted to marry him. She wanted to have children with him.

She wanted to live the life she'd hoped to have with him.

At the end of the first week of his imprisonment, she joined a protest outside the gaol with a large group of women, including May, Rosanna, Ita and Esther, who'd sent her a note when she heard about Joseph's arrest. Much to her astonishment, Alice Kelley came too, saying that the actions of the Black and Tans and the Auxiliaries had been utterly disgraceful and dishonoured anyone who'd ever fought with them in the war. Which meant that her late husband had been dishonoured too. She stood side by side with Winifred as they sang songs to encourage the prisoners and held up placards urging the release of everyone inside. The police and guards, perhaps mindful of the fact that the protesters were all women, didn't try to disperse them, but allowed them to sing and shout.

Winifred hoped Joseph could hear them. And that somehow he'd know that she was out there waiting for him.

He was released in December, on a cold, wet day when the pavements were slick with melting sleet and Winifred shivered every time she looked out of the window of Kelley's Fine Fabrics. She was late getting home, partly because of the weather and partly because they'd been busy, and at first she didn't notice the man standing in the shelter of the doorway in East Essex Street.

Then he moved out of the shadows, and she cried out, first with nerves and then with delight when she realised who he was.

'They had no reason to detain me, no space to keep me, and prisoners against whom they could make a much better case.'

'Stop talking and come inside.'

She led him up the stairs to their rooms, which were empty because Thomas had stayed out with work colleagues and Annie had already left for her cleaning job.

'I was terrified you'd catch something awful and die,' Winnie said as she made him tea.

'I wasn't all that hopeful about living myself. Though I was more afraid they'd shoot me. But I kept thinking of you.' He put the enamel mug on the table and reached for her hand. 'You kept me going, Winnie.'

'I love you,' she said.

'I love you too. I thought about you every day.'

'Did you hear me singing?'

'You sang? You were with them?'

'Only some days,' she admitted. 'I thought you might hear my caterwauling above the others.'

'I did hear something akin to an animal being slaughtered.' He grinned at her.

'Beast.' But she smiled. 'Oh Joseph, it's so good to have you here.'

He pulled her towards him until she was sitting on his lap. She could both see and feel how much thinner he was, but his good eye danced with mischief and his smile warmed her heart. She leaned forward and kissed him. He kissed her back, pulling the pins from her hair so that it fell to her shoulders and sliding his hand beneath the thin fabric of her blouse.

'Joseph Burke!' She pulled back and looked at him.

'Winifred O'Leary.'

She led him to the bed she'd once shared with her sisters.

He kissed her on the lips and she put her arms around him. She'd been so scared that he might never come back to her that she was afraid she was imagining it now. But she wasn't imagining the thrill that holding him so close gave her. She wasn't imagining the love that flooded her heart and made her body tingle. It felt so right to be in his arms. And, she reminded herself as he kissed her again, she should have been his wife by now.

Joseph exhaled with happiness and relief. Then he laid his head on the pillow.

In the time it took her to remove her boots and lie beside him, he'd fallen asleep.

She looked at the gentle rise and fall of his chest. She moved closer and put her arm across him.

He slept on.

He didn't wake until the next morning. Neither Winifred sliding gently from the bed nor Annie and Thomas coming home woke him. Winifred's parents had been shocked to see him in the house, but even more shocked at how thin he was.

'The poor boy,' Annie murmured as they watched him sleep. 'These are such terrible times to be living in.'

She said the same to him when he finally woke, after Thomas had already left for work.

'I know, Mrs O'Leary,' he said as he ate the thick slice of bread she put in front of him. 'But they will get better. We have right on our side.'

'When did that ever mean anything?' she asked. 'I'm feeling that things will get worse before they get better. Worse for you, worse for us, worse for my daughter.'

He glanced at Winifred, who was putting on her coat.

'I won't let anything happen to Winnie,' he told her.

'You won't be able to stop it,' said Annie.

'I couldn't bear it if you were in danger.' Joseph turned to Winifred. 'You're the light in my life.'

She blushed.

'I don't want to be responsible for them raiding this house either,' he said.

'They wouldn't find anything if they did,' Annie pointed out.

'But I wouldn't stand by if they came for you.'

'They won't come for me,' said Winifred.

'They might if you were my wife.'

She stared at him. 'What are you saying?'

'I want to marry you more than anything in the world,' he told her. 'But maybe it would be better to wait until this is over. I don't want to put you or your family in danger, Winnie.'

'It's never going to be over,' she said. 'That's why I think fighting is so stupid. And that's why the Volunteers get married no matter how young they are. They know it'll never end and they want their girlfriends to be their wives.'

'It will end,' insisted Joseph. 'There's a different atmosphere in the city now. You must be able to feel it yourself.'

'I don't know what I feel right now,' said Winifred. 'Either about the war or about you deciding you don't want to marry me.'

'I *do* want to marry you. I said that. I don't want to put you in danger, that's all. If you were married to me, if we were living together . . . they could arrest both of us. And your mam and dad. I'd hate if anything happened to them because of me.'

'Don't you think I'm just as likely to be arrested as your fiancée as your wife?'

'No,' said Joseph. 'You'll be living here in a house that's safe. That's never had any banned material. That's never sheltered anyone. That's never been raided. You're not in any organisations. They'll have no reason to come near you.'

'But—'

'And I promise you, by this time next year it'll be over. You'll be my wife before then.'

'Joseph—'

'I need you to be safe,' he said. 'I need not to worry about you.'

'He's right,' said Annie.

'But what – we're not to see each other?' asked Winifred. 'We're to pretend the other doesn't exist?'

'I'm not saying that,' said Joseph. 'I couldn't bear not to see you. But let's just carry on as a courting couple, seeing each other once a week, being careful.'

'We could be careful even if we were married,' said Winifred. 'Joseph, everyone knows we're engaged. And there are plenty of married Volunteers. Not being your wife won't protect me.'

'We can put it about that you've cooled on marriage since I was arrested,' said Joseph. 'That I'm trying to win you back. Listen to me, Winnie. When they raided the house, they threw my mother against the wall and pointed guns at Ita and Rosanna. Who knows what might happen if one of those trigger-happy Black and Tans or Auxiliaries got twitchy? I don't want to risk it, not with you. And not with your parents either.'

Winifred looked at her mother. Annie put her arm around her and hugged her tight.

'He's protecting you,' she said as she released her again. 'And me and your da. He's doing the right thing.'

'Six months,' said Winifred finally. 'That's all. If we haven't won this damn war by then, we either get married or we're finished for good.'

'Winnie . . .'

'I'm not waiting forever,' she said. 'And I'm not going to worry about you forever either. So we either get married next summer – which is when your mother wanted, so she should be happy – or we don't get married at all. And if that means a choice between the armed struggle and me, then so be it, it's a choice you'll have to make.'

Her expression was fixed. Determined.

'Of course, we might have won long before then.' Joseph smiled at her.

'We might.'

'But if not . . .' He nodded. 'I'm doing this for you.'

'The fight isn't for me,' she said. 'The fight is for everyone else.'

'This part is for you.'

He kissed her, even though her mother was watching.

She put her arms around him and held him as close as she dared.

Chapter 9

Dublin, winter 1920

She told Alice Kelley that the engagement was off.

'Oh no.' Alice looked at her in shock. 'Why? I thought you loved each other.'

'I can't marry someone who keeps getting carted off to prison.'

'What if he needs you?'

'He doesn't need me in gaol,' said Winifred. 'He has his gaggle of sisters to look out for him.'

'But you went to the prison to sing for him. I went there to sing for him too.'

'I went to sing for everyone,' said Winifred. 'What they're doing to prisoners is wrong.'

'I'm sorry,' said Alice. 'I really am. I wish everything could go back to normal.'

But what *was* normal? Winifred wondered. And how different was Alice's normal to hers? She thought of her employer's husband, killed fighting for the British, who had right on their side in the Great War. It didn't matter how righteous they might have been then, Joseph had remarked when she spoke of it to him; it didn't mean they had right on their side when it came to Ireland. In fact, he'd said, they were very much in the wrong.

'I've received threats,' Alice added when Winifred said nothing.

'Threats?' Winifred's eyes widened. 'From who?'

'From whom.' Alice had corrected Winifred's grammar from the first day she'd started in the shop, telling her that her clients wanted well-spoken staff attending to them. 'From your republican friends, I presume. After all, it was they who attacked the shop.'

'They didn't, though,' said Winifred. 'It was a random stone. Joseph came in to make sure no one was hurt, and he had the window repaired. He wouldn't have done that if it had been a deliberate attack.'

'Perhaps he wanted to throw us off the scent.'

'You can't really believe that,' said Winifred. 'You like Joseph. You encouraged me to keep seeing him. And you protested outside Kilmainham with me.'

'Who else would have threatened me, though?' asked Alice.

Winifred didn't want to say that it could be friends of Alice's who supported the Crown and objected to her stance outside the prison.

'What did they say?' she asked. 'Did they come to you here at the shop? Or at home?'

'At the choir,' said Alice. 'A note was left in my coat.'

'At your church choir!' Winifred looked at her in surprise. But the fact that the note had been left there made her even more certain that it was someone Alice knew rather than a republican sympathiser.

'I'll try to find out if it was anyone from our . . . the republican side,' she said.

'How? Now that you've broken it off with your rebel soldier, nobody will tell you anything.'

'We're not getting married,' Winifred said. 'At least, not yet. But we'll still see each other from time to time. He thinks I'll be safer that way.'

'None of us is safe, Miss O'Leary. Not you, or me. It doesn't matter which side you're on or how much you try to distance yourself from your young man.'

'Do you have the note that was left in your pocket?' asked Winifred, not wanting to continue this line of conversation with her boss.

Alice hesitated, then opened her handbag, which had been beneath the counter, and took out a folded piece of paper. She handed it to Winifred.

WE'RE WATCHING YOU, it said in red ink. There was nothing to indicate whether she was being watched by loyalists or republicans.

'Do you have any . . . any enemies?' Winifred looked at her in bewilderment.

'It's a church choir, Miss O'Leary, not the field of battle. Of course I don't have enemies.'

'I honestly don't understand it,' said Winifred. 'Maybe it's just some eejit who wants to frighten you for some reason. I can't help thinking the republicans would be a bit more specific if they were threatening you. It's a mystery to me.'

Alice's eyes narrowed as she looked at the note again. Then she sniffed it and frowned.

'You might be right,' she said thoughtfully.

'In what way?'

'Obviously I don't have enemies.' She repeated her earlier assertion. 'But I'm thinking . . . Marjorie Wilson.'

'Who's Marjorie Wilson?'

'She's a stuck-up madam.' Alice sniffed. 'She thinks she's the best singer in the choir, but she's not, not by a long chalk. I got a solo part ahead of her. She was furious. And this paper . . .' She sniffed it again. 'It smells of her cologne. Acqua di Parma. She got it in Italy when she was there with her husband last year. She boasts about it.'

Winifred tried to keep a straight face, but she couldn't help herself and started to laugh.

'What's so funny?' demanded Alice.

'Only that we're here wondering which side in this awful war might kill us, but your note could be from a resentful chorister. Which is sort of normal in a very abnormal way.'

'Oh!' Alice's eyes widened. 'It's a bit like Mrs Christie's book.'

'Mrs Christie's book?' Winifred looked puzzled.

'*The Mysterious Affair at Styles.* Everybody's reading it,' said Alice. 'Edward's mother sent it. It's a detective mystery. With a Belgian detective.'

'I must tell my sister Rosie. She lives in Belgium, remember?'

'The mystery is set in England,' said Alice. 'But perhaps it can be bought in Belgium too. I have to say, it was very clever and thrilling. I hope Mrs Christie writes more books. Anyway,' she replaced the note in her handbag, 'people can be horrible to each other and it doesn't have to be political. It can be a question of money. Or, in Marjorie Wilson's case, envy.'

Winifred was beginning to feel sorry for Marjorie, who was now Alice's chief suspect. But as she'd replaced Joseph and the other republicans as her employer's target, she wasn't going to say a thing.

'You have a sister in England too, don't you, as well as the one in Belgium?' asked Alice.

'Mary-Jane,' confirmed Winifred. 'She's a big reader. I'll tell her to look out for Mrs Christie's book. My other sister, Katy, is in Meath.'

'Yet you want to stay here in Dublin yourself? Waiting for your man? Even though you're not engaged to him?'

'I still love him,' said Winifred.

'Then he's worth waiting for.' Alice took a deep breath. 'Now come along, Miss O'Leary. We don't have time for idle chit-chat. We have a shop to run.'

The following week, without any notice, Katy came to visit. She came alone, and Winifred was shocked at her appearance. Her sister looked older than her twenty-seven years, her face gaunt and her once luxuriant hair thin and brittle.

'Is it the war?' she asked later that evening when their mother had gone to clean the steps of the Empire Palace and their father was in the local pub, having the two glasses of beer he allowed himself at weekends. 'Or is it your husband that has you looking so terrible?'

'The war isn't helping,' said Katy. 'It's putting everyone under strain. But Reid . . .' She undid the buttons on her blouse and showed Winifred the bruises and weals on her arms and shoulders where her husband had beaten her. 'His drinking is getting worse. He's a violent man who hid it until I married him, but now he treats me like I'm his to do with whatever he likes.'

Winifred felt her jaw clench with rage for her sister. And rage at herself too, for suspecting something but not saying anything.

'What are you going to do?' she asked.

'I have choices, do I?'

Winifred shrugged helplessly.

'Bloody men,' said Katy. 'Bloody drunken men and their sense of superiority. When they've nothing to be superior about. Nothing at all.'

It was Annie who, when she came home and saw the bruises for herself, said what Winifred was thinking.

'Leave him,' she told Katy. 'Leave him right now. Before he does anything else to you. Before he does worse.'

'He'd come looking for me.'

'And if he did?' Annie snorted. 'He'd have me and your da to answer to.'

Tears filled Katy's eyes. 'I thought you'd say I made my bed and I should lie in it. Isn't that what most women are supposed to do?'

'Not my daughter,' said Annie. 'The idea of you lying in it with someone who could do that to you fills me with shame.'

'I'm expecting a baby,' said Katy.

Annie and Winifred looked at her in dismay.

'After it's born,' Katy said. 'I'll come then.'

'Katy, *a stór*, the last time you were pregnant, when you lost the baby, did the same thing happen? Did he hit you?'

'He thought it was a girl. He thinks this one is a boy. He won't do anything. He wants me to have it.'

'He's already done something!' cried Winifred. 'How long gone are you?'

'Five months.'

Annie and Winifred exchanged glances. Katy didn't look five months pregnant. She didn't look pregnant at all. Winifred wondered if she was eating properly and if the baby

116

was getting the nourishment it needed. Annie was concerned that Reid's treatment of her daughter had affected the growth of the child.

'You should stay with us, Katy. Don't risk it.' Winifred's voice was filled with consternation.

'I can't.' Katy shook her head. 'He'd only haul me back. Besides, he hasn't actually beaten me like before. Only my arms and shoulders. Afterwards it will be worse.'

'Mary, Mother of God.' Annie blessed herself rapidly. 'It's bad enough he's hitting you anywhere. I can't let you go back to him. I can't.'

'You must,' said Katy. 'I promise you, I'll leave as soon as the baby is born.'

'And you'll bring the craythur with you?'

'Of course.'

'What about Tom?' asked Winifred.

'He's still on Conaghty's farm,' said Katy. 'There's lots of work for him there.'

'Send him back to me,' said Annie. 'I don't want him close to this. And I'll not let a young boy think it's right to hit a woman.'

'Noel Mulvanney is coming up to Dublin next week. I'll send Tom with him.'

'Do that,' said Annie.

Winifred took her sister's hand in hers and squeezed it, choking back the tears that she didn't want to fall.

The days were almost at their shortest, the nights at their longest, and the violence of the war in the cities and the country increased with every passing hour. Although Annie was anxious about Katy, she was glad to have her son back with her and was pleased that Tom, who had grown tall and strong in the country, had now got a job as an errand boy for Russell's grocers on Sackville Street. That meant that he could walk most of the way with Winifred every morning and sometimes meet her on the way home too. Winifred liked having her brother with her. He wasn't, she told him, as irritating as he had been when he was younger, and he was useful around the house too.

'I'm a man now,' Tom said as he poked the coals on the fire. 'I can look after you and Ma when Da's not here.'

Winifred was about to say that they didn't need looking after, but seeing the proud look on her brother's face, she kept her mouth shut and instead hugged him so tightly he protested that she was suffocating him.

When the two of them got home to East Essex Street a few days after his arrival, hurrying across the city because flurries of snow had begun to fall, Winifred was surprised to see her sister Marianne warming her feet at the small grate.

Marianne squealed with delight at seeing Tom.

'You've grown so much!' she exclaimed as she got up to hug him. 'I hardly recognise you.'

'And I don't recognise you at all.' He squirmed away from her hold.

'Ah here.' Marianne made a face at him. 'Surely you remember your big sister?'

He shook his head.

'You don't remember sleeping in the same bed as me?' she demanded. 'Top to tail? Your face against my feet?'

'I dream of feet,' he told her solemnly. 'I thought it was in my head. Not that they were yours.'

Marianne laughed and cuffed him around the ear. He stuck his tongue out at her.

'When's Ma due back?' she asked Winifred, who was hanging her coat on the peg. 'I didn't think she'd be out this late.'

'She usually goes out when I get in,' Winifred reminded her. 'She's doing some extra this week because everywhere is busy with Christmas.' She smiled. Even with a war on, people looked towards Christmas for a little joy.

'I have to tell her my news.'

'What news?'

'You'll have to wait. I can't tell you first. But it's good news.'

Winifred looked at her doubtfully. As the youngest O'Leary girl, Marianne liked to be the centre of attention. But she wasn't at all sure that whatever news her sister had would be welcomed by their mother. She didn't ask Marianne to elaborate, but waited until both their parents were home and seated close to the fire for her to share it.

'I'm going to America,' said Marianne. 'In the new year.'

'You're what?' Her mother looked at her in astonishment. 'How did this come about? What does Dr Desmond say? Why did—'

'Would you stop asking questions, Ma?' Marianne shook her head. 'Dr Desmond will wish me good luck. He'll be happy for me.'

'But—'

'I met a man,' said Marianne. 'I'm going with him.'

'Marianne O'Leary!' Her mother looked at her in horror. 'You are *not* going to America with a man! Are you mad?'

'I'm not going with him as Marianne O'Leary,' said Marianne. 'I'll be going as Mrs Keogh. We're getting married first.'

'You most certainly are not!' retorted Annie. 'You're fifteen years old. How old is this man?'

'He's seventeen.'

'He's a boy,' said Annie. 'And you're a child.'

'I'm working and earning my own money,' said Marianne. 'And I'm living in Dr Desmond's house. I'm not a child any more.'

'You're too young to get married and you're too young to go to America.'

'I'm not too young to get married,' said Marianne. 'There are plenty of girls younger than me married, and going to America too. What's for me here? Staying in service at Dr Desmond's waiting for this stupid war to end? I want to do more with my life. In America, I will. And I won't have to be afraid that I'll be shot every time I cross the road.'

'You'd only be shot by accident.' This time it was her father who spoke.

'Exactly!' Marianne gave him a triumphant look. 'Just like you! Neither the Brits nor the Irish can shoot straight. I'd be safer hiding behind a coal sack than walking along East Essex Street.'

'Don't be silly,' said Annie.

'It's the truth.'

'And this boy you've met and want to go to America with. What does he do?'

'He's a barber. He'll get work in America, I know he will.'

'A barber!' exclaimed Winifred. 'How did you meet a barber?'

'He comes to Dr Desmond's house,' said Marianne. 'He's a good person.'

Annie looked at her daughter thoughtfully. 'And does he care about you?'

'He loves me and he wants to marry me.'

'You'd get married before Winifred?' her father asked.

'Of course,' said Marianne. 'If I was to wait for Winifred, with all her shilly-shallying, I'd never get married at all.'

'You're not marrying anyone at fifteen years old,' said Annie. 'I don't care how many girls you think you know who are married at your age; you're too young. And you're not going to America either. You can wait until you're sixteen and after Winnie and Joseph are married.'

'But she said she wouldn't get married until the war was over.' Marianne's voice was plaintive. 'That could be years and years.'

'Next summer at the latest,' said Winifred. 'That's when we're marrying.'

'Oh, the war will be over then, will it?' demanded Marianne. 'That's likely, isn't it, when they're still raiding the barracks and the police raid us back and when they do dreadful things and pretend it's to keep the peace. Not that the police are the only ones. I've heard our side doing some dreadful things too.'

'What dreadful things?' asked Winifred.

'You're going out with one of them,' said Marianne. 'You can't be so ignorant.'

'I'm not ignorant.'

'All right, then, I'll tell you. Mrs Desmond's cousin, her that lives in Mayo, was seeing a soldier. The republicans came around to her house and told her to stop seeing him, that she was a traitor. She didn't stop. They came back to the house one night and pulled her outside and cut off all her hair.'

'I've heard of that,' said Thomas. 'It's dreadful if it's true.'

'It's true all right, and I'm not going to wait for people

121

to cut off my hair.' Marianne ran her fingers through her chestnut locks.

'Your barber boy is a Brit?' Annie looked aghast.

'No,' conceded Marianne. 'But he's not a republican either. He doesn't care. He has friends who are soldiers.'

'Mary, mother of Jesus, what have you got yourself into?' demanded Annie.

'No more than what Winifred has with Joseph Burke,' retorted her daughter. 'I want to go to America and that's that.'

'Maybe the girl should go,' murmured Thomas to his wife.

'You know what will happen? They'll go and he'll abandon her and she'll be in a worse state. Probably with a child too. And I don't care what she says, she's only a chisler herself and she's not ready to be married or a mother.'

'I'm more ready than Winnie.'

'I was ready before, but Joseph was arrested,' Winifred reminded her.

Marianne gave her a dark look. 'I don't know,' she said. 'You were never one for the boys. You don't love him the way I love Danny.'

'Of course I do!' Winifred was outraged. 'How dare you say that, Marianne O'Leary!'

'Winnie's affairs are none of your business, Marianne,' said her mother. 'Now listen to me, young lady, you'll go back to Dr Desmond and you'll work hard and you'll not even think about getting married and haring off to America until you're sixteen.'

'I'd be safer there,' grumbled Marianne. 'You don't know half of what's going on in this city.'

'I certainly do,' said Annie. 'Don't I hear it every day at the theatre.'

'And you,' Marianne looked at Winifred, 'you don't know either.'

'My fiancé and his family are involved in the fight for Irish freedom,' Winifred said. 'I think that means I know enough.'

'And you're all prepared to sit here and wait,' said Marianne. 'But I want to go and live. Like Mary-Jane and Rosie. They have good lives in England and Belgium. Everyone is better off out of here.'

'It will be better when we win the war,' said her father.

'*If* we win,' said Marianne. 'Not everyone thinks we will.'

'We will.' Winifred looked at her sister. 'We'll win because we have right on our side and the people are on our side, and in the end we'll have a free country and you won't want to go to America because everything you'll need will be here.'

Marianne, Annie and Thomas looked at her in astonishment.

'I never thought I'd hear that from you,' said her father. 'It seems that going out with the freedom fighter has changed your views after all.'

'I hate violence and I'm as sick of this war as the next person,' said Winifred. 'And . . . and I didn't even realise I'd started to think this way. But sometimes you have to fight. So the more of us who get behind it, the better. Including you, Marianne O'Leary. And Ma is right, you're a child and so is your boyfriend. Do you really want to be having babies in America with nobody around to help you?'

'I'd be a good mother. Just like Ma.'

'There's plenty of time,' said Annie. 'Give it till you're sixteen. If this war is still going on then, you can leave.'

'I'm not sixteen for months,' wailed Marianne.

'You'd drive a woman to drink,' said Annie. 'Go back to Dr Desmond's. We'll talk about it again.'

Marianne shrugged as she picked up her coat and pulled it around her. Then she walked out of the room, leaving silence in her wake.

Chapter 10

Dublin, Christmas 1920/New Year 1921

Although an underlying air of tension hung over the city, Dubliners were attempting to make the most of Christmas, and the shop-owners of Sackville Street had made an effort to decorate their windows and add a little festive spirit. Alice and Winifred worked hard to ensure that the window of Kelley's looked appropriately traditional, with a large crib in the centre of the display surrounded by bales of fabric topped with papier-mâché leaves to create multicoloured palm trees. By Christmas Eve, everyone who wanted to buy material to make new clothes for Christmas Day had already done so, and there were very few customers. Alice used the time to do a stock-take and decide what fabrics she'd discount in the days after Christmas, while Winifred tidied the stockroom and made suggestions about what kinds of deals to offer.

She was moving bales of linen when she heard the tinkle of the shop bell and the murmur of a male voice. She stopped what she was doing and stood immobile, her heart beating rapidly. Men rarely came into Kelley's. The shop's clientele was almost exclusively female, and women always collected their own orders.

The door to the stockroom opened, and Alice poked her head around it.

'A gentleman to see you, Miss O'Leary,' she said.

Winifred's heartbeat accelerated still more. There was no man who needed to see her. Not for anything good. She thought briefly about trying to leave through the side door that led onto a narrow laneway, but that door was locked and the key was in the shop. She took a deep breath and walked out of the stockroom.

'Hello, Miss O'Leary.'

'Joseph!' This time her heart raced for a different reason. 'I didn't expect to see you today. And certainly not here.'

'It's Christmas Eve,' he said. 'I've finished work. I was hoping you might like to join me.'

'I've still another hour to go,' she said.

'Oh, don't be silly, Miss O'Leary.' Alice beamed at her. 'Go off with your young man. I can finish up here.'

'That's very kind of you, but . . .'

'I mean it,' Alice said. 'Go. Enjoy yourself.'

'Are you really sure?'

'Go before I change my mind,' said Alice.

Winifred pulled the apron she'd been wearing over her head and hung it on the coat stand, in place of her fawn coat. Joseph held the coat for her while she put it on.

'Are you going anywhere nice?' asked Alice.

'It's a surprise,' said Joseph.

'A nice surprise?'

'I hope so.'

'Here you are, Miss O'Leary.' Alice opened a drawer

beneath the counter and took out a pair of red wool gloves. 'I was going to give these to you later, but you'll have use for them now.'

'Oh.' Winifred took the gloves and pulled them onto her hands. 'Thank you, Mrs Kelley. That's very kind of you. I don't have anything for you,' she added anxiously. 'I didn't think . . .'

'I wasn't expecting anything,' said Alice. 'Now off you go. Happy Christmas.'

Winifred followed Joseph out of the shop. A light dusting of snow covered the street, but the flakes falling from the grey sky were sparse and it didn't look like there'd be much more.

'Just as well you threw my gloves into the river,' remarked Joseph. 'Otherwise you wouldn't be able to wear those.'

'I said I was sorry about that.' Winifred made a face at him. 'I regretted it as soon as I did it, because they were beautiful gloves. But I was mad at you.'

'I don't like you being mad at me, but I do like you being feisty,' he said.

She laughed and held him closer, then asked him if it was all right to walk the streets of Dublin together. On the other occasions they'd met, usually outdoors in a park despite the darker winter days, they'd arrived and left separately. They hadn't been to Bewley's since Joseph's arrest.

'It's Christmas,' he replied. 'Even the Brits aren't out looking for trouble. We'll be fine.'

'So where are we going?' she asked. And then, as a truck carrying soldiers drove by, 'I thought you said they weren't out.'

'I said they weren't looking for trouble,' he reminded her. 'Don't worry, Winnie. Everyone's a little more relaxed this week. We're meeting other people too, if that's all right with you. We're going to have tea with Anthony and Bridget.'

'That will be nice,' she agreed. 'I haven't seen him in an age.'

'He's been busy.'

'Working or fighting?'

'Both.'

'And you?' she asked.

'Planning,' said Joseph.

'Anything I should know about? Or, more to the point, anything I shouldn't really know about?'

'Nothing special,' he replied. 'We're continuing our attacks on barracks and anywhere there are British soldiers or policemen, of course, but I'm not an active part of that. At least, not right now.'

'I read in the *Journal* that there was talk of a truce.' She gave him a hopeful look, but he shook his head and said that wasn't going to happen.

'They've declared martial law in the south of the country, and they burned Cork city in reprisals for the last ambush,' he said. 'But I truly do believe there isn't long left in this fight, Winifred. And that we'll win it.'

'I hope so.' She squeezed his arm. 'Let's not talk about it. Let's pretend there's nothing going on.'

Which they did, ignoring a battalion of soldiers marching down the opposite side of the street and the jeers of a gang of youths who were following them.

'Here we are.' Joseph stopped outside the Gresham Hotel, where wreaths of holly and ivy decorated the entrance, the green leaves and red berries bright against the pale stonework.

'The Gresham? We're having tea in the Gresham?' Winifred looked at him in astonishment.

'And why not?' he replied as he led her up the steps. 'Aren't we as entitled as anyone else to have tea here?'

'I've never been inside it before,' she murmured. 'If you'd told me, I would have worn something better.'

'You look lovely, Winnie,' he said. 'You always do, no matter what you wear.'

She leaned her head briefly on his shoulder and waited with delight as the doorman opened the doors for them and waved them inside. The atrium was buzzing with the conversation of groups of stylish men and women seated at small tables. The muted colours, large mirrors and huge chandeliers gave the impression of a grand town house, while the warm air meant that she immediately took off her new gloves and smiled with delight.

'This is lovely,' she said. 'Are you sure it's all right for me to be here?'

'Of course.' Joseph steered her towards a table in the corner. 'And here's my good friend already waiting for us.'

Winifred saw Anthony stand up. The two men shook hands, and then Anthony kissed Winifred's, which made her laugh.

'And may I introduce you to Miss Bridget Lafferty,' he said.

The young woman, who'd remained seated, now stood up too. She was tall, with bright blue eyes and a soft peaches-and-cream complexion. She wore a pale pink blouse with a ruby brooch at the throat, and a lilac skirt that fitted her slender body to perfection.

'Pleased to meet you,' she said.

Winnie recognised her accent as being a northern one, and she glanced at Anthony.

'Miss Lafferty is staying with family in Sandymount while she studies at Trinity College,' he said.

'Classics,' said Bridget. 'I plan to teach.'

'Education for women is very important,' agreed Winifred, even as she processed the fact that Bridget's family were wealthy enough to send her to college, which put the other woman in a very different social class to her. And which meant that there were professions open to Bridget that were firmly closed to Winifred herself. 'How did you and Anthony meet?'

'By accident.' Bridget smiled. 'I fell off my bicycle and landed at his feet.'

'A lucky accident for me,' said Anthony.

'I agree.' Bridget flashed a wide grin at him.

A young waitress brought them tea and sandwiches and Winifred basked in the unaccustomed luxury of the setting she found herself in.

Regardless of the War of Independence, Dublin – and Ireland – was changing, she thought. Women at college. Women wanting to be teachers. And despite the undoubtedly shameful levels of poverty that racked the city, there was reason for hope too, because there were families like hers, working families, able to survive. More than survive, she thought, as she looked around her. They were doing better. Because here she was, sitting in the Gresham Hotel as though it was her right. And that was a good thing. Places like the Gresham should be places that anyone could go to. Places like Trinity College, too.

She felt a surge of pride in herself and her country and the possibilities that lay ahead of her despite the current circumstances.

'Oh,' said Bridget suddenly as she saw a man approaching. There was an immediate frisson of tension at the table.

'Nobody to worry about.' She stood up. 'Mr Yeats, how good to see you again.'

The man was in his fifties, his long face partially hidden by the broad-brimmed hat he was wearing. As he arrived at the table, he removed the hat to reveal greying hair.

'Miss Lafferty,' he said to Bridget. 'The pleasure is all mine.'

'Thank you. These are my friends.' She introduced them, and Mr Yeats nodded to each of them.

'I'm a friend of Miss Lafferty's uncle,' he said. 'I've painted for him.'

Winifred thought he looked very refined for a painter, and almost said so.

'And you've painted him too.' Bridget giggled.

'That I have.'

'Painted him?' Winifred frowned.

'Mr Yeats does portraits,' said Bridget. 'Well, sometimes. He did one of my uncle for his birthday, and my aunt says it's the best she's ever seen.'

'Oh.' Winifred was grateful she hadn't opened her mouth sooner and betrayed her assumption that the man painted walls and buildings. She swallowed hard to hide the embarrassment she felt at even thinking such a thing. Because obviously a man like Mr Yeats would be a painter of people and not of walls.

'And you, Miss O'Leary, what do you do?' he asked after Bridget had invited him to sit with them for a while.

Winifred told him about the shop.

'You're an artist too,' he said. 'The colours and cut of the fabric, the design of the dress . . . a work of art.'

'I'm just a shop girl,' said Winifred, even though she liked the idea of clothes and fabrics as art. 'My work isn't artistic.'

'I love art,' said Bridget. 'It's life.'

'There's only one art, and it's the art of living,' said Mr Yeats. 'And I'm glad to see that despite everything, that's what you young people are doing.' He took a notebook and pencil out of his coat pocket and begin to sketch, using firm, confident strokes. The others were silent for a while, but as he continued to draw, they began to talk in low tones about the coldness of the weather and the delight of being able to sit in the warm hotel.

'Here you are.' Mr Yeats tore the page from his notebook and handed it to Winifred. It was a sketch of her standing behind a shop counter, a length of fabric in her hands, and her eyes widened as she looked at it.

'Is this how you see me?' she asked as Joseph took it from her to see it for himself. 'Because I look sad.'

'Everyone looks sad right now,' said the painter. 'Your sadness is reflected in your eyes, Miss O'Leary. But . . .' he took the drawing from Joseph and added a few more strokes, 'you can also look like this.'

He handed it to her again and she smiled. He had cleverly changed the shading so that the sadness had changed to a look of determination and made her appear stronger.

'That's more you, Winnie,' said Joseph. 'I saw that look the very first day I came into the shop and you lambasted me about your broken window.'

'I'd like to think so.' She examined the drawing again. 'Thank you, Mr Yeats. I'll do my best to live up to this.'

'My pleasure,' he said. 'I like sketching new people. Now,' he added as he stood up, 'I'd best be on my way. I'm meeting some friends. I was early, that's why I inflicted myself on you. It was good to see you, Miss Lafferty. Give my regards to your uncle.'

'I will,' Bridget said. When Mr Yeats had left, she smiled at Winifred. 'You should keep that. Maybe one day it'll be worth a fortune. More and more people are buying paintings by Jack B. Yeats.'

'Oh,' Winifred said. 'I didn't realise.' Because she had heard of him, of course she had, the brother of the poet whose work was so well regarded. It must be nice to be part of a family that didn't have to work for a living, she thought. Who could dabble in poetry and art instead of selling fabric or labouring or painting walls. 'He's very well known.'

'Not well known enough if you didn't recognise the name,' said Bridget.

'I wasn't thinking . . .' Winifred certainly wasn't going to confess now to having first thought he was a labourer. 'Of course I'll keep it.'

'I have an oil painting myself,' said Bridget. 'He did it when he stayed with us for a few days. It's hanging over my bed.'

They talked then about painting and poetry, theatre and books. Although she hadn't read as widely as either Bridget or, indeed, Joseph, who was a voracious reader, Winifred had read enough to be able to hold her own in the conversation. Once again she was grateful to Annie, who'd made sure that all her family was well educated, and that her daughters treasured the few books they had.

But when politics reared its head, as was almost inevitable, she allowed her mind to drift, imagining a world in which sitting in the Gresham having tea and sandwiches would be a norm for her and her sisters. And her own daughters and granddaughters too.

In the icy January that followed. Winifred saw hardly anything of Joseph. She went out very little, averting her eyes from soldiers on the streets as she scurried from the shop to her home, sometimes with Tom beside her, sometimes alone. Every time the soldiers passed her by, she felt her body stiffen as though she was guilty of something other than being in love with Joseph Burke. Which, given that he was in their view an insurrectionist, was itself something to feel guilty about.

Then the news arrived that despite her promise, Marianne had left Dr Desmond's and was on her way to America with her now husband, Danny Keogh. Annie cried when she heard, saying that she couldn't believe Marianne had got married behind her back, and the very least her daughter could have done was come and say goodbye. It was ridiculous, she said, that girls could be married at just twelve years of age when they were nothing more than children themselves, and it was very hard on her to have three daughters in three different countries, with Mary-Jane in England, Rosie in Belgium and now Marianne in America. 'If she ever gets there,' she wailed. 'Sure, going to Queenstown to get the boat is probably less safe than the journey across the sea. Cork is as bad as Dublin right now. She could be set on by anyone.'

'She'll be well protected,' Winifred said, while thinking nothing of the sort and wishing Marianne had confided in her so that she could've throttled her.

'At least I've still got you, Winnie,' said her mother. 'You were always the most reliable of my girls.'

Reliable because I do what I'm told, Winifred thought. Because I don't rock the boat. Even though it deserves to be rocked. And even though I still believe in the concept of a quiet life. But it was hard to have a quiet life in a time of war, when you were constantly on edge and every loud noise made your heart race and your hands shake.

She shared this thought with Alice Kelley one afternoon, and Alice nodded and said that she felt the same. She added that the Great War was the worst of it for her, because hadn't she spent the entire four years of it worrying about her husband only to have him get killed in the end?

'I'm sorry,' Winifred said. 'It's been much worse for you than me.'

'Men start wars, but women suffer through them,' said Alice. 'And I know it was terrible on the battlefield, probably a million times worse than we could ever imagine, but I wonder why it is that it has to come down to fighting in the end.'

Winifred was about to reply when the bell above the door jangled and a woman stepped inside. Her heart almost stopped as she recognised Agnes Burke. She couldn't think of any reason that the woman would call to the shop unless it was with news of Joseph. And the only news around these days was bad news.

But Agnes smiled at Alice, who welcomed her as a new customer, asking if she could help.

'I want something in green,' said Agnes. 'For curtains to go in my dining room. But I'm sure Miss O'Leary can help me, seeing that we're almost family.'

Alice glanced at Winifred, who introduced Agnes as Joseph's mother.

'I'm pleased to meet you,' said Alice. 'I'm sure we can help you, and at a favourable price too. Fetch the curtain material, Miss O'Leary.'

Winifred recalled the dining room of St Anthony's Place and selected a fabric she thought Agnes would like. When her future mother-in-law had inspected it and pronounced it suitable, she cut the required length, then folded it neatly and wrapped it in brown paper.

'You're a good worker, Winnie,' said Agnes. 'You know what you're doing. And you wrap a very nice parcel.'

'Thank you,' said Winifred.

'I need something else,' said Agnes. 'Not expensive. It's to divide a space,' she added.

'We have muslin if you don't need it to be too heavy,' said Winifred.

'Cut a few yards of muslin for me, so,' said Agnes.

'How many is a few? Two? Three?'

'Make it five. I want it bulky enough.'

Winifred went into the stockroom and returned with a bale of muslin. She cut five yards and folded it carefully.

'I can add it to your parcel,' she said.

'No. I want it to go somewhere else,' said Agnes. 'Would you be able to deliver it today for me?'

'We can get a delivery boy to do it,' said Alice, who'd been watching Winifred cut and package the material.

'I'd prefer Miss O'Leary to deliver it personally,' Agnes said. 'I want to be certain it gets to the right address. Perhaps she could do it later this afternoon? And maybe deliver my own parcel tomorrow? Of course I'll pay for her services. Oh, and Miss O'Leary?'

'Yes.'

'If you wouldn't mind adding this to the package, I'd be very grateful. You'd save me a trip.'

Agnes took some additional folded material from her big handbag and handed it to Winifred, who registered that there was something wrapped inside. As she felt the weight of the material, and the shape of what it enveloped, her heart began to beat faster and she didn't even try to hide the worry in her eyes.

'Just bundle it up there,' said Agnes.

'But—'

'I'm in a bit of a hurry,' the other woman said.

Winifred glanced at Alice, but her boss was filling in the ledger and hadn't noticed the exchange of material. She opened her mouth as though to speak, then closed it again and placed the wrapped object on the folded muslin.

When she'd finished tying up the parcel, Agnes handed her an envelope. 'So you know where to go. No need to write an address on the package itself. There's a letter in the envelope too.'

Winifred looked at the name and address, then returned her gaze to Agnes.

'You can do it on your way home,' said the older woman. 'It's a slight detour, I know. But no bother to you to take an extra walk. You're a young girl and you're fit.'

Winifred put the letter in the pocket of her coat, which was hanging on the wall. Her mind was racing. She knew the reputation of the area she'd be delivering the parcel to, and she was very worried about what it now contained.

'Is everything all right, Miss O'Leary?' asked Alice as Winifred wiped her hands on her skirt.

'Of course.' Winifred didn't look at her. Nor did she look at Agnes.

'It's cash on delivery,' Alice told Mrs Burke. 'Or thirty days' credit for customers with accounts. Unfortunately you don't have an account, but I'm sure we could set one up for you, given that you'll be related to Miss O'Leary soon.'

Agnes took a large purse from the pocket of her coat.

'I'm happy to pay cash,' she said as she handed over the money. 'It's always better that way. And of course, here's some money to cover Miss O'Leary making the delivery personally for me.'

When Alice asked where the fabric was being delivered to, and Winifred told her, she looked at her in consternation.

'Why is she asking you to go there?'

'I . . . The Burkes do a lot of charity work,' said Winifred. 'Perhaps . . .'

'Charity work!' Alice gave her a disbelieving look.

'I honestly don't know, Mrs Kelley.'

'Leave early, before it gets dark,' said Alice. She didn't say anything more.

Winifred was relieved that Alice wasn't being inquisitive, and even more relieved at leaving early, because she knew her mother would be furious at the idea of her walking to North King Street in the dark, and equally furious with Mrs Burke for asking her to do it. She put the package in a straw bag and checked the letter in her pocket, then left the shop and walked briskly across the street.

The city was busy, but Winifred didn't make eye contact with any of the people walking by. Nor did she gaze, as she normally did, at the motor cars that drove by, envying the freedom they gave to the people who could afford them. Finally turning into North King Street, she raised her eyes and saw women standing in the doors of the tenement buildings, their shawls halfway down their backs, their blouses open to show their cleavage.

She tried not to stare. Annie had warned her many times about Dublin's red-light district, but Winifred had never walked alone through the area known as Monto before. She'd been told that many of the customers of the kip-houses were policemen, or British soldiers, while a good number of the people who actually lived here were part of the republican movement. Which meant that, in more ways than one, it was a tinderbox.

She counted off the numbers of the houses until she reached a three-storey building where half a dozen women stood on the steps. She couldn't help thinking that they must be freezing in the cold January evening, but the women – scarcely older and possibly even younger than herself – didn't seem to care.

'I have a package for Maud Higgins,' she said to a girl whose cheeky smile reminded her of Marianne, despite the fact that she was attired in a low-cut dress and high heels, clothes that Marianne, for all her occasional brazenness, would never dream of wearing.

'Have you now?' the girl said. 'And what d'you want me to do about it?'

'Tell Mrs Higgins I'm here?' suggested Winifred.

'Or maybe you should just hand it to me.'

'I have to give it to Mrs Higgins herself. I'll wait while you get her.'

'You can stand on the step there, but make sure you don't take any business from me!' An older woman wearing a tight-fitting red dress laughed.

'I . . . won't,' said Winifred.

'A lot of them around here like us innocent,' said the woman. 'You look innocent.'

'I'm not that innocent,' snapped Winifred. 'But I'm tired and cold and I've things to do.'

'All right, all right, keep your drawers on.' The woman shrugged. 'I'll get Maud for you. Chrissie, you go inside. Your regular will be here any minute.'

She went into the house, followed by the girl, while Winifred stood on the pavement outside, stamping her feet to keep out the cold. The street was busy as men strode by, stopping sometimes to look at the girls who stood outside almost every single tenement building before going inside with one of them. It wasn't that Winifred had been entirely unaware of the fact that prostitution was rife in the city – some of the girls came to Sackville Street, after all – but she'd never seen so many in one place. She remembered Alice talking to a customer about it once and saying how disgraceful it was that there were supposedly more than fifteen hundred girls working in the district. But, she thought suddenly, with so much poverty in the city, maybe it wasn't all that surprising.

A man walked briskly towards her, and with a sense of shock she realised that, despite his hat and muffler, she recognised him. He was the owner of a tobacconist's near Kelley's Fabrics, a family man, she thought, but clearly not. Or perhaps a man with 'needs'. Marianne, on her occasional visits from Dr Desmond's, had occasionally told stories of men and their needs that made Winifred blush.

He hurried up the steps and into the brothel, not noticing Winifred as she shrank into the shadows, trying to make herself invisible. He was quickly followed by another man, cap pulled down low so that he was unidentifiable, and a few moments later by a third – tall and well built, with a black moustache, and not, it appeared, in the slightest bit worried about being seen.

It seemed to her an age since the woman had gone to get Maud Higgins. She wondered if she simply hadn't bothered and was with a client instead. And if that was the case, what was she to do with the package she was guarding in her straw bag? Bring it back to Agnes? She couldn't possibly do that. Agnes would be furious with her and probably decide that she hadn't tried to deliver it at all. Besides, having got this far, she certainly didn't want to walk the city further with it.

Nor did she want to make her relationship with Agnes any worse than it already was. But she resented her future mother-in-law putting her in this position. And what about Joseph? The question had been lurking in the back of her mind ever since Agnes Burke had handed her the package. Did he know that his mother had asked her to carry a gun across the city? Because that was the object that had been so carefully concealed in the material Agnes had given her. And if so, did he approve? After all, despite them occasionally meeting up, their relationship was meant to be cooler than before, and that was supposedly for her safety. Exactly how safe would he think bringing arms to a brothel in Monto was?

It was another five minutes, and Winifred's anxiety level had reached an all-time high, before a slender woman who looked to be in her early forties appeared at the door. She was dressed entirely in black, but the colour wasn't severe on her. In fact, it flattered her slightly olive complexion and her piercing blue eyes.

'You have a package for me? Who sent it?' Her accent was as piercing as her eyes.

'And a letter.' Winifred took the envelope from her pocket and handed both it and the package to her.

'Who sent it?' repeated Mrs Higgins.

'I'm sure the letter is signed.'

'You can't tell me?'

'I could,' said Winifred. 'But I'm not sure I should.'

'Aren't you the good little patriot.' The woman laughed.

Winifred suddenly realised that Agnes hadn't given her a description of Maud Higgins, and that she could be handing both the letter and the package over to anyone. Which could lead to absolute disaster. But it was too late now, and she told herself that the woman in front of her had such a commanding presence she had to be the right person.

'You've done what you came to do,' said Maud. 'You should go now. This really isn't a place for a girl like you to be out on her own.'

'You don't say,' muttered Winifred under her breath. She turned and hurried along Church Street towards Merchant's Quay and home.

Her mother was getting ready to go out when she arrived at East Essex Street. Winifred said nothing about her mission, and Annie was too preoccupied with her own affairs to notice the look of relief on her daughter's face as she slipped off her coat and hung it up.

As soon as her mother had left, Winnie sat down and took off her boots, allowing them to fall to the floor with a thud.

Then she stretched her feet towards the fire until she could feel them eventually heating up.

Never again, she muttered. I'm not cut out for this. So never, ever again.

Chapter 11

Dublin, January 1921

Alice didn't mention the parcel the next day. They were surprisingly busy, with a steady stream of women coming in to buy fabric in the January sale period, and there was no time for chat or gossip.

'I think this is going to be a good year for the shop,' said Alice as she closed the till for the day. 'I don't know—'

But she didn't have the chance to finish the sentence, because at that moment the door burst open and half a dozen armed Auxiliaries stepped inside. They were big men, in caubeen berets and khaki uniforms, and they took up the entire space in front of the counter. They were armed with rifles slung over their shoulders or pistols at their waists. Alice and Winifred looked at them in horror.

'Alice Kelley?' The tallest of them leaned towards her, causing her to step back as she acknowledged who she was. Winifred, standing in the doorway to the stockroom, tried to make herself unnoticeable. 'We've a warrant to search the premises. We've reason to believe you're hiding weapons here.'

'What?' Alice looked at them from astonished blue eyes. 'I keep bales of fabric here, not boxes of guns.'

'We'll see if you're right, won't we?' He lifted the wooden slat of the counter and allowed it to bang open, stepping past Alice as though she wasn't there.

'We don't . . .' Winifred, shrinking even further against the wall, shut her mouth as the man looked at her. With a sense of horror, she realised that she'd seen him the previous night at North King Street. He'd been the third man to enter the brothel. Had he seen her? Recognised her? Was that why they were here? Was this all her fault? She felt her mouth go dry, and when she tried to swallow, it was as though there was a stone in her throat.

The man gave no sign of recognising her as he and the other Auxiliaries went to work, upending Alice's stock of fabrics, pulling out boxes and searching cupboards without finding anything, while Alice wailed that they were destroying the place.

'You.' He pointed at Winifred. 'Turn around.'

'Why?'

'Do what you're bloody told.'

'But I—'

He took her by the arm and pushed her against the wall. Until that moment, it hadn't really registered with her that she and Alice were two women alone with six men, but now it did. And she was suddenly more afraid than she'd ever been.

'Now let's see what you might be hiding.' He pulled at her blouse, and Winifred screamed.

'Get your hands off her!' Alice's shriek was loud and piercing as she ran at him. 'I am a war widow and my husband was killed fighting for England. You might have fought along-side him yourself. So let go of my employee at once and get out of my shop. You know there are no weapons here. You've searched everywhere.'

The Auxiliary laughed, and released his hold on Winifred.

'Not quite everywhere,' he said as he put his arms around Alice instead. 'You ladies are known for the places you try to hide things.'

There was a peal of laughter from the rest of the men as Alice used her fists to no avail on their leader.

Winifred, who'd edged towards the door, opened it and began to shout for help.

'We're Irishwomen!' she called. 'Being assaulted in our own shop! We've done nothing wrong.'

One of the Auxiliaries yanked her by the arm and sent her crashing to the ground. Then the leader dragged Alice into the street with him and flung her on top of Winifred, who gasped at the weight of her boss's body landing on her own.

At that moment, the sound of gunshots reached them, and the Auxiliaries looked in the direction of O'Connell Bridge.

'What in God's name is that about?' One of the younger men glanced at his leader.

'This effing country.' The leader grasped his rifle and turned away from Alice and Winnie. 'Come on, we can deal with these two another time.'

The Auxiliaries formed into a small marching group and began to run towards the bridge.

'This isn't over,' their leader called back to the two women, who were still lying on the pavement. 'We'll be back.'

More shots were fired in the distance. Alice and Winifred stayed where they were. When it was clear that nobody was coming back, Alice groaned and pulled herself upright, gasping aloud as she put her hand to the ground.

'Are you all right?' asked Winifred, who had also managed to sit up.

'I . . . Except for my wrist.' Alice's breath came in nervous gasps as she tried to flex it, wincing at the pain.

'Are they still shooting?' asked Winifred.

'Yes, but we don't know who started it. We don't know why.'

'It doesn't matter,' said Winifred. 'If it hadn't happened, they would've . . .' She was unable to finish the sentence, but she was thinking of the stories of the soldiers who'd raped and beaten women they believed were helping the republicans, and Marianne's insistence that sometimes they'd had their heads shaved too. Yet these men were supposedly there to keep the peace, and no matter what they thought of the Irish, they surely couldn't have intended to abuse her and Alice in broad daylight. And then she remembered the heat of the Auxiliary's breath on her face and his grip on her arm, and she thought of his jaunty gait in Monto the previous evening, and she knew that he was perfectly capable of it.

They were still sitting on the pavement when two men rounded the corner and stopped abruptly.

'Miss O'Leary.' The shorter of the two spoke to Winifred. 'Are you all right? What happened?'

Winnie recognised him as being the Volunteer who, along with Anthony, had replaced the window in Mrs Kelley's shop. She frowned as she tried to remember his name.

'We were attacked.' It was Alice who replied, in a high voice. 'Bloody Auxiliaries turned my shop over. And for nothing.'

'Mrs Kelley?'

'Do you know me?' She was suddenly wary.

'I know your shop,' he said. 'And I know the name on it.'

'Padraig,' said Winifred suddenly.

'That's right. Padraig Shanahan.'

'You know each other?' Alice's voice was sharp.

'Not really,' said Winifred. 'We're acquaintances.'

She was glad that today, for whatever reason, neither Padraig nor the man who was with him was wearing an Irish army uniform. She couldn't help thinking that the sight of it, after what they'd already been through, would've given Alice an attack of the vapours. And perhaps she'd think that knowledge of their acquaintance was what had brought the Auxiliaries to the shop.

'Can I help you?' Padraig extended his hand.

Winifred nodded, and he assisted her upright. She brushed down her skirt, glad that it was more dusty than dirty. But then she realised that her blouse was torn, and she pulled it over her chest with trembling fingers.

'And you?' Padraig reached down to Alice, but when he touched her hand, she yelped.

'It's my wrist,' she said with a sob. 'It's very sore.'

'Let me see.' Padraig gently took her hand in his, then grimaced. 'Perhaps it's just sprained, but you may have broken it,' he said.

'No!'

'I could take you to the hospital.'

'But . . . but the shop. And Miss O'Leary. Winnie.'

'I think we should shut the shop for the rest of the day,' said Winifred. 'It's getting late anyway. You need to have your wrist treated, Mrs Kelley.'

'Why did they do this?' The tears that had been brimming in Alice's eyes started to fall. 'Why?'

'And what made them stop?' asked Winifred. 'There were shots. What was that all about?'

'Soldiers fired at civilians at a checkpoint on the bridge.' The other man spoke for the first time. 'We don't know why.'

'Is everyone all right?'

'I'm sure people were hit. You don't fire indiscriminately at civilians and not hit anyone.'

'This is just awful,' wailed Alice. 'I can't take it any more.'

'Don't upset yourself,' said Winifred. 'It'll be all right.'

'It'll never be all right!' Alice cried.

Winifred agreed with her. But she wasn't going to say so.

'Let me take you to get your wrist seen to.' Padraig's voice was calm and soothing as he helped Alice to her feet. 'Miss O'Leary is right. You should shut up shop for the day. Francie will help her.'

'Francie O'Reilly,' said the other man. 'I'll make sure everything is secure, don't you worry.'

'Thank you.' Alice sniffed.

She allowed Padraig to lead her away, while Francie watched as Winifred began to tidy the shop.

'You're Joseph Burke's girl, aren't you?' he said as she replaced boxes of buttons in their cubbyholes.

'I . . . Yes.'

'I'm sorry this happened. Do you know why?'

'They said the shop was known as a place where arms were kept,' she said. 'But it's not. It . . .' She stopped. She wasn't going to say anything about Agnes and the gun.

'Don't fret yourself,' said Francie. 'Let's do what we can here.'

They worked together in silence, Francie shifting the bales and picking up buttons and hooks while Winifred refolded fabrics that had been in parcels ready for delivery to customers. The Auxiliaries had torn them open, leaving the contents bundled on the floor. The last piece she folded was the green fabric that Agnes had chosen the previous day. She was suddenly glad that she'd planned to take it to St Anthony's Place herself and hadn't written the address on the brown paper packaging.

When it was safely tied up, she turned the sign on the door to 'Closed' and locked it behind her.

'Do you want me to walk you home?' asked Francie.

'I'll be fine,' she said.

'If you're sure.' He gave her an apologetic smile. 'I need to get to Terenure. I hope the trams are still running, especially if there's been trouble on the bridge.'

'Thank you for taking the time to help me,' said Winifred.

'You're very welcome.' Francie tipped his cap and walked away.

Once again Winifred moved through the city with a parcel under her arm, not making eye contact with anyone. Although she was shocked by what had happened, her mind was quite suddenly calm, her walk steady and confident. She crossed the street to avoid a group of RIC constables standing outside the Pro-Cathedral, and then hurried past the increasingly dilapidated tenements towards Temple Street and St Anthony's Place.

She was stopped at a checkpoint a couple of hundred yards from her destination.

'And who have we here?' The soldier looked at her, but his expression was bored.

'I'm delivering a parcel.'

'Where to?'

'The convent,' Winifred replied without even thinking.

'Let me see it.'

He took the parcel from her and ripped it open. Winifred pulled her coat more tightly around her, hiding the tear in her blouse.

'What's it for?' asked the soldier as the green fabric spilled onto the ground.

'I don't know,' said Winifred. 'I don't ask. I just deliver.'

'On your way,' said the soldier. 'Don't stay out after the curfew.'

'I won't,' said Winifred.

She walked quickly past him and didn't slow down until she reached the convent building.

Winifred walked up the steps and rang the bell. A young postulant opened the heavy oak door.

'I have a parcel of fabric for Mrs Burke. Could you give it to her?'

'You may give it to her yourself.' The postulant's voice was soft, her accent French. 'Follow me.'

Winifred stepped inside.

The smell of beeswax polish was a welcome relief from the stench of gunpowder that lingered in the air, and she inhaled the soothing aroma as she followed the nun along the corridor that linked the convent with the Burkes' house. The postulant knocked on the door to the house, and it was Agnes herself who answered it.

'Miss O'Leary.' She looked surprised.

Winifred stepped into the house and the nun closed the

door firmly behind her. She heard the sound of a key being turned.

'I see you have my fabric,' said Agnes.

'The Auxiliaries raided the shop earlier. It was only because of some other incident that they left without . . . Well, I don't know what they were going to do. Mrs Kelley may have a broken wrist. We were both thrown to the ground.' Winifred's voice trembled for a moment, then she cleared her throat and spoke more firmly again. 'I was stopped and searched on the way here. That's why I thought it was better to come to the convent. I didn't realise there was a connecting door.'

'It's used occasionally,' said Agnes. 'The nuns have a policy of "see no evil, hear no evil". They never put themselves in danger. But they do allow us to enter or leave by the convent from time to time.'

'Fortunately for me,' said Winifred.

'I'm sorry about the raid on your shop. But I commend you on your quick thinking in getting here. I presume you managed to deal with that other little matter?'

'Yes.'

'Excellent,' said Agnes. 'I was just about to sit down to a cup of tea. I'm sure you could do with one to warm you up.'

Winifred nodded, and followed her into the Yellow Room.

'Were you seen going to Mrs Higgins's?' asked Agnes after she'd poured the tea.

'I'm sure I was,' replied Winifred. She told Agnes that she'd seen one of the Auxiliaries there too, and wondered if he'd recognised her, 'In any event, there has to be some link with you, Mrs Burke,' she added. 'And the result of all this is that Mrs Kelley has gone to hospital to have her wrist seen to.' She choked back a sob. Here in the warmth of St Anthony's Place, feeling safer from the world outside, the unexpected composure she'd felt until now was beginning to crack.

'There's no need to cry, Miss O'Leary.' Agnes couldn't keep her impatience out of her voice. 'Everyone is being raided. This house was raided, you know that. It's an intimidation tactic.'

'It's hard to believe it was a random intimidation the day after you gave me a gun to deliver to the red-light district.' Winifred spoke as firmly as she could before taking a hanky from her bag and blowing her nose. 'There has to be a connection. And I'm not sure why you asked me to do it at all, given that Joseph and I are supposed to be keeping some distance between us.'

Agnes sat back in her chair and observed the young woman in front of her. Even though Winifred had looked as though she were going to collapse into a torrent of sobbing, she'd regained her composure, and there was a new-found determination about her, a confidence that hadn't been there before. Which, given what she'd just gone through, surprised Agnes. And Winifred wasn't wrong in questioning if there was a connection between her trip to Monto and the raid on the shop. Agnes was asking herself the same question.

'I'll try to find out if there was a particular reason your shop was targeted,' she said. 'But a lot of these raids are completely random. The Auxiliaries need to justify their existence.'

'Why did you ask me to deliver the gun?' Winifred put her cup on the table.

'It was a pistol for a Volunteer who needed to make an escape,' replied Agnes.

'But why did *I* have to deliver it?' demanded Winifred. 'I'm sure you've plenty of people available for stuff like that.'

'I'd like to think so.' Agnes sighed. 'But it's hard, Miss O'Leary. Young Volunteers are lifted off the streets all the time. Houses are raided, as you know yourself. We needed someone to do something urgently, and I thought of you.'

'Did you ask Joseph if I should do it?'

'No.'

Winifred raised an eyebrow, and to her astonishment, she saw a faint colour rise in Agnes's cheeks.

'He would have agreed.'

'He most certainly would not.'

'Aren't you ashamed?' Agnes hid her discomfiture with a question of her own.

'Of what?'

'Of not doing more?'

'I'm doing the best I can,' retorted Winifred. 'And gun running is totally against my principles. At least, being used as an unwitting gun runner is.' She exhaled sharply. 'But one thing's for sure, I'm not going to stand back and let those louts come into the shop and beat me and my employer up for no reason.'

The door opened and May and Ita walked in. May was carrying her baby, but put him into the perambulator that was alongside the wall when she saw Winifred.

'Miss O'Leary had some trouble today,' said Agnes. 'She needs a little care and compassion.'

'Don't we all,' murmured Ita. She gave Winifred a warm smile. 'What trouble did you run into?'

Winifred told the story again and May looked anxious.

'It feels like things have intensified. There are spies all over the place,' she said. 'Nobody is above suspicion.'

'What was in the letter?' asked Winifred.

'Letter?' echoed Agnes.

'I delivered a letter too,' Winifred reminded her.

'Information,' said Agnes. 'Nothing more.'

'I didn't ask to be dragged into this,' said Winifred. 'But now that I am, you have to tell me everything.'

And so Agnes, who'd always considered Winifred a luke-warm republican at best, and hadn't thought she was good enough for Joseph, explained how they helped Volunteers who were trying to evade the Crown forces by hiding them, providing them with weapons sourced from other sympa-thisers, and printing propaganda in the boiler room. Winifred had known this already, but the depth of the family's involve-ment had never been laid out before her so starkly and specifically before, not even by Joseph.

'And of course May has her work with Cumann na mBan too,' added Agnes. 'Supporting Volunteers, helping with safe houses, disseminating propaganda.'

'You said that the nuns have a "hear no evil, see no evil" policy,' said Winifred. 'But you're practically using the house as a kind of rebellion HQ.'

'That's an exaggeration,' said May. 'Besides, the nuns are on the side of peace, and the only way there'll be peace is for us to take back control of our own country.'

'The postulant who let me in seemed to be French.'

'It was originally a French order,' said Agnes.

'Do you want to be part of it?' asked May abruptly. 'Do you want to join Cumann na mBan?'

'No.' Winifred was adamant. 'But I do want my country to be governed by Irish people. I certainly don't want to answer to those who would allow women to be treated the way Mrs Kelley and I were treated. I'd like a country where we had more rights and more of a say. And where women who were working in places like Monto had rights too. I want a country where someone like me can have her own shop. Where my children can stay in school longer. And where people like the Countess aren't in gaol.'

'You want Utopia,' said Ita. 'We just want a republic.'

And then the door to the Yellow Room opened and Joseph walked in.

Agnes suggested that she and her daughters move to the kitchen and allow her son and his fiancée a little time together. The two younger women got up immediately, Ita winking at Winifred as she went past.

'So?' Joseph looked at her when they were alone. 'Why are you here?'

'They kept you in the dark.' She proceeded to tell him about her trip to North King Street and the raid on the shop, while he listened in silence, his expression growing grimmer by the second.

'Were you hurt?' he demanded when she finished. 'Did any of those men lay a finger on you?'

'I was probably in more danger from the ones visiting the floozies at Mrs Higgins's,' said Winifred. 'Although at least they were paying customers.'

'I hate to think of what you and Mrs Kelley went through,' said Joseph. 'But I'm very proud that you stood up for yourselves. I'm not happy that my mother felt she could involve you, though. She had no right to do that.'

'No, she hadn't,' said Winifred. 'But she's so convinced she's right, nothing else matters. Unfortunately,' she added, 'that's how the British seem to think too. That because they're right, they can do what they like.'

'We're making progress in this war,' Joseph said. 'I know it appears grim at the moment, and I know everyone is worried because the British have more troops, but I promise you things are moving in our direction. Remember that headline in the American newspapers that were sent to us? "British violence unabated during holiday season but Irish people are still undaunted"? We're winning popular opinion around the world, and by God, yes, we're undaunted.'

'I didn't feel undaunted when the Auxiliaries came into Kelley's and tried to search us.' Winifred said. 'I was terrified.'

'I understand.' Joseph held her close. 'I wish that hadn't happened.'

'So do I.'

'They're panicking,' he told her. 'That's why they're going after everything and everyone.'

'Really?' She leaned against his shoulder. 'I thought it was because they had some information. That's far more likely.'

'It was wrong of my mother to use you like that,' said Joseph.

'I never wanted to be involved,' said Winifred. 'But now that I am, I'll do my best. Only when I know what I'm doing and why, though. I won't be used as a puppet.'

'Winnie.' He held her face between his hands. 'Are you sure?

Because it's dangerous, and I don't want to put you in danger, remember?'

'When the door opened and the Auxiliaries burst in, I thought we were going to be killed,' she admitted. 'Or maybe worse.' She swallowed hard and he hugged her tight. 'I think I've already been in the kind of danger you were hoping to avoid.'

'At least we had people nearby,' Joseph said. 'It was good that Padraig was there so quickly.'

'He was giving Alice the glad eye afterwards,' Winifred told him, a sudden note of amusement in her voice.

'You're joking! He's only a kid, and she must be all of thirty.'

'She's twenty-nine.' Winifred dug him in the ribs. 'Which, the way things are going, is what I'll be by the time we actually get around to marrying. Even Marianne is married ahead of me now, and she really is a child.'

'Have you heard from her? Has she arrived in the States?'

'No word yet,' said Winifred. 'Ma is beside herself.'

'I'm sure she is. If I hear anything from New York, I'll let you know straight away.'

'What would you hear?' asked Winifred.

'Not much,' Joseph admitted. 'But we have lots of people in America who support us and who keep in touch, so I'll put the word out.'

'She was always headstrong,' Winifred said. 'Always wanted to be someone and do something spectacular. And now she has.'

Joseph moved his head closer to hers.

'I don't need spectacular,' he said. 'I just need you.'

'Do you?' asked Winifred. 'I wonder sometimes.'

'You're what keeps me going,' said Joseph. 'Knowing that I'm building a better Ireland for you and for our children. That's what's important to me, I swear to you.'

She looked up then and he kissed her. And even though there was frost on the outside of the window, and the trees in the garden were bare, Winifred felt her body warm as though it was midsummer.

Chapter 12

Dublin, spring 1921

Winifred took the tram to Rathmines to visit Alice, who was staying at home while her wrist healed. Alice's house was in the middle of a terrace off Kenilworth Square, and Winifred, who'd never been there before, thought it was an astonishingly large space for one woman on her own. Not that Alice was entirely on her own; she had a live-in maid who did the housework as well as cooking light meals.

It was the maid who answered the door and brought Winifred into the parlour where Alice was sitting, her arm in a sling.

'I'm so glad your wrist isn't broken,' Winifred said.

'So am I. Things are bad enough without the worry of broken bones.' Alice shook her head. 'I don't know what this country is coming to, Miss O'Leary. I really don't.'

Winifred said nothing, unsure of where Alice's loyalties really lay. On the one hand she'd supported the prisoners in Kilmainham. Yet did she blame the rebels for starting the war and inciting violence, or did she blame the British for the actions they'd taken against them? It was hard to tell, as

Alice's approval seemed to waver between the two depending on her mood.

'Violent thugs,' she said. 'They should be ashamed of themselves.'

'The Auxiliaries?'

'Of course the Auxiliaries!' cried Alice. 'They're supposed to uphold the law, but what they did to us was disgraceful. I'm glad you weren't more badly hurt yourself. How do you feel now?'

'I still ache all over, but I think I was more winded than anything,' replied Winifred.

'I simply do not know why they targeted my shop.' Alice shook her head. 'Unlike the note in my coat, I can't place the blame for this on Marjorie Wilson. I realise that you're the girlfriend of a rebel, Winnie, but in reality you hardly see him, and it's not as though you're involved in insurrection and violence yourself.'

Winifred thought of the gun wrapped in muslin that she'd brought to North King Street. She also noted that her employer had called her by her Christian name again.

'I thought briefly about hanging a Union Jack outside the shop,' Alice continued. Winifred shot her a horrified look. 'Along with a tricolour,' she added. 'To show that we don't support one side or the other. But then I realised that we'd be hated equally by both sides.'

'Yes,' said Winifred. 'We would.'

'Besides,' Alice said, 'you *do* support one side over the other.'

'I have to,' said Winifred.

'But in your heart?'

'I used to want to be neutral,' Winifred confessed. 'But you can't be, can you? You have to choose.'

'And you choose a republic.'

'Yes.'

Winifred looked at Alice, wondering if the older woman was going to fire her. Alice's loyalties had to be more with the British, despite what had happened in the shop. Her husband had died for them in the Great War, after all.

'I see de Valera is back from America.' Alice changed the subject slightly as the maid brought in tea and poured cups for both of them. 'Wanting the republicans to take on the British in a military fight rather than guerrilla warfare.'

'We'd lose,' said Winifred. 'The British troops would vastly outnumber us.'

'Is that what your young man says?'

'It's what anyone with half a brain says.'

'And yet we fight them on the streets.'

'It's a better tactic.'

'You seem remarkably well informed.'

'I read the papers, that's all.'

It was strange to be here talking about guerrilla tactics with her boss, thought Winifred. And then the conversation moved towards talking about marriage, which, she thought, might be even stranger. Although Alice had always been a generous employer, the relationship between them didn't usually stray into the personal. But now she reminisced about her own marriage and her late husband. It hadn't been a love match, she confessed, more of a coming together of two people who didn't know if they'd see each other again. And yet, she said, she missed him, although she wasn't sure how he'd have felt about her owning a shop, which his family looked down on as 'trade'. Nevertheless, her father-in-law still paid her an annual stipend.

'I don't think Mr Burke will ever be in a position to do that for me,' commented Winifred.

'Make sure you're looked after,' Alice told her. 'Women need their own means. We can't be dependent on men. This war is bad for all of us,' she continued. 'Men and women alike. And I've come around to thinking that it would be better if the English left Ireland to its own devices. After all, the Irish are never going to accept things the way they are, and what's the point in the English staying in a country where nobody wants them?'

'Joseph says it sends a bad signal if they can't keep control of a neighbouring country,' remarked Winifred. 'It would show that the Empire was unstable.'

'Empires never last,' said Alice. 'Think of the Romans. Think of the Egyptians. Anyway, what I'm saying is that the best way to end this is for the Irish to win. And so if there's anything I can do for your rebel husband-to-be and his cohorts, I'm willing.'

'Mrs Kelley!' Winifred looked at her in astonishment. 'Are you serious?'

'Yes, I am,' said Alice. 'I'm ready to fight for the cause.'

'It could be a trap,' Agnes said when Winifred came to the house to tell her of Alice's offer. Once again she'd been stopped at a checkpoint, but this time the soldier manning it had simply nodded her through when she told him she was delivering material to the nuns, which meant that she'd had to enter through the convent again.

'I don't think so,' said Winifred. 'Mrs Kelley was furious about the raid on the shop and how we were treated.'

Joseph, who was sitting with them, took her by the hand.

'Winnie and I haven't been out together since Christmas Eve,' he said. 'And that's to keep her out of harm's way. I'm not sure how it will work out if we start using Kelley's as a safe place, or a weapons store.'

'We've already established I'm in harm's way,' said Winifred. 'All the same, I'm not sure how keen Mrs Kelley will be about having boxes of guns in the stockroom. But she's certainly happy for the shop to be used as a communications centre. Lots of women come in every day. It would be easy to pass on information.'

'That might work,' agreed Agnes.

'The whole plan was to keep you away from the centre of things, Winnie.' Joseph sighed.

'Too late,' his fiancée replied. 'I'm already there.'

And so, as the fighting grew more intense, while at the same time rumours of peace talks and truces and an end to the war permeated the city, Winifred and Alice accepted and passed on intelligence to the republican army. From time to time, when absolutely necessary, they sheltered Volunteers in the stockroom, making a space for them behind the bales of fabrics and allowing them to enter and leave through the almost hidden door to the narrow laneway behind the building. Winifred occasionally brought guns from the house in St Anthony's Place, always wrapped in plenty of muslin and carefully packaged, although as she remarked, any soldier worth his salt would realise that muslin didn't weigh as much as the parcels she was carrying. But although she was terrified of being found out, she walked confidently through the streets, her head held high, ignoring both troops and Volunteers as well as anyone else around her.

Which made it all the more shocking that she was in St Anthony's Place when the Burke home was raided yet again.

It was Ita who warned them of the advancing battalion which had cordoned off the area and was making house-to-house searches.

'I don't want them to find you here,' said Agnes.

'I don't want them to find me either.' Winifred knew that she'd be under suspicion forever if she was caught in the house. And suspicion might fall too on the nuns who'd let her use the convent as a point of entry. Not that the nuns weren't well able to look after themselves, she acknowledged; so far the British troops had never even tried to search the convent, and Winifred doubted they'd get past the front door if they did.

'Come on.' Joseph held out his hand to her. 'We'll have to hide you.'

'But they'll find me here!' she gasped as they hurried towards the room where the Countess had been concealed.

'Not at all.' He winked at her. 'We've a much better place than that.'

He led her to the boiler room, and she felt beads of perspiration break out on her forehead as they raced past the big furnaces that supplied the heat to the convent. The perspiration wasn't only because of the intense heat. The soldiers had searched the boiler room when they'd imprisoned Joseph. They'd be sure to search it again. But he carried on and stopped at a rusting iron gate set into the wall. It was partly obscured by various pieces of equipment, but not completely out of sight.

'Where are we going?'

'You'll see.' He took a large key from a hook on the wall and opened the gate. Stepping through, she realised they were in a small cellar.

'My God,' she gasped. 'Do you store ammunition here? Or hide people? Or—'

'Stop chattering,' he said. 'We don't use it at all because it's not ours to use. Look.' He pointed at another iron gate, also locked. As her eyes grew accustomed to the gloom, which was broken by faint light coming through slats high in the wall, Winifred gave a muffled cry. She was standing in a crypt, where engraved stone tombs and statues of angels took up most of the space.

'We're under the convent here,' explained Joseph. 'When we were children, we used to play here, until the nuns found out and locked the gate.'

'You played here?' She shuddered. 'Weren't you terrified?'

'Not really.' He shook his head. 'May used to tell stories about the angels and we didn't actually realise at first there were bodies in the tombs.'

'Oh my God.' She shuddered again.

'Anyhow, they locked the gate, but my father kept the key. He checks on it from time to time.'

'Checks on it? Or hides people here?'

'Only once,' admitted Joseph. 'That was when Cathal Brugha was on the run. It wasn't safe to keep him in the house itself.'

'And you want me to stay here? On my own? In the dark?' Her voice shook. She didn't want to admit that she was afraid of the dark. Given everything else that was going on, it sounded childish and pathetic.

'The dead won't hurt you,' said Joseph. 'It's the living you should worry about.'

She nodded mutely.

'Behind that one there,' he said, nodding towards a stone

sarcophagus adorned by carvings of the Angel Gabriel. 'You'll be well hidden.'

'I hope so.' She swallowed hard and then walked gingerly towards the tomb, trying to keep her steps steady.

'I'll be back as soon as they've gone,' said Joseph.

'All right.' She sank down behind the stone and rested her head on her knees. If she kept her eyes closed, she told herself, she wouldn't know it was dark at all.

She heard the gate lock behind Joseph.

The sudden thought that the entire family might be arrested almost made her cry out. Because if they were, who would know she was here? Alone. With only the bodies of the dead nuns for company.

She'd been scared at first, but now, crouching behind the tomb, she realised that the main emotion she was feeling was fury. She shouldn't have to be hiding here from soldiers from another country. Joseph's family shouldn't have had to hide the Minister for Labour and the Minister for Defence in their home. She realised with a sense of shock that if she'd kept one of the many guns she'd moved around the city over the past few weeks, she wouldn't have thought twice about using it now. She didn't know if that was a good or a bad thing.

For a woman who'd wanted a quiet life, she'd certainly changed her tune, she thought. Yet maybe that was what war did to you. It revealed a depth of feeling you never knew you had. It turned you into someone you never thought you could be.

She couldn't be sure how much later it was when she heard the voices of the soldiers.

'Look everywhere,' the officer in charge said. 'We've found incriminating material here before.'

There wasn't a lot of space in the boiler room for the soldiers to search. Winifred heard them moving Mr Burke's tools and then one of the soldiers remarking on the heat from the furnaces. His footsteps drew closer to the gate, and he gave a cry before rattling it. Winifred shrank further behind the stone sarcophagus.

'What's this?' he asked.

'Nothing.' It was the officer who spoke again. 'It leads to a burial chamber for the convent. It's locked on their side. We checked it out the last time we were here; the mother superior brought us down. Damn creepy if you ask me, keeping their dead so close.'

The soldier moved away.

'Copies of *The Freeman's Journal*. Nothing else,' a third voice said.

'Pity. I wouldn't have minded taking Burke in again. He's an arrogant sod. As for his mother, I wouldn't trust her as far as I could throw her.'

'The tip-off was for Mountjoy Square and the surrounding area,' the soldier reminded him. 'I'm sure we'll pick up enough Fenians without Burke.'

'That won't stop him. Or any of them,' said the officer. 'Though I'd love to get that mother of his. Wasn't Private Fairfax shot by a woman only last week? There he was, walking along Harcourt Street minding his own business, when she takes a gun from the perambulator she's pushing and shoots him there and then. Just as well she was a terrible shot, or he'd be dead. As it is, he was lucky they were able to get him to hospital and get the bullet out of his shoulder.'

'The women are the worst,' agreed the soldier.

'The female of the species is deadlier than the male,' the officer chuckled. 'And in this case it's probably true. But even though the Burke women are definitely rebels, there's nothing in the house we can usefully use to arrest them.'

'Why are we still doing this?' The soldier suddenly sounded bored. 'They don't want us here and we don't want to be here. What's the ruddy point of it all?'

'That's enough from you, Morton,' said the officer, his voice crisp. 'We do as we're commanded to do. And we've found all we're going to find here. Which is sweet Fanny Adams. So we may go.'

Winifred heard them march out of the boiler house and allowed herself to breathe again.

Whatever tip-off the soldiers had received, it hadn't been about her.

Now all she had to do was wait until Joseph came and let her out.

It was only a few minutes before curfew when she arrived back at East Essex Street. The streets had been swarming with soldiers, and she'd been afraid that she'd be caught up in another of their checkpoints or barricades. But she was empty-handed and walking quickly, and it was only a couple of men who'd had too much to drink who took any notice of her, calling to her that she could do worse than warm herself with them.

She ignored their calls and jeers as she strode on. She wouldn't tell Joseph about them when next she saw him. He'd been unhappy at letting her walk the streets on her own at night, even though she'd lied to him and said she felt perfectly safe.

169

'Safer than hiding behind the body of Sister Alphonsus anyway,' she'd added. 'Certainly safer than waiting for you to come and get me. You took so long, I was afraid I'd be left there forever.'

'Sorry,' Joseph said as he wiped a cobweb from her shoulder. 'We wanted to make sure they were gone.'

'Did they take anything from your house?'

'Nothing to take,' he told her. 'We've been very careful ever since the last time. We burn everything in the furnace and May doesn't leave any of her propaganda lying around.'

Winifred had nodded, and then he'd kissed her before watching her leave.

Now, as she let herself into the house, she felt the strength leave her body and she couldn't wait to sit down.

But there was someone already hunched on the worn chair beneath the window. And she gasped as she saw that it was her sister Katy. Her hair was shorn, showing a large gash on the side of her head. Her face was pale and her expression blank. She seemed to be folded in on herself, a shadow of the woman she'd once been. Annie was sitting on a stool beside her, holding her hand.

'What happened?' asked Winifred.

'That bastard Reid.' Annie spat the words out. 'He beat her again and this time he nearly killed her. I knew she shouldn't have gone back to him. I knew I shouldn't have let her.'

'Mother of God,' said Winifred. 'How did you . . .'

'Mona Mulvanney told us,' said Annie. 'She heard your sister screaming last night. She sent word up this morning, and your father hired a horse and trap to get her. She'll not be going back, that's the God's honest truth. The lying bastard told Mona's husband that Katy'd been with an English soldier. Said she deserved it.'

'Are you all right, Katy?' asked Winnie.

Katy said nothing.

'It's the bang to the head,' Annie told her. 'She's . . . well, I don't know how she is really.'

'She should be in hospital,' said Winifred.

'I know. But what can we do? Sure the hospitals are over-flowing with casualties from the shootings as well as people who are sick. She's my daughter. I'll take care of her.'

'How about Dr Desmond?' asked Winifred. 'Perhaps he could help.'

'After the way Marianne left him?'

'He's still a doctor,' said Winifred.

'It's too late to get him now,' said Annie. 'The curfew is in place.'

'Damn the curfew. I'm going to ask him anyhow.'

'It's late. He won't come.'

'I'll make him come,' said Winifred. 'What about the baby?' she asked suddenly.

At her words, a tear trickled down Katy's face.

'No baby,' she said, her words slurred. 'I've lost my baby.'

'I shouldn't have let her go back to him.' Annie choked back a sob. 'It was always a mistake to think he'd be different, even if he thought she was carrying a son this time.'

'I'm getting the doctor. If Katy's lost her baby, she needs medical attention right now.'

'I'll kill that cowardly bastard.'

Winifred hadn't seen her father standing in a darkened corner of the room. But now he stepped into the flicker-ing light.

'I'll go back there tomorrow and I'll tear him limb from limb and I don't care what happens to me.'

Annie said nothing.

'I'm getting the doctor now,' said Winifred.

She walked out of the room and pulled the door behind her.

Although soldiers patrolled the streets, they were otherwise deserted. Winifred hurried towards St Stephen's Green, keeping in the shelter of the buildings and ducking into doorways, trying to stay as inconspicuous as possible. She avoided three different patrols, the last close to Dr Desmond's home. When she reached it, she ran up the steps that led to the grey-painted Georgian door and pressed on the large white button to ring the bell.

It was almost a minute later before the door opened and a housemaid looked at her. For a moment, Winifred's tiredness overwhelmed her, and she thought the young girl in front of her was Marianne. But then she realised that this girl's hair was fairer, her face longer and her eyes a penetrating blue.

'I need to see Dr Desmond,' she said. 'It's urgent.'

'The doctor's not at home,' said the girl, in a soft Cork accent. 'And it's late.'

'Not at home to visitors, I'm sure,' said Winifred. 'But he's needed urgently for a patient.'

'Urgent cases go to hospital,' said the girl. 'And you can't be urgent if you managed to get here yourself. How did you get here anyway?' Her tone was accusing. 'How did you get past the soldiers during curfew? Are you a spy?'

'Don't be silly,' said Winifred. 'I'm nothing of the sort. I'm . . . My sister used to work here.'

'What's that to do with anything?'

Winifred was getting annoyed. Young girls these days were a lot cheekier than she'd been, that was for sure. She'd never have spoken to anyone the way this one was speaking to her.

'Just get him,' she said. 'I can't stay on your doorstep forever.'

'I told you—'

'Dolly, what's going on?' A tall woman walked into the hallway. She was wearing a mid-length skirt and a white blouse, with a woollen cardigan wrapped around her shoulders.

'Mrs Desmond?' asked Winifred. 'I'm Marianne's sister. My other sister has been badly beaten and she needs—'

'Marianne?' The woman stepped closer. 'Marianne O'Leary?'

'Yes,' said Winifred.

'That girl caused me nothing but trouble,' said Mrs Desmond. 'Upped and went with only a week's notice. And she had far too many notions about herself. Clearly it's a family trait. Do you realise what time it is? Nobody is out now. And my husband certainly isn't going to wherever it is you come from to treat another O'Leary.'

'She was beaten by her husband,' said Winifred. 'She's lost her baby. He hit her on the head. She's . . . she's very poorly.'

'Then you should take her to hospital.'

'How?' demanded Winifred.

The woman looked at her.

'Please.'

'I'll speak to my husband, but he'll tell you the same as me.'

She turned away from the door, but the housemaid stayed where she was. Winifred looked past her to the elegantly decorated hallway of the doctor's home. The black and white tiles were the same as the Burkes', but a much larger chandelier

173

hung from the ceiling of the doctor's house, and there was enough room for a long table, on which was placed an enormous vase of fresh flowers as well as carved bronze figures. Further along were a couple of chairs upholstered in rose-pink satin. Being a doctor was a profitable profession, thought Winifred. And her heart suddenly sank, because even if Dr Desmond had helped her father four years earlier, there was no reason for him to put himself in danger to help her sister now.

What had she been thinking?

She was such a fool.

But at that moment, the doctor himself appeared and gave her an enquiring look.

'Miss O'Leary,' he said. 'It's a while since we've met.'

'Indeed it is.' She nodded. 'And I'm sorry for coming to you at this time and in this way, but I'm so worried about my sister and I—'

'William, there's a curfew. You shouldn't be going out,' said Mrs Desmond.

'I know,' said the doctor. 'But there's also a woman in trouble, Hetty. And you know how I feel about violence against women.'

'I . . .' Hetty Desmond looked at her husband and then at Winifred, who was clasping and unclasping her hands. 'This damn country,' she muttered.

Dr Desmond moved towards her and kissed her lightly on the cheek.

'Don't worry. I'll be back soon.'

'One day you'll go out and you won't come back.' Mrs Desmond rubbed the back of her neck. 'Be careful.'

'As always,' said the doctor, then turned towards Winifred. 'Let's go, Miss O'Leary. I have a car.'

Winifred had never been in a car before. Like the majority of the people in the city, she walked everywhere, although if she was going a long way, she sometimes took the tram. But a car was a complete luxury – she'd heard someone once say that there were about 3,000 of them in Dublin, but she found it hard to believe that many people could afford one.

She followed Dr Desmond to where it was parked, and climbed into the front while he started it.

'If we're stopped at a checkpoint, you're my nurse,' he said as the vehicle moved off. Winifred gripped the door and nodded, but she was too overcome by actually being in a car to say anything at all.

They were almost at East Essex Street before they were stopped, but Dr Desmond spoke firmly to the soldiers and told them that a pregnant woman needed his attention. Winifred could hardly believe that they allowed the car to pass by, but they did.

'Not all the soldiers are like the Black and Tans or the Auxiliaries,' said Dr Desmond when she said this to him. 'Most are decent people. But war does terrible things even to decent people.'

He pulled up outside their building and she got out of the car, wondering if anyone could see her. They'd think she'd come up in the world. At least until they knew why Dr Desmond was here.

Annie sighed with relief to see him and thanked him over and over again as he examined Katy.

'You say her husband did this?' he asked when he'd finished and Katy was resting.

'Yes,' said Annie.

'He should be in gaol.'

'But nobody will put him there,' said Annie. 'They'll blame Katy. They never blame the man. They'll say it's the drink. It's not the drink. It's his nature.'

'I need to get her to a hospital,' said the doctor. 'She's been badly beaten and lost a lot of blood. I really can't say . . .' His voice trailed off.

'He tried to pretend she'd been with someone else,' said Winifred. 'I know my sister. She wouldn't have done anything like that. And even if she had,' she added, 'how dare he beat her? What gives him the right?'

'She's his wife,' said Dr Desmond. 'That gives him the right.'

'It'll be different in the new Ireland.' Winifred clenched her fists. 'Everything will be different.'

'If only I believed that,' said Dr Desmond.

Chapter 13

Dublin, spring/summer 1921

Dr Desmond had arranged for Katy to be brought to hospital, where they diagnosed concussion, a cracked rib, severe bruising and soft tissue damage, as well as the loss of her baby.

'My beautiful daughter,' wailed Annie after they'd told her they were keeping Katy in for a while. 'That man has destroyed her.'

'Katy's strong,' said Winnie. 'She'll recover.'

'She can't have children,' Annie said. 'Not now.'

'I should hope not!' exclaimed Winnie. 'She's never going back to him.'

'Even if she did,' said Annie, 'and not that I'd let her, the doctor at the hospital said that her injuries mean that she won't be able to.'

'Oh,' said Winnie.

'And there was a bleed on her brain.' Annie's voice shook as she said the words. 'That's why she's struggling to speak.'

'Will she recover from that?'

'Maybe. Over time.'

'I hope that shitehawk rots in hell,' said Winnie.

And Annie agreed.

Thomas O'Leary arranged transport for himself to Katy's home the following day. Despite Annie urging him not to go, saying that Reid would be just as violent towards him and that he wasn't in a fit state to defend himself, her husband was adamant.

'I'm not going alone,' he said. 'Paddy Dwyer is coming with me.'

Paddy, who had worked with him at the docks, was an enormous bull of a man.

'Don't kill him, so,' said Annie. 'I'd love it if you did, but you'd be the one who'd end up in gaol. Be careful.'

Thomas kissed her and then Katy, and made his way to the quays, where Paddy was waiting with the car his brother-in-law had lent him.

They drove in silence out of the city and then along the quiet country roads that led to Kells. It was peaceful, and Thomas was enjoying the smell of the unfurling spring flowers and the fresh water of the rivers instead of the stench of the Liffey and the unrelenting Dublin smoke.

But beautiful and all though it was, he thought, bad things still happened. And he wanted his son-in-law to pay for what he'd done to Katy.

When they got to the small cottage, though, there was nobody there. A few hens scratched around at the side of the building, but they were the only signs of life. Thomas pushed open the door and saw dirty crockery piled in the Belfast sink beneath the window. In the single bedroom, the bed was stripped back to the horsehair mattress.

'Has he done a runner?' asked Paddy.

'I don't know. Maybe he's out in the fields.'

But the only person they met was Noel Mulvanney from the adjoining farm, whose wife had been the one to let them know what had happened to Katy.

'He left this morning,' Noel told them. 'Before it was light. I was out myself and I saw the trap outside his door and him clambering onto it.'

'Where did he go?' asked Thomas.

'I don't know,' replied Noel. 'I'll ask around, but he wasn't a popular man in these parts. Your girl is well shot of him.'

'I know,' said Thomas. 'But I wanted to let him know what I thought.'

'Perhaps it's better you don't,' said Noel, with a glance at Paddy. 'Perhaps it's better to walk away.'

Thomas said nothing as he returned to the cottage and turned it upside down looking for anything that would give him a clue as to where Reid had gone. But there was nothing. In the end, the only thing he could do was to put Katy's meagre selection of clothes into a pillowcase and bring them back to Dublin with him.

A few days later, Esther called to the shop to buy some material to divide up her rooms in Dorset Street some more. Winnie hadn't seen her friend for weeks, and she was concerned that Esther looked tired and her eyes lacked their usual sparkle.

'I'm pregnant again,' Esther told her when they went for a cup of tea together in the new café that had opened around the corner from Kelley's Fine Fabrics. 'And I'm exhausted.'

'But you're happy to be pregnant?'

'Henry's delighted.'

'You're not?' Winifred had noticed the hesitation in Esther's voice.

'I am. But . . .'

'What?'

'I'm worried,' confessed Esther. 'Is it right to be having children while there's a guerrilla war going on? Is it safe?'

She was asking the question that Winifred herself asked every single day when she got up: 'Is it safe?' And of course the answer was that nobody knew if it was safe or not. There were reports all the time about civilian casualties, of people being accidentally shot, of being in the wrong place at the wrong time. Winifred didn't feel that she could comfort her friend as much as she would've liked. And knowing that her sister would never have children now, Winnie felt even less able to comfort Esther, because it suddenly seemed to her that having a child was a privilege. And that would be something to remember, she thought, when and if she got pregnant herself.

'Jesus, Mary and Joseph, Winnie, poor Katy,' said Esther when she told her. 'Here am I moaning, and that girl's gone through pure hell.'

'I suppose not all men are bastards.' Winifred gave her friend a wry smile.

'Ah, I suppose they're not. I'm lucky with Henry, I know I am. And I'll love this baby as much as Arthur. But sometimes . . .' She sighed.

'Sometimes it all gets too much,' said Winifred, taking her friend's hand. 'And yet we have to carry on.'

'Carry on at home and carry on with the feckin' war. It's too much carrying on. And none of it the right sort.'

Winifred laughed.

'Although I do wish those bastarding Brits would piss off home,' Esther added.

'Esther!'

'You'd think they'd have had enough of us by now, wouldn't you?'

'You would,' agreed Winifred.

'I worry about Henry.' Esther lowered her voice. 'Working in Dublin Castle. He hears things. And he passes on information. I'm afraid he'll be caught.'

'Who does he pass information to?' asked Winifred. She saw the flicker of anxiety in Esther's eyes. 'Don't tell me. I don't need to know.'

'I'm sorry, Winnie,' said Esther. 'You're my friend. We don't have secrets. But these are Henry's secrets, not mine.'

'I understand,' said Winifred. 'I really do.'

'Nothing is simple any more.' Esther refilled their cups. 'Not that it ever was, I suppose. Anyhow, Henry's doing his bit, along with a lot of the girls in Dublin Castle.'

'The girls?' Winifred looked at her in surprise.

'Sure half of them are in Cumann na mBan.' Esther grinned. 'The men simply don't suspect a pretty girl of being an informer or a spy. The place is riddled with them.'

'If the women are on the case, we'll have the war won before Christmas.' Winifred smiled at her. 'So I don't know what you're worried about at all, Esther Boland.'

'You're dead right. Anyhow, let's talk about something else. What's the news with you and Joseph? I thought you'd get married quickly after what happened last year.'

'It's complicated,' said Winifred, who went on to explain

Joseph's reasons for wanting them to stay apart. 'Though I honestly don't think it makes any difference now. Not when I . . .'

'You what?'

'I do a little myself,' admitted Winifred. 'Not much. Just odd bits and pieces.'

'You should just get on with it and marry him, so.'

'I'd like nothing more. But I can't leave Ma and Katy right now. I need to help them.'

'Of course you do. But don't keep him waiting forever. I love being Mrs Boland. I want you to be Mrs Burke.'

'When this war is over, we'll be two old married friends,' said Winifred. 'We'll talk about our children and our husbands instead of the Brits and bullets.'

'Absolutely.' Esther smiled and the dimples reappeared in her cheeks. She raised her cup. 'To us,' she said.

'To us,' Winifred echoed. 'And to the end of the war.'

And yet the fighting continued. The republicans' intelligence network was widespread, and they continued to ambush British troops at various locations around the country. Although the official line was that the British were on the verge of winning, they never seemed to be in control of events.

Even at Kelley's Fine Fabrics, the customers would shake their heads and say that the guerrilla war could go on forever because the British would never win and the Irish would never lose.

'Although I've heard that the Brits are wavering,' said Thomas one evening after his tea. He'd been far more vocal about the war in the last weeks, more supportive of the Volunteers.

Winnie, who was helping Katy with her own tea, looked at him questioningly.

'In what way wavering?' she asked.

'That there's a lack of commitment,' said Thomas. 'That they're losing the stomach for the fight. The politicians are getting anxious at the reports in the foreign press calling out the atrocities that the RIC and their cohorts are committing. They don't want to lose the ear of the Americans. They've always loved America.'

'Another part of the Empire they lost,' observed Annie.

'That's why Dev has spent so much time courting the Yanks,' said Thomas. 'There's a lot of support for Ireland there.'

'Are they seriously wavering, d'you think?' asked Winifred as she handed Katy a cloth to wipe her face.

'Who knows.' Thomas shrugged. 'It's the first time I've heard it said inside, though. They don't think I'm listening when I'm pushing the trolley around, but I am. And right now they're worried, that's for sure.'

'Interesting,' said Winnie, then turned her attention back to her sister.

It was more than two weeks later before Winifred saw Joseph again. He was waiting for her outside the shop, his cap pulled down over his forehead.

'Oh!' she cried in delight. 'I didn't think I'd see you until next week.'

'I couldn't stay away,' said Joseph. 'I missed you too much.'

'I thought you'd be too busy to miss me,' she said.

'I'm never too busy to miss you.' He pulled her close, still in the shelter of the doorway, and kissed her.

'How are things in the shop?' he asked as he released her again. 'Any problems?'

'Not a sign of an Auxiliary or even an RIC officer,' she said.

'When we were perfectly innocent, we were raided. And now that we're not, we're being left alone. Actually, I can't help thinking that Mrs Kelley is quite enjoying being a secret spy.'

'She's a remarkable woman,' said Joseph. 'I can understand why her sympathies might lie with the Crown, but her help has been invaluable.'

'She changed utterly after the raid,' Winifred told him. 'But I suppose being attacked and thinking the worst could happen will do that to a person.'

'I'm very glad it wasn't worse.' Joseph squeezed her arm. 'Oh Winnie, I wish we could be together. Given everything that's happened, we should be.'

'Funny you should say that, because I had tea with my friend Esther and we talked about it. And afterwards, all I wanted to do was haul you into a church there and then. But at the moment I need to be home to help with Katy. Ma can't manage on her own.'

Joseph had been horrified when he'd learned what had happened to her sister, and had asked if there was anything he and his family could do, but Winifred had replied that they were managing for the moment themselves.

'How is she?' he asked now. 'I feel sick to the stomach whenever I think of it.'

Winifred told him that Dr Desmond was hopeful Katy's speech might ultimately improve, as the bleed hadn't been as serious as they'd first thought, but for the moment she needed nursing at home.

'Which I'll help with, of course.' She looked at him hesitantly. 'It's why I think we should wait till summer like we planned for the wedding.'

'I understand.'

184

'Oh don't! Don't be understanding. Just say that you want to carry me off yourself!'

'Winifred O'Leary! I do actually want to carry you off. And I want to be with you and kiss you and caress you and love you the way you should be loved.'

'Oh.' Winifred felt herself blush.

'In the meantime, take good care of your sister.'

'She's strong,' said Winifred. 'And independent too. So that helps.'

'All you O'Leary girls are independent.' He smiled at her.

'Maybe. Look, we'll just get married as your mother wanted, with a breakfast in St Anthony's Place and photographs in the garden. And who knows . . .' she gave him a hopeful look, 'with me and Mrs Kelley on the case, maybe we'll be a republic by then.'

'If sheer determination won things, you'd have the Brits on the run already.' Joseph grinned at her.

'My father thinks they're wavering. That's the other thing I wanted to tell you. He overheard two officers talking about it the other day. They're not committed to carrying on.'

'Who were the officers?' Joseph looked at her intently.

'I don't know.' Winifred shook her head. 'He doesn't usually hear anything much, you know that. But he was having a cigarette break and so were they . . . It was just a fragment of a conversation, but it's interesting, don't you think? If they can't carry on . . .'

'They'll carry on just long enough.' Joseph shook his head. 'If your father hears anything else, you'll tell me, won't you? I'm not asking him to actively spy, absolutely not. But he's in the Custom House. He may well hear useful information.'

'It's records, not policy they deal with in the Custom House. It's hardly a hotbed of gossip.'

'Everywhere there are people is a hotbed of gossip.'

She made a face at him, and he grinned.

'The war will be won on the back of gossip,' he said. 'It's far more useful than guns in the end.'

As the weeks rolled past, Winifred's time was spent helping Katy to talk again; passing information and hiding arms and ammunition in the shop; and in her actual job of measuring and cutting fabrics – something that kept her very busy, as with Easter falling early that year, customers were keen to buy fabrics for curtains and cushions, dresses and blouses.

It was disconcerting, however, to walk into the storeroom and know that there were rifles hidden in bales of silk or velvet. Or to occasionally meet the anxious eyes of a Volunteer hiding before he could be moved somewhere safer. Whenever a new customer came into the shop, Winifred would know if they were there to collect a pistol, because they would show their Cumann na mBan pin – a slim bronze brooch with the letters CnB wrought around a rifle. The women were always polite, and although some were as serious as Joseph's sister May, many of them were bright and cheerful and looked exactly like any other young woman out shopping. It struck her that in normal times they'd be using muslin and calico to make dresses, not to hide guns or bullets. They'd be talking about the latest fashions or the news from England, where so many of them, like Winifred, had relatives. War made you look at everything through a different prism. It shifted your perspective. It made you feel alive and mortal at the same time.

After her conversation with Joseph, however, she did ask her father if there were any other useful nuggets of information coming out of the Custom House.

'Who wants to know? You? Or your boyfriend?'

'I told him about that gossip. He thought it was interesting. He wondered if you'd heard anything else.'

'Not content with almost turning you into a Volunteer, now he wants me to join his merry throng?' Thomas dipped bread into the yolk of the egg he was having for his tea.

'He's not trying to recruit you to do anything dangerous.' Winifred hadn't told her parents the full extent of the operation now running out of Kelley's Fine Fabrics. She knew they'd disapprove. Not because they were against what was happening, but because they wouldn't want her to put herself in danger. She suspected that both of them knew more than they were letting on, but that they preferred to remain unaware. Anyhow, they had enough to worry about with Katy.

'I only hear chatter,' said Thomas. 'And if the half of it was true, either we'd all be dead by now, or the Brits would have left us to rot. So it's not exactly useful. They were laying bets on how long FitzAlan would last.' He said the last words casually as he dipped his bread in the egg again.

Winifred knew that Lord Edmund FitzAlan-Howard had just been appointed Lord Lieutenant of Ireland, the first Roman Catholic to hold the post. It was definitely interesting that they didn't think he'd be in the position for long.

'First and last Catholic is what they're saying,' said Thomas. 'Not because they think he's not up to it, but because they don't think there'll be a Lord Lieutenant for much longer. You can say that to your young man. Maybe it'll slow them down on their attacks if they think the Brits are already on the way out.'

Or maybe it'll make them even more determined, thought Winifred, but she said nothing.

At the start of May, Ita Burke caught a bad cold, which went to her chest and left her feverish and struggling for breath. The only saving grace, Agnes repeated over and over again, was that it wasn't tuberculosis, which was rampant in the city. But when Ita was moved to hospital, she was afraid that she might catch it there anyway, and spent her time with her rosary beads in her hands, begging the Virgin Mary to take care of her daughter.

Winifred hoped that Ita would recover too, both because she got on better with her than with the other Burke girls, and because she and Joseph had tentatively agreed a July date for their wedding and they didn't want to postpone it again.

'I feel we're doomed every time we set a date,' she told Katy one evening. 'It's not as though we're having a huge society wedding. All I want to do is get married.'

'But you want it to be a lovely happy day,' said Katy, enunciating each word slowly and carefully.

'It'll be happy anyway.'

'In these times, when everything's so grim, people look forward to something a bit special.'

'Marrying Joseph is special enough.'

Katy smiled, even though one side of her mouth didn't move.

'Was your day with Reid special?' asked Winifred. 'I don't remember it.' She hadn't been there, the day having been just for adults.

'I was happy,' said Katy. 'I thought he loved me.'

'When did he start beating you?'

'The first time I got pregnant. If I'd any sense, I'd have left him there and then.'

Although they were no longer trying to hide the fact that they were a couple, Joseph and Winifred didn't actually announce another engagement. Nor did they meet in the shop any more, although sometimes he would wait for her outside Clerys.

It was always a lovely surprise to find him there, and when she left work on the evening of 24 May and saw him waiting, her heart lifted with joy.

'It's good to see you,' she said as he fell into step beside her. 'How is Ita?'

'Improving, but slowly,' said Joseph. 'She'd be better off in the country, away from the city air.'

'Do you have relatives she could go to?'

'I know almost everyone in Dublin has family in the country, but we don't.'

'Nor do we.' Her hand, holding his arm, squeezed it gently. 'Katy moving to Reid's place in Kells was the furthest we got.'

Joseph smiled, then his face became serious again.

'I wanted to see you so you could tell your father not to go to work tomorrow,' he said.

'What?' She looked at him in surprise.

'Better to stay home.'

'Is it an operation? I haven't had the hint of one in all the information going through the shop.'

'I wasn't involved in the planning of this,' said Joseph. 'I can't give you details.'

'But you know something's going to happen?'

'They say there won't be loss of life, but you know how these things turn out, Winnie. With the best will in the world, people panic and make mistakes.'

'What people? What mistakes might they make?'

'Look, I honestly can't tell you. All I am saying is that your father should stay home. I don't want him caught up in anything.'

'Maybe he knows about it already,' remarked Winifred. 'After all, he told me about FitzAlan and . . .' Her eyes widened. 'You're not going to do anything to the Lord Lieutenant, are you? Not because of anything my father said?'

'Not that I'm aware of,' said Joseph.

'If I tell him not to go to work, he'll want to know why. He'll go anyway,' she added. 'Just so's you know. But I'll tell him.'

'I'd feel much better if he wasn't around.'

'Will it be bad?'

'Jesus, Winnie, it's a war. Everything's bad.'

'But you keep saying it's getting better.'

'It can be pretty shit in the meantime.'

'Joseph Burke!'

'Please, Winifred. Tell him to stay home.'

'All right,' she said. 'But I'll be wasting my time.'

Winifred was right. Thomas O'Leary looked at her with indignation and said that there was no chance of him not going to work. 'Besides, if I don't show up, they'll ask questions.'

'You can be sick for one day,' she said.

'I'm never sick,' said Thomas, which was perfectly true.
'But—'
'If I stay away and something happens, people will know that I knew,' said Thomas. 'So ye'll all be under suspicion. It's better that I go in.'

Winifred nodded slowly. He had a point.

She still wished Joseph had told her what was planned.

Chapter 14

It was almost one o'clock in the afternoon the following day when Thomas O'Leary began pushing a trolley-load of documents in large cardboard boxes along one of the corridors of the Custom House. He was thinking that he needed to oil the squeaky wheel when he heard the sound of people running into the building. He stopped, his hands on the top of the pile of boxes, and listened to a fusillade of gunshots ricochet from the walls.

'Dammit,' he muttered. 'Winifred's boy was right.'

As he stood hesitantly beside the trolley, a dozen men dressed in trousers and jackets, caps on their heads and boots on their feet, rushed into the corridor, waving pistols and shouting. He raised his hands as the leader ran towards him, pointing his gun.

'You!' he cried. 'With me.'

Thomas kept his hands up as he was marched to the main hall of the building, where other staff were huddled.

'On the floor!' cried the Volunteer. 'Quick now, or I'll shoot. And keep yizzer mouths shut. No chattering.'

The staff lay on the floor in silence and watched the Volunteers, nervy and agitated, pile bales of cotton and sprinkle them with petrol. Thomas's eyes narrowed. Were the feckers going to burn the place? he asked himself. And if they did, what would happen to all the records kept there? True, they were records kept by the British, but they related to Irish people: births and marriages and deaths and landowners and business arrangements and all sorts of important information. It would be a crime to lose it.

If only Joseph had told Winifred what was going to happen, perhaps he'd have been able to . . . Well, no, he conceded. He wouldn't have been able to prevent it. And he understood why it was happening. They were striking at the heart of the administration. But he couldn't help feeling conflicted about it.

He heard more shouts from the outside of the building, and more gunfire. He raised his head. The men inside looked anxious.

'The Auxiliaries have arrived!' cried one.

'It's all right.' Another spoke more calmly. 'There are battalions outside providing cover.'

'We're striking a blow against the oppressors!' shouted a third. 'With all the records burned, they'll never be able to govern us.'

The assembled staff exchanged worried looks.

'Are they mad or what?' muttered Thomas.

A whistle blew, and one of the Volunteers threw a match on the nearest bale of cotton, which took light immediately. The crowd of people in the hall screamed, and despite the yells of the Volunteers to stay where they were, they scrambled up from the floor and tried to flee the building. More pistol shots rang out, this time accompanied by the sounds of rifles from outside.

'The Auxiliaries,' said Thomas to the middle-aged woman who was clutching his arm. 'They're battering their way in.'

'We'll all be killed,' she cried. 'If not by the lunatics in here, then by the thugs out there.'

'If we're not roasted alive,' observed Thomas.

The republican pistols were suddenly silent. Thomas saw one of the Volunteers check his weapon, and realised that they'd run out of ammunition. He laughed internally at the thought of dispatching men to sack a building with so little firepower, but he was also furious on their behalf. They shouldn't have been sent to do a job without proper equipment. Nevertheless, if their objective was to burn it . . . well, they were succeeding. The smoke around them was blackening, and it was becoming increasingly difficult to breathe.

'We have to get out of here,' he said. He began to sidle towards the nearest exit, glad that he was partly hidden by smoke.

'Hey, you!' A young Volunteer coughed. 'Stay where you are!'

'And be incinerated?' retorted Thomas. 'Not bloody likely.'

To his astonishment, the man threw himself at him and tried to grapple him to the ground again, but the woman turned on the Volunteer and scratched his face with her long nails.

'Feckers!' she cried. 'Rebel feckers! This is my job. This is my work.'

'You're working for the enemy,' he spat at her. 'And this is our coup.'

He began coughing again, and Thomas took the opportunity to drag the woman with him towards the exit.

194

'Don't shoot!' he yelled as he moved forward. 'We're workers. Don't shoot!'

Then, amid the smoke, he saw one of the Auxiliaries. The man was pointing a rifle at him.

'Don't shoot!' echoed the woman beside him, her voice panicked.

As they stood with their hands up, Thomas felt a sudden impact in his shoulder. He was spun around, away from the woman, and crumpled to the floor, pain ripping through him.

'I should have listened to Winnie,' he said, as everything went black.

The plumes of smoke were visible across the city. Winifred and Alice stood outside the shop and watched them rise towards the sky.

'Oh my God,' murmured Alice. 'What have they done?'

'It's mostly the second battalion of the Dublin Brigade.' Edie Hawkins, who owned the nearby florist's, joined them. 'Apparently this was Dev's idea. He was calling for a big action.'

'But what?' asked Winifred. 'What's happening?'

'They're burning down the Custom House,' said Edie. 'But they'll be trapped inside. It's a bloody suicide mission.'

Alice closed the shop and the women joined the throng of people crowding the quays to watch the building burn. As the copper dome collapsed, many of the crowd cheered. But all Winifred could think was that her obstinate father had gone to work despite Joseph's warning, and that there was already talk of dead and wounded.

* * *

195

When she got home, Annie was pacing the floor and Katy was trying to comfort her.

'Have you heard anything?' Katy asked.

Winifred shook her head.

'This is madness!' cried Annie. 'Why did they do it?'

Winifred told her what Edie had said about Dev's desire for a big action. 'And people are saying that if all the records are destroyed – like when they destroyed the tax offices earlier this year – well, then the British have no means to govern.'

'Foolish, foolish arrogance!' Annie said. 'Those are our records too.'

Winifred said nothing.

'And your fiancé knew, but he didn't say anything.'

'He told Da not to go to work,' Winifred reminded her.

Annie collapsed onto the wooden chair beside the table.

'He'll be all right,' said Katy. 'I know he will.'

'He's too old for this,' said Annie. 'He wouldn't be able to run away.'

'He wouldn't run away in any case,' murmured Winifred.

'I'll go and see what's happening.' It was Tom who spoke. 'I'll find Da and bring him home.'

It was dark when Tom returned, but to the absolute relief and astonishment of the women, Thomas was with him. Their relief turned to despair when they saw his injuries. The bullet that had felled him had clipped the top of his shoulder, and he'd lost a lot of blood, though the wound wasn't fatal. But he had been kicked where he lay, and according to Tom, who'd spoken to bystanders, he'd then been dragged into the street, where he'd been left propped against a sack of coal.

'It's a miracle you found me, son.' Thomas coughed, a consequence of the smoke he'd inhaled during the attack. 'But I always knew someone would get me eventually.'

'You need a doctor,' said Katy.

'Half of Dublin needs a doctor.' He coughed again.

'I'll disinfect your shoulder,' said Winifred.

She went to the shelf and took down a bottle of antiseptic, pouring some onto a cloth.

'Ah, Jesus, woman, now it's you who wants to kill me!' cried her father.

'Sorry,' said Winifred.

She dabbed at the wound, which was deeper than she'd hoped. Then she pressed another piece of cloth to it and bandaged it in place.

'You have a bad habit of getting shot,' Annie told her husband.

'I don't get out of the way quick enough.'

Winifred also cleaned the cuts on his face. There was a clear impression of a boot on his side, and the skin was already turning purple around it. She used the arnica that her mother had rubbed on Katy's bruises a few months earlier to treat that.

'We're a somewhat unfortunate family,' murmured her sister when she finally replaced the antiseptic and the arnica on the shelf.

'Don't you worry about me,' said Thomas. 'I'll be better before I'm twice married.'

In bed that night, Winifred allowed her worries about Joseph to replace her worries about her father. Although he'd told her he hadn't taken part in the planning of the fire, she was aware from the talk on the streets that the Dublin Brigade had been heavily involved in the subsequent action, and he could have been there at some point. There was so much confusion in the city that it was entirely possible Joseph was wounded too and nobody had been able to tell her about it.

I'm worn out worrying, she thought as she shifted uneasily in the bed. And worn out worrying about who I should be worrying about most.

The following day as she walked to the shop, she could see the smoke from the Custom House still rising in the sky. The streets were filled with men from the RIC, the Black and Tans and the Auxiliaries, and she was sure that their orders were to round up as many sympathisers as possible. She hoped Joseph wouldn't be among them. She hoped she wouldn't be among them either.

Joseph called to East Essex Street the following evening. Winifred flew into his arms, hugging him tightly in her relief that he was all right.

'I hope you're happy.' Annie looked at him angrily. 'Your little stunt has made things even worse, as well as getting my husband shot.'

'Shot?' Joseph released his hold on Winifred and looked at Annie in horror. 'Thomas was shot?'

'Yes. He was coming out of the building with a woman and an Auxiliary took a pot at him. And then . . .' she was shaking with anger, 'then someone beat him up.'

'Can I see him?'

It was Winifred who led Joseph into the other room and pulled back the curtain to show her father lying on the bed.

'I'm sorry about your injury,' Joseph said to him. 'How are you feeling?'

'How d'you think I'm feeling.' Thomas's breath was rasping. 'I've been shot and kicked to within an inch of my life. I've breathed in a year's worth of smoke in less than an hour. I'm hardly in the best of health, am I?'

'We hoped there'd be no civilian casualties,' said Joseph.

'Jesus, man, you can't be that naïve. In all honesty, there was such mayhem there was a good chance that one of your crowd could have shot me just as easily. Or certainly burned me to death.'

'We wanted everyone evacuated.'

'That was never going to happen. How many died?'

'As far as I know, only five. But a hundred captured.'

'You burned the place down. You achieved your aim, even though you've destroyed vital information.'

'Shouldn't you be in hospital?' Joseph knew the older man had a point.

'I probably should,' Thomas wheezed. 'But I'm more concerned about getting back to work. If there's work to get back to. Your fine plan has left us without jobs.'

'It wasn't my plan.'

'Collective responsibility,' said Thomas. 'You were part of it.'

Joseph said nothing. Thomas was right.

'I have to go to work now,' said Annie from the doorway. 'Afterwards, I'll walk by. See what's going on.'

'It's still chaotic,' said Joseph.

'If nothing else, you're a master of understatement,' said Annie. She put on her coat and kissed her husband on the forehead. 'I'll be back soon.'

* * *

Joseph brought Winifred to the Palace bar on Fleet Street, where he bought her a sherry to steady her nerves. The place was full of Dubliners, and the only topic of conversation was the burning of the Custom House. Joseph and Winifred sat at a round table facing the shelves of spirits that gleamed beneath the muted lights. Winifred felt the warmth of the sherry revive her, and she allowed a small sigh to escape her lips.

'I'm very sorry about your father,' said Joseph, after he'd taken a gulp from his pint of stout. 'He was unlucky.'

'You warned us,' said Winifred. 'Da didn't listen.'

'He's surrounded by British sympathisers all day,' said Joseph. 'He probably thought it wouldn't amount to much. They all take us for fools.'

'Not everyone who works there is a sympathiser,' protested Winifred. 'A lot of the senior administration staff are, of course. But aren't there plenty of spies there too? And my father definitely doesn't think you're a fool,' she added. 'He believes in freedom just as much as you. He has a different way of going about it, that's all.'

'His way, whatever it is, would go on forever,' said Joseph.

'I know.' Winifred sighed. 'Oh Joseph, I know you have to do what you have to do, but . . . try not to get arrested or shot.'

'I'll do my best.' He put his arm around her. 'Truly I will.'

She set her glass down on the table and leaned her head against his shoulder. 'Maybe Marianne had the right idea after all in getting away from this.'

'Do you want to leave Ireland?' asked Joseph.

Winifred said nothing.

'Winnie? Do you want to go?'

'Would you?' she asked. 'If that was what I wanted, would you leave?'

It was Joseph's turn to be silent for a moment, then he turned and held her face in his hands.

'If that's what you want, that's what we'll do. We could go to America like Marianne. I could join one of the fund-raising organisations there.'

'You'd do that for me?'

He nodded.

'I wouldn't ask you.' She took his hand in hers. 'I wouldn't ask you and I wouldn't feel right about going myself. I'd love to,' she added, 'but that's just a personal thing. We have to stay. We have to see this through.'

'I love you, Winnie.' Joseph took her other hand. 'I've never loved anyone more.'

She smiled at him.

'I love your beauty and your strength, and I love how you make me have to think about what I believe in.'

'Fine words, Mr O'Leary.' She smiled again.

'And I love your courage and your conviction and the fact that even though you didn't want to take part in anything, you and Mrs Kelley became involved.'

'She's a revelation.' Winifred laughed. 'I never would have thought the shop would become part of the struggle and that she'd be so . . . determined about it. She'd give May a run for her money!'

'If it wasn't for the women, for you and Mrs Kelley and May and everyone in Cumann na mBan, we wouldn't be where we are now,' said Joseph. 'I sometimes think what you do is braver than going into battle. Because you're doing it all while pretending that you're doing nothing.'

'Truthfully, I don't feel brave at all,' said Winifred. 'I'm scared witless most of the time.'

'Lloyd George is coming under a lot of pressure,' said Joseph. 'The whole British government is. Their journalists are coming over here to see how it is for themselves instead of relying on propaganda from the administration. Apparently one of the Cabinet members said recently that the reports upset his nerves. We want those nerves upset. The burning of the Custom House is good propaganda. So maybe they'll feel forced into talking. Into negotiating.'

'Everything you say is right, but there were talks in December and they got us nowhere. Why should this be different?'

'Perhaps it won't be,' acknowledged Joseph. 'But there's something in the air, Winnie. A shift in thinking. I can feel it.' He looked around the pub. The conversation was as animated as ever. 'Can't you feel it too?'

'Maybe.'

'You see! I know things are going to change. I just know it. We'll be married as we planned and move into rooms of our own, and we'll raise our children as Irish children, and everything will be fine, I promise you.'

'You do?'

'Absolutely,' said Joseph.

'I want to believe you.'

'I always mean what I say.' He leaned across the table and kissed her.

When Winifred got home from work the following day, she was concerned to see that Katy, who was doing her best to look after their father, had placed a cold flannel on his forehead.

'He's too hot,' she said. 'It may be a fever.'

Winifred checked the wound in his shoulder and noticed that, despite the antiseptic she'd used on it the previous night, it was now red and swollen. She applied more antiseptic and re-dressed the wound.

'Let's keep him as cool as we can,' she said. 'I'll see if I can get him some honey.'

She hurried out of the rooms and along the street to the herbal store on the corner. The owner, Mr Jessop, gave her a small jar of honey and made up some papers of quinine, which he said might also help.

Her mother was home when she got back and had taken over the task of keeping Thomas cool. Winifred mixed one of the quinine papers with water and Annie gave it to her husband to drink.

'Should we try to get Dr Desmond to call again?' asked Winifred.

'That man comes to us out of the goodness of his heart,' said Annie. 'We can't keep imposing on him.'

'But Da needs help,' said Winifred.

'Let's wait until morning,' said Annie. 'Perhaps things will be better then.'

Winifred nodded. She was tired, and she wanted to believe that the quinine and honey would work.

Thomas wasn't any better the following morning, but nor was he worse. However, when she got back from the shop that evening, he was delirious, and she immediately went out again to call on Dr Desmond.

The young maid, Dolly, recognised her and told her that the doctor and his wife were both out.

'Can you ask him to call to us. It's urgent.'

'It's always urgent with you O'Learys,' said Dolly. 'Why the doctor even bothers, and him so busy with proper patients, I don't know.'

Winifred wanted to give the girl a clip around the ear for cheekiness, but she held herself in check.

'Just ask,' she said. 'Thank you.'

It was the following day before Dr Desmond came to East Essex Street, and by then Winifred, Katy and Annie were struggling to keep Thomas cool, while despite the honey and the quinine, the wound on his arm was oozing.

'The infection is spreading,' said the doctor when he looked at it. 'His lungs have been damaged by the smoke. And the fever . . .'

'Will he be all right?' asked Katy.

'I'll give him something to help.'

In the bed, Thomas's breaths grew shallower.

The women looked at each other anxiously.

Thomas died three days later.

They held a wake in East Essex Street. Annie laid him out in his best suit and boots, and men who'd worked with him at the docks as well as some of those who knew him at the Custom House showed up to pay their respects. Over and over again they told her they were sorry for her troubles and spoke warmly and generously of Thomas. 'A good man' and 'a decent man' were the phrases most used, and they gave comfort to Annie, and to Katy and Winifred too. They shook hands with young Tom and told him he was the man of the house now, and each time they did, he stood up a little straighter. The other O'Leary girls, Mary-Jane,

Rosie and Marianne, were of course unable to be there. Winifred had sent telegrams to inform them of their father's death, and their shocked responses were left on the mantelpiece of the main room.

Annie provided sandwiches and beer for the mourners, although she worried about the cost now that Thomas's wage would no longer be coming into the house. She worried about being able to keep the rooms, too. But she kept her worries to herself as she accepted the words of comfort that were being offered.

She was speaking to Father O'Doherty, who would be conducting the funeral service the following day, when the door opened again and she saw the tall, imposing figure of Agnes Burke. Her husband, John, was beside her, and they were followed by Joseph, Ita and Rosanna.

'Mrs O'Leary,' Agnes said. 'I'm sorry for your troubles.'

'Thank you,' said Annie.

'I didn't get to meet your husband as much as I would have liked,' said John. 'What time we spent together was enjoyable. I'm sorry too.'

Joseph, Ita and Rosanna all shook her hand, then moved out of the way to allow others to pay their respects.

Joseph put his arm around Winifred. 'How are you?' he asked.

'It doesn't seem real.'

'I know. I'm so very sorry, Winnie. Your mother . . . is she doing all right?'

'Ma is a rock,' said Winifred. 'But even rocks get worn away over time.'

Any further conversation was silenced by Father O'Doherty beginning a decade of the rosary. The murmured cadences of the prayers and the rhythmic clack of beads filled the room. Winifred found herself repeating the words over and over, and even though she'd never truly believed in them, they were a comfort.

Then Oscar Sheridan, who'd worked with Thomas years earlier, took out his tin whistle and began to play 'Boolavogue', a haunting ballad commemorating the rebellion of 1798, which had been a favourite of Thomas's and which he had always sung at celebrations. The mourners joined in, their voices strong together, while Annie wiped the tears from her eyes.

Oscar continued with a variety of tunes, some poignant and some more cheerful, then Ita Burke stepped forward and asked if she could sing. Annie nodded, and as Ita's clear voice rang out, the rest of the room stood in silence.

She sang 'The Parting Glass', a song that had originated in Scotland but was popular in Ireland, particularly at funerals. Oscar picked up the tune on his tin whistle, but the rest of the mourners, who had joined in with every song until then, allowed Ita to sing on alone.

'Fair play to ye,' said Oscar at the end, as he led the applause. 'That's a great send-off for Thomas. It's a pity he couldn't hear it himself.'

'Maybe he could, Oscar,' murmured Annie. 'Maybe he could.'

As curfew drew close, the mourners began to leave. Agnes Burke approached Annie.

'I want to give you this.' She took a brown envelope from the pocket of the light coat she was wearing.

'What is it?' asked Annie.

206

'Take it.'

Annie took the envelope and opened it. She glanced at Agnes and then back at the envelope and the money it contained.

'What is it?' she repeated.

'A donation. For you,' said Agnes.

'I don't accept charity.'

'It's not charity. Your husband was killed as a result of being shot by occupying forces. It's only right that you should be compensated.'

'There's compensation for everyone who's shot?' Annie gave her a look of disbelief.

'Not everyone,' said Agnes. 'But people who . . . people whose circumstances warrant it. And yours do.'

'I'm sure there are plenty more deserving than me,' said Annie.

'I'm sure there are too,' said Agnes. 'But I don't know them personally. I do know you. And I knew your husband. You will be family. So I spoke to some of the women in my group and we arranged a collection, because it was the right thing to do.'

Annie looked at the money again. Then Katy, who had been standing just behind her, reached out and took the envelope.

'Thank you,' she said in her now slow, laboured way. 'It's very generous of you and your group.'

'Katy—'

But Katy held up her hand and stopped her mother before she could say anything else.

'No money will replace my father,' she told Agnes.

'I realise that. I know it's hard. I wish it hadn't happened. But we're in times of war and terrible things are part of our lives.'

'It's very generous,' repeated Katy. 'Thank you. And thank your group.'

'It's the least we could do,' said Agnes. Then she beckoned to Ita and Rosanna and the three of them left.

'I'll see you tomorrow at the funeral,' Joseph told Winifred. She nodded.

'I love you,' he said.

'I know. I love you too.'

Following on their telegrams, letters arrived from Rosie, Mary-Jane and Marianne.

Rosie's letter was full of French phrases of sorrow, although she did say that Papa (as she now called him) had lived a good life, which was a great comfort to all of them.

Perhaps I will be able to come back to Dublin for a visit. The newspapers here talk of 'La Guerre d'Indépendance Irlandaise' and reported on the burning of the Custom House. I felt it very deeply in my heart when I read it. Most of the newspapers are very supportive. I hope that despite what happened to mon cher Papa, you are all safe and well.

Rosie xxxx

Two letters from Marianne arrived on the same day, although they'd been posted weeks apart. The first was full of the news that she and Danny had settled in Philadelphia ('Philadelphia!' exclaimed Annie. 'Weren't they going to New York? Where exactly is Philadelphia?'), where he'd got a job as a barber, and that Marianne herself was now working as a hairdresser and manicurist. ('In the name of all that's holy,' Annie continued when she read this, 'what does Marianne know about hair and nails? And what sort of women is she meeting?')

The second letter was in response to the news of Thomas's death saying that she was very, very sorry. 'But honestly,' she wrote, 'it was inevitable sooner or later that someone in the family would be killed. Although I thought it would be Winnie because of her consorting with rebels. I was right to have left for the safety of America no matter what you all said. But I'm sending a big kiss to you, Ma, and maybe one day you'll come to America too.'

'That girl is soft in the head,' said Annie. 'Maybe it's just as well she left.'

'It's good to know she thought I'd be killed,' said Winifred. 'She hasn't a clue really, has she?'

'I wish she hadn't gone,' said Annie. 'I wish Mary-Jane and Rosie hadn't either. But they're safe and we're not.'

'We've had our share now,' said Winifred. 'Even Da said that the British government is losing the stomach for the fight. So maybe, just maybe, all this violence and killing will stop soon.'

'In that case, let's pray that our father was one of the last of them.' Katy reached out and squeezed her sister's hand.

And although they both knew that was unlikely, they were also conscious of a different feeling in the city. A feeling that something had changed, that viewpoints were shifting.

'Henry says they have a choice,' said Esther, who had come into the shop one afternoon to buy fabric and begun discussing the situation with Winifred and Alice. 'They can pour yet more men and resources into trying to quell every action we

209

take, or they can start peace talks. And it looks very much like they're going to try to talk.'

'But would they be serious about talking?' asked Alice. 'It wouldn't just be a tactic to catch us off guard?'

'They're struggling to maintain any sort of order,' said Esther. 'They don't have proper records, they don't know who to trust, they're losing the support of the British press – well, some of it anyhow. The Dublin Castle propaganda machine is putting out stories that get sillier and sillier and everyone knows they're not true. So they're . . . um . . . floundering, I think Henry said.'

'I don't believe a word I read in the papers any more,' said Alice. 'If they're supportive of the British, then they say it'll only take a few more weeks for order to be restored. And if you're to believe the *Journal* or the *Bulletin*, the Brits will be hightailing it back to Blighty on the next boat.'

Winifred and Esther both laughed.

'Well you might laugh,' said Alice with mock severity. 'But I hope you're right, Mrs Boland. We all need a break. Now, listen to me, I know you really like that plain calico, but I do have a lovely patterned one I can do you for the same price.'

And the conversation turned to fabrics, which cheered them all up immensely.

King George V made a conciliatory speech at the opening of the new parliament in Northern Ireland the following month in which he appealed for forbearance; to forgive and forget, to bring an era of peace and goodwill. Reading it in the newspapers, Winifred couldn't help thinking that it was very different in tone to anything that had come out of Britain in a long time. Then Lloyd George followed with a letter to

Éamon de Valera, leader of the largest Irish party, suggesting a conference to discuss the future of Ireland.

Joseph and his family viewed this with a mixture of hope and trepidation. Despite being as tired of war as the O'Learys, they were prepared to continue to fight for their freedom. And so, along with everyone else in the country, they gathered to talk among themselves, telling each other what was acceptable and what wasn't, hoping that de Valera wouldn't sell out or that Lloyd George wouldn't impose impossible conditions for a truce.

'We're in a strong position,' Agnes said. 'We can keep going, but they're getting it in the neck now with the losses they're incurring. If I was a British mother, I wouldn't want my son coming here to be shot at.'

De Valera and Lloyd George met. They agreed terms, making certain concessions on both sides.

The truce was signed on 9 July.

A couple of weeks after that, Winifred and Joseph were finally married.

Chapter 15

Dublin, summer/autumn 1921

July 1921

Dear Rosie,

You asked me to write to you about the wedding. I'm so excited at actually being able to write the words 'the wedding' because the most important thing is that it actually happened!!! There were so many obstacles that even with the signing of the truce I wasn't sure we'd manage to go through with it. Right until the last minute I was waiting for something awful to stop it.

And it was more than I ever dreamed of!

We walked to St Michael and John's in glorious sunshine, and people shouted out good wishes. The colours from the stained-glass windows lit up the altar, and even though you know I'm not really religious, I did feel that there was something very special about the moment when Joseph and I stood there and promised to be faithful to each other. He is such a good man, Rosie. I'm proud to be married to him.

Afterwards we got a trap to St Anthony's Place. It was wonderful to go up Sackville Street and not see any soldiers!!! I have to say that Mrs Burke organised everything perfectly and the breakfast in the Red Room was really elegant. I felt like a proper lady. The table setting was magnificent, with her best china, cutlery and glasses and a beautiful floral arrangement. The nuns baked the cake for us and it was lovely. I felt like somebody really important, that all this was being done for me and Joseph. Anthony was his best man and he looked very handsome. I'm wondering will the next wedding be him and Bridget. She's very elegant and wore a really lovely wide-sleeved blouse. I was quite taken with it, though obviously my own was beautiful too. (I don't think I can look elegant, though, Rosie, no matter how much I try!) Bridget caught my posy when I threw it over my head. Maybe we'll become couples who visit each other's homes for tea. Doesn't that sound posh?

The only disaster was first thing when Ma was ironing her blouse – why she had to wait until the morning of the wedding to iron it I don't know. Anyway, she was distracted by Tom, who was throwing his ball against the wall, and she left the iron for a moment to cuff him around the head. But she hadn't realised that she'd left it partly on the blouse and it burned the collar. So in the end she had to wear her patterned Sunday blouse instead of the cream ones the rest of us had. She was quite upset by it, but I didn't mind. I couldn't quite believe I was finally putting on the skirt and blouse I had to take off last November. The skirt was looser on me than back then, but it was still a good fit. I'm enclosing a photograph for you taken in the garden of St Anthony's Place. You can see that Ma is dressed differently. My skirt was a beautiful plum colour, like that quilt you used to like so much, and Bridget's was a little paler. She had it made herself for the day because she wore the one for November all during the winter. I think she thought I wasn't going to get married. Or maybe she thought that Anthony would break it off with her, given his reputation as a flirt. But actually I think he's very much in love with her. And why wouldn't he be? She's pretty and intelligent. We all look very serious in the photograph because we weren't supposed to move, but we laughed a lot and had great fun. And although I'll never, ever say it to Agnes Burke, a summer wedding was probably a lot more fun than a winter one would have been. Because it was really nice to sit in the garden and enjoy the silence of no explosions and no gunfire.

I am very much hoping that with the start of our married life coinciding with the end of the war it will be a happy time for all of us (I'm saying 'end' even though it's still just a truce at the moment and there are still occasional raids and forays). Anyway, I'm keeping my fingers crossed that we'll have nothing but peace and contentment in the years ahead. There are days, Rosie, when I feel the heaviness of the last two years weigh upon me, when everything still seems dark and impossible and I find it difficult to get out of bed.

But I never say anything about this. I don't like to think of Da and how he lived through so much during his life only to fall when there was some hope in sight. My heart aches at the injustice of it and I know Ma's heart aches too, even though she's very strong and says that we all have to die sooner or later and that he had five years

214

after being shot during the Rising that she didn't think he'd have. I never thought of it like that, but if Dr Desmond hadn't been around then, Da would have bled to death. So perhaps Ma's right. But I still feel the loss very keenly. Of course Joseph lost family over the course of the war, and he's lost many friends, especially in these last months. But he still has his parents. Everything has affected him too, but he's a much more positive person than I am. When he feels the darkness, he takes out his harmonica and plays a tune. He's really very good at it. He plays the mandolin too. Whenever I struggle to wake up in the mornings, he stands at the end of the bed and plays 'For me and my Gal' to urge me from beneath the covers.

I love him very much, Rosie. The only thing I'd change, if I could change anything, would be where we live. At the moment, we're at St Anthony's Place with Mr and Mrs Burke. We'd been planning to rent a room in Dorset Street, but Mrs Burke pointed out that there was plenty of space in the house for us and that it was madness paying rent for inferior accommodation when we could live with her with our own room and a big garden. Of course, she's right, but I was looking forward to having a place of our own. It was the garden that made me agree, because it's so lovely to be able to sit out there, and there was nowhere we could rent with a garden. The places we could get didn't even have a yard. Even though St Anthony's Place is in the heart of the city, the garden is beautiful, and it's quiet and peaceful. I told Joseph I didn't want to live with his mother forever (after all, she is very, very bossy) and he agrees, but he also thinks it's a good opportunity for us to save a little money. And even though he has his own job, he helps his father with the boiler house too, so this is a good plan for everyone.

Katy is doing a lot better. I think she enjoyed the wedding, but there is no doubt that Reid's attack has changed her. She's slower in her speech and she has to think before she answers a question. But she looks like herself again, and now that her hair has fully grown back, you wouldn't know that she has such a dreadful scar. She was really worried for a time that Reid would come looking for her, but we heard that he's gone to Belfast to work at the shipyard. I don't know how he will fare there, because it's said that Catholics are often dismissed, but he's the kind of person who'll find a place for himself no matter what. He'll probably say he's a Protestant!

This is the longest letter I have ever written. I hope you are well, darling Rosie. I was very glad to hear of the safe arrival of Léonard junior. Perhaps one day you will come to visit us here in Dublin.

Your loving sister,

Winnie

August 1921

Dear Winnie,

Hello from Philadelphia, where Danny and I are doing very, very well. We have made good friends among other Irish people here and Danny has opened his barber's shop. My hair salon will be beside it. We are proper business people, even though we're young. Danny is an excellent barber and I am learning about cutting hair – I will be gcod at it because I like making women look beautiful.

Everything is bigger and brighter here, and although they have gone through some hard times, there is lots of hope and optimism. So much more exciting than Ireland! My best friend is from County Cork. Her name is Brenda. She sounds like an American when she speaks, but then sometime when it's just her and me she sounds like someone from Cork all over again. I have an excellent American accent!

Much love to you and Ma.

Your sister,

Mrs Marianne Keogh

PS I am enclosing a photograph of me taken outside the barber's shop. My dress is buttercup yellow and my hair is in a style they call 'shingle' M xxx

September 1921

Dear Mary-Jane,

Thank you for your letter and for the photograph of your family. You all look very well and happy and it is funny to see you sitting in your chair with your feet in water to stay cool. The weather has been good here, but not as hot as England, it seems.

Joseph and I are well settled in now. In answer to your question, at the time of writing I am not expecting, although everyone makes remarks about 'little ones'. It's really quite rude, isn't it, asking women this question? After what happened to Katy and her babies, I believe that children

217

truly are a gift, and I do hope to have them, but we don't have plans to start a family yet.

We are still with Mrs Burke as it is a practical arrangement. I am doing my best to be accommodating to all the Burkes and I think they are doing their best to make me feel welcome. Every so often, though, Joseph's mother looks at me in a speculative way, and I can't help thinking she feels I'm not good enough for him.

I left Mrs Kelley's after I got married. It seemed like the right thing to do, especially as I had to redecorate rooms in St Anthony's Place for us. I miss the buzz of the shop, and I definitely miss having my own money, but it's nice to be a lady of leisure for a while. It also means I can spend more time with Katy. She's still improving. You'd hardly know what had happened to her except when she has to think of a word, or when you realise she struggles with her arm, an after-effect of the minor stroke that his beating caused. But she looks well again, Mary-Jane, and that's such a relief.

I'm happy that as I write this to you, I'm in the garden at St Anthony's Place, the sun is shining, the flowers are in bloom and the sky is blue.

Your loving sister,
Winnie

October 1921

Dear Mrs Kelley,

Thank you for your letter. I am sorry that the new girl hasn't worked out for you. I can't believe she stole money from the till. I have spoken to Joseph and he is happy for me to return to the shop for a time as he respects you very much. Therefore I will be there next Monday at 9.30 a.m. as requested.

Yours faithfully,
Winifred Burke (Mrs)

Chapter 16

Dublin, winter 1921/spring 1922

Winifred was happy working in the shop again. She liked being away from St Anthony's Place and the watchful eye of Joseph's mother, and she liked earning her own money and having a sense of independence. Her mind was lighter as she walked to work every day, even though the winter was drawing in and the days were getting colder. Now that she was a married woman, Alice gave her greater respect, and indeed the two of them regarded each other as friends rather than employer and employee, sharing confidences in a way they hadn't before. Alice asked about Winifred's life with the Burkes, questioning how she was getting on in a house of which she wasn't the mistress.

'It can be difficult,' Winifred admitted. 'I thought Mrs Burke was simply opinionated about politics, but the truth is she has an opinion on everything. And she delivers it in such a way that even when I agree with her, I want to argue. I spend a lot of time biting my tongue.'

'Oh, I was the same with Edward's mother!' exclaimed Alice. 'She disliked the way I did things, the food I served . . . she was a difficult woman. Still is. But I have to keep in with her because . . . well, because of the money.'

'That's understandable. And before that, when your husband was alive, you did it because you loved him. Like me and Joseph.'

'In the end, my marriage was more like a business arrangement than anything else,' observed Alice. 'Edward went off to fight and left me behind for months at a time, and I had to live my own life without him. It was always disconcerting when he came home. He expected me to look after him, to do everything he wanted, how he wanted. But I was used to living by myself. I didn't like being told what to do by someone who was hardly ever there.'

'At least Joseph didn't have to go away to fight,' remarked Winifred as she folded yards of white linen.

'And maybe when the Treaty is signed, the fighting will be over for good.' Alice's voice was full of optimism. 'And you and me, Winnie, we'll have done our bit to bring it about.'

The Irish delegation to negotiate a treaty with Britain had been in London since October, and the various twists and turns of the discussions were being hotly debated in Dublin. When the final agreement was reached in December, and twenty-six of the thirty-two counties effectively became a free state in the British dominion while the other six remained sovereign to Britain, there was uproar in St Anthony's Place.

'That happened because de Valera didn't go himself!' cried Agnes in fury. 'Michael Collins and the rest of the delegation have signed our country away. I didn't support the Volunteers so that our ministers would have to swear an oath of allegiance to the King. Or to have an English royal representative or governor general or whatever they want to call him being part of our government. I fought against being part of the British Empire and this treaty keeps us in it. Collins should be ashamed of himself.'

'De Valera is furious too,' said May. 'Though it's not because of the Treaty itself; it's because they signed it without telling him what was in it first. As they had the right to do, of course. But it was a mistake. And our history is littered with mistakes.'

'This isn't going to turn out well.' Joseph, sitting on the sofa beside Winifred, took her hand. 'It might be a rocky road ahead yet.'

'Can we please not talk about it for just one night?' asked John, who'd walked into the room while Agnes was in full flow. 'Can we not simply sit here and pretend that everything is perfectly fine?'

Winifred shot him a sympathetic look.

But for once his view prevailed, and the conversation turned to *Heartbreak House*, a recent play by the renowned George Bernard Shaw that Joseph and Winifred had gone to see the previous week.

'The critic was right,' Joseph said. 'It was long and wordy.'

'Like Dev,' said Winifred, which made them laugh.

'Did you enjoy it?' asked Ita.

'It was interesting,' Winifred said.

'You fell asleep!' exclaimed Joseph.

'Only briefly,' she admitted. 'I can't quite get my head around Mr Shaw's imagining of the world. Death rays and destruction seem fanciful.'

'Death rays!' Agnes looked at her. 'What on earth is that man on about now?'

'Maybe if we had a death ray, the English would think twice about being here,' said Rosanna in amusement.

'It destroyed dynamite,' Joseph told her.

'Totally mad,' said Ita.

'I enjoyed his other play more,' remarked Winifred.

'Which other?' asked John. 'He's written a lot.'

'*Pygmalion*,' replied Winifred. 'I loved the English social-climbing in it, and how their accents mattered so much. And I love the idea that a flower girl could pass herself off as a duchess once she changes how she speaks, except that she talks about the things she knows and Professor Higgins's family is completely flummoxed by her.'

'It's a very funny play,' agreed John. 'Agnes and I went to see it when it was on first.'

'What I liked was that the young lady did well for herself,' said Agnes. 'And she stood up to those silly men. I like to think she married nobody and set herself up as a teacher of linguistics after all.'

Winifred and May both laughed at Joseph and John, who made despairing faces at Agnes's commentary.

'Well, even if *Heartbreak House* wasn't as amusing as *Pygmalion*, it was nice to be at the theatre,' said Winifred. 'It felt almost normal. And people were in good spirits.'

'For however long that lasts,' murmured Agnes.

'No more of that.' John held up his hand. 'No politics, remember.'

Agnes looked as though she was going to disagree, then shrugged.

'I'm tired,' Winifred announced. 'I think I'll go to bed.'

'I'll join you shortly,' said Joseph.

Fifteen minutes later, he walked into the bedroom and put his arms around her, drawing her close.

'I love you, Mrs Burke,' he whispered.

'Don't call me that.' Winifred giggled. 'It makes me think of your mother.'

'Jesus wept.' He made a face. 'I think you've put me off what I had in mind for tonight.'

'Surely not.' She began to unbutton his shirt and then allowed her hand to slide lower. 'No,' she said. 'Definitely not.'

'You're a witch, Winnie.'

'That I am,' she said, and lay back on the bed and pulled him towards her.

Politics took second place to her first Christmas as a married woman. The Burkes invited the O'Learys to their house for dinner, where Agnes served mixed root vegetables from the garden followed by a bread pudding that she'd made herself.

'I'm sorry there's no meat,' she said. 'It's hard to get.'

'You're a good cook,' said Annie. 'And this is an excellent meal, thank you.'

Annie herself had managed to obtain oranges and nuts at the market earlier in the week, and they ate those afterwards.

'Perhaps supplies will improve in the new year,' she said.

She regretted the remark when it led to another of the Burke family's impassioned political discussions. When Winifred glanced at her mother, Annie winked at her and she dissolved into a fit of the giggles that had Agnes and her daughters looking at her in astonishment, because Winifred wasn't known for being a woman who laughed very much. In fact, the female

Burkes would often say to each other, she usually had a perpetual look of worry on her face. Winifred, had she known, would've said there was plenty to worry about.

But not during those few weeks, where she felt almost light-hearted.

The Treaty was passed in January, much to the fury of those who opposed it. Éamon de Valera immediately resigned as president of Ireland and challenged the right of the Dáil to ratify it at all. Even though Winifred joined the cheering throngs outside Dublin Castle to see the arrival of the provisional government for the handover from the British, she knew that the Burkes were very much opposed to the Treaty and she worried about the consequences. Agnes had refused to come to the castle, but Joseph had accompanied her.

'Say what you like, but it's exciting to see our own people walk in and take over,' she said to him as the taxi cabs bringing Michael Collins and the rest of the government swept up and the crowd cheered wildly. 'It's a historic moment for us.' She took her hat from her head and waved it in the air.

'I wish I could believe it will turn out as well as you think it will,' he said. 'I'm afraid that any gains we eke out will somehow be clawed back, because we're a free state in the Empire, not a sovereign republic in our own right.'

'I'm aware that might happen,' said Winifred. 'Alice and I discuss it ourselves, you know. Political conversation isn't solely the preserve of the Burkes!'

'Indeed it's not,' conceded Joseph as the crowd pushed forward to get a better view and he had to hold on to Winifred to avoid being separated from her.

'And I think it's a mistake for Cumann na mBan to be against it too.' Winifred had to raise her voice. 'Oh look, there's Collins now. He's very handsome, isn't he?'

'Is that how you decide?' Joseph laughed. 'Based on looks?'

'I might.' She grinned. 'It is exciting. I don't care what you say.'

And that day, it was. But in the weeks that followed, the chasm between those who supported the Treaty and those who opposed it grew wider. Despite her admiration for Collins, and the fact that she knew her own mother was in agreement with him, Winifred knew she had to align herself with the Burkes and their views. After all, she was living in their house. And as she acknowledged to herself one evening after another heated debate over the dinner table, it wasn't as though they were wrong. The Treaty was inherently flawed. But it seemed to her that at least it was a step on the road. And that was progress.

People everywhere were arguing. In pubs, in cafés, in shops, in homes, the pro- and anti-Treaty perspectives were debated. And friendships were splintering because of it. Including the one between Joseph and Anthony.

Anthony believed that Collins had done the best he could, but Joseph argued that the Treaty was storing up trouble for the future; that what had resulted, a state independent from the United Kingdom but still part of the Empire, wasn't what had been proclaimed by Pearse and the others in 1916.

'Do we want to placate the dead or move on with the living?' asked Anthony one afternoon as they sat smoking in the garden of St Anthony's Place. 'Give it time, Joe. We'll change things.'

'I know you believe that'll happen. But I don't think it will.'

'Winnie agrees with me,' said Anthony.

'It's what her mother thinks, and Winnie will never say a word against her mother.'

'You used her during the War of Independence to further your aims and you'll use her again because you're blinkered. Your whole family is blinkered. You're not the man I thought you were, Joseph Burke. You won't be happy until the entire British army has been slaughtered and half the Irish population with them. And you'd betray your own wife if you had to.'

'I'll have no need to betray my wife because she's a proud Irishwoman and she'll always do what's right.'

'What you tell her is right.'

'Don't talk nonsense,' said Joseph. 'Besides, weren't you the one calling for greater force from the brigades during the war? For the burning of barracks? For the assassination of Royal Irish Constabulary members? What's changed you?'

Anthony was silent.

'It's Bridget, isn't it?' The realisation suddenly came to Joseph. 'Her family . . . her connections . . . being from Ulster . . .'

'It's not Bridget,' said Anthony, but his voice lacked conviction before he looked up and met Joseph's gaze without flinching. 'There are more people on the side of this Treaty than against it. If you fight, you'll be putting us back years.'

'If we don't fight, the effects of the Treaty will be with us for years,' said Joseph. 'We'll be leaving unfinished business for our children and their children after them. We need to deal with this properly once and for all.'

'You're wrong,' said Anthony. 'You're standing in the way of peace. And I can't support you, Joe.'

'Surely—'

'No!' Anthony shook his head. 'You can pick your side, but you can't pick your friends.'

He stood up and walked away, slamming the iron gate behind him.

Winifred, who'd heard the raised voices and seen Anthony leave, stepped into the garden.

'Are you all right?' she asked.

'Do you think I've taken the wrong road?' Joseph turned to her. 'Do you think we should swallow our principles and accept this treaty?'

'I want to accept it,' she said, 'because I want this to be over. I don't want us to lose our friends and fight our countrymen. You know Ma thinks it's the right thing to do so that the fighting ends. I understand her point of view. I want to be able to see her and Katy without worrying that your family think of me as a traitor.'

'They don't think that.' Joseph shook his head. 'And I won't take up arms against any Irishman. But . . .'

She put her arms around him and leaned her head on his chest. 'You can't make that promise, can you?'

'I . . . I hope I can. But whatever the circumstances, I promise to keep you safe.'

'I want us to move on with our lives and leave all this behind,' she told him. 'I want us to have our own home. Our own family too, some day. I want—'

'You're as bad as the British with your list of demands,' he said, a sudden dry humour in his voice.

She smiled.

'I want us to be happy, Joseph. But you won't be until you've done everything you possibly can to deliver the freedom you think we deserve.'

'We need to be able to work independently of them, Winnie. To make our own laws, to keep our own money, to have our own head of state. These are important things. If we don't get it right now, when will we have the chance again?'

'I'll always be on your side,' she told him.

'And I'll always love you,' he said before he kissed her.

Chapter 17

April 1922

Dear Winnie,

Your friend the Countess Markievicz visited Philadelphia today. She gave a talk at the church hall and I went along because seeing her was like seeing a link to home. I know this is my home now, but I think about you all very often. Anyway, there was a band to greet her and lots and lots of Irish people. Since I've been here I've met many of them but suddenly they were all in the one place. I got talking to a girl called Martha Clune. Her family lived in Arran Street where we lived before we moved to East Essex Street and I think I remember playing with her! Isn't that amazing? All this distance and I meet someone I knew when I was six.

Anyway, the Countess talked against the idea of the Free State and everyone here agrees with her. She said that as long as Ireland is part of the British Empire she'll always be a rebel and everyone cheered. She's here to raise money. She raised a lot of it today.

I know I didn't care much for what was going on when I was in Dublin, but now I find I want to know. I've joined an Irish women's club here and we bake cakes and sell them as fundraisers. You'll laugh at me baking cakes. You know I was never interested.

Are you on the anti-Treaty side? I think you must be because the Burkes hid the Countess. But I can't know for certain. If you are, tell me and maybe I can send some of our fundraising money to you.

In other news, we are doing very well with the barber's and hairdresser's. American women like to look their best. So it has been a good move for me. Even better if there's still trouble in Ireland. You will see from the address that we have moved again. The new rooms are much better than the others, but we are hoping to get a small house of our own.

Can you imagine it, Winnie! Me, living in a house. With my own garden! I feel so lucky. I hope you are well and happy.

Tell Ma I was asking for her. Tell her also there's no sign of a baba yet. I'm too busy for that sort of thing and I'm using what I learned from working with Dr Desmond to make sure it doesn't happen.

Your loving sister,
Marianne

June 1922

Dear Winifred,

Thank you for your letter.

It was worrying to read that the anti-Treaty forces occupied the Four Courts last month. The papers say that

231

they are hoping for a confrontation with the British that will bring down the Treaty. But as I write to you, they are under siege. Are they still? It's all such a terrible mess. I'm so glad your Joseph is not there, even though you told me that the Burke family is anti-Treaty. What does Mama say? I know all she ever wanted was for the fighting to stop, so I think she must be for the Treaty. That puts you in a difficult position, chérie, no?

How is Katy? Has her husband ever come looking for her? She's in a difficult situation too, isn't she? Married to someone who's run off. It means she can't get married again, even if she wanted to. Although good that he has gone, the violent porc!

My pregnancy is going well and I don't feel at all ill, although occasionally tired. I'm glad to hear your news too! We are very grown up now, all of us married and having babies. I know you are very early on and so you are not saying anything to anyone yet. A wise move. And yes, childbirth is painful. But you forget that, you really do. Especially if you have a good doctor. I hope our children will have the chance to meet sometime. Do you want to have a boy or a girl? Léonard prefers girls, which is unusual, I think. He says boys are nothing but trouble!

Keep well, ma soeur adorée. Stay safe in these troubled times.

Love always,

Rosie

Winifred had expected that sooner or later she'd get pregnant, even though she'd hoped it would take a little longer. She'd considered writing to Marianne to ask her what methods Dr Desmond recommended, but it was Alice who told her what she needed to know. She hadn't brought it up directly with her boss, but Alice had asked her outright if she had any plans for a family. When Winifred replied that she would like to be a mother, but not quite yet, Alice nodded.

'You can't leave it up to chance,' she said in the brisk tone she used when she was ordering new fabrics. 'Chance, it seems, is on the side of men, and men are quite happy to have their wives pregnant.'

'My sister in America says she's using something to stop it. But I always thought there wasn't much you could really do to prevent it. It just happens when you . . . when you're with your husband.'

'It didn't happen to me.'

Winifred looked at her in surprise. She'd always assumed that Alice's childless state was a result of Edward being sent off to war.

'Of course him being at the front didn't help,' agreed Alice. 'But before then, and on the times he came home, well, Winifred, with the amount of times we did it together, I should most definitely have become pregnant if I hadn't taken steps to prevent it.'

'What steps?' Despite her embarrassment at Alice's comments, Winifred was intrigued.

'You buy a sponge in the chemist,' said Alice. 'Then you soak it in olive oil and you . . . you insert it before you go to bed. The olive oil slows down the man's seed.'

Winifred made a face.

'It isn't always effective,' Alice conceded. 'But it was effective enough for me.'

'But didn't you want children?' asked Winifred. 'I know I'm not in a rush, but I do think, especially after what happened to my sister, that it's important to have a baby of my own.'

'I didn't want them particularly,' said Alice. 'Even less did I want to produce them like shelling peas from a pod.'

'Alice!'

'Have you read about a woman in America who is trying to make birth control normal? She's founded something called the Birth Control League. Her view is that liberating women from constantly having children allows social change. And indeed, she's right. Think of all our Cumann na mBan friends. Some of them will go on to be wonderful mothers, I'm sure, but others will want to stay socially active. And that's very difficult with a family.'

'The Burkes seem to manage,' observed Winifred. 'Having children didn't stop Agnes and May.'

'True,' conceded Alice. 'But even if you don't want to be active, you don't want to be pregnant all the time either. So if you want my advice, use a sponge. There are other things you can soak it in,' she added, 'but olive oil is easily available and nobody questions you.'

'I see.'

'I'm being selfish,' said Alice. 'I don't want to lose you as an employee. You're the best I ever had.'

Winifred smiled, then hugged her friend.

She bought sponges and olive oil that evening.

And for a time, it worked.

* * *

Joseph had known that she wanted some time before having children, and he didn't have a problem with that. Nevertheless, he was ecstatic when she told him of her pregnancy. He put his arms around her and said that she'd made him the happiest man in the world.

'Happier than when I married you?' she asked.

'That was the happiest day of my life,' he said.

'But this makes you happier?'

'It makes me feel . . . that we're a unit, Winnie. You and me and the baba. We're a proper family.'

'I'm a bit scared, to be honest,' she said.

'Don't be,' said Joseph. 'I'm with you. I'll always be with you.'

Agnes Burke set out a special tea for her, telling her that she had to look after herself and the baby and that she would have to give up her job at Kelley's shop.

'I spoke to Mrs Kelley and she says I can continue to work until I start to show.'

'I'm not sure that's advisable . . .'

'Mrs Burke.' Winifred looked at her steadily. 'Members of Cumann na mBan take part in protests and other activities while they're pregnant. All I'm doing is standing behind a counter. I think I'll be perfectly well.'

'What do you think, Joseph?' asked Agnes.

'I think Winifred is perfectly capable of deciding for herself,' he said.

Annie and Katy were delighted with the news too.

'You'll be a wonderful mother,' Katy told her.

'I hope so.' Winifred made a face. 'I want to be, but I sometimes think . . .'

'What?'

'I'm not very maternal,' confessed Winifred. 'I don't go soft in the head like some women when I see babies.'

'The minute the baba is in your arms you'll be maternal,' said Annie.

'Really?' Winifred looked at her.

'Without a shadow of a doubt,' said Annie, and hugged her.

Winifred was finding pregnancy easier than she'd expected, and although she eventually began to let out her skirts, it was difficult to tell she was pregnant at all.

'You lucky thing,' Esther said to her one day when they met. 'Look at me. I swell up like a hot air balloon, whereas you look like you've just put on an extra pound.'

Esther was now pregnant with her third child and Winifred couldn't deny that she was very large.

'Agnes is worried that I'm not showing enough,' she confessed. 'She's making me drink a glass of Guinness a day.'

'It helps with your iron,' said Esther.

'I hate the taste.' Winifred grimaced.

'I quite like it myself. A tot of brandy is good too.'

'The only spirit in the house is whiskey, and only Mr Burke drinks that,' said Winifred. 'I'm grand, Esther, honestly. I feel great.'

'And what about the shop?' Esther looked at her with interest. 'You're still working there, aren't you?'

'For the time being,' said Winifred. 'It keeps me busy and takes my mind off what's to come. Tell me the truth, Esther, is it really awful?'

'I'm not going to lie,' said Esther. 'It feels like you're being ripped apart. But then you have a baba and, oh, I don't know, Winnie, it seems to ease away.'

'And afterwards? What about . . . you know . . . afterwards?'

'Well, of course you have to go to the church a month after and be blessed,' Esther said. 'It's a load of aul' codswallop but it keeps them off you long enough to feel able for it again. I'm only in the door when Henry's ready to go for it.'

'Don't you like it?' asked Winifred.

'I did at first, but Henry is very demanding. I like the break, if I'm honest.'

'Joseph is . . . tender,' said Winifred. 'He's being very careful with me now.'

'You two lovebirds make me sick.' But Esther smiled. 'I hope our babas will be friends, Winnie.'

'I hope so too.'

As the days grew warmer, Winifred felt as though the atmosphere in the city was heating up too, that it was a tinderbox of suppressed emotions that could explode at any moment.

At the end of June, it did.

Michael Collins had been utterly unable to persuade the anti-Treaty forces to leave the Four Courts, and in what everyone later accepted was a point of no return between the provisional government and the anti-Treaty side, he eventually ordered the shelling of the building.

'I can't believe he's doing this to his own people,' said Joseph when the bombardment commenced. 'He knows the men in there. He fought side by side with some of them. He knows why they're there. He's borrowed the damn artillery from the British themselves and started a civil war.'

Agnes was incensed. 'Irishmen and Irishwomen gave their lives for this!' she said through gritted teeth. 'To have that traitor fire on them on the orders of the British . . . I knew nothing good would come of this treaty. I knew it. As for those who were there and working for the British government, they should be ashamed of themselves.'

'Have you both forgotten that my father used to work at the Custom House?' asked Winifred. 'He never thought that he worked for the British. He worked for Ireland.'

'I didn't mean your father,' said Agnes, in a tone that Winifred thought meant she did.

'We can't apportion blame to anyone,' said Joseph. 'We need to convince good Irishmen to do the right thing.'

'Perhaps they can negotiate some kind of truce,' suggested Winifred.

'Isn't that what Collins did?' demanded her mother-in-law. 'He negotiated the Treaty and he negotiated badly.'

'Dev should have gone instead. Everyone knows that. The only reason he didn't was so that he could wash his hands of it all. He's a sleeveen with motives of his own.'

'Since when did you get so interested in what Dev should and shouldn't have done?'

'Since I became pregnant,' said Winifred. 'I don't want my child to grow up in a hellhole of a country with a double-crossing leader.'

'You'll want your child to grow up in a republic,' Agnes said. 'One that has the interests of the people at heart.'

'I do feel that Michael Collins has the interests of the people at heart,' said Winifred.

'That's your mother speaking. I know the O'Learys are on the side of the Free State.'

'Like me, they're on the side of Irish people not killing each other. But it doesn't look like that's the way things are going.'

'I don't want to argue with your mother,' she said that night when she and Joseph were alone together. 'I don't want to argue with you either. But I won't have her talking about Ma as though she's some kind of traitor.'

'She doesn't think that.'

'She does. And I know she's thinking I am too. I've seen her watching me.'

'Watching you?'

'She follows me around. I'm sure she thinks I'm passing information to anti-Treaty supporters.'

'You're paranoid. It's because you're expecting.'

'That's not why I'm paranoid,' she said. 'It's because I have reason to be. I'm telling you, Joseph, she spies on me. I caught her coming out of our room the other day. She said she was putting fresh camphor in the wardrobe, but I didn't see any. She was checking up on me, I swear to you. And so do Ita and Rosanna.'

'You're getting things out of perspective,' he told her. 'All she's doing is making sure you're keeping well.'

'I hope you're right.'

But she wasn't at all certain.

Large crowds had gathered around the public buildings on the Liffey quays as the bombardment continued, but Winifred stayed away, not wanting it to appear as though she supported one side or the other.

However, it was hard to ignore when the sound of the guns was so loud they could be easily heard in the shop.

'We'll all be deaf before this is over,' said Alice. 'I really think—'

But what she thought was lost in the sound of a massive explosion that rocked the building and echoed around the city.

'Jesus, Mary and Joseph, what was that?' said Winifred, her hand instinctively covering her belly.

'Somebody's blown something up.' Alice's voice was shaky. 'Let's wait a moment.'

When they plucked up the courage to go outside, the two women saw a cloud of black smoke rising into the sky, along with what they initially thought were huge flakes of ash but later realised were official papers that had been destroyed in the explosion.

'I can't believe it's all happening again,' said Winifred as they looked in horror at the devastation. 'And the worst of it is that we're fighting each other.'

'Maybe that's what the British meant when they said the Irish were ungovernable,' murmured Alice.

'You can't believe that.'

'I believe that we had peace in our hands and we sabotaged it. And I'm sorry to say, Winifred, that your husband is on the losing side. Because eventually the pro-Treaty side will win. They have the support of the British, after all.'

'I know,' murmured Winifred. 'It's just that Joseph and his family . . . they have principles.'

'Worth dying for?' asked Alice.

'You thought Ireland being free was worth . . . well, maybe not dying for, but worth putting yourself at risk for,' Winifred pointed out. 'You helped it to happen.'

'And now we've got our freedom, what's the point in throwing it all away for a principle?'

'If we don't have principles, what do we have?' asked Winifred.

'Padraig says—'

'Padraig?' Winifred looked at her in surprise. 'You're still seeing him? I thought you and he . . . Well, I asked before and you didn't say, and—'

'Because I didn't want you thinking I was spying on you.'

'Spying on me!' Winifred stared at her. 'Why would you be spying on me?'

'Padraig supports the Treaty,' said Alice. 'He thinks anyone who doesn't is a traitor.'

'Oh. I thought most of Joseph's battalion were anti.'

'There are more people for it than against it,' said Alice. 'I'm sorry again, Winifred, but you've picked the losing side.'

'I'm on both sides,' Winifred reminded her. 'I want a compromise.'

'There'll be no compromising. Not now.'

'So what are you saying?'

'Either you're for the Free State or you're not. In the end, you'll have to make a choice. And if you throw in your lot with the Burkes, then perhaps it's better if you don't come back to the shop. Because I can't have it caught up in another war. Look at this!' Alice gestured towards the Four Courts. 'The anti-Treaty side will always find an excuse to keep fighting. It's all they know.'

'Joseph doesn't want to fight other Irishmen,' said Winifred.

'But he will,' said Alice. 'And it'll be the biggest mistake of his life, and yours.'

'The Treaty can be changed.'

'Not without a lot more bloodshed, and I'm not prepared to be part of it. Also,' she looked at Winifred appraisingly, 'I'm not sure you should be part of it in your condition. Certainly being on your feet all day isn't a good idea any more.'

'Alice! I'm pregnant, not ill. And you said I could work until it became too obvious.'

'It's beginning to matter now,' said Alice. 'You should stay home, look after your health and try to persuade your husband and his family to see sense.'

'But—'

'It's better this way.'

'Are you letting me go?' asked Winifred.

'I suppose I am,' said Alice.

The two women looked at each other.

'I'm sorry,' said Alice for the third time. 'But it's for the best if you don't come here any more.'

'I see.' Winifred looked again towards the Four Courts and then back at the shop.

'You'll be better off at home,' said Alice. 'It's more appropriate.'

'You want me to leave now? Just like that?'

'Yes, I do.'

Winifred went back into the shop and swapped her apron for her coat.

'So this is goodbye,' she said.

'I suppose it is,' said Alice.

The two women looked at each other wordlessly.

Then Winifred drew herself up, turned around and walked away.

Chapter 18

While the Four Courts was being bombarded by the provisional government's National Army, commanded by Michael Collins, there were pitched battles on the streets of the city. Units of the Dublin Brigade took over buildings around the Sackville Street area as strategic positions. De Valera, who'd declared that he was going to serve as a Volunteer, and Cathal Brugha, the former defence minister, joined the anti-Treaty forces. The fighting on Sackville Street was intense, and once again the buildings in the surrounding area were pockmarked by bullets and the sound of gunfire echoed through the air.

Winifred, although unhappy at having to leave Kelley's Fine Fabrics, worried for Alice's safety and hoped that she'd closed the shop and wasn't in any danger.

'There's been a call to arms at Barry's Hotel.' Joseph, dressed in his uniform and carrying a pistol, strode into the Yellow Room, where she was knitting a baby bonnet in a fine white wool. 'They're assembling battalions.'

'But you can't fight!' she cried. 'You only have one good eye.'

'I can see well enough,' he said.

'You promised not to fight.'

'There's no other option.'

'But—'

'I have to go, Winifred. It's my duty.'

'Oh Joseph. Please don't get killed.'

'I won't.'

He kissed her quickly on the cheek, and she watched from the window until he'd walked out of the gate and pulled it closed behind him.

As he made his way to Gardiner Row, where the hotel was situated, Joseph did his best to keep out of sight of possible National Army forces. Approaching it, he could see that the glass had been knocked out of the windows and replaced with sandbags, with rifles protruding between the bags.

I hope to God they don't shoot me! he thought, at the exact moment a shot rang out. He flinched, then realised it had come from behind him, and ran towards the door, which was slightly ajar. He half fell inside and almost collided with Countess Markievicz, who was standing in the hallway wearing her green uniform.

'Mary, Mother of God,' he panted as he sank to his knees. 'That was close. The feckers nearly got me.'

'Mr Burke.' She slammed the door closed behind him. 'We meet again. In battle this time, rather than hiding in your house.'

'It's always an honour to see you.' He stood upright and extended his hand. 'Even in these circumstances.'

'I don't know that meeting me is an honour.' She smiled at him and clasped his hand in hers. 'But I hope fighting with me will be.'

They were trying to control the area leading to Sackville Street, one of the officers told them. They would fortify the hotel and the surrounding area to the best of their abilities. They barricaded the doors with the hotel furniture and Joseph took up his position behind one of the sandbagged windows, while the Countess was led to another area of the hotel. He suddenly remembered the moment when Winnie had discovered her in St Anthony's Place. The look of guilt on both women's faces – the Countess for having spilled the ink and Winnie for having seen her.

I'm doing this for you, Winnie, he thought. And if I die, I'll die thinking of you.

Winifred was in their room at St Anthony's Place. She'd shut the door behind her so that she could cry without her mother-in-law looking at her as though she was crying for the other side. Agnes and her daughters, meanwhile, said decades of the rosary in the garden and called upon the Mother of God to protect the republicans. As the rhythmic chant of their prayers wafted through her bedroom window, Winifred wondered which side God was on. After all, she thought, her own mother was praying for victory too. Only she was for Collins and the provisional government and there was no changing her mind about it. Not that Winifred tried. She was too conflicted about it herself.

There is no God, she decided as she put her hands over her ears to block out the Burkes' prayers. There can't be. And if there is, he's a warmonger himself. Otherwise how could there have been a world war? And how can there be so much hatred and conflict? No, she concluded, prayers were a waste of time. She wasn't going to bother with them any more.

* * *

245

Winifred would forever afterwards associate the summer months with the smell of smoke and gunpowder. It seemed to have lodged in her nose, so that even on days when the fighting abated, she could still smell and taste it. She associated it too with the constant fear that someone would come to the door to tell her that her husband had been killed. But when the bang on the door came, it wasn't with the news she dreaded, but to inform them that the garrison staff had decided to evacuate Barry's Hotel that night and that Volunteers would be making their way to St Anthony's Place with sensitive materials.

'Of course,' said Agnes. 'As many as need shelter.'

'Is my husband with them?' asked Winifred.

'Lieutenant Burke is helping with the evacuation,' the messenger replied. 'Be ready.'

Joseph and the Countess were sitting side by side on a table in one of the rooms on the top floor of the hotel. She was dishevelled, her hair falling into her eyes, the pins that had kept it in place having long since fallen out. There were dark smudges on her forehead, and beneath her unbuttoned jacket, her cream blouse was filthy. Joseph's jacket was unbuttoned too, his shirt equally dirty.

'We're hopelessly outnumbered,' he said, after taking a long drag from a cigarette. 'We're going to evacuate. I never thought it would end like this.'

'Nor did I,' she said. 'Although I understand the allure of making some kind of peace. But the Free State arrangement can't last, and when it collapses, we'll be back to where we are now.'

'Still fighting.' Joseph handed her the cigarette and she took a puff.

'Still fighting.' She grinned. 'They call me a rebel, and I am. A rebel for a free and independent republic.'

'We will have it,' said Joseph.

'I hope so,' said the Countess.

After a final puff of the cigarette, Joseph went to join the commanding officer, Captain Murphy, in the room where documents and arms had been stored.

'We're guarding them tonight, and in the morning we'll take them to your home,' said the captain. 'We'll have them moved from there as quickly as possible afterwards.'

'And how are we going to transport them?' asked Joseph.

'We'll commandeer a vehicle. At least, you will.'

Joseph nodded. Commandeering transport was one of his better skills.

In the meantime, however, he and some of the other republicans laid mines in the hotel. The owner, Annie Farrington, who had refused to leave when it was first occupied and who regularly bemoaned the fact that they were using her good furniture as a barricade, watched as Joseph placed a mine in position.

'Please don't blow it up,' she said. 'I still owe the banks money. If the hotel ends up as rubble, I'll have to pay them back and won't have any way of doing it. I appreciate you're doing what you feel you have to do, but surely to God ruining me any more than I'm already ruined isn't part of it.'

Joseph looked at her. Her face was pale and her eyes red-rimmed from crying.

'Are you coming with us?' he asked.

'I am not,' she said fiercely. 'I'm staying with the hotel. If the place is going up, I'm going up with it.'

She reminded him of Winifred.

He looked at the mine he'd laid.

'Don't worry,' he said. 'They won't go off.'

'Why?'

'I've detached them.'

'Truly?'

'I wouldn't lie to you. I don't want you going up with the building either. But you should leave and come with us. You'd be safer.'

'And let the Staters ransack the place?' She shook her head. 'This is my hotel. It was my hotel before you took it over and it'll be my hotel when you go.'

'I'm sorry we've caused you trouble,' said Joseph.

'You weren't my most profitable guests.' Annie gave him a rueful smile, then went back up the stairs.

Dawn was creeping over the rooftops of the city, but Agnes Burke was already prepared for the arrival of whatever materials would be stored at her home. Her heart was racing, both from nerves at potentially hoarding ammunition and grenades, and with relief that Joseph was still alive and hadn't been shot during one of the many gun battles of the past few days.

Her husband kissed her as he went to the boiler room, where there were now additional concealment areas in the floor. He'd dug them out after the house had last been raided and placed heavy equipment over the trapdoors. Ideally it would have been good to use the crypt as a storage area, but neither he nor Agnes wanted to compromise the nuns.

It was nearly eight o'clock when Winifred saw a bread van pull to a halt outside the house and a man in a brown shop coat jump from the driver's side. It took her a moment to recognise Joseph, and she rushed to open the gate.

'Quick!' he cried before she had time to say anything. 'We need to unload.'

And then men were running into the house with boxes and crates, which they passed from the back of the van. The entire operation took less than fifteen minutes, but when they'd finished, the room where Agnes had sheltered so many Volunteers in the past was packed with boxes.

'Someone will be along later to move them,' Captain Murphy told her. 'They're not safe here.'

'I understand.'

'Thank you,' he said.

When they'd gone, Joseph took off the shop coat and heaved a sigh.

Winifred put her arms around him and kissed him, not caring that Agnes was standing impatiently behind her.

'I was so worried for you,' she said.

'I was perfectly safe the whole time,' he assured her.

'I doubt that.'

'I was. And not only safe . . .' he grinned suddenly, 'but also the procurer of fresh bread!' He opened a box he'd left in the hallway to reveal a couple of loaves. 'Baked this morning.'

'Was the van driver one of ours?' asked Agnes as she inhaled the aroma of the bread.

'I don't know,' said Joseph. 'I waved my gun at him and told him to get out, and he did.'

'You robbed the van?'

'I borrowed it,' he amended.

'It doesn't matter,' said Agnes. 'Let's celebrate your return with some bread and jam and a pot of tea.'

* * *

Winifred had assumed that the documents and ammunition would be in the house for a few days, and she'd spent the last couple of hours telling herself not to think about the fact that St Anthony's Place was practically an armoury, but at six o'clock that evening, a different group of men from the Dublin Brigade began to move the boxes again, this time loading them into a red van marked *Swastika Laundry*. The vans were a familiar sight in the city, as the small hotels in the surrounding area often used the company for their laundry requirements. As the van drove away, Winifred felt a physical sense of relief, and her shoulders, which she only now realised she'd had hunched up all day, finally relaxed.

She put her hand on her belly.

'It's all right, baba,' she said. 'At least for now.'

They were sitting in the Yellow Room listening to Joseph's account of the last few days when the banging started at the door. Joseph and his mother exchanged glances, but it was Winifred who got up to answer it.

'We're searching these premises.' The Free State soldier at the door pushed past her, knocking her sideways. He strode down the hallway and into the Yellow Room.

'Burke,' he said to Joseph. 'Where have you been?'

'Here,' replied Joseph. 'Tending to my pregnant wife.'

'Don't lie to me.'

'He's not lying,' said Winifred from the chair where she'd sat down again, the gentle swell of her belly obvious to anyone who looked.

The soldier, barely out of his teens, stared at her in embarrassment and then ignored her as he began to search the

250

room. A dozen others fanned out and commenced their own searches. But although they spent over an hour in St Anthony's Place, they found nothing, not even the trapdoors in the floor of the boiler room, where John was shovelling coal into the furnaces, sweat pouring down his face.

'We know you were involved, Burke,' the young soldier said to Joseph when they were leaving empty-handed. 'Don't think we won't get you sooner or later.'

But they didn't, even though Joseph took part in more operations aimed at disrupting the National Army. He had devoted himself entirely to the cause, and his only income was what he was getting from the republicans. Fortunately, from Winifred's point of view, Mr Burke's job wasn't under threat, and the nuns occasionally gave the family extra food, so they were still living reasonably well. And it was fortunate too that they hadn't been asked to hide any more documents or people, so that despite the regular raids on St Anthony's Place, the soldiers always left empty-handed.

'They've shot Collins.'

Winifred had just walked in the door when May, who was putting on her coat to leave, told her the news.

'Collins? Michael Collins is dead?'

'How many other Collinses do you know?' asked May. 'This is great news.'

'No it's not,' said Winifred. 'A man is dead.'

'A traitor,' said May. 'Ambushed at Béal na Bláth by our forces in Cork.'

'That's terrible. You mightn't have agreed with him, but he had his principles.'

251

'Jesus wept. You don't see it, do you? He was an obstacle. He's been removed.'

'No,' said Winifred. '*You* don't see it, May. You've made a martyr out of him, and those Free Staters you despise so much are going to rally around him. There's nothing more powerful than a dead hero.'

'We've lots of dead heroes of our own,' May told her. 'Terence MacSwiney, Cathal Brugha shot last month—'

'We could paper the walls with lists of names of dead heroes,' said Winifred. 'But what good is that to the living?'

'My mother said you went to see your mother and sister yesterday. Are they feeding you this nonsense? Your brother, too? Because you sound like a Free Stater yourself. Have you been passing information? You creep around the house listening at doors, and God knows what you do with what you hear. You're a danger to us all, Winifred O'Leary.'

'It's Winifred Burke, and don't be so stupid, May,' said Winifred. 'My mother and sister are as entitled to their views as you are to yours. My brother is a child. And I'm the wife of someone who's probably going to get killed. In the end, his death will mean nothing, because history will be written in whatever way suits the victors. And that's going to be the Free Staters, because they have more support and are better equipped. How the hell is a badly organised guerrilla army that has to commandeer bread vans and laundry vans going to win against people with cannons?'

'We'll wear them down the same way we wore the Brits down,' said May. 'I thought I was wrong about you when you started to help us, but you're a dangerous woman, Winifred, and it was a mistake for my brother to marry you.'

'Strangely enough, he doesn't seem to think so.'

'He deserves your unconditional support,' said May. 'It's a pity you can't give it to him. And a worry too. Are you trying to turn him against us? Have you already succeeded? If so, it would be better if you both left this house.'

'That's not your decision to make,' said Winifred. 'And you know perfectly well where Joseph's loyalties lie. In any event, I'd do nothing to put this family in danger, even if the family itself seems to embrace it.'

She walked out of the kitchen and slammed the door behind her.

She called to see Esther the following day, picking her way through the rubble that lined the streets but thankful that the battle appeared to be over for now. Her friend looked harassed, her elder child toddling around the rooms, the baby crying in the lined drawer she was using as a cot, and signs of her third pregnancy very evident.

The air hung hot and heavy, and Esther continually pushed damp hair from her forehead.

'I feel like I'm living the same day over and over again,' she said while Winifred made tea.

'I know.' Winifred nodded. 'Every time we think there's an agreement, somebody says it's not the agreement they want and the next thing you know they're shooting at each other.'

'I'm not talking about the war, you eejit. I'm talking about being bloody pregnant. My body is wrecked with it. And Henry . . .'

'What about Henry?'

'Well, he seems to think that as long as I'm pregnant, that's his job done,' replied Esther. 'We used to want to do things together, but now he expects me to be at home all the time looking after the children while he goes out with his friends.'

'To meetings?' Winifred spooned tea into the battered tin teapot.

'Meetings? Meetings in the pub!' Esther snorted. 'Honestly, Winifred, it's like I don't exist any more.'

'I'm sure that can't be true,' Winifred murmured. 'Henry loves you.'

'Oh, take off those rose-tinted spectacles! They're the same ones I was wearing when I got married. It seemed like the right thing. I wanted to do it. And yet . . . well, it's not what I imagined. It was at first,' she added, 'before the children. But now . . . Don't get pregnant again, Winnie, that's my advice.'

'I thought you liked being a mother.' Winifred glanced at the baby as she put the tea in front of her friend.

'I do,' said Esther. 'But it takes over our lives. Why are we supposed to sit at home with children all day when men do what the hell they like? Who made that rule?'

'Maybe it was an Englishman.' Winifred made a face. 'Maybe before the English came here, women ruled the roost.'

'I doubt that very much. The problem isn't which country men come from. It's the men themselves.'

'I do hope you're wrong, at least where Joseph is concerned,' Winifred said as she rested her hand on her belly. 'If you don't want more children, Esther, haven't you ever tried—'

'Jesus, Winnie! You're not talking about getting rid of it? I'm not going to some woman who'd ply me with gin and then do God knows what so that I bleed to death. And if I didn't bleed to death, Henry would kill me anyway.'

'I'm not talking about getting rid of your baby! I'm talking about not getting pregnant in the first place.'

'I know there are ways,' said Esther. 'But Henry doesn't approve. And nor does the Church.'

'Who says you have to tell him? I said nothing to Joseph the first time I used the sponge. And the Church can stay out of it. A bunch of men who know nothing.' Winnie went on to describe the method to Esther, who listened with interest.

'I'll have to try something. I can't . . . I need a break, Winnie. I'm so feckin' tired all the time.'

'I'm getting tired myself now,' said Winifred. 'I think it's the heat. And everything that's going on around us. I hope things will be different when my baby is born. But I'm not holding out a lot of hope.'

'I used to think the best of everyone.' Esther took a sip of her tea. 'Now I think the worst. It's a terrible way to be.'

As her pregnancy progressed, Winifred wondered if Esther was right in her assessment of men. Despite still asking her how she was feeling every morning, Joseph's attention was now more fixated on the progress of the political situation, and the continuing aggression between the nationalists and the republican factions. Although pitched battles and raids continued through the autumn and winter, the Free State formally came into existence on 6 December; two days later, Northern Ireland rejoined the United Kingdom. The new Irish government met at Leinster House, where a message from King George was read out. But attacks and skirmishes between pro- and anti-Treaty sides persisted, with no sign that they were going to stop.

Unlike the previous year, when there had been a sense of hope at St Anthony's Place, that year's Christmas was bleak and uncompromising. The O'Learys weren't invited to visit, and Agnes, who was suffering with a bad chest infection, hadn't felt any desire to provide a festive meal. Ita was also poorly, and so Winifred, helped by Rosanna, did the cooking. Although both Agnes and Ita had improved a little by Christmas Day, conversation around the table was subdued. It seemed that even the Burkes didn't have the energy for yet more talk about war and politics. They were conscious of Winifred's conflicted emotions – and as May and Agnes often said to each other, her conflicted loyalties. As a consequence, she was left out of a lot of their conversations and felt more isolated than ever. They were conscious too of the friendships that had been affected by the split between the factions. Although Cumann na mBan members were officially against the Treaty, May's closest friend, Hetty, was ardently for it, and the two women hadn't met or spoken since the explosion at the Four Courts. May clearly missed her friend, and was even sharper than usual in her conversations. In another family row, the relationship with Agnes's brother and his family, which had once been cordial, was now frigid, as they had been big supporters of Michael Collins and considered his assassination to be treason.

Nobody had the strength to keep up with the shifting alliances, and in the short days and long nights of winter, nobody even cared what they were any more.

After the meal, Winifred went up to her bedroom and lay on the bed, closing her eyes but quite unable to sleep. Hers wasn't the only family that had taken different sides but it was difficult to be living with one when they thought your sympathies were with the other. Over the last few months, she hadn't been to East Essex Street at all. She was using her now advanced pregnancy as an excuse. But the reality was that she was afraid of being targeted by the anti-Treaty side, even though she was living in an anti-Treaty house.

It was nearly an hour before Joseph joined her.

'Are you all right?' he asked.

'I've never been so tired in my life,' she told him. 'I desperately want to go to sleep and not wake up until all this is over.'

'I know the feeling,' he said as he took off his shoes and lay down beside her.

'You don't,' she said. 'You're out there getting shot at, and even if it scares you, it also exhilarates you.'

'It really doesn't.' He put his arm around her. 'I'd much rather be here with you.'

'Would you?' She turned to look at him. 'Would you really? Because sometimes I think that you all secretly want this fight to go on forever.'

'I absolutely don't.' Joseph's words were vehement. 'I don't want to be planning strikes on police stations or breaking windows or anything like that. I want to be working for a better Ireland, one where everyone, no matter who they are, can prosper. One where there's education for all and where those in need are looked after.'

'Isn't that what the Bolsheviks want in Russia?' Winifred propped herself up on her elbow. 'And their war has been going on for five years. I can't bear the idea of us fighting each other while our child grows up.'

'We're not Russia,' said Joseph.

'But we could be.'

'Do you want to know how I really feel?' He put his hand on her belly.

'Tell me.'

'I don't think us republicans will win this war and have things how we want. But we have to keep the pressure on the British to change the Treaty so that Ireland is a sovereign republic and not a free state within the Empire. That's what's most important to me, Winnie. To know that our country is standing on its own two feet. So if there's a compromise to be made, I'll be happy to make it. Because I don't want our child to grow up in a country at war with itself either.'

'Promise?'

'I promise.'

'Thank you,' she said.

'Happy Christmas.' He kissed her gently on the mouth. 'You're the most important person in the world to me. And you always will be.'

Chapter 19

Dublin, spring 1923

Her baby was born in January, on a bright, cloudless day when the birdsong in the garden mingled with the sound of gunfire in the streets. The labour had been surprisingly easy – intense, yes, and painful too, but less tiring, Winifred thought, than nine months of being pregnant. When she heard the bellowing cry of her child, she couldn't quite believe that she was a mother, but she was overwhelmed by emotion as the midwife placed her tiny daughter in her arms.

'I will do everything I possibly can to keep you safe,' she whispered. 'I won't let anything bad happen to you. I'll die myself first.'

Despite the antagonism between her and her mother-in-law, Agnes had assisted the midwife at the birth and complimented Winifred on how well she'd done, telling her that she was a strong woman and that the baby was a real fighter, something she clearly got from her father. Winifred was too tired to say anything in return.

Ita and Rosanna tiptoed into the room and cooed with delight at the sight of them together.

'Can I be godmother?' asked Rosanna. 'Ita already is to May's eldest. It's my turn.'

Winifred had thought of asking Katy, but it was so long since she'd seen her and her mother, and because of the conflict between the families, she decided it was easier not to. So she nodded and Rosanna danced out of the room with delight.

'My clever, clever wife,' said Joseph when he was allowed in to see her. 'She's the prettiest baby I've ever seen.'

'I thought it was just me thinking that,' said Winifred.

'Absolutely not,' Joseph assured her. 'Luckily for her, she takes after you.'

Winifred laughed, and her husband smiled.

'Her future will be good,' he said.

'Will it?' Winifred looked up at him.

'No matter how things turn out, I'll make sure of that.'

She sent word to her mother that her baby had been born and told her that she would come to see her when she was able. Annie replied with a note saying that she was always welcome. Agnes knew that despite Winifred's anxieties about being caught up in fighting, she planned to go to East Essex Street as soon as she was recovered enough, and reminded her that it was important to have her daughter baptised before she took her anywhere.

'I told Rosanna she could be godmother,' said Winifred. 'I suppose she'll want James to be the godfather, if that's all right with Joseph.'

James was Rosanna's fiancé, the two of them having got engaged on her birthday a few weeks earlier. If Joseph and Anthony hadn't fallen out over the civil war, she knew her husband would have wanted him to be the godfather, but as it was, he agreed that Rosanna and James would be perfect.

The following day, while she was still confined to the house – even though she felt perfectly well and would have liked to go to the church herself, no matter that it wasn't the done thing and that she continued with her absolute lack of faith in God – Winifred handed her baby over to her sister-in-law to be baptised and sat quietly in the Yellow Room until their return.

It was a surprisingly quiet day, with no background gunfire or explosions to silence the birds, who were singing loudly in the bare branches of the trees. Winifred felt almost peaceful, a warm rug around her knees, her body more her own than it had been since she'd first realised she was pregnant.

Agnes had baked a cake and made sandwiches to celebrate her granddaughter's christening, and she set them out on the table shortly before the godparents and baby were due back.

'We're here!' Rosanna strode into the room, a beam stretched across her face. 'I'm finally a godmother. Rosanna Ita is now a Christian.'

'Who?' Winifred looked at her in surprise.

'Rosanna Ita.'

'But I told you I wanted to call her Anne Alice,' said Winifred.

'I'm her godmother and it's my choice,' said Rosanna. 'Besides, everyone's called Anne these days. Rosanna is much more unusual.'

'Not to me it's not,' said Winifred. 'I have a sister called Rosanna. She lives in Brussels. You know that already.'

'So your baby is named after both of us.' Rosanna smiled at her.

'I'm not calling her Rosanna,' said Winifred.

'Don't be silly,' said Agnes. 'It's a lovely name.'

'But it's not the name I chose!'

'Rosanna is right about calling her Anne,' said Agnes. 'You've already got an Annie and a Marianne in your family. As for Alice, it's too much of an English name. Surely you can see that?'

'Was this actually your idea?' demanded Winifred. 'And are you telling me you won't call my baby the name I picked because it sounds English?'

'There's a Princess Alice,' said Agnes. 'It wouldn't do to name a republican baby after a princess.'

'Oh for God's sake!' Winifred was both annoyed and exasperated. 'When will this family learn that not everything is a republican issue.'

She said the same to Joseph when he arrived home.

'It was very cheeky of them, but it's too late now,' he said. 'She's been named.'

'Well, I'm not calling her Rosanna,' said Winifred. 'She's my baby, and if they won't call her Anne, I'm picking another name.'

'What are you going to call her then?'

'Brenda.'

'What?' He stared at her in absolute astonishment. 'What sort of a name is that? I've never even heard of anyone called Brenda.'

'My sister in America has a friend called Brenda,' said Winnie. 'It's unusual. I like it.'

'You know she's always going to be Rosanna to my mother and sisters.'

'And she's always going to be Brenda to me.'

'Oh Winnie.' His face broke into a grin. 'It's a lovely name.'

'Do you really like it?'

'Yes,' he said. 'I do.'

She knew he was humouring her, but she didn't care.

She went to see her mother the following month. As she walked along the street, pushing the huge navy-blue perambulator that had been in the Burke family since the turn of the century, her eyes took in the absolute devastation of the city. There were more facades than actual buildings, she thought, anxiously aware that they were crumbling around her and suddenly terrified that a huge slab of concrete would fall on her and her baby, killing them both. She felt her heart start to race and her breath came in short gasps, and she had to stop and wait until the dizziness passed and she was able to continue her walk.

Annie was waiting for her at the door of the tenement.

'Winnie!' she cried, stepping out to greet her. 'It's so lovely to see you again.'

'And you.' Winifred hugged her mother fiercely.

'Leave the perambulator in the hall and bring the baby up with you. She's beautiful. Is she good? Does she sleep? Is she colicky? How are you managing with her?'

'When you stop asking questions, I might be able to answer one,' said Winifred as she followed her mother into their rooms.

'It's my job to ask you questions. And your job to answer them.'

And she did. She felt a welcome calmness as she showed off her baby to her mother and Katy in the cosiness of East Essex Street and talked about things that had nothing to do with war and freedom. It was a relief to be with people who

263

loved her for who she was, and who weren't trying to turn her into some republican rebel.

'And yet you always were rebellious,' said Annie with a smile when Winifred said this to her.

'I was not. Didn't I stay here when Mary-Jane and Rosie moved off, and when Katy got married? And when Marianne ran away to America? Wasn't I the only one to be a good daughter to her parents?' Winifred glanced at her sister, suddenly afraid she might have upset her by mentioning her ill-fated marriage, but Katy was smiling.

'Oh, you're a saint all right.' Annie laughed.

Winifred did too.

And in her head, East Essex Street became a place to be herself again, even though she really didn't know who that person was any more.

She was feeling happy and contented as she pushed the perambulator along the quays and headed back to St Anthony's Place. Every so often she blew kisses at her baby, who was sleeping soundly. Crossing Parnell Street, she stood back to allow a short file of children following a young boy on a tricycle go past. The girls had pillowcases with red crosses sewn on them tied around their heads, and the boy riding the tricycle carried a flag with the words *Red Cross* written on it in shaky lettering. There was a small cart attached to the tricycle and inside the cart was a rag doll.

'Do you need any injuries fixed, missus?' asked one of the girls. 'We're nurses.'

'Ah no, I'm grand, thanks.' Winifred smiled at them and nodded at the doll in the cart. 'I'm sure you need to take your patient to hospital.'

'He was shot in the leg,' said the boy on the tricycle. 'But we'll bandage him up.'

She didn't know whether to be horrified or amused by the children playing at tending to injured civilians. What have we come to? she asked herself. And then, as Brenda gurgled in the pram, she smiled and blew another kiss at her. Regardless of everything, she thought, life goes on. And in this mixed-up world of war and violence, you have to find happiness where you can.

She was still thinking this when she opened the door to the house and found it in complete disarray.

'What happened?' she asked.

'Those feckin' Free Staters!' Agnes spat the words out. 'They came for Joseph.'

'What?' Winifred felt the blood leave her face, and she held on to the banister for support. 'Who came for him? When? Where is he?'

'That bastard Padraig Shanahan. A man who was supposed to be his friend.'

'No!'

'Yes,' said Agnes.

'Where did they take him?'

'I don't know.' Her face crumpled. 'It was bad enough when the British were taking our boys, but now . . . now I don't even know who to ask.'

'I'll go and find out,' said Winifred.

'You can't,' said Agnes. 'It's getting late. It'll be dark soon. You can't go out on your own in the dark, and you just after having a baby.'

'And how are we to find out anything otherwise?' demanded Winifred. 'Look after her. I'll be back soon.'

She walked down Sackville Street, her head high, ignoring the groups of men clustered together, knowing that some or all of them were armed. She assumed they were the National Army and that therefore they had been the ones to take Joseph, but she didn't look at them even though her heart was filled with rage. Turning into Sackville Place, she stopped outside Kelley's Fine Fabrics. There were bullet marks in the walls, but the window had miraculously survived intact. She recognised her father's paintwork.

She took a deep breath and pushed the door open. The bell jingled, and a moment later Alice Kelley stepped out from the storeroom.

'Mrs Burke. Winifred.' She looked at her in surprise. 'What are you doing here?'

'Where's my husband?' asked Winifred.

'I'm sorry?'

'Padraig came for him. Where has he taken him?'

'I . . . Really, you can't come in here and start demanding—'

'But your husband's merry band of warriors can come to my home – my *home*, Alice – and drag my husband off without telling us where?'

'I'm sorry, but Joseph is a traitor.'

'Oh for God's sake!' Winifred looked at her furiously. 'He disagrees with something. It doesn't make him a traitor.'

'King George gave his blessing to the Free State,' said Alice. 'Being against it is wrong.'

'Fine. All right. My husband is wrong. But where is he?'

'How should I know?'

'Alice . . . please.' Winifred hadn't wanted to cry, but she couldn't stop the tears from rolling down her cheeks. Alice looked at her in silence.

'I don't know where he is,' she said again. 'But I'll try to find out. I'll send you what information I can.'

'Thank you,' said Winifred.

'He's in the wrong,' repeated Alice.

'I don't care,' Winifred said. 'I just want to know where he is.'

Alice nodded.

Winifred walked out of the shop.

When she arrived home, May had turned up, and all the Burke women were on their knees saying decades of the rosary.

'You took an age,' said Agnes as Winifred took the baby from her and kissed her. 'Have you any news?'

'No. But—'

Even as she spoke, there was a loud rap on the door. The women looked at each other anxiously. Then Agnes went to open it.

'Mrs Burke.' The young man outside was wearing a republican uniform. 'Francie O'Reilly is my name. I've come to tell you that Joseph is in Mountjoy gaol. But there's talk of sending him to Maryborough instead.'

'Jesus, Mary and Joseph,' said Agnes. 'That's in Portlaoise. Why?'

'Mountjoy is already overcrowded, and they don't want to add to it. Or to the supporters outside.'

Just as when he'd been imprisoned in Kilmainham and Winifred had joined the throng of women at the gates, crowds continued to mass outside the prisons, shouting words of encouragement to the prisoners and singing the rebel songs that had once also been sung by their gaolers.

Winifred, standing at the door to the Yellow Room, recognised

Francie O'Reilly as one of the men who'd rescued her and Alice when the Auxiliaries had come into the shop.

'Maryborough is more than fifty miles away,' she said to him. 'How am I supposed to visit him?'

Francie shrugged.

'Are you sure that's where he's going?' asked May.

'I can't be certain, but I'll find out. That's what I do,' he told her. 'I find out where the prisoners are and I tell the families.'

'How can we get him out?' asked Winifred.

'You can't. I'm going to be honest with you. They're being made an example of. We're trying to out-English the English when it comes to how they're being incarcerated and punished. The Staters need to be seen to be in control.'

'Are you a Free Stater?' asked Winifred.

'I'm an Irishman,' said Francie. 'I don't like to see another Irishman in prison. But these are the times we're in.'

'I truly can't believe it,' said Agnes. 'Joseph would have helped those boys in the past.'

'It's different now,' said Francie. 'I'm sorry for it, but it is. I'll be back when I know more.'

When he'd gone, Winifred took off her coat and hat and hung them on the hook. Then she went up to her room and lay on her bed with Brenda beside her, thinking that their joint happiness had been very fleeting.

Joseph had always known that he'd be arrested again eventually, and so the arrival of soldiers from the National Army hadn't surprised him. What had surprised him – although perhaps, he thought, disappointed might be a better word – was being arrested by Padraig Shanahan. He and Padraig had served together in the third battalion during the War of Independence. They'd looked out for each other. Had drinks with each other. Joked with each other about the things they'd do together when the war was over. Not in their wildest dreams did they envisage one of them arresting the other.

'*Et tu*, Paddy?' Joseph had said after a short scuffle in which Padraig had punched him in the face.

'You chose the losing side, Joe,' said Padraig. 'You've betrayed all of us.'

'That betrayal works both ways. The signing of the Treaty was a betrayal. Collins knew it was a mistake and he did it anyway.'

'It was a stalemate!' cried Padraig. 'Without it we would have been locked in a war with the Brits forever.'

'And now we're locked in a war with each other.'

'I don't have time for this.' Padraig shoved him towards the truck parked outside St Anthony's Place. 'I'm taking you to Mountjoy.'

'Home from home,' said Joseph. 'Sure I can hardly wait.'

Even though Mountjoy seemed to him even more crowded and insanitary than Kilmainham, Joseph wasn't expecting to be transferred to Maryborough. As he looked up at the forbidding grey building, he wondered if it was a worse place to be. It didn't take him long to decide that it was, especially as he was far from home now. And he doubted there'd be the same number of people protesting outside the Portlaoise prison as there were outside Mountjoy either.

'Prisoner 570,' said the guard. 'This is second floor, E wing. You're in Cell 1.'

'Ah.' Joseph smiled at him through his swollen lip. The

punch he'd received from Padraig had left him with a cut over it, as well as a black eye. 'The executive suite,' he said as he was pushed into the cell. 'Thank you for your hospitality.'

'Shut up, you rebel traitor.' The guard locked the door.

'We were on the same side until recently,' said Joseph. 'I'm hardly a traitor.'

'There's a government in this country and you're fighting it,' the man reminded him. 'So we don't want the same thing. You want anarchy.'

'I really don't.'

But the guard had gone, leaving Joseph to his own devices.

There was a thin mattress in the cell, and he sat down on it. He wished he'd been able to say a few words to Winnie before they'd taken him. He'd encouraged her to visit her mother that day, despite the tension between the Burkes and the O'Learys. He felt it was essential for her to be part of her own family as well as his. He knew that living at St Anthony's Place sometimes overwhelmed her, and it was important to him that she didn't lapse into a spiral of misery that she couldn't climb out of. She wouldn't be the first woman it had happened to, especially after childbirth and particularly over the last few years. And so he fretted that he hadn't been able to reassure her that he'd be all right. He knew she'd be worried about him. He could imagine her now, sitting in the Yellow Room, picking at a non-existent thread on a cushion, her mind racing and thinking nothing but the worst.

Mind you, he thought as he looked at the damp walls of his cell and the threadbare mattress on the floor, there isn't a big step from here to the absolute worst. So maybe Winnie won't be too far wrong in her imaginings.

Chapter 20

Portlaoise, spring 1923

A few weeks after Joseph's transfer, Winifred left the baby with her mother while she, Agnes and May took the train to Portlaoise to visit him at Maryborough. The train was crowded, and she was uncomfortably warm in her gabardine skirt and blouse. She'd folded her coat and put it on the rack above the seat, but despite the heat, she kept her hat firmly on her head for the entire journey.

They weren't the only passengers going to the prison. When they alighted at the station, many of their fellow travellers began to walk towards the large building with its castellated turrets almost a mile away. May's husband, who had a friend in Portlaoise, had organised a pony and trap for them, and the driver was waiting in the street outside.

'Up ye get,' he said as he assisted the women. 'I hope ye had a good journey.'

'As good as it could be,' said Agnes.

Green leaves were beginning to unfurl on the trees that lined the pitted road to the prison. Birds called to each other over the sound of the trap, and Winifred was glad of the slight breeze on the back of her neck as they passed those who were walking. She was surprised at the numbers, either groups or people on their own, and as she thought of how many men had been interned without trial, she felt anger ball up inside her.

'Here we are.' The driver jumped to the ground, then helped the ladies descend.

With dozens of families milling around the entrance, the scene was chaotic. The guards didn't seem to have a system, or even care very much who had come or which prisoner they wanted to see. In any event, none of the visits seemed to be organised. Even though Agnes had a letter saying she had permission to see prisoner 570, the guard she gave it to shrugged and told her he wasn't sure where Joseph Burke was.

'Cell 1, Level 2, East Wing,' Winifred informed him.

He stared at her without speaking, his eyes full of contempt.

'So now you know, you can go and get him,' she said.

'We don't have to bring him to you.'

'You'd bloody better,' said Winifred.

The guard laughed dismissively and walked away, the letter still in his hand. The three women were unsure if he'd return, but after ten minutes, he appeared again and led them inside to a cold room.

'Wait here,' he said, walking out and shutting the heavy door behind him.

The women looked at each other anxiously.

'We need to get him out of here,' said May.

'Help him escape, d'you mean?' asked Winifred. 'With a key in a cake? Like de Valera back in 1919?'

'Don't be silly,' said Agnes. 'Of course we can't help him escape. But there has to be a way to have him released.'

'If there was a way, wouldn't every prisoner be released?'

They stood in silence. As the cold seeped into their bones, they retreated into their own thoughts.

A further ten minutes later, the guard returned, accompanied by Joseph.

Winifred cried out and rushed to him, but the guard held her back.

'No consorting with the prisoner, or the visit ends,' he said.

Winifred took a step back.

'Hello, Winnie,' said Joseph. 'You're looking well.'

'You're not,' she said.

He smiled at her and shrugged.

'Mother of God, son, what have they done to you?' Agnes looked at him in consternation. 'Your poor face is ruined.'

'They've given me the beating they said I deserved, but sure that's no more than anyone here is getting. They're feeding me, but it's nothing you'd recognise as food. And they're betraying all the principles we've ever stood for—'

His words were cut off by the guard, who'd been standing at the wall and who now pulled Joseph's arm up behind his back.

'Not another word, Burke,' he said. 'You're lucky to be alive.'

'We're praying for you,' said May. 'A decade of the rosary every night.'

'You too?' Joseph asked, glancing at Winifred.

'I say different prayers,' she told him.

He smiled at her again, and then winked.

Even though her heart was breaking, she smiled in return.

'We've brought you some things,' said Agnes. 'Bread. Clean clothes. Newspapers.'

'I'll take them,' said the guard.

'You will not. He's entitled to food and clothes.'

'I'll take the newspapers.'

'Just as well,' said Joseph. 'I doubt the news is good.'

'The Countess has published some cartoons,' said May. 'Excellent ones, showing what's happening.'

'Good for her,' said Joseph.

'And I brought you these,' said Winifred. 'Your harmonica, so that maybe you can have a bit of music. And an autograph book. I thought maybe . . . well, you'll have friends here and they can sign it for you. Or you can use it for your writing. You've never had time for your writing, and maybe now . . .'

'Locked up with nothing to do will motivate me?' He nodded. 'I'm impressed that you're finding a positive side to this for me, Winnie.'

'Don't joke.'

'I'm not,' he said as he took the book from her. 'I like this. Thank you. How's our daughter?'

'She misses you.'

'She probably doesn't even notice I'm not there.' Joseph's voice was suddenly bleak.

'She does,' insisted Winifred. 'I tell her that her daddy will be home soon. I miss you too. And I hope you'll be out of here before too long.'

'I hope so too. But when I am, I won't treat the people who are guarding me with the same disrespect as they're showing to loyal republicans.'

'Shut it, Burke,' said the guard. 'Time for you to go, missus. I'm sorry you married this loser.'

'I'll never be sorry I married you, Joseph,' said Winnie. 'You'll always be my one true love.'

'Until she finds someone else,' the guard told him when the women had left and he was escorting Joseph back to his cell. 'She's a good-looking woman. She won't wait forever.'

Chapter 21

Dublin and Portlaoise, spring 1923

Brenda was a blessing, there was no doubt about it. If it wasn't for her and her calm and sunny nature, Winifred knew that the strain of Joseph's internment would be wearing her down every day. But she had to be bright and cheerful for her baby daughter, and she did her best to make every day a good one for her. Even though the baby was only a few months old, Winifred spoke to her as though she was an adult, talking to her about her father, telling her stories of how brave he was, and saying that when he got home, he'd be able to play the harmonica and the mandolin for her.

She sat with her in the garden as often as she could, and at least twice a week pushed her to East Essex Street, where Katy, who was enchanted by the baby, loved to play with her.

'She's an absolute treasure,' Katy said one morning when they were together. 'And as bright as a button.'

'She is, isn't she?' Winifred couldn't keep the pride from her voice. 'I know all mothers think their children are wonderful, but Brenda really is.'

'I adore her,' said Katy.

'If it wasn't for Reid, you'd have had children of your own by now,' Winifred said. 'And you'd have been a wonderful mother. Before I had Brenda, I wasn't too sure about it myself, but now, I'd never be without her. I can't imagine what it's like for you.'

'I've accepted not having children,' said Katy. 'But I think of the ones that might have been and I know they were with me for a time. And so I remember them.'

'Oh Katy.'

'I was such a fool over Reid,' she said. 'I believed him when he first apologised for hitting me. I never thought he'd do it again.'

'Have you heard anything at all from him?'

'Not a thing.' Katy shook her head. 'I truly did think he'd come to Dublin and try to haul me back. I was prepared for it. I rehearsed in my head the things I'd say. But he hasn't come. You remember he was supposed to have gone to Belfast?'

Winifred nodded.

'Well, I heard that he went to America. To New York.'

'In that case, hopefully he'll never come back.'

'Hopefully not,' said Katy.

'Are you happy?' asked Winifred. 'I know Reid was a bastard, but you did have your own home. And now you're back here with Ma and Tom.'

'Sure wouldn't one of us have wanted to look after Ma when she got a bit older anyway,' said Katy. 'As it is, her and me look after each other. And Tom . . .' she smiled, 'Tom looks after both of us. He takes being the man of the house very seriously.'

'Ah, he's a pet really.'

'And we're doing all right, Winnie.' Katy leaned forward and put her arm around her sister's shoulders. 'We're staying strong. You're staying strong. And Joseph will be home one day, I'm sure of it.'

That same day, Winifred went to see Alice Kelley again.

She pushed the door open and manoeuvred the perambulator inside. At the jangle of the bell, Alice came out of the stockroom.

'Winifred,' she said.

'I couldn't come before,' said Winifred. 'I was too . . . Everything was too difficult. But I wanted to say thank you for finding out what had happened to Joseph. For sending Francie O'Reilly to our house.'

'It was the least I could do. How is he now?'

'He's in Maryborough,' said Winifred. 'It's not the best place, Mrs Kelley, there's no pretending it is. And the treatment they get isn't good. But at least I know where he is and I've seen him.'

'I truly am sorry,' said Alice. 'I always thought he was a good man.'

'He still is.'

'This war is worse than the last. It's fractured everything. The country. Families. Friendships.'

'I know,' said Winifred. 'I thought *we* had a friendship, Alice, but you were always my employer.'

They looked awkwardly at each other.

'I'd better go,' Winifred said. 'My baby will need to be fed soon.'

'I'm happy that you have her.'

278

'So am I.'
'Winifred . . .'
'Yes.'
'Stay out of trouble.'
'I'll do my best,' said Winifred, and left the shop.

April 1923

Dearest Rosie,

It's lovely to hear from you again. Thank you for your good wishes for Rosanna, who I call Brenda. It's a long story. Congratulations on the birth of your second child. I'm very happy to be an aunt again. It would be nice for us to see our nieces and nephews one day. Ma is doing well, but she's aged since Da died. I'm glad Katy is with her, and Tom too. You wouldn't recognise him, he's got so tall and handsome. He's working in Smith's, the news-agent's, and he's doing well. Katy has a few hours' washing-up work, and Ma is still cleaning the steps at the theatre. It's called the Olympia now – after the ending of the War of Independence, the name Empire Palace was far too British for an Irish theatre.

I'm glad that you're safe and well and happy in Belgium. How I long to be somewhere else myself. Dublin is a nightmare. Ireland is a nightmare. Marianne was right to leave for America when she did, even though I thought she was making a mistake at the time.

I've only seen Joseph once since he was moved to Maryborough. Perhaps that's a good thing. Sometimes people call to the house with messages from him, so at least I know he's alive. But I find it hard to put the image

279

of the prison out of my head, and the stories coming out of all the gaols are hard to hear.

The so-called provisional government abolished the Supreme Court and its judges, and the president of the executive council, Mr William Cosgrave, said that 'we are not going to treat rebels as POWs'. So this means they can do what they like to people in prison, people who have still not been charged with any crime, and there's nothing anyone can do to stop them.

All the gaols are very crowded and I don't know what they're going to do if they keep detaining people. There's nowhere to put them.

Mrs Burke and her daughters continue to pray, but I can't do it. Especially because the Church has said that the republicans are guilty of murder and assassination. As though the National Army hasn't murdered and assassinated people itself! I realise that neither side should be murdering or assassinating anyone, but you can't say it's wrong for some and not for others. The hypocrisy of the Church makes me ill.

I got talking to a woman on the train home from Portlaoise. She has one brother in Mountjoy and the other is with Joseph in Maryborough. I went with her to Mountjoy yesterday and we stood on the North Circular Road, waving our flags and singing songs. The prisoners have dug out the window frames so they can lean out and shout back. It's very encouraging, for them and for us.

I do wish Joseph was there, even though I know the conditions are horrible. But they're horrible in Maryborough too and I can't go there every night to shout my support. That's the thing, though, Rosie, there is lots and lots of support for the men. Not necessarily because they're against the Treaty, although there's support for that, but people don't think we should be locking up our own.

It seems my life is a complete cycle of one fight after another.

But at least I have my lovely daughter to give me hope.

Love from your sister,

Winnie

Joseph's spirits had been lifted by Winnie's visit, and by her bringing his harmonica and the autograph book. He'd already begun to fill it with inspirational quotes and the signatures of his fellow inmates, some of whom included pen-and-ink drawings and cartoons mocking life in the prison, which was every bit as harsh as he'd expected it to be. When it was cold, it was too cold. When it was hot, it was too hot. The food was poor, the bread stale, and although the rat problem wasn't as bad as it had been in Frongoch years earlier, they still made frequent appearances.

The prisoners were, however, allowed to mix with each other, and in the evenings, Joseph often played the harmonica while the inmates sang along to songs like 'Kevin Barry', which commemorated a boy of eighteen who was hanged in Mountjoy in 1920, and 'The Wind that Shakes the Barley', a haunting melody made all the more dramatic by the acoustics of the stone walls.

The difficulty for all the internees was knowing that they'd fought side by side with the guards who were now imprisoning them. It left a bitter taste in Joseph's mouth, and he couldn't help wondering if the people of Ireland would ever be able to forgive or forget what they were doing to each other.

He still believed he was right to reject the Treaty. But he wished there'd been another way to change things.

Chapter 22

Dublin, summer/autumn 1923

Winifred was sitting on a rug in the garden, watching her five-month-old daughter as she tried to launch herself forwards. Over the last few days, Brenda had become very active, clearly wanting to get around by herself even if she wasn't quite ready to crawl yet. Winifred delighted in her attempts, holding her hands and encouraging her as much as she could. Being with the baby made her laugh and forget the continuing civil war and the internment of her husband.

The kitchen door banged open and Ita came running out.

'You'll never guess!' she cried.

'Joseph has been freed?'

Ita's face, which had been lit up with excitement, darkened momentarily.

'No, but as good as,' she said. 'Frank Aiken has told the brigades to stop fighting and go home.'

'He's given up?' Winifred looked at her sister-in-law in astonishment. 'The chief of staff of the republicans has called an end to it? The Free Staters have won?'

'Dev agrees. He said that more fighting would be in vain and that military victory should be with . . .' she hesitated, 'with those who have destroyed the republic.'

'So it was all for nothing,' said Winifred. 'All those deaths. And people like Joseph incarcerated. What does your mother think?'

'She doesn't want to accept it, but she will,' said Ita. 'We all have to, Winnie. We backed the losing side.'

'We did what we thought was right.' Winifred spoke automatically, even though she'd never been sure of what was right. But the idea that the civil war was over, that there would be no more fighting on the streets, and above all, that Joseph would soon be home was seductive.

'Francie O'Reilly is going to call to the house later with more information,' said Ita. 'But at least Joseph will be freed. Isn't that wonderful?'

The wind rustled through the trees and a cloud of apple blossom fell onto the rug. Brenda closed her fist around the tiny flowers and gurgled in delight.

'Yes.' Winifred was too dazed by the unexpected news to feel excited yet. 'It's wonderful. Oh my goodness, Brenda!' She picked up the baby and held her high in the air. 'Daddy's coming home!'

The news that the war had ended left the prisoners in Maryborough with mixed feelings.

'When will they let us go?' Paudie McLoughlin asked Joseph.

'I really don't know. I'm betting they'll eventually release us without ever having charged us at all.'

'I want to get home,' said Paudie.

'Don't we all.'

Joseph took his autograph book from his pocket and unfolded a piece of paper that was tucked behind the cover. It was the sketch that Jack Yeats had done of Winnie a couple of years earlier. She'd slid it between the pages of the book before giving it to him, and looking at it always filled him with resolve.

'Hey, you, Burke, you're with me,' shouted a guard, and Joseph replaced the sketch in the autograph book before slipping it into his pocket. 'You're being moved.'

'Not released?' asked Joseph.

'Chance would be a fine thing.'

'Where am I going?'

'None of your business. Get your stuff. Now.' The guard shoved him in the back.

Joseph gathered up the spare clothes that were folded on his mattress before joining another thirty or so men waiting outside the block.

'What's this about?' he murmured to the man nearest him.

'No idea.'

'Wherever we're going has to be a step up.'

'You're joking, right?'

'I probably am,' agreed Joseph.

They were marched from the prison and loaded onto wooden-sided transport trucks.

'Where are you taking us?' Joseph called out to the driver, who turned around to face him. 'Anthony?' He looked at his former friend in astonishment. 'What are you doing here?'

'What does it look like? I'm transporting prisoners to new accommodation.'

'Where?' asked Joseph.

Anthony didn't answer.

'For God's sake. Telling us where we're going won't change anything.'

'Knowing won't change anything either,' said Anthony as he secured the tailgate of the truck.

'The war is over. We should be released.'

'You're traitors,' said Anthony. 'You made things much harder.'

'Do you feel good and righteous?' asked Joseph. 'Treating your friends and colleagues like this?'

'You made a choice.'

'And you've made one too. To allow the Brits to dictate to us. To accept a deal that isn't a deal. To—'

'Shut your mouth.' Anthony drew a pistol from his belt. 'All of you are to keep quiet. You're criminals, not soldiers.'

'We're political prisoners, not criminals,' said Joseph.

'You once believed in everything Michael Collins stood for,' said Anthony. 'You would have defended him with your life.'

'And you once brought Cathal Brugha to my home and asked me to shelter him,' Joseph reminded him. 'My parents, me and my sisters would have defended him with our lives too. But your side shot him.'

Anthony fired his gun into the air, then got into the cabin of the truck. He started the engine, and the convoy of vehicles drove slowly out of the prison gates. Even though it was cold in the unsheltered back, Joseph and the other prisoners enjoyed the feeling of fresh air on their faces. After all, as one of them said, it might be the last fresh air they'd ever experience.

* * *

'He's been transferred to the Curragh,' Francie told the Burkes when he came to St Anthony's Place later that evening. 'There's more space there, although God knows for how long. They reckon there's over ten thousand interned now in various camps and gaols.'

'But why aren't they being released?' wailed Winifred. 'The war is over.'

'The Free State wants to punish them.'

'Haven't they been punished enough? The conditions they've been kept in? Rancid food? What more can they do to them?'

'I really don't know,' said Francie. 'I think they're trying to figure out how to neutralise them.'

'Neutralise?' Winifred moistened her lips with her tongue. 'Do you mean execute? Surely the government wouldn't stoop so low.'

'It would be a big mistake,' he agreed.

'Maybe they're moving them there to process them for release,' said Rosanna, who was bouncing Brenda on her lap.

'It's certainly closer to home,' said Winifred.

'But there's no train,' Agnes pointed out. 'So it's harder to get to.'

'It's still about half the distance,' Winifred said. 'It feels better.'

'Whatever you say.' Agnes indulged her daughter-in-law more these days. She was conscious that, hard though it was for her to know her son was a prisoner, it was even harder for Winifred. So she went easier on her than before.

'Maybe the conditions are better too,' said Winifred.

'Maybe,' said Agnes, without conviction.

*　*　*

The conditions weren't better. The camp had been handed over by the British the previous year, and the buildings were in poor repair. Many of the windows didn't have glass, something that Joseph reckoned might not matter too much in the warm days of summer but would mean it would be cold come the icy December winds that cut across the flat landscape. He hoped he wouldn't be there long enough to have his suspicions confirmed.

As he took his place in a long hut that seemed no better than a hay shed, Anthony walked up to him.

'You can sign out,' he said.

'What?'

'You can sign out. All you have to do is sign a declaration that you'll renounce being a republican and you can leave. Nothing more will be done. You'll be home to Winifred by tomorrow. You'll be with your little girl too.'

'You know I have a daughter?'

'I heard,' said Anthony. 'Listen to me, Joseph, these places are death traps. You'll become ill, everyone does. You could die here. Is that what you want from your life?'

'No,' said Joseph. 'But the life you're offering me isn't the one I want for my wife and daughter either.'

'You always were a stubborn fool.' Anthony shook his head, then turned and walked away.

'Right,' said Joseph as he rejoined the group of men who were also assigned to his hut. 'Who's in charge here?'

Chapter 23

Tintown internment camp, the Curragh, July 1923

Darling Winnie,

Well, despite everything, we are still here. Still prisoners of the state. I don't think they know what to do with us. The guards have allowed us to get on with it, and we have organised ourselves as best we can with a command structure based on our ranks. We are allowed to cook (this is not a big concession; our food rations are woefully inadequate, and what cooking is done is unappetising). My mother would be horrified at what I am currently eating. If you can send parcels, please do. Toiletries and clothes along with any type of food you can manage would be very welcome. More stationery too, if that's at all possible.

I have no idea how long I'll be here.

My hut, Tintown 3, is no better or worse than any of the others, although I would describe conditions as primitive. We have arranged activities among ourselves, and I am teaching some of my colleagues to play the harmonica. A women's group sent us a few additional ones. (The local women have a prisoners' support group, and they try to improve conditions as well as occasionally sending us items like soap – and harmonicas!) I am also learning French, though I doubt I'll ever get the opportunity to use it, unless your sister Rosie comes to visit! It is, however, a very graceful language. Certainly the language of love, not war.

I hope you are keeping well and that Rosanna Ita (Brenda) is thriving. I promise you, Winnie, that I will come home to you. And I cannot wait to kiss your darling lips again.

Your loving husband,
Joseph

August 1923

Dearest Joseph,
It is always good to get your letters, although sometimes they are delayed and then two arrive together. And sometimes they are censored, although I can usually guess what you're trying to tell me. Despite the terrible conditions you're living under, I'm pleased to say that your penmanship is very elegant. Though I would rather you were here than a million of your letters, no matter how beautifully written they are.

I am enclosing a photograph of Brenda. Isn't she pretty in her knitted coat and hat? It's pale pink. Katy did it for me. She has taken to knitting to calm her nerves and also keep her fingers active when she's at home. I didn't know it before, but Reid also broke her hand in one of his attacks. She now suffers from rheumatism in it. I count myself so very lucky that I married you and not a man like him. There is still no word of him, which is a good thing.

I presume you heard that Dev has been arrested again? He was trying to make an election speech when they grabbed him. Honestly, it's like there are more prisoners than free men in the country right now.

Out here, there are lots of protests at the conditions under which you're being kept. Maud Gonne MacBride has organised a campaign for the release of prisoners, and there are regular parades through the streets protesting the situation. I don't know if you know that she was arrested in April for 'painting banners for seditious demonstrations' and 'preparing anti-government literature'. Unlike you, however, she was only kept captive for twenty days. I'm not sure if it was because she's a woman, or because she was Yeats's lover, or MacBride's wife – perhaps it doesn't look well to keep the wife of someone who was executed in 1916 in prison. Or maybe they still don't like putting the Anglo-Irish behind bars. The Countess (I do love that woman) is also vocal about the conditions for prisoners. Of course, she has experience of them herself. I have gone on many of the marches and there is something very powerful about being with people who all want justice. I have my own placard. It says 'Free Our Brave Political Prisoners Now'. Of course we still sing outside Mountjoy and Kilmainham. I wish you were there so that I could perhaps see you at the window with some of the others. And yet the conditions are so bad that I'm afraid you would be worse off. Though I'm sure you don't think you could possibly be worse off.

I long to see you and to have you close to me again.
Your loving wife,
Winnie

Tintown internment camp, the Curragh, October 1923

Darling Winnie,

I have joined with our compatriots being held here and in other prisons for over five months since the cessation of hostilities without being charged, and we have agreed to go on hunger strike. Please do not worry about me. It's been building up to this and I am relatively fit and well.

This is our pledge:

We pledge ourselves by the living republic to the lives of our comrades that we will not take food or anything except water until we are unconditionally released – all we are about to suffer we offer to the glory of God and for the freedom of Ireland.

There are more than three thousand of us refusing food. They will have to release us. It is unconscionable to keep us without charge for another day. We are in fine spirits, and not eating what they call food here is no great hardship anyhow.

I think of you and of our daughter every day.
Your loving husband,
Joseph

Chapter 24

Dublin, winter 1923

Joseph and his fellow prisoners in the Curragh were not the only ones to go on hunger strike. In prisons and camps around the country, internees were refusing food and demanding to be released. Winnie considered joining the strike herself, even as she remembered only a few years earlier thinking it was something she'd never do. But her mother-in-law begged her not to, saying that Brenda needed at least one parent who wasn't starving themselves to death. Agnes was torn about her son's decision, supporting his motives while still wishing he wasn't doing it. She, along with Winifred, May and Katy, protested almost daily about the prisoners' continued incarceration, standing outside Mountjoy and Dublin Castle, marching in support of the hunger strikers and demanding to know why, with the civil war at an end, people were still being held.

'There's no sympathy for them,' said Winifred as she and Katy sat in the Gresham Hotel in early November. The evening had already drawn in and darkness was beginning to fall over the city. They had spent nearly three hours outside the GPO with their placards, and Katy had insisted on getting some tea afterwards. They'd left the placards at the side of the hotel before going in. 'Everyone's tired of fighting, they're happy to accept the Free State, and nobody cares about political prisoners any more,' she added. 'I feel like we're shouting into the wind.'

'That's not true,' said Katy. 'There were plenty of women outside the GPO today.'

'But the state itself doesn't care,' said Winifred. 'Even the Church – not that I give a damn what priests say – is totally against them now. I heard that anyone who dies because of the strike won't be buried in consecrated ground.'

'Joseph won't die,' Katy assured her.

'It's been almost a month,' said Winifred. 'Nobody can survive more than a month without eating. And despite what he says, it isn't as if he was strong anyway. You know how easily he catches cold, and Tintown is bitter now. Everyone says so.'

'I'm so sorry,' said Katy. 'I really am.'

'I understand why he's doing it. They should be freed. It's disgraceful that they haven't been. But the government has to appear to be strong, and they won't care if their political opponents starve themselves to death. And here I am,' added Winifred, 'having tea with you as though I was a lady of leisure and my husband wasn't dying.'

Katy reached across the table and grasped her sister's hand. The two women stayed as they were for a moment, and then, to their surprise, a man stopped in front of them.

'Miss O'Leary,' he said.

Both looked up at him.

'Do you remember me? Jack Yeats.'

'Of course I remember you.' Winifred cleared her throat. 'It's good to see you again.'

'Are you well?' he asked.

'I . . . Yes.'

'Are you still Miss O'Leary?'

'No.' She shook her head. 'Mrs Burke.'

'Congratulations.'

'I'm not sure that's exactly the right word.'

'Oh, why not? May I join you?'

When this time she nodded, he pulled up a chair.

'What's the problem?' he asked.

She told him about Joseph and the others in Tintown, and how scared she was that he was going to die, and how abandoned she felt by the state, who saw the anti-Treaty citizens as opponents rather than people.

'I'm so sorry,' said Yeats. 'I wish there was something I could do to help.'

'There's nothing,' said Winifred. 'But thank you for saying it.'

'Where are you living now?' he asked. 'Are you safe yourself?'

'Oh yes. There hasn't been a raid on St Anthony's Place since they arrested Joseph. And we haven't been involved in anything . . . subversive ourselves. I'd support the state now if the state supported me.' She glanced at Katy. 'My parents and my sister were in favour. My father has passed away since we last met.'

'I'm sorry to hear that. It's a difficult situation you're in.'

'Aren't we all in difficult situations these days?'

'Indeed.' He stood up. 'I hope it turns out well for you, Mrs Burke. I hope your husband gets what he's looking for.'

'Thank you.'

Yeats raised his hat and moved away.

'Nice man,' observed Katy.

'Too old for you.' Winifred gave her a weak smile, and then glanced at the clock on the wall. 'I'd better get back. Ita is looking after Brenda, and she's not really the maternal sort.'

'I thought you told me she'd got engaged,' said Katy.

'That still doesn't make her maternal,' said Winnie. 'At least, not yet. Rosanna is better at looking after children, but of course she won't call Brenda by her proper name; she insists on calling her Rosanna too.'

'Poor Brenda,' said Katy. 'She'll be so confused when she's older.'

'Living with the Burkes would confuse anyone,' said Winifred. 'Both Rosanna and Ita want to get married next year. They're hoping Joseph will be released before then. It doesn't seem to occur to them that if he isn't released, he'll have starved himself to death. I don't want to be a widow, Katy.'

'I don't want you to be one either.'

'In his last message, Joseph told me to be happy. He said that if he died, I was to find happiness with someone else. He said I deserved that at least.'

'Oh Winnie. I'm sure . . .'

'None of us can be sure of anything,' said Winifred.

'Would you?' asked Katy. 'Find someone else?'

'There'll never be anyone for me but Joseph. And I won't even think it while there's still hope for him.'

'I understand.'

'What about you? Would you find someone else?'

'Even if I could, with Reid still out and about there some-where, who'd have me?' Katy shook her head. 'I'm too old,

I'm crocked, and I can't have children. Besides,' she added, 'I'm not going to repeat my mistake. I never want to be close to a man again either.'

'It's so sad,' said Winifred. 'Your husband was a bad man and he got away with it. Mine is a good man and he'll probably die for his beliefs.'

'I know you don't pray, but I will,' said Katy as they got up to leave. 'I prayed for deliverance from Reid and that prayer was answered. So maybe this one will be too.'

There was frost on the inside of the window. Joseph could see a spiderweb of ice spinning its way across the glass, blurring the image of the dark sky outside, making the stars themselves fuzzy. But not when he looked through the hole in the window. There the stars were bright points of light. The same points of light that could be seen everywhere in the world, not just in Tintown. He wished he could see them more clearly. His fingers moved up his face and touched the socket where his glass eye should be. He wondered what had happened to it. Why he hadn't put it in. Why the empty socket was so painful.

'Burke.' He felt warm liquid on his lips, but when he looked down, he didn't have a glass in his hand. 'Burke.'

He realised his good eye was closed. But how, he wondered, could he have seen the sky and the stars if his eye was closed?

'Drink this. It's Bovril.'

He opened his eye to see a guard standing over him, an enamel mug in his hand. He touched his face again. He could feel the glass eye in its socket, where it should be.

'Only water,' he whispered through cracked lips. 'Only water.'

'You said you were going on hunger strike until you were released,' said the guard. 'You've been released, Burke.'

Joseph stared at him, not really understanding what was being said.

'You and your comrades. You're being released. Drink this.'

'Trick?' he murmured.

'No trick,' said the guard, his voice less brusque. 'We're letting you go.'

Joseph was still having trouble understanding what was being said to him. But he felt the rim of the cup against his teeth, and the savoury aroma of the beef drink was too much to resist. He swallowed, then gagged.

'That's it, Burke,' said the guard. 'Back to the land of the living with you. You'll be out of here in a few days. Your transport is already arranged.'

It was the end of the week before he and the other hunger strikers were fit to be released, although as he said himself, fit was pushing it a bit – all of them had problems with their vision and hearing, and they found it difficult to walk as far as the truck that was bringing them to Dublin. But at least they were finally being let go. He could hardly allow himself to think of spending the night at home again, of lying in bed beside Winnie, feeling the warmth of her body against his. And of seeing his daughter, who was nearly a year old by now. He hadn't expected to be interned for so long. Five months in Maryborough and the same in the Curragh. Almost a year of being locked away from his family, and for what? Certainly once the first Dáil had convened as the governing body of the Free State, there was no going back.

And there'd be no more fighting. Not by him. Not by anyone close to him.

He'd lost this particular war. But he wanted to be able to shape the republic so that it wasn't a mirror image of Britain. He wanted it to be inclusive. He wanted it to be a country where everyone was cherished. Where the state looked after the poorest.

First, though, he wanted to go home.

Winifred was almost sick with anticipation. She knew that Joseph and his fellow inmates were due to arrive in Dublin that afternoon. Francie O'Reilly had told her that they'd be released outside Dublin Castle. May had organised for a Cumann na mBan group to meet them there, and although Winifred would have preferred to see Joseph for the first time in months on her own, she appreciated the idea of the internees being welcomed by the people who had protested daily for their release.

And so here she was standing outside the gates of the castle, Brenda in her arms, waiting impatiently for the transport truck to arrive. The women were singing as they always did, and they continued to hold placards calling for the release of all the prisoners. The National Army soldiers around the castle watched them carefully, but didn't engage with them.

At last the truck arrived, to wild cheers from the assembled crowd. Winifred felt herself being carried forward in the surge, and she tightened her grip on her daughter. The tailgate was lowered and the men, their clothes too big for their bodies, began to emerge. She looked anxiously for Joseph, suddenly afraid that things hadn't worked out and he wasn't there. When she eventually saw him, she gasped in both shock and relief.

He was the thinnest of the lot. His face, always gaunt, was hollow, and clumps of his previously thick hair had fallen out. She pushed her way towards him, calling his name, although she knew he couldn't hear her above the noise of the crowd.

Then he turned towards her, blinking in the sunlight.

'Joseph!' she cried. 'We're here.'

She saw him register the sound of her voice, and she pushed forward again until she was beside him and putting one arm around him while still holding on to their daughter.

'Joseph. My Joseph.'

'Winnie.' His voice was raspy. 'You came.'

'Of course I came, you absolute eejit,' she said. 'How could I not? We've arranged a trap to take you home.'

May, who'd stuck close to Winifred, embraced her brother.

'Welcome back, Joseph,' she said. 'You're a true hero of the republic.'

'I wouldn't quite say that.' He blinked again. 'We didn't get what we wanted.'

'You got lots of attention,' said May. 'The world's press was focused on what was happening here. And you've been released, that's the main thing. Now we're going home. Come on.'

She led the way through the throng, who continued to cheer the returning men and reach out to pat them on the back.

Joseph climbed unsteadily into the trap and sat down.

'Dada.' Brenda waved her arms.

He looked at Winifred and the baby.

'Dada.'

'How does she know?' he asked.

300

'We've been talking about nobody but her dada for almost a year,' said May. 'Of course she knows.'

'To be exact, she calls every man she sees Dada.' Winifred smiled. 'Eventually she was bound to be right.'

Chapter 25

It was a jollier Christmas. For the first time since the Rising of 1916, the undercurrent of imminent or actual war wasn't the main topic of the conversation around the table. Most of the chatter concerned the family, and the upcoming nuptials of both Rosanna and Ita. Agnes had suggested that a double wedding might be nice, but Rosanna said she wasn't going to share her special day with her sister. Ita joked that she wasn't offended by that, and Rosanna said she wasn't being offensive, merely stating a fact.

'I wouldn't want to overshadow you, Ita,' she said. 'Not on your wedding day.'

'Oh! You don't think I'd be overshadowing you?'

'You could,' agreed Rosanna, flicking her fingers through her long wavy hair. 'But I look better in photographs.'

'In your dreams,' Ita laughed.

Winifred listened to them baiting each other, enjoying the banter that had been missing from their lives for so long.

The following day, she and Joseph went to East Essex Street, where Annie fussed over her son-in-law in a maternal way that Agnes hadn't. She made sure he had the chair closest to the fire and made him a beef broth that she insisted was from her own special recipe and guaranteed to put some skin on his bones. She wanted to hear about his experiences in Maryborough and the Curragh, and much to Winifred's surprise, because Joseph had been reluctant to talk about it much, he related stories of casual cruelty towards the prisoners that made her grasp his hand and squeeze it tightly.

'I'm really sorry,' Annie told him. 'I know we were on different sides, not that I ever picked a side as such, more that I thought the Treaty was the best way to go. That's what Thomas would've thought too. But treating people the way you were treated was wrong.'

'Everyone did things they're ashamed of now or will be in the future,' said Joseph. 'We can all claim we did them with the best of intentions. Even the burning of the Custom House.'

'Even that,' agreed Annie. 'I heard some of the things they said about the prisoners. I'm not sure that any of those intentions were honourable.'

'We have to put it behind us and move forward for the good of the country,' said Joseph. He began to cough violently and put his mug of broth down on the table. 'Sorry. I can't shift this damn cough.'

Winifred shot him an anxious look, and when the bout of coughing finished, he told her not to worry.

'I'm used to my dodgy lungs,' he said.

'You need to build yourself up.' Annie took the mug and added more broth to it. 'You should wear flannel against your chest. Hold on,' she added. 'I have some.'

'I really don't think . . .'

But he didn't have a chance to finish the sentence, because

Annie had already opened the chest of drawers and taken out a roll of pink material.

'I'm not sure . . .' Joseph looked at it doubtfully.

'Nobody will see the colour under your shirt,' she said. 'And here.' She handed him a square piece of cloth on a cord. 'It's the holy scapular of St Joseph. I got it from the Pro-Cathedral when I heard you were being released.'

Joseph took the cloth and looked at it. The fragments of cloth were violet and gold; the image of St Joseph holding the baby Jesus was embossed on the front of one gold segment while the papal crown decorated the other.

'It will protect you,' said Annie.

'I should have had one before now,' he quipped.

'God was looking over you,' his mother-in-law said. 'And I want him to keep looking over you so that you can look over Winnie and your little girl.'

'I'll always look over her,' promised Joseph. 'Now that I'm back and the war is at an end, I'm going to find work again and make sure we're a solid family.'

'Good,' said young Tom.

'I believe you're working in Smith's now,' said Joseph.

'I'm changing jobs. I've been offered a position with the railways.'

'Even better. I'd like to take Winnie on a trip.'

'Where to?' She looked at him enthusiastically.

'Cork perhaps?'

'The rebel county?' Tom made a face. 'You wouldn't think of anywhere less troublesome? After all, that's where Collins was assassinated.'

'Shouldn't the whole idea of moving on mean that we don't associate every place in Ireland with some issue of the war?' demanded Winifred. 'I'd love to go to Cork. I've never been.'

'Neither have I,' said Joseph. 'But I met a lot of Cork men in prison and they all talked about how beautiful it was. At least before the Auxiliaries tried to burn it to the ground back in 1920. Actually,' he added, 'I met men from all over Ireland, and all of them talked about how beautiful their home county was. And not that I don't love Dublin with all my heart, but right now, you can't really call it beautiful, can you? Not with half the buildings nothing more than rubble.'

'It will be again,' Annie said. 'When we rebuild.'

'There's so much rebuilding to do.' Winifred's voice was thoughtful. 'Not just of buildings, but our lives. And ourselves.'

The week after Christmas, a delivery boy arrived at the gates of St Anthony's Place and rang the bell. Agnes, who'd been polishing the brass on the door, took the square brown paper parcel from him and brought it into the house, where Joseph and Winifred were sitting in front of the Yellow Room's large fire.

'It's addressed to you,' she said, looking at Winifred.

'Me? Who's it from?' asked Winifred in surprise.

'I don't know.'

'A secret admirer?' Joseph raised an eyebrow.

'Certainly not. It looks like a picture frame.' Winifred frowned. 'I didn't order a frame. It must be a mistake.'

'It's very definitely addressed to you, though.' Joseph pointed to the label. 'Look. Mrs Winifred Burke, St Anthony's Place.'

'How strange.' Winifred began to untie the string around the parcel, but the knots were too tight, and in the end Joseph got a knife and cut them. She pulled the paper gently away and then gasped in astonishment.

She recognised herself in the painting. Or at least she recognised the impression of a woman wearing a brown coat and brown hat, a cup of tea in her hand, that looked like her.

'Goodness!' exclaimed Agnes. 'It's you.'

'There's a note,' said Winifred. She picked it up and read it. '"To Mrs Burke. I've sketched you once and painted you once. I hope you like this. Best wishes to you and your husband. I heard he was released. Jack Yeats."'

'Jack Yeats? The painter? He's the man who did this.' Joseph took the sketch from his jacket pocket and unfolded it.

'I met him in the Gresham,' recalled Winifred. 'I went there with Katy. He remembered us from before.'

'It's very presumptuous of him to paint your portrait,' said Agnes.

'It's not exactly a portrait.' Winifred looked at it critically. 'And it's not exactly me either, is it? It's a woman having a cup of tea.'

'It's definitely you,' said Joseph. 'He's got you so well. The way you hold your cup. The way you tilt your head.'

'I hope you and he—'

'Oh for heaven's sake!' Winifred shot an exasperated glance at her mother-in-law. 'I told you. Katy and I were having tea and he said hello. And the time before, Joseph was with me along with Anthony and Bridget.'

There was a moment's silence at the mention of Anthony's name. Although some friendships were being slowly repaired following the war, Joseph hadn't seen Anthony since the day he'd arrived at the Curragh. And he didn't want to see him either.

'Well, it's a very generous gift. Mr Yeats is becoming quite well known,' said Agnes. 'But I'm not sure you should accept it, Winifred.'

'I don't see why not,' said Joseph. 'I think it's a lovely picture and we should hang it in our bedroom.'

'Are you sure?' asked Winifred.

'I am.'

He didn't wait, but went to the boiler room and took a picture hook, nails and a hammer from the workbench. Then he hung the picture of Winifred over their bed.

Chapter 26

Cork, summer 1924

It was the following year before Joseph was finally able to fulfil his promise to bring Winifred on a holiday, something he hoped would release the pent-up anxiety that still hadn't entirely left her. He booked tickets on the train from Kingsbridge to Cork and a room in a small hotel on the banks of the Glashaboy River. Mr Burke brought the family to the station on a trap and told them to have a wonderful time.

The platforms were full of people who, now that they could do so more safely, were anxious to be on the move again. Winifred settled into her seat, Brenda on her lap, and looked out at the scenery flashing by. After being surrounded by nothing but scarred grey buildings, she was enchanted by the emerald green and vivid yellow of the fields as the train passed through the countryside, never having seen so much open space before. She imagined life in the small towns and villages she saw, wondering how it had been for them during the war, and thinking of the stories Katy had told her about life in the country. Beautiful though it was, she wasn't at all sure she'd like it herself, even though the land was so green and vibrant compared to the drabness that was the city.

Nevertheless, she was delighted to arrive at the picturesque country hotel where they were to spend the three nights of their break.

The hotel was a two-storey whitewashed building with a thatched roof and a riverside garden filled with flowers. The sound of the water rushing over the stony bed was soothing, as was the birdsong that filled the air. It was calm and relaxing, and for the first time in a long while, Winifred felt a weight lift from her shoulders. The middle-aged couple who ran it, Malachy and Bridie O'Sullivan, welcomed the Burkes warmly and showed them to a small room under the eaves, where they'd placed a wooden crib for Brenda.

'And what a lovely name she has,' said Bridie. 'After St Brendan, is it?'

'Yes,' said Winifred, judging it was easier to agree than to explain how she'd chosen the name at random.

'A great saint altogether,' said Bridie. 'And a proud Munster man, even if he was from Kerry.'

Joseph smiled. Rivalry between the counties in every province of the country was legendary.

'There'll be a meal for you at six o'clock,' continued Bridie. 'If you don't mind me saying, you both look like you need a bit of a rest first. And then some proper home cooking.'

'Is she casting aspersions on *my* home cooking, d'you think?' asked Winifred when they were alone in the room together. 'How does she know it's awful?'

'It's not that bad,' said Joseph, even though he crossed his fingers behind his back. 'But then anyone from outside

Dublin thinks they know best when it comes to putting food on the table.'

'I suppose they have a better chance of getting fresh produce,' conceded Winifred. 'And I did catch a great smell of newly baked bread when I came in. D'you think there'll be bread and jam for tea?'

'And more, I hope,' said Joseph.

'It's so good to be alone with you again.' She leaned her head on his shoulder.

And even though she wasn't strictly speaking the truth, because Brenda was trying to climb his leg, he agreed.

There was indeed bread and jam and more. Bridie provided eggs and cuts of cold meat, as well as mugs of strong, dark tea. Two other couples were staying at the hotel, and all six guests sat at the long table in the front room. Conversation was stilted at first, but then turned to easy topics like fishing and farming, neither of which the Burkes knew anything about. They didn't contribute much, but listened with interest while making sure that Brenda, who had been provided with mashed egg on a slice of brown bread, didn't annoy the other guests.

It was, Winifred thought, a welcome change from meals around the table at St Anthony's Place, and it was lovely to sit with people who didn't know anything about them and who consequently didn't make her feel as though she was an interloper into the group.

Later that night, when Brenda was sleeping, Joseph and Winifred sat outside in the warm summer air and chatted to one of the couples, Matt and Delia Murphy, who were from Killester on the north side of Dublin and who'd spent a week on Matt's cousin's farm in nearby Bandon before coming to the hotel.

'Well, I say my cousin, but he's just some connection with the family,' said Matt as he lit a cigarette and then offered one to Joseph. 'I really don't know a lot about farming myself. I'm a bit of a bluffer.'

Joseph took the cigarette and said that he had sounded knowledgeable enough.

'Only from what Frank told me,' Matt admitted.

'You're obviously a quick learner.'

'You have to be in this country.' He laughed. 'Will we take a turn along the riverbank? It's such a nice evening.'

The two women decided to stay where they were, and they sat in silence for a moment as they watched their husbands stroll away. Then Delia, a pretty young woman who Winifred reckoned was three or four years younger than her, asked about Brenda.

'She's the loveliest baby ever,' Winifred replied. 'So good and so placid.'

'We've been married six months and I'm not expecting yet.' Delia placed a hand on her own flat belly.

'It's good to have some time on your own,' said Winifred. 'Get to know each other. Your husband is quite a bit older than you, isn't he?'

'He's thirty-five.' Delia nodded. 'Fifteen years. But he's a good man and he'll look after me. He was married before,' she added. 'His wife died in childbirth.'

'Oh.'

'So I'm hoping . . .'

'I'm sure everything will be fine for you,' said Winifred.

'We say that, don't we?' Delia pushed a strand of her fine

311

blonde hair from her eyes. 'But we put our lives at risk all the time when we have children. And yet that's our job.'

'Our job?' Winifred frowned.

'I mean, what's the point of being a woman if you don't have a baby?'

There was plenty of point, thought Winifred. Over the last years women had shown that they could be fighters, protesters, negotiators and members of Parliament as well as mothers. She said this to Delia.

'I can't imagine a mother rushing onto the streets with a gun.' Delia shuddered.

'Well, Countess Markievicz did, but I suppose she didn't have a baby under her arm at the time.'

'Nevertheless,' said Delia, 'her job really was at home. She only had one child, didn't she?'

'And a stepson, I believe,' said Winifred. 'The girl was sent to her grandmother. Well, she's a woman now. The same age as me, I think.'

'I think she was crazy,' said Delia. 'She should've been with her husband and baby, not taking part in riots and making speeches.'

'And yet she achieved a lot,' said Winifred. 'So, like I said, a mother but also a person.'

'The most important thing for me is to be a mother,' said Delia. 'Mattie wants a son.'

Winifred nodded. Men always wanted sons, although Joseph had never said this to her and was besotted with Brenda. Still, she was sure he'd like a boy.

'I read that carrots and red beet are good for having boys,' she said.

'Really?' Delia's blue eyes opened wide.

'And garlic for getting pregnant in the first place.'

'Garlic? Where would I get garlic?'

'I don't know,' admitted Winifred. 'It's just something I read.'

'Do you read a lot?'

'A good deal.'

'I don't like reading,' said Delia. 'But the information is useful, thank you.'

'You're welcome.'

'I think I'll go to my room now. I want to be ready when Matt gets back.'

She got up and went inside, but Winifred stayed where she was, thinking about the younger woman's words. There was no question but that she was happy to be a mother, but there had to be more to life for a woman than having babies. Yet Delia was only echoing how politicians, who were being influenced more and more by the Church, seemed to be thinking these days. That women, the very same women who, like Winnie, had smuggled guns to the rebels and put themselves in danger for the republic, should now stay home and have their lives ruled by their husbands.

I'm happy to ask Joseph's opinion on important matters, she thought, and it's right for women to share things with their husbands. But I'll never let myself or my children have our lives ruled by any man.

It was nearly thirty minutes later when Joseph and Matt returned, and at that point Winifred herself said that she'd go inside. The two men sat on the bench she'd vacated, Joseph stretching his legs out in front of him while Matt puffed on a cigarette. Joseph had refused his offer of another

313

one. He was feeling the benefit of the clearer country air on his lungs.

'Well now,' said Matt as he released a stream of smoke into the night sky, 'with the war over, you say you want to be involved in workers' rights. In the trade union movement.'

'It's important,' said Joseph. 'We need a country where everyone is valued, not just the elite few. And from my experiences, every man has his own part to play. Every man can learn. Every man should be counted.'

'Where do you expect to work when your health is improved?'

'I don't know yet,' he admitted. 'Unfortunately I won't be able to do much physical work. My lungs were already weak going into prison, and those months in Tintown didn't help.'

'I admire you for the hunger strike,' said Matt. 'I couldn't have done it myself.'

'The first few days are the hardest,' said Joseph. 'After that, you get used to it. And after a couple of weeks, you slip in and out of what's real. I thought I was talking to Pearse and Connolly half the time, but I was just rambling aloud to myself.'

'I'm involved in the labour movement,' said Matt. 'I'll put feelers out, see if I can find anything for you.'

'That's decent of you,' said Joseph. He took out a piece of paper and wrote his name and address on it before handing it to the older man. 'Thank you.'

'No,' said Matt. 'Thank you for sticking to your principles. You may have been wrong – I'm reserving judgement on that – but people won't forget why you and men like you did what you did.'

'Perhaps,' said Joseph. He got up from the bench. 'I'd better go up to my wife.'

'I'll stay out here for a time.' Matt lit another cigarette from the butt of the first. 'See you tomorrow.'

Winifred was drifting in and out of sleep when Joseph came into the bedroom, but she opened her eyes as he got into bed.

'Nice evening?' she asked.

'He seems like a decent fellow,' said Joseph. 'Of course, it's hard to trust anyone completely, even now.'

'I know. Although his wife seems to be very . . . very . . .'

'What?' Joseph looked at her curiously.

'Passive,' said Winifred. 'She wants to have babies for him. His first wife died in childbirth.'

'Ah.'

'If I died in childbirth, would you find someone else to have babies with?'

'I didn't marry you to have babies,' said Joseph.

'No?' She raised an eyebrow.

'Well, yes, but not exclusively. I married you because you're a woman with a mind of her own.'

'That's the problem.' Winifred propped herself on her elbow and looked at him seriously. 'A lot of women aren't really allowed to have minds of their own. We're supposed to think whatever it is our husbands tell us to think.'

'Chance would be a fine thing.' Joseph laughed.

'You know what I mean.' She gave him a dig in the ribs.

'I've been surrounded by strong women all my life,' he said. 'I expect you to have minds of your own.'

'But I'm not sure the government does. And I know you're

interested in how things will change in our Free State – hopefully to be a republic – but you've got to take account of women too. And not just as people popping out babies.'

'I was talking to Matt just now about that selfsame thing,' said Joseph. 'Well, not so much about women, but about work and unions and how workers need to be organised and look after themselves. There are lots of women working now, and they should have rights. And those who are at home should have rights too. So it's something I want to pursue in the future. He says he has contacts and he might be able to help me.'

'Always fighting for something.' But her tone was teasing.

'I can't help it. And I'm very serious about it.' He smiled, and gathered her close. 'We have a great future ahead of us, Winnie Burke. Don't you ever forget it.'

'How could I when you remind me of it, you big strong man.'

He kissed her.

She kissed him back.

Chapter 27

Dublin, summer 1927

June 1927

Dear Mary-Jane,

I can't believe you've finally written a full-length letter. Ma has received all your postcards, of course, and she's kept every one, despite them being of places in England. She likes the colour ones of the red buses best. Anyway, I am glad to hear that all is well with you and that you're thinking of a return trip to Ireland. We would be so happy to see you. Things have changed a lot since you left, but you know that, of course. There is some rebuilding going on in the city, but the truth is that we are an impoverished nation. I'm sure you'll think we're very backwards in comparison with London.

Will you be able to bring your children? It would be lovely for them to meet. Brenda is four now and the prettiest, cleverest baby in the world. I know everyone says that about their own children, but she really is clever. She only has to hear a word once and she can repeat it. She also knows what they mean. She can write a little too, and her letters are really well formed. So I'm not just being a proud mama to say that she's clever, because she is! (The Burkes still call her Rosanna – even Joseph does when he talks to his mother or father about her. He thinks I don't know, but I do.) Kitty, her sister, is quick and clever too, even though she's only two. While Brenda is thoughtful and placid, Kitty is always into things. You won't yet have heard that I also have a son, John. He was a somewhat unexpected arrival, born early a few weeks ago. Nevertheless, he is a very loud, lusty baby who screams for attention, but when he is picked up he is the sweetest thing. I put him and Kitty in the pram and Brenda walks beside us.

I hadn't really expected to be a mother of three children by now. I had intended to space them a little more, but surprisingly I'm good at being pregnant and good at having children and they're a great joy to me. I love seeing Joseph reflected in them! Strangely, although he was interned for the first year of Brenda's life, I see him most in her. Kitty is like you. John is the image of his grandfather Burke.

I met a woman a few years ago who said that our job was to be mothers. I don't agree with that, but I get so much pleasure from watching my children grow that it has changed my ambition if not my view. I used to want to own a drapery shop. But now I want to work harder to make the world better. Not just for my children, but for others too.

I've joined a group that discusses women's rights. We meet once a month and send letters to politicians. Unfortunately, the damn Church is taking far too much of a front seat in talking about women, and they're listened to more than women themselves, which is disgraceful. There's a lot of stuff about a woman's place being in the kitchen (they've clearly never tasted my cooking; Agnes insists on doing it because I'm still so awful!) and having babies. I honestly think many of our politicians would be happy to see us all at home, pregnant and silent.

I suppose you heard about our general election? Nobody won a clear majority and Éamon de Valera says this means that Irish people want to get rid of the oath of allegiance. The Burkes definitely do. So do I, and so does Ma – it's actually quite silly, don't you think, when we have our own government now to swear loyalty to a foreign king? Though maybe you think differently, living in England. It's complicated, isn't it? The two countries were tied to each other for so long, untying them is very difficult. You think it's just a matter of saying 'get it done', but it's not. It's in memories and how we've lived together, what people want and expect, and how they go about things in the future.

I'm sorry, I'm rambling on. It's ages since I've written a letter.

It's a long time since I've heard from any of my sisters. Rosie's last letter came at Christmas (has she written to you? I think she's very happy in Brussels and she seems to adore Léo), and I haven't heard from Marianne since last summer. I know it hurts Ma that she doesn't write often, because Ma writes to her. But that's Marianne for you.

I look forward to seeing you soon!

Your loving sister,

Winnie

September 1927

Dear Winnie,

What a lovely time we had in Dublin, and how kind it was of your mother-in-law to let me and the children stay at St Anthony's Place. They had such fun and they adored your babas – not that Brenda wants to be thought of as a baby; you are right, she is very grown up and serious for a four-year-old.

You live in a beautiful house with a wonderful garden. You landed on your feet with Joseph despite everything. He is a good man and his father is the sweetest person I know. But you're right about Agnes – she's a tartar. I'd like to say she has a heart of gold, but I'm not sure about that. The way she quizzed me about England and about being married to an Englishman! I thought at first that she considered me a spy. Can you imagine me as a spy? I'm far too open for that.

It was great to see Ma again and I was surprised at how well she looks. She's a strong woman, don't you think? And Katy too. Reid was an absolute swine for treating her the way he did. She's still Katy, but I see what you meant about her being slower and having to think before

320

she does anything. Nevertheless, it's good that she has a job she likes, and that with Ma and Tom earning too, there are no real money worries at East Essex Street.

What a lovely day we had by the sea. That's the disadvantage of living where we do, you can't get to the seaside easily. I miss the sea. I miss the sound of the waves and the smell of salt in the air. And I miss walking along the promenade with an ice cream. We've holidayed at the seaside ourselves, but it's not the same as catching the tram to Kingstown. Sorry, I should call it Dún Laoghaire now. I do like it there. If I ever return to Ireland, that's where I'd like to live. It's funny – my roots are in Ireland, and yet I've put down roots here too. My husband is English. My children are English. Even my accent is a little bit English. I didn't realise that until I got home.

Perhaps next time Wilf will come too and see what Ireland is like himself. Because, of course, he reads the papers and they're not always complimentary. He knows they can't be telling the whole truth, because he knows me and I tell him everything. And yet when you're brought up a certain way, it's hard to think differently.

Dearest Winifred, you know how bad a correspondent I am. I will continue to send cards to Ma, but remember that all my family is always in my thoughts.

Your loving sister,
Mary-Jane

Mary-Jane's visit had brightened up the summer for Winifred, who'd enjoyed going out with her sister and their children and derived a certain perverse amusement at listening to their

English accents at St Anthony's Place. She'd seen her mother-in-law bless herself when she heard some of their more English phrases, and that had made her laugh.

There had been a lot of laughter in St Anthony's Place during Mary-Jane's visit, mainly because there had been so many children there all the time. May had visited with hers, and Rosanna had called by more than once with her own baby. Ita hadn't yet had children of her own, and Winifred wondered if she ever would; she had never been the strongest of the Burke girls, and perhaps she either couldn't or wouldn't get pregnant.

Of course she could be using the sponge soaked in olive oil method that had worked, albeit imperfectly, for Winifred herself. The more she thought about it, the more it seemed to Winnie that being able to decide when you had children would be a good thing, and that there should be more research into pregnancy and motherhood and women's health. She made a note to raise it at her next women's group meeting, but she mentioned it to Joseph first.

'Are you telling me you don't want any more children?' he asked.

'No.' She shook her head. 'I love my babies and I'd be happy to have . . . well, one more anyway. But I was thinking about the future. Their future. We have two girls, and what if they want to have jobs and do well for themselves?'

'And not get married at all?' Joseph frowned. 'In that case, they won't have children anyway.'

'You'd hope,' said Winifred.

'Winifred Burke! Are you suggesting that a daughter of mine would have a baby out of wedlock?'

'It happens,' said Winifred. 'Obviously I don't want it to happen to my children—'

'It would be a disgrace!' exclaimed Joseph.

'It would certainly be a disaster. For Brenda or for Kitty. But not for the bowsie that got them pregnant.'

'What d'you mean?'

'Fallen women is what we call them,' said Winifred. 'But they're not fallen. At least, not the way we mean. They've fallen for a man and believed his lies and then they're the ones who suffer afterwards. That needs to change.'

Joseph looked at her thoughtfully.

'And if they do get married but don't want to have babies straight away, there should be advice on that,' Winifred continued. 'Not whispered stories between women. Proper medical advice from doctors. Also,' she added, 'we need to support women like Katy.'

'How do you mean?'

'Her husband beat her, Joseph. Yet nothing was done about it precisely because he was her husband.'

'I know that's wrong,' agreed Joseph. 'But—'

'There's no but,' said Winifred. 'Men like that are criminals and should be treated as criminals. And women like Katy shouldn't be told to put up with it.'

'Is this the kind of radical idea your group discusses?'

'We haven't until now. But we will. You and your friends who are trying to shape the republic – and especially your slithery pal Dev – aren't listening to what matters to us,' said Winifred. 'We were there supporting you and marching for you and advocating for you while you were fighting and while you were in prison. And we were spying and providing shelter and ammunition. We sacrificed a lot. But now that the wars are over, he's pushing the women away. The Countess . . .' Her voice trailed off. She was still upset about Countess

Markievicz, who had died in July from complications after surgery. It seemed such an inappropriate way for a woman like her to die, and it was unfair that she should be taken so soon. 'The Countess would have wanted freedoms for women,' she continued now. 'She would have wanted us to reach our potential like she did.'

'Not every woman is the Countess,' said Joseph.

'But every woman deserves a chance,' countered Winifred. 'I worry that there are too many men's voices in government. And they're being influenced by the Catholic Church – nobody elected priests, so why should they be involved at all? Meanwhile men make decisions that affect women, but they don't notice the effect themselves. And it's not just women at home,' she added, warming to her theme. 'It's women in work. We need to make sure that we have better support for women at work. Better support for women at home. Better support for women in general.'

'My goodness.' Joseph looked at her with respect. 'You've really thought about this.'

'Of course I have,' said Winifred. 'We have our own country now. We want to make it a good one for every person. I've heard you and your trade union pals talk about it. But you always talk about the politics, never the social side. And I think about my friend Esther, who had a baby a year because that's what she thought was expected of her. The truth is that many men seem to want women at home worrying about their children so that they can't interfere in the things men themselves are doing. Well, Joseph Burke, we have to interfere one way or the other. Unfortunately I'm the woman at home with children, so I can't really march into the Dáil and demand things, but I can make sure that my husband will demand things for me. It's not ideal, but it's better than nothing.'

'You're amazing,' said Joseph.

'I'm all talk, no action,' confessed Winifred. 'Our group is a talking shop and we write lots of letters, but we don't get out and make actual change.'

'That's not true,' he said. 'Sometimes words inspire action. And you've given me lots to think about.'

Chapter 28

Dublin, summer 1931

Winifred was peeling potatoes in the kitchen of St Anthony's Place, lost in thought about Joseph's latest plans for union reform, when Agnes came in, her face pale.

'What?' Even though Winifred tried not to catastrophise these days, Agnes's expression was grim.

'It's May,' she said. 'She has consumption.'

'May!' Winifred looked at her mother-in-law in astonishment. 'May? Not Ita?'

'She was helping in the slums,' said Agnes. 'Bringing milk to children. She must have picked it up there.'

'Dear God.' Despite her well-observed lack of faith, Winifred blessed herself. Over the years, tuberculosis had been a deadly killer in Dublin city. It had always been both a relief and a surprise to her that the O'Learys and the Burkes had avoided the disease, even though Ita and Joseph were prime candidates given their 'delicate' chests. She was very aware that in the early part of the century, 12,000 people in Dublin alone had died from it. It had been one of the many things that she'd worried about in the days when Joseph was interned and she'd felt the weight of his absence pressing down upon her. But she hadn't even thought about it in months. And now, out of the blue, May, strong and vibrant May, who was never ill, had succumbed. It didn't seem right.

'What about Ita?' she asked. 'Is she all right?'

'I don't know about Ita,' said Agnes. 'I haven't heard from her or Rosanna. But, oh Winnie – my lovely daughter!'

'Have you seen her?' Winifred couldn't help herself. She stepped back from her mother-in-law, fearful of infection herself.

'Last week,' said Agnes. 'She was all right last week.'

'Oh God.' Winifred looked at her. 'You should go to your room too,' she said. 'Just in case.'

'If I'm infected, it's too late,' said Agnes. 'Too late for all of us.'

Winifred was scrubbing the floors and surfaces with Jeyes Fluid to disinfect them when Joseph came home from work that evening. He was as concerned as her.

'I wonder if we can get May into a sanatorium,' he said. 'I'll see what I can do.'

'I'll keep disinfecting,' said Winifred. 'Your mother is isolating in her room. I left some food outside the door for her.'

He nodded.

'This is one of the reasons women have lots of children. They expect some of them to die.' She looked at him, her eyes full of tears. 'But my heart will break if any of my babies catch it. Brenda was helping your mother around the house yesterday. And then she was helping me with the two littlest.

327

I didn't have Una and Patricia in the last couple of years just to make up the numbers. I wanted all of them. Kitty is strong, and so is John, but . . . but it doesn't matter how strong you are if it gets into your lungs. Oh Joseph, after what happened to you in Frongoch and Tintown, you have to be careful.'

'We're doing all we can,' Joseph tried to reassure her. 'And perhaps my mother isn't infected.'

'I talked to your father earlier. He's moved into the Blue Room.'

'Good,' he said. Then he put his arm around his wife. 'Don't worry. Everything will be all right.'

But it wasn't.

May was sent to the sanatorium in Peamount, outside the city. Three weeks later, Ita, who'd met her briefly after she'd become infected but before she developed symptoms, followed. And a month later, Agnes herself was admitted.

Like most Dubliners, Winifred knew of the existence of the sanatorium, which had been built earlier in the century to cope with the high levels of tuberculosis in the city. Until now, she'd never personally known anyone who'd been sent there. Visiting was forbidden – the patients were kept isolated from the rest of the community. Many of them said that being separated from their families was the hardest part of the disease. However, once a week Joseph cycled the twelve miles each way so that he could see his mother and sisters at the window of the building.

'They're well,' he'd say to Winifred and his father when he returned. 'They're well and we're well.'

Winifred was watching her children like a hawk, particularly Una, who caught colds easily and who was, in her mother's words, 'chesty'. But so far the little girl remained healthy. In fact all of the children were healthy, for which Winifred was profoundly grateful.

Annie was horrified when she heard about the Burke women.

'All the time we lived in much worse surroundings and none of you caught it,' she said. 'I was terrified you would, when you were younger. I thought *I* would those months when I was in a workhouse and nothing more than a child myself. But I didn't and we didn't. And we were lucky that your father got his job and we got the rooms we did and we weren't crammed together like so many others. It gave us a chance.'

'When it's your time, it's your time,' said Katy, who was sitting in the corner of the room knitting. 'Reid should have killed me, but I survived. Joseph survived a hunger strike. It's all part of God's plan.'

'Don't start with God's plan,' Winifred snorted. 'What sort of God has the kind of plans your God seems to have? Plans where people struggle for life, struggle through life and then die a horrible death? Seems to me that God is a psychopath.'

'Winifred Burke! You can wash your mouth out with soap,' exclaimed her mother even as she blessed herself. 'God is kind and loving—'

'Oh, don't give me that!' retorted Winifred. 'A kind and loving God would wave his hand and get rid of this disease. And he wouldn't have had you in a workhouse when you were younger either. Or—'

'We pulled ourselves up,' said Annie. 'You have to remember that. God helped us.'

'And what about the people he didn't help?' demanded Winifred.

'I'm going to say the rosary for Mrs Burke and her daughters,' said Annie. 'And none of your nonsense will stop me.'

With Agnes in the sanatorium, Winifred took over the running of St Anthony's Place. Although she'd always played second fiddle to her mother-in-law when it came to domestic matters, she was competent at organising the daily maintenance and administration of the house, though having her doing the cooking was a trial for everyone. Even Brenda, who was stoic and accepting, asked if somebody else couldn't cook the cabbage because it was terrible. But over time, Winifred's culinary skills improved and eventually she became, if not a good cook, a capable one. Her speciality was a fish stew that she flavoured with herbs from the garden, and a coddle made with vegetables also grown in the garden. Although she missed Agnes, she felt liberated by not having her constantly looking over her shoulder or criticising her or lecturing her about the economic and political situation, even though this made her feel guilty for being disease-free herself. She also found it easier to play with the children, not feeling that she had to be as solemn and serious as she was when the older Mrs Burke was around. Nevertheless, she hoped that her mother-in-law might be one of the lucky ones who recovered, even if the consequence would be remaining frail for the rest of her life. Illness frightened her. Incurable illnesses frightened her even more.

The children noticed the absence of their grandmother, and their reaction was to run a little wilder than they otherwise would have done. More than once, their grand-father had to shoo them out of the boiler house, although he indulged John and allowed him to accompany him on his rounds of the convent, checking every single radiator every day.

'I want to be a boiler man when I grow up,' John told him, and Mr Burke shook his hand and said that he was sure he'd be an excellent one.

The children stayed healthy, although Winifred paid special attention to Brenda and Kitty, who were at school and mixing with others, taking their temperatures as soon as they came home and doing her best to make sure they had as much nutritious food as possible. It was a difficult, worrying time, and yet, thought Winifred, somehow more stable than those that had gone before.

They were living day to day, continually waiting for news about May and Agnes and Ita, but, thought Winifred, the wonderful thing about these days was that Joseph came home every evening. While she worried about her mother-in-law and sisters-in-law, she didn't worry any more about her husband, so the day he didn't come home until very late, she was in a state of high anxiety, convinced that something dreadful had happened.

'Not at all,' he said, taking her by the hands and then kissing her. 'I'm changing jobs, that's all.'

'Changing jobs? For what?' She looked at him in astonishment.

'You know Dev has started up a new paper? *The Irish Press*? He's offered me a position in the dispatch department.'

'Dev has? But doesn't he know that you're not his biggest fan?'

'I was on his side about the Treaty.' Joseph shrugged. 'He wants loyal people.'

'Are you loyal to Dev or loyal to the country?' asked Winifred.

'I'm hoping it's going to be the same thing,' said Joseph. 'Plus it's more money.'

'Oh.'

'Which puts us in a much better place for the coming years,' he said.

'If it wasn't for this awful disease, we'd be in a great place,' she told him.

'Everything will work out,' he promised. 'You'll see. It will be fine.'

Winifred could see that Joseph was happy in his new job, and that made her happy too, as she said to Katy when they went for a walk along the seafront at Sandymount one afternoon. Also, she added, he had now taken to writing letters to the paper about workers' rights and other social matters.

'Really?' Katy looked surprised. 'We get the paper most days and I haven't seen any of them.'

'That's because he writes under a pseudonym,' Winnie told her. 'He calls himself Mr Winston O'Leary.'

Katy laughed.

'I've taken to calling him Mr O'Leary at home.' Winifred chuckled. 'I told him I might change the children's names to O'Leary too. He said that wasn't a bad idea. I know he was joking, but actually, Katy, he's very progressive.'

'You're lucky with him, you know.'

'I do know,' said Winnie. 'Although it can be a bit wearying sometimes. Now that he's the chairman of the trade union newspaper section, they sometimes have meetings at the house. The feckin' arguments they have, you wouldn't believe. And then I bring them in sandwiches and say that I hope they're rehearsing the arguments for equal opportunities for women at the newspapers, and they quieten down.'

'And are they?'

'Arguing for equal rights? The famous Mr O'Leary wrote a letter about that too.'

In fact Joseph was a prolific letter-writer, much to Winnie's delight. But when she said to him that perhaps he was all work and no play, he also joined the trade union band. When he came home with a band uniform, she insisted he try it on.

'I never thought I'd be pleased to see you in a uniform again,' she said as he stood in front of her, the brass buttons gleaming.

'I never thought I'd be pleased to wear one,' he admitted.

'Now let's take it off,' said Winifred, and undid the buttons one by one.

She was assembling the ingredients for the fish stew when she heard a loud rap on the communicating door between the convent and the house. During the war years, the nuns had occasionally knocked on that door, either to deliver bread or to allow her to visit the house unseen. Nobody had knocked since Agnes had gone to the sanatorium, and the unexpectedness of it made Winnie's heart race. She wiped her hands on her apron and opened the door, her eyes widening in surprise at the sight of the mother superior standing there.

333

'You're keeping the house well,' remarked the nun when Winifred welcomed her and invited her into the Yellow Room.

'Would you like some tea?' Winnie asked.

'Thank you, Mrs Burke.'

Winifred checked on the youngest children, who were still down for their afternoon nap, before making the tea and bringing it to the nun, who was seated beside the unlit fire.

'Are you warm enough?' she asked. 'I could light it if you like.'

'It's a perfectly warm day,' said the mother superior. 'No need.'

'How can I help?' asked Winifred when she'd finished pouring the tea.

'First of all I wanted to ask about Mrs Agnes Burke,' said the nun. 'I know she's been in the sanatorium for weeks now. And her daughters too.'

'They're not any better but not any worse,' said Winifred. 'It's such a terrible disease. You think perhaps there's an improvement and then there's a setback, and of course not being able to visit them is difficult.'

'Please let them know that we're praying for them,' said the nun.

'I will.'

'We pray for you too.' She smiled, and the severity of her face eased. 'We've always prayed for your family, Mrs Burke. Mr John Burke has been a good worker and we have confidence in him. We like him. Even during the darkest days of the wars we had confidence in him. In Mrs Burke too.'

'Do you have confidence in me?' asked Winifred.

'You're a very different woman, but yes, we have confidence in you. You're a good mother.'

334

Winifred wasn't sure the mother superior was being entirely honest about that. Certainly not if she was aware that she'd caught Brenda, Kitty and John shouting in through the bars of the mausoleum the other day, trying (they insisted) to wake the sleeping nuns.

'I'm glad you have faith in me,' she said.

'We certainly have faith in your ability to look after your family,' said the nun.

'I'm pleased to hear that.'

'To that end . . .' Mother Superior replaced her cup on its saucer, 'I wanted to tell you about some changes that will be happening in the convent that will affect you. Mr Burke is aware that change is coming but I thought it would be useful to speak to the woman of the house myself, and explain things more fully to you. It will be easier, in turn, for you to give him the exact details.'

From the tone of her voice, Winifred feared that the changes wouldn't be good ones.

'We may not be staying here,' the nun continued. 'The order has been looking at our situation and at the situation in other countries. They want us to spread our word and our work overseas. There are concerns about Europe, about the faithful there.'

'You don't mean because of Mr Hitler, do you?' Winifred frowned. The news had been full of his rise in Germany, and when Joseph wasn't talking about de Valera and his right-wing tendencies, he was worrying about Hitler and fascism.

'Among others,' said the nun. 'The world is heading for chaos, but in Ireland, at least, the people are faithful. Some of us will stay but some will go. And we need the money, you see.'

'The money?'

'We have been offered a substantial amount for the convent.'

'You'd sell the convent?' Winnie looked at her in horror.

'It's not something that will happen immediately. But you're a woman with a young family and you need to think ahead.'

'You mean this house will be sold too?'

'It belongs to us,' said the nun.

'How long do we have?'

'I really don't know. It depends on the buyers. A few weeks, perhaps a little longer. But of course, Mrs Burke, the new government has talked a lot about clearing the slums and building homes for people to live in. I'm sure you'll find somewhere suitable.'

The mother superior was referring to the government's limited public housing programme, which had resulted in a number of flats being built in the city and additional homes further outside. Joseph and his trade union colleagues had been active in campaigning for better housing, but as far as Winifred knew, he hadn't thought he'd be needing it for his own family.

She did know that there were far more people looking for housing than there were available houses for them. And how, she thought, was she going to find somewhere for herself, Joseph and their five children in just a few weeks? And what about Mr Burke? Would he want to come with them too? And then there was Agnes, in the event that she recovered enough to be discharged from the sanatorium. Would they be able to find anywhere big enough for all of them? She'd grown accustomed to the space that St Anthony's Place provided. It would be difficult to go back to living in two rooms again. If she could even find two rooms.

'You're a resourceful woman.' The nun smiled at her as

all these thoughts passed through Winifred's head. 'As resourceful as your mother-in-law in your own way. I'm sure you'll come up with something.'

'Thank you.' Winifred didn't know why she was thanking her. After all, she'd just told her she was going to lose her home. And she hadn't offered any help or suggestions about what she should do about it.

'The blessing of God upon you, dear,' said the mother superior as she got up from the chair. 'I'll pray you find somewhere suitable.'

But as she watched the older woman sweep out of the house in a flurry of black robes, Winifred wondered how they possibly could.

Joseph was shocked that evening when Winifred told him about the nun's visit.

'I never thought they'd leave,' he said. 'I never thought we'd have to leave either. Which is a poor reflection on me.'

'Your father isn't getting any younger, and even if they weren't going to sell the convent, we'd probably all have had to move when he couldn't cope with the boiler any more,' Winifred pointed out. 'This has just brought it to a head sooner.'

'I should have realised it would happen.' Joseph frowned. 'And now that I have to think about it, I'm thinking about everyone in the country, not just us. People here have no right to a home, no matter how hard they've worked. We're all dependent on private landlords to provide us with accommodation, and private landlords can do what they like. I appreciate that this house belongs to the nuns,' he added, 'but it's been our home for a long time.'

'I know.'

'It was cowardly of her to come and tell you this instead of saying it to Da,' said Joseph. 'She's asking you to do her dirty work for her.'

'And yet they've been good to us,' Winifred reminded him. 'During the war they turned a blind eye to what was going on. They baked bread for us. They—'

'I don't believe you're defending the religious now,' said Joseph. 'You're the one who's usually against them.'

'I'm defending the people, not the institution, and not that they really need me to,' said Winifred. 'But in the end, they look after themselves.'

Before Joseph had the chance to reply, his father walked into the room. Joseph looked at his wife enquiringly, but she shook her head. She certainly wasn't going to say anything to John about the latest bombshell when he was tired after a long day. Besides, although he was always unfailingly polite and cheerful with her, she knew he was also deeply concerned about his wife and daughters, and a housing crisis wasn't something he needed to be burdened with just now. Maybe that was why the nun had come to see her instead of him.

Winifred wondered if there would ever be a time when life wasn't throwing impossible situations at them. She got up and made some tea for John, then went upstairs to check on the children. Brenda and Kitty were still awake and reading *The Secret Garden*, a book that Brenda's teacher had loaned her. Brenda was reading aloud and Kitty was looking over her shoulder, her lips moving silently to the words.

'Sleep, you two,' said Winifred, pulling closed the heavy curtain at the window.

'It's early,' protested Brenda.

'We've just got to a good bit,' said Kitty. 'Mary has found a boy in a hidden bedroom!' Her face was flushed with excitement.

'Well, her discovery will have to wait until tomorrow,' said Winifred.

'But Ma—'

'Sleep.' Winifred's voice was firm.

She drew back the curtain that divided the bedroom – a curtain she'd made herself, remembering as she'd done so the one in East Essex Street. That curtain had separated the children from their parents; in this case it simply separated the two older girls from the two babies. Una was sucking her thumb as she slept, while little Patricia suddenly opened her eyes and looked at her mother.

'Sleep for you too,' whispered Winifred, stroking her on the cheek until her eyes fluttered closed again. She then checked on John, but there was no fear of him being awake; he invariably went out for the count as soon as his head hit the pillow.

The ringing of the bell at the gate sounded through the open window, and she hurried down the stairs, glancing at the grandfather clock in the hallway.

Nobody ever came with good news at this hour, she thought, and then hoped that she was wrong.

Chapter 29

Dublin, summer/autumn 1931

She wasn't wrong.

May's husband, Michael, accompanied by his eldest son, stood outside.

'May died this afternoon,' he said when they'd gone into the Yellow Room. 'She took a turn this morning. It was very quick in the end.'

Winifred felt the tears well up. She and May hadn't seen eye to eye over a lot of things, but she was devastated to hear that she'd died.

'I'm so sorry.' She hugged Michael. 'She was a woman of strong beliefs, and a tireless worker.'

'My wife? And Ita?' John asked.

'I only got news of May.' Michael's voice was ragged. 'I was expecting it, of course. I'd always expected it from the moment she went in there. But I hoped . . .'

'Have a drink.' Joseph went to the cupboard and took out a bottle of Powers whiskey. He poured a finger into glasses for himself, John and Michael. Then, as Winifred looked at him, he poured a finger for her too.

'And a tot for the boy,' she said. 'He needs something.'

He did as she asked, then asked his brother-in-law about the arrangements for the funeral. Michael drank the whiskey in a single mouthful and said that he'd let them know when they were finalised.

'If there's anything I can do to help, just let me know,' said Winifred.

'That's kind of you,' said Michael. 'I know you two didn't get on.'

'We didn't agree on lots of things,' said Winifred. 'But that doesn't matter. Caring for each other is what does.'

Ita died a few weeks later, and Agnes lost her battle with the disease shortly afterwards. Winifred wondered if it was from sorrow as much as TB itself. She felt that the Burke family, once so strong, was crumbling around her. She was weighed down with sadness for her husband and her father-in-law, and for Rosanna, who sobbed throughout the funerals. (Although she also thought that Rosanna was a terrible drama queen, because she attempted to make the days about her and her grief while seeming to forget about her father, who was broken-hearted at the loss of his wife and daughters.)

'And yet if people don't die, then where's the space for the living?' Mr Burke said one day when Winifred put a plate of stew in front of him. 'Where's the space for all your kiddies if us old folk don't leave?'

'I suppose we all have our time,' agreed Winifred. 'It's just that the older you get, the more you realise how short it really is.'

* * *

The mother superior of the convent attended Agnes's funeral, and a few days later came to the house to say that the nuns would be leaving the convent in six weeks' time so that the new owners could take possession.

'However, we will be paying Mr Burke an additional month's wages to help with your finances, which we feel is more than generous,' she said. 'We hope you find exactly what you need.'

'She said it as though she was doing us an immense favour,' said Winifred to Esther, who was now renting a house in the Liberties area of the city. It was a narrow two-storey building with an outside toilet and a private yard. Even though it was small, Esther was delighted with it, as it gave her and her brood of nine children some privacy. But to Winifred, accustomed as she was to the large rooms and even larger garden of St Anthony's Place (as well as an indoor lavatory), Esther's home was cramped and inadequate.

'Ah, you'll find something, Winnie,' said Esther. 'Sure don't you always fall on your feet.'

'Me! Fall on my feet! Are you joking?'

'You do,' protested Esther. 'Look at you now, with your husband and his good job and your well-spaced-out children.'

'I wouldn't say they're that well spaced out. I seem to go for one every two years, which wasn't the original plan at all.'

'Better than me,' said Esther. 'I never did get the hang of the sponge.'

'How's Henry?' asked Winifred.

'Ah, sure, you know yourself. Pullin' the divil by the tail. He's calmed down a bit the last couple of years, but sure the children would drive anyone to drink.'

'They're lovely, though,' said Winifred. 'Your girls are very pretty. And every one of them healthy.'

'They take after me for looks and him for strength.' Esther gave her a smile. 'Anyway, Winnie, I bet you'll do all right on the house.'

'I hope so,' said Winifred. 'I asked the mother superior to give me a reference, and to be fair to her, she did. It says we're a lovely family.' She grinned.

'And so you are,' said Esther. 'One of the best.'

'You're one of the best too.' Winifred hugged her friend. 'I'll call around again soon.'

'I've applied for one of the corporation's new houses,' Joseph told her that night. 'There's a lot of people looking for one, but our references are good. We've the one from the nuns, and I managed to get Todd Andrews to sign for me too. He was at the Curragh at the same time as me – though the clever bugger escaped – and he's been appointed to the Department of Industry and Commerce. He's a good man.'

'That doesn't mean he'll get you a house.'

'No, but it's helpful,' said Joseph. 'Between him and the nuns, I'm feeling hopeful.'

Winifred nodded, and tried to feel hopeful too.

As the time for their departure from St Anthony's Place came and there was still no word about a house, Winifred grew more and more worried. Her anxiety transmitted itself to the children, who were cranky and more mischievous than usual. John climbed the wall that surrounded the garden and fell from it, necessitating a trip to the hospital to check that

343

his arm wasn't broken. Kitty, who'd been given a second-hand doll's perambulator for her sixth birthday, put both Una and baby Patricia in it, causing it to tip over and spill them onto the pavement – that was another hospital visit. And Brenda, normally so responsible, decided she wanted to write her own book, took a bottle of ink from the dresser and dropped it on the kitchen floor, where it smashed and formed a spreading blue lake. She then walked into it and traipsed her inky footsteps along the hallway and onto the Axminster rug in the Yellow Room. When Winifred saw the mess, she remembered her encounter with Constance Markievicz, and the Countess's mishap with ink. It seemed so long ago, she thought as she cleaned up, and yet she could see the woman as clearly as though she were standing in front of her. (The memory didn't stop her bellowing at Brenda, who burst into tears and was joined in her sobbing by the rest of her siblings.)

Winifred felt guilty about making her children cry, but she knew she'd never have lost her temper with Brenda if it hadn't been for the stress she felt over finding somewhere to live.

'You can always move in with us,' said Annie when she went to visit her one Saturday, bringing all five children with her. Joseph was at band practice – he always said that playing music helped him think.

'I can't inflict us all on you, Ma,' said Winifred. 'There isn't room, and . . . well, look at those children!'

Annie laughed. Brenda and Kitty were reading together, but John and Una were fighting, rolling along the floor, shrieking at each other. Patricia, in her mother's arms, was watching them, her eyes wide.

'I heard of new rooms on Dorset Street,' said Katy. 'That wouldn't be far.'

'Did you? I went to look at some last week, but they were gone before I got there.' Winifred had been dispirited to arrive and discover the rooms were no longer available.

'You could go now,' said Annie.

'I wouldn't bring the children with me,' said Winifred.

'I'll look after them,' said Annie. 'Katy can go with you.'

'We'll get the tram up O'Connell Street,' said Katy. 'I don't have the legs to walk all the way.'

'If you're sure.'

Mrs O'Leary was adamant, and the two sisters walked out of the tenement to the tram.

'Except for the bullet marks on the GPO, you'd hardly know there had been a war,' said Katy.

'Two wars,' remarked Winifred. 'Two wars and a Rising, in fact. And O'Connell Street the centre of so much of it.'

'In my head I still say Sackville Street,' admitted Katy. 'But O'Connell Street is so much better.'

When they alighted from the tram, they walked to the address in Dorset Street where the rooms were to let. But even as they stepped through the front door, Winnie felt a blanket of dread wrap itself around her. The building was damp and musty, and very little natural light made its way through the grimy windows.

Yet the rooms were spacious, even if the floors were uneven, and she told herself that plenty of Jeyes Fluid and carbolic soap would clean them.

'Come back on Monday with the first week's rent,' said the landlady. 'You'll have yourself a lovely place to live.'

*   *   *

345

She went home, telling herself that she'd done the best she could. There was no sign of Joseph, which surprised her. She fed the children and made herself a cup of tea, trying not to feel sad at the idea of leaving the warm and welcoming kitchen, her favourite room in the house where she'd lived for the past ten years.

When Joseph did arrive, he serenaded her with his harmonica, playing one of her favourite songs, 'Ol' Man River'.

'You're in a happy mood,' she said when he finished the tune with a flourish then put his arms around her and kissed her.

'Because I have good news,' he said. 'It's not confirmed yet – I won't have official word until Monday – but . . . we've been allocated a house.'

'Seriously?' She looked at him in disbelief.

'Very seriously,' he said. 'In Crumlin.'

Winifred had a vague idea where that was.

'Three miles south of the city,' Joseph told her. 'Not too far from your ma.'

'Three miles, though. It's practically the country.'

'Dublin is growing,' said Joseph. 'And we have to move with the times.'

He and Winifred walked there the following day and stood in front of the newly constructed semi-detached house. It had two bedrooms and an indoor bathroom, with, Joseph said, a bath and a geyser for hot water.

'It has a garden too.' He led her around the side of the building. 'We can grow our own vegetables.'

Winifred stood at the end of the garden and gazed at the house, already visualising where she would put things,

346

how she would allocate space, and what she might grow in the garden. She couldn't quite believe that this could be their new home, even when Joseph brought her inside and showed her the neat kitchen and dining area and separate front room, before going up the stairs to the bedrooms and bathroom.

'Of course it's not as big as St Anthony's Place,' he conceded when they were outside again. 'It will be a little cramped. But I can afford the rent.' He looked at her anxiously. 'What do you think?'

'It's ours,' she murmured. 'Yours and mine. It has hot and cold water. It has a bathroom.'

'Yes,' he said. 'It has. And yes, it's ours.'

'And the government has provided it. We're paying rent to them, not a landlord.'

'There's talk of building twenty thousand homes,' said Joseph. 'Not all are houses, of course. Some are flats. But it's the end of slums and landlords. It's a new start. We didn't get everything we wanted, for all our fighting, but we're making progress. We're a country in charge of its own destiny.'

She nodded.

'So what do you think?' he asked again.

'It's beautiful.' She turned to him. 'I can't believe this. I'm going to be living in my very own house, provided by our very own government. And yes, we're practically in the country out here.' She waved her hands expansively towards the Dublin mountains in the distance. 'But I'm sure I'll get used to it.'

'I'm sure you will.' He grinned at her.

'What about your father?'

'What d'you mean?'

'Well, when we talked about having to leave St Anthony's Place, he said Rosanna had offered him a bed with her. But to be honest, I didn't think he sounded thrilled by the idea.'

'Really? I thought he'd prefer to be with Rosanna.' Joseph looked surprised. 'She's renting half a house on the north side of the city, and she has fewer children. It would be quieter for him.'

'Ah Joseph, are you mad? Your da loves our children, especially John. I think he'd prefer the option to live with us.'

'But he hasn't actually said that.'

'Because we hadn't got anywhere when we talked about it,' said Winifred. 'Listen to me, Joseph, your da has been lovely to me always. If he wants to live with Rosanna, I don't mind in the least, but I'm happy to have him with us if that's what he wants.'

'It'll be crowded,' warned Joseph.

'Not as damn crowded as that awful place in Dorset Street.' Winifred shrugged. 'We could put a bed in the parlour. He could share with John. The older girls in one bedroom. Patricia with us.'

'I love you, Winnie Burke.'

'I know you do. Now stop trying to kiss me on a public street. You'll have us arrested before we even move into our new home.'

When Rosanna heard about the Crumlin house, she and James turned up at St Anthony's Place with their children.

'It's right that you should be retired,' she told her father as they sat around the table in the kitchen. 'You've worked all your life and you're entitled to some rest now. It's not like you're a young man any more.'

'Thank you for pointing that out,' said John.

'And if you want to live with us, you're very welcome,' continued Rosanna. 'We're hoping to get a council house ourselves. We don't have the pull that Joseph does, of course, with his friends in high places.'

'I don't have any pull,' said Joseph. 'I applied like everyone else.'

'But your application was supported.'

'The nuns were good,' he conceded. 'As well as a notice to quit, they gave us references.'

'They could do the same for us,' said Rosanna.

'Except you're not renting from the nuns,' Winifred pointed out.

'You mean we're not living for free.'

'Nor are we.'

'You're living off the back of my father.'

Winifred looked at Rosanna in surprise. There was a resentment in the younger woman's voice she'd never heard before.

'Did you want to live here yourselves?' she asked.

'It wasn't an option, was it?' said Rosanna. 'You were here and popping out children at will. You took up all the space.'

'Don't be silly, Rosanna,' said her father. 'Winifred has been very good to me. She was very good to your mother too. And so if she wants to offer me a place to live, I'd be happy to accept.'

'Of course,' said Winifred.

'That's good.' Rosanna looked pleased. 'It's about time you paid back.'

She got up from the table, followed by her husband, and

called to the children, who'd been playing with their cousins in the garden.

'I'll miss it.' She turned back towards her father. 'I'll miss this place and I'll miss you and I miss our mother and . . . .' She burst into tears. 'None of it is how I wanted.'

'Very little of life is how we want it,' said John. 'Don't cry. I'll visit you. It's not that far.'

'We'd love to have you.' She threw her arms around him and sobbed again.

'Rosanna . . .' James put his arm awkwardly around her. 'You're upsetting the children. We should go.'

And indeed, the youngest of the large group of children who had run towards the house were crying too, their wails adding to her sobs.

'Come on.' Joseph swept Una into his arms. 'Stop that horrible noise and I'll give you an apple.'

Una looked at him from brown eyes that were so like her mother's.

'Apple?'

'Yes, apple,' said her father. 'But only if you stop crying.'

'Can I have an apple too?' asked Kitty.

'You can share. You can all share.'

Suddenly he was surrounded by children demanding apples. He went to the dresser, where there were a couple in a bowl, cut them into thin slices and divided them amongst all of them, including Rosanna's.

'Well now.' Rosanna sniffed and dabbed at her eyes. 'I'm glad all that's settled. 'We'll leave you to work out the details of your move. James, hurry up and put our three in the pram. They'll never walk all the way home.'

'It was lovely to see you,' said Winifred.

'You too.' Rosanna's tears had gone and her smile was as sunny as it had ever been. 'We can't wait to see your new home. We hope you're very happy there.'

'Thank you,' said Winifred.

She heaved a sigh of relief when they'd gone.

She kept the curtains from St Anthony's Place. There were more than she needed, but she planned to alter what she could and use the unwanted fabric to cover chairs or make counterpanes for the beds. At least, she planned to cut it to size and allow someone else to do the sewing. It grieved her that after so long working for Alice Kelley, she'd never managed to master the art of needlework.

She left her father-in-law looking after the children while she went out to do some shopping. But she didn't stop at any of the stores along O'Connell Street, instead making directly for Kelley's Fine Fabrics. She hadn't been to the shop since she'd come to thank Alice for the information on Joseph's whereabouts after his arrest, and she didn't even know if it still existed. But it was there, and still with the same window that he'd had replaced, and the same signage that her father had painted. Faded and cracked now, and needing to be redone, but the sight of it catapulted her back in time as she remembered how frightened she'd been when the stone had come through the window, and how she'd been instantly attracted to Joseph Burke, even if she hadn't wanted to admit it to herself. She remembered, too, the raid on the shop, and lying in the gutter with Alice, convinced they were going to be raped and killed. And she remembered how her employer had been part of it all afterwards, allowing the shop to be used to move guns and ammunition.

They should always have been on the same side, her and Alice. It was a pity things had turned out the way they did.

The door to the shop opened and a woman walked out, a brown paper package under her arm. She held the door wide for Winifred, who hesitated for a moment, then stepped inside.

A young woman stood behind the counter. She was about sixteen or seventeen, her long hair plaited and coiled around her head.

'Can I help you?' she asked.

'May I,' murmured Winifred.

The girl blushed.

'May I help you?'

'Is Mrs Kelley here?'

'She's in the stockroom. I'll get her for you.'

The girl disappeared. Winifred looked around. Nothing in the shop had changed. There were still bales of fabric on the shelves. The big white clock continued to tick on the wall. And the brass ruler was still set into the smooth wooden countertop. She ran her fingers along it.

'Miss O'Leary. I mean, Mrs Burke.' Alice stood in front of her. An Alice whose dark hair was now liberally sprinkled with grey but whose features were as fine as ever. 'Winifred. What are you doing here?'

'I was thinking about fabric and cutting, and I thought of here.'

'What do you need fabric for?'

'My new house.'

Alice turned her attention to her assistant. 'Helene, will you take charge for a short time while I deal with Mrs Burke.' She turned to Winifred. 'Would you like tea?'

'Tea?'

'Yes, tea.' Alice's words were abrupt. 'There's a tea shop around the corner and—'

'I know it,' said Winifred.

'Shall we?'

'Yes.'

They walked in silence to the tea shop, and sat in silence at the round wooden table while the waitress busied herself bringing a pot of tea and biscuits.

'I didn't expect to have tea with you,' said Winifred.

'I didn't expect to see you at all.'

'No. I haven't been in this part of town much lately.'

'But you've been here, in the tea shop.'

'Alice, I didn't come to talk about tea shops.'

'You came to buy fabric.'

'Where else would I come?' asked Winifred. 'Although I wasn't sure the shop would still be here.'

'Why shouldn't it be?'

'I thought you might have moved on.'

'Heavens, girl, I didn't move on through two wars; why would I move on in peacetime?'

'Good point,' said Winifred.

'I'm surprised you came back to me for fabric, though. I thought you hated me.'

'I never hated you. We had different views, that's all.'

'You were influenced by your husband and his cohorts.'

'Perhaps. Or perhaps I believed they had a point. But no matter what, it was wrong to imprison Joseph without charge for almost a year. To send him back to me as a skeleton. But,' she added, 'you helped me find out where he was. And I'll always be grateful for that.'

'It was the least I could do. I believe he's working for *The Irish Press* now.'

'How on earth did you know that?'

'Contacts,' said Alice.

'Francie?'

'Padraig.' Alice held out her hand so that Winifred could see the wide gold band that had replaced the narrow one she'd worn previously. 'We got married.'

'Oh!' Winifred looked at her in surprise, then smiled. 'Good for you. I hope you're very happy.'

'Some people don't hope that,' said Alice. 'They think I was crazy to marry a man younger than me. They think he'll leave me.'

'Why would he do that?' asked Winifred. 'You're a good woman.'

'As are you,' conceded Alice. 'How have things been for you?'

Winifred told her, and Alice exclaimed at her being a mother of five, and then they talked about the new house in Crumlin and how Winifred planned to use the old curtains from St Anthony's Place.

'Do you still have the green brocade that your mother-in-law bought?'

'Yes.'

'Use that for your parlour curtains,' said Alice. 'It would be spectacular.'

'That's what I was thinking myself,' said Winifred. 'I can cut it, of course, but I wondered if one of your sewers would make them up?'

'I'll get Miss Shaw to do it. She's the best I have.'

'Thank you. I didn't want to make a mess of the fabric by doing it myself.'

'It was never your strong point.' Alice smiled.

'Are you still living in Kenilworth Square?' Winifred asked as she freshened their tea.

'Yes. It will always be my home.'

'And Padraig is happy there?'

'Sometimes it's difficult for him,' admitted Alice. 'He's working for the government now. But the truth is, I have more money than him. So he resents that, but he also likes what the money can bring.'

'Do you still get a stipend from your late husband's family?'

'Yes. That was for life.' Alice smiled. 'I look on it as his gift to me.'

'Lucky,' murmured Winifred.

'And you'll be lucky too.' Suddenly Alice reached across the table and took her hands. 'Maybe we were on different sides for a time, but we've come through it, Winifred. Through all the wars and the troubles they brought. The division and the hatred and the unfairness of them. And . . . well, we've come through the peace too, which might have been just as hard. We've come through it because we're strong women and we always will be. Women who know what they want and how to get it.'

'Oh Alice, I've never known what I wanted. I never had a plan. I met Joseph by chance and I fell in love with him by chance and I became a rebel by chance because of him. And then I became a wife – eventually – and a mother. But I never had a plan.'

'Maybe you should make one for the future.'

'The only plan I have is for the quiet life I always wanted. For my children to have a better one than me. No wars. No fighting. No guns or fugitives in the house either.'

'And yet for that to happen, we have to be vigilant,' said Alice. 'I'm involved in a league—'

'A league! Alice! What sort of league? I was in a women's group myself for a while, but when Joseph's mother got sick and with having to be so watchful of the children . . . well, I didn't have time for it.'

'My league helps women. Women who've had violent husbands, who have nowhere to go.'

'Oh.'

'If you'd like to join us when you move to Crumlin . . . You won't be far from me, will you?'

'A mile or so,' said Winifred.

'We meet on Wednesday evenings,' said Alice. 'You should come.'

Winifred thought about Katy.

'Yes,' she said. 'Once I'm there, I will.'

'And bring me your fabric, and I promise you, you'll have the most wonderful curtains.'

'Thank you,' said Winifred.

'I'm glad you came,' said Alice.

'So am I.' Winifred smiled. 'So am I.'

Joseph had organised a horse and cart to take the family and their furniture to their new house. Each of the children was given their own parcel to carry, while Brenda and Kitty were also tasked with looking after the younger ones and making sure nothing was left behind.

'Because,' Winifred warned each child, 'if anything gets left behind, the owner does too.'

Kitty's fingers tightened around the books she was holding. Winifred was certain that her second daughter wouldn't mind being left behind so long as she had a book to read. She spent most of her time in a world of her own, blissfully unaware of what was going on around her. Brenda was the considerate one, always keeping an eye on the others, doing things before anyone realised they needed doing. John was like his grandfather. Practical. Loved mechanical things. Una was fun-loving and pretty. Patricia, even though she was a baby, was thoughtful.

I'll do my best to ensure you all have a good future, she said to herself. I'll work with Alice Kelley and her group to make sure that no matter what you do in life, you'll be able to do it on your own terms.

Joseph and his father were still loading boxes onto the cart. Winifred walked through the house to check that everything had been packed. She stood at the door of the bedroom. The slanting sun highlighted the space on the wall where the painting of her had hung. She wondered if she was still the woman Jack Yeats had seen. She wanted to be the less anxious version he'd sketched of her. She thought perhaps that now she was, even though the end of the wars hadn't brought about an easier life for her or her family. But one day it might.

She closed the door and went downstairs, stopping at the small room where she'd first seen the Countess. She could hear the rebel woman's voice echoing in her head, saying that Mrs Burke would have her guts for garters for spilling the ink. She smiled. She wasn't at all like the Countess, but she liked to think that perhaps some of her strong, dynamic spirit had rubbed off on her eventually.

She continued to the kitchen and then stepped into the garden, enjoying the feel of the late-morning sun on her shoulders. She'd miss the garden the most. The one at the Crumlin house could never compare with it. She checked herself. She'd make it compare. She'd plant apple trees and cherry blossom and roses. And lots and lots of vegetables. It would be a spectacular garden. Her garden.

The door to the boiler room was open. She walked along the pathway towards it and stepped inside. The boilers were silent, not needed now that the convent was empty.

She moved towards the iron gate that led to the crypt. She remembered hiding from the soldiers among the dead nuns, terrified that she'd be found and even more terrified that she wouldn't. It seemed like a complete lifetime ago. As though it had happened to another person. But it hadn't. It had happened to her, Winifred O'Leary, who hadn't wanted to be involved in anything but who'd ended up smuggling guns, sheltering republicans and singing rebel songs outside prisons.

And somehow it had turned out all right.

She was a survivor.

She always would be.

She went back into the house again. Joseph was standing in the hallway.

'Where on earth were you?' he asked. 'We're ready to leave.'

'Saying goodbye,' she told him. 'I didn't really want to live here, you know. I spent some of the worst days of my life here. But some of the best too.'

'All my days after marrying you have been wonderful,' said Joseph. 'Even the ones in Tintown.'

'The lengths you went to to get away from me.' She grinned at him.

'I know.' He grinned back. 'Come on, Winnie. A new life beckons!'

She followed him along the hallway. Her eye caught sight of something blue in the corner. A child's shoe. Patricia's, she knew. She was always wriggling out of her shoes.

She stepped outside. The cart was loaded and the children were sitting together.

'Everybody got everything?' she asked.

'Yes!' they shouted.

Winifred laughed and clambered onto the cart beside her husband.

Joseph turned to the children sitting in the back. 'Everyone here who's meant to be here?' he asked.

'All here!' they chorused in reply.

The driver of the cart tapped the horse, and they began to move.

Joseph took out his harmonica and started to play.

Winifred recognised the rousing tune of 'A Nation Once Again', which she and the other women protesters had often sung outside Kilmainham prison. She hadn't dared believe then that Joseph would be released. She hadn't dared believe he'd be released from Maryborough or the Curragh either.

But he had.

And here we are, she thought as she put her arm around his waist. Still alive. Still together.

He missed a note, smiled, then continued playing as they turned onto O'Connell Street, where workers continued to rebuild the battle-scarred buildings.

As the horse and cart stopped briefly on the bridge before heading south, Winifred gazed up the river towards East Essex Street, then turned back to look in the direction they'd come from. All of her life, good and bad, had been lived in the city. Now she was moving away from the streets and buildings that were so familiar to her. But she wasn't anxious, she was excited.

I've come a long way, she thought. Now it's time to move on. And with Joseph at my side and my children all around me, I know I'm ready for whatever comes next.

Acknowledgements

Thanks to Joan O'Flanagan Loughlin for her information
and research on family trees

The National Library of Ireland

And my family, as always

Author Note

The Woman on the Bridge is a novel inspired by the life of my grandmother and the stories she told me about her youth. Although it is based on true events, it is a work of fiction. Any historical errors are entirely mine.

Bibliography

I relied a lot on oral family history in writing this novel but also found the following very helpful:

Women and the Irish Revolution, ed. Linda Connolly (Irish Academic Press)

Markievicz Prison Letters and Rebel Writings, ed. Lindie Naughton (Merrion Press)

The Split: From Treaty to Civil War 1920–23, ed. Tommy Graham, Brian Hanley, Darragh Gannon, Grace O'Keeffe (Wordwell)

Glossary

1916 Rising
An armed uprising against British rule in Ireland with the intention of creating an independent republic

a stór
An Irish term of affection

Auxiliaries
A paramilitary unit of the RIC made up of former British army officers

Black and Tans
Former British soldiers recruited to reinforce the RIC

Boland's Mill
A strategic republican position during the 1916 Rising

Caubeen
A style of beret

Coddle
A traditional Dublin stew usually made from sausages, rashers (sliced back bacon), potatoes and onion

Craythur
Someone deserving of sympathy, or helpless in some way

Cumann na mBan (The Women's Council)
A paramilitary organisation of Irish women working with the Volunteers

Custom House
A stately building on the north bank of the Liffey where government records were maintained

Dublin Brigade
The Dublin division of the Volunteers

the Four Courts
The courts building on the river Liffey that also housed the Irish Public Record Office

Free State
The twenty-six-county state established by the Anglo-Irish treaty of December 1921, under which Ireland was a dominion of the British Empire

Frongoch
An internment camp in Wales to which Irish republicans were sent after the 1916 Rising

GAA (Gaelic Athletic Association)
An amateur sporting organisation that promotes indigenous Irish games

Inghinidhe na hÉireann (Daughters of Ireland)
A nationalist women's organisation that merged with *Cumann na mBan* in 1914

National Army
The military army of the pro-treaty side, also called the Free State Army

Pearse and Connolly
Two of the seven signatories of the 1916 Proclamation of Independence, both executed by the British

the Plantations
The confiscation of Irish-owned land by the British Crown and its subsequent colonisation with settlers from Britain

Pro-cathedral
St Mary's Pro-Cathedral – the main Roman Catholic cathedral in Dublin

RIC
The Royal Irish Constabulary was the police force in Ireland from 1822 to 1922. It was under the authority of the British Administration and had a more military structure than conventional police forces

Sheila O'Flanagan

Sleeveen
A sly, devious person

the Volunteers
A military organisation set up by Irish nationalists and republicans